REAL LIFE CRIME

SCENE INVESTIGATIONS

FORENSIC SCIENCE CASE FILES

REAL LIFE CRIME

SCENE INVESTIGATIONS

FORENSIC SCIENCE CASE FILES

Abbeydale Press

ISBN: 978-1-8647-201-4
ISBN: 1-86147-201-3

1 3 5 7 9 10 8 6 4 2

Published by Abbeydale Press
An imprint of Bookmart Ltd
Blaby Road, Wigston
Leicester LE18 4SE
England

Every effort has been made to contact the copyright holders for the pictures. In some cases they have been untraceable, for which we offer our apologies. Thanks to the following libraries and picture agencies which supplied pictures:

PICTURE LIBRARIES
AFP/EPA, Associated Press, AP Worldwide, Black Museum, Culver Pictures, Mary Evans Photo Library, Jack Hickes Photography, Fairfax Ltd, Getty Images, Illustrated London News, Hulton-Deutsch Collection, News Ltd of Australia, Peter Lomas, Popperfotos, Portfolio Pictures, Press Association, Rex Features, Frank Spooner Pictures, Syndication International, Suddeutscher Verlag, The John Frost Collection,Topham and UPI/Bettmann

THE AUTHORS
Frank Smyth, Allan Hall, Ray Black

Printed in Thailand

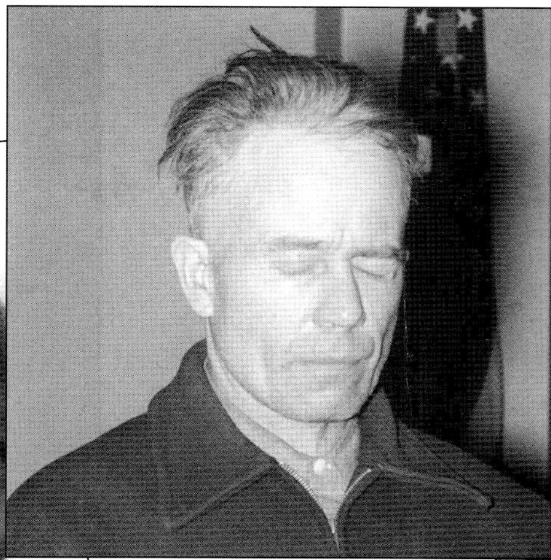

Contents

SECTION 1
Indelible Evidence

LAB DETECTION 8
Scientific Evidence

DNA EVIDENCE 22
Fingering Criminals

WILLIAM HEIRENS 32
The Mama's Boy

HAROLD SHIPMAN 42
Doctor Death

SECTION 2
Amazing Team Work

KAREN PRICE 50
Face Value

DR PERERA 58
The Arrogant Dentist

PETER FALCONIO 67
Outback Ambush

SECTION 3
Too Few Clues

SILENT WITNESSES 78
The Maggot Murder

GORDON HAY 86
Marks of Death

EMMETT-DUNNE 96
A Deadly Affair

GEORGI MARKOV 102
Murder by Umbrella

MURDER INC. 110
Cheapskate Killers

SECTION 4
Drawn Out Cases

JOHN LIST 122
The Murderous Dad

DE LA BECKWITH 130
Third Time Unlucky

SAM SHEPPARD 138
A Travesty of Justice

BILLIE-JO JENKINS 146
Blood Spatter Clues

DAMILOLA TAYLOR 154
Too Scared to Talk

SECTION 5
Crimes of Horror

CONSTANZO 162
Voodoo Murders

JOHN CHRISTIE 170
10 Rillington Place

PETER KURTEN 180
Düsseldorf Monster

EDWARD GEIN 186
The Secret Hunter

ED KEMPER 196
The Headhunter

SARAH PAYNE 206
Forensic Fibres

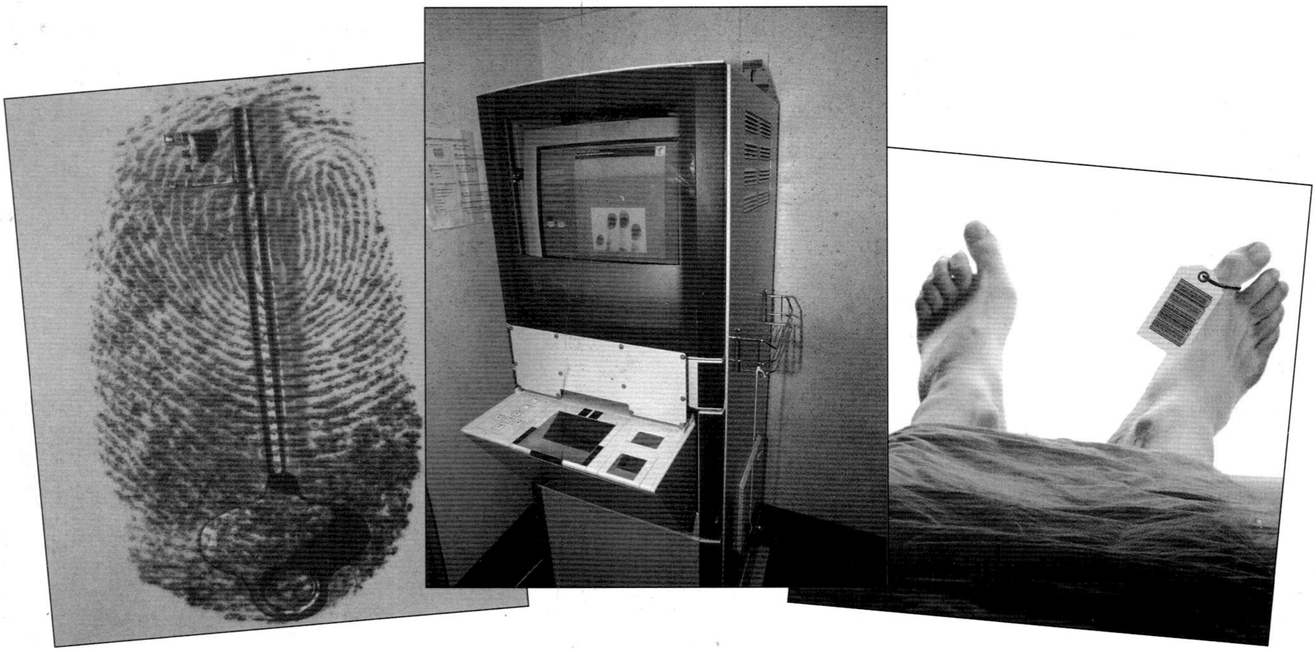

Preface

As technology becomes more and more advanced, the harder it becomes for a perpetrator of a crime to escape unnoticed. For example, forensic science can determine who dropped the sticky sweet paper, who left a fingerprint on the front of the aquarium, whose footprint was embedded in the damp earth, whose blood it is on the broken pane of glass. Answering these types of questions is exactly what forensic science is all about.

Forensic science is the study of an object or objects that relate to a crime. The carefully trained forensic analyst will collect vital clues from the crime scene, preserve them so that they will not become tainted before arriving at the laboratory and then painstakingly analyse every scrap of evidence. This forensic evidence is very often crucial to the determination of whether a person is guilty or innocent.

This book gives details of the use of early forensic knowledge right up to the innovative methods used today. Through the use of DNA the reality of being able to tie a person to the scene of a crime without a shadow of doubt is starting to be realised. In some cases a defendant will plead guilty when confronted with the knowledge that the police have strong DNA samples to use as evidence, thinking that the jury will conclude that such information is infallible. The cases in this book offer graphic details of not only the crimes but also how the police went about solving them.

INDELIBLE EVIDENCE

LAB DETECTION
Scientific Evidence

From Henry Faulds' original pioneering ideas on fingerprinting to the ultra-modern process of DNA testing was a quantum leap that was accomplished in little more than a century. It is a leap that has spelled nothing but bad news for society's villains, now unable to rely on a good alibi.

No-one on earth laments the passing of the "good old days" more than the professional criminal. For as time has gone by, so the arm of the law has grown ever longer thanks to the miracles of forensic science. Applying chemistry, physics, biology and pathology to sleuthing has combined to give us space-age methods of divining criminal acts and, thereby, bringing the perpetrators of them to justice. Just as the safebreaker in early-Victorian times would scoff at the very idea that a single fingerprint could lead him to swing from the gallows, so the murderer of the 1970s didn't realise that within a decade a single drop of blood would give sleuths his very genetic make-up in the process now known as DNA.

Before science was applied to crime the catching of society's miscreants was pretty much a hit-and-miss affair. Unless a murder weapon or stolen property was found upon the culprit – or he was marked by the signs of struggle with his victim – there was every likelihood that he would get clean away with his misdeed. One of the earliest and most significant crime-fighting techniques to be taken on board by police authorities all over the world must, of course, be the process of fingerprinting. In 1864 in India a servant of Her Majesty's empire named William Herschel noted that no two fingerprints are ever alike and began using the system to pay pensioned Indian Army soldiers who could not read and write; the presence of their right index finger print each payday testified to their identity. His system was improved upon some years later by a dour Scotsman named Henry Faulds, who in 1880 wrote to *Nature* magazine suggesting that this might be a way of identifying 'society's criminal elements". There followed a certain amount of acrimonious squabbling between the two gentlemen as to who had rights to the aforementioned "discovery" but, nonetheless, between them they had discovered the system of logging criminals that is still in place today.

It was a third individual, Sir Francis Galton, who took the "dab" out of the realms of the possible into the practical. In 1892 he published a book called simply *Fingerprints* which proved conclusively that no two were ever alike. That same year the first murder ever to be solved by fingerprinting was committed in Necochea, Argentina. A woman named Francesca Rojas ran into the hut of her neighbour screaming that her two children aged four and six had been murdered. She put the blame on a man named Velasquez who she said had been pressuring her to marry, saying that she had returned home from work and found the children dead in bed. Velasquez was tortured by the local police but he maintained his innocence. Colin Wilson, author of *The Mammoth Book of True Crime*, takes up the story: 'A police

---

THE ARM OF THE LAW HAS GROWN EVER LONGER THANKS TO THE MIRACLES OF FORENSIC SCIENCE

WILLIAM HERSCHEL NOTED THAT NO TWO FINGERPRINTS ARE EVER ALIKE AND BEGAN USING THE SYSTEM

Below: ***A celebrated case in which 'dabs' found at the crime scene proved the undoing of kidnap-killer Arthur Hosein.***

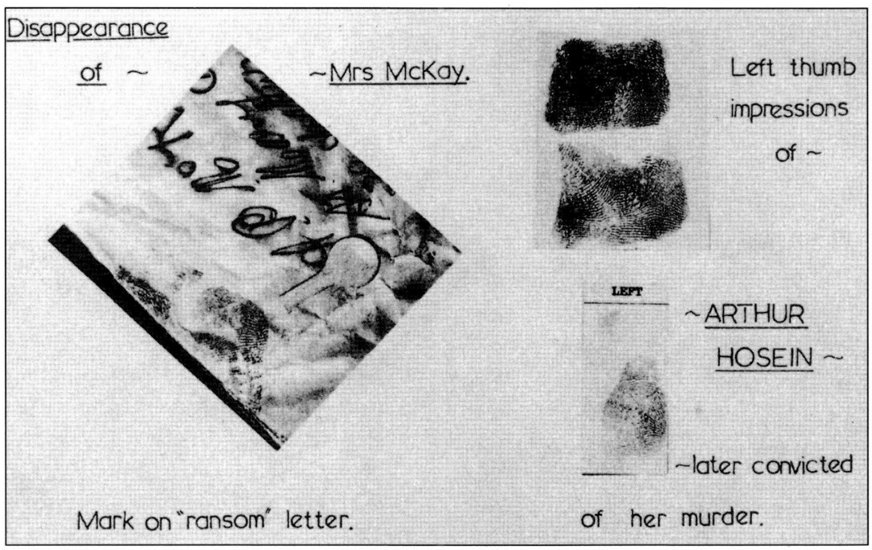

Opposite: ***Henry Faulds, founding father of modern detection.***

Above: ***Dusting a bottle for fingerprints – the film left behind clearly shows the imprint.***

inspector named Alvarez went out to investigate from La Plata. And he knew something about the work of a Dalmatian named Juan Vucetich, head of the Statistical Bureau of Police in Buenos Aires who had developed his own fingerprint system after reading an article by Galton. Alvarez went into the woman's hut and searched for clues. All he could find was a bloody thumb-print on a door. Alvarez sawed off the portion of the door and took it back to headquarters. Then he sent for Rojas and made her give a thumb-print. Alvarez knew very little about classification, but it was quite obvious that the two prints were identical. When he showed the woman the two prints through a magnifying glass, she broke down and confessed – she had murdered her two children because she wanted to marry a young lover who objected to them. This Argentine Lady Macbeth, who tried to rid herself of illegitimate children and an unwanted lover with one blow, obviously deserves to stand very high on a list of the world's worst women."

Nowadays the FBI in America is the repository of the most fingerprints on earth, over 200 million of them that can all be accessed by the major law enforcement agencies in the country within minutes. The FBI handles 30,000 fingerprint enquiries each day using laser beams to scan 80 fingerprints a second to find a match. In Britain there are some two-and-a-half million fingerprints on file on the police national computer in Hendon.

SOPHISTICATED DETECTION

While the collating and keeping of fingerprints has grown more technical, so has their retrieval from crime scenes. Iodine fumes and niohydrin spray can be used to lift prints from porous surfaces. Even lip-prints can be classified and there is a case of a hit-and-run driver in America where the lip-prints of the victim were taken from the bumper of the suspect's vehicle. But only two per-cent of crimes are solved by fingerprints today, even though their importance cannot be underestimated.

A single print was enough to trap John Cannan in Britain in 1987 for the abduction and sex murder of newlywed Shirley Banks. Cannan, 25, was caught driving the woman's car but claimed to have purchased it at an auction. He insisted he had never met the woman – she was missing, presumed dead – and police were still on the hunt for clues. A police search of his flat in Bristol turned up a dossier from a private detective Cannan had hired – and on it was a single fingerprint. This was matched from prints that were taken from the dead woman's home and office. Paul Jobbins, a senior fingerprint officer with Avon police, was gratified to see his work lead to Cannan being sentenced to life imprisonment for murder and rape.

After the evolution of fingerprinting came blood as the next weapon in the arsenal of law and order. Its unique properties, which enabled scientists to develop serums against diptheria and snake bites, could be used to identify the perpetrators of crime using simple laboratory tests. Initially the process merely told investigators whether blood was human or animal – as in the case of a French murderer who was sent to the guillotine in 1902 after a test showed that the blood he was covered with was not from a rabbit as claimed but from a human being – and soon blood was classified into three separate groupings thanks to the research of the Austrian-born scientist Dr. Karl Landsteiner. Landsteiner, who emigrated to America, received the Nobel prize in 1930 for his work in classifying blood – a boon to doctors, hospitals and patients, but no less a landmark discovery for sleuths. His OAB system categorised humans as having type O, type A or type B blood groups, all classified according to their immunological properties.

Twenty years before this, in 1910 in England, came the first British murder trial at which blood was to play a crucial role. Isabella Wilson, a 70-year-old junkshop keeper, was found brutalised and strangled to death in the back of her premises in Slough. A shifty character named William Broome, who had designs upon acquiring the shabby store, was a chief suspect in the murder but had moved away on the day she was found dead. Police later tracked him down to Harlesden in North London where a prostitute friend gave him an alibi that he had been with her when the old lady was being killed. But Dr. William Wilcox, the chief expert on bloodstains at the Home Office, found traces of blood under the victim's fingernails – traces which he matched to scratches on Broome's face. Broome probably did not derive any satisfaction from the fact that, as he mounted the gallows to be hanged for the murder, he had gone into the criminal history books as the first villain to be brought to book by blood.

MISSING EVIDENCE

Another famous murder case was once solved because of the *lack* of bloodstains. A famous French criminologist named Alexandre Lacassagne plotted the correlation between blood spots at a crime scene and the position of the victim at the time of death. For instance: blood dropped vertically from a stationary object makes a circular spot with ragged edges. The greater the distance the blood has to drop, the greater the crenellations. If blood moves from a moving object it leaves spots resembling exclamation marks indicating the direction the victim was heading in. Thanks to Professor Lacassagne, police forces were able to draw up charts for crime scene detectives to reconstruct what had happened to murder victims.

Such a chart came in useful for the examination of 43-year-old Catherine McCluskey, found lying in the middle of the road in Glasgow on July 29 1950. At first appearances the corpse seemed to have been dragged along the road by a car or lorry, a long trail of blood marking her path along the tarmac.

Professor Andrew Alison, the pathologist working on the case, examined the body and he concluded that her injuries were not consistent with having been knocked down by a hit-and-run driver. He surmised that she had either been bludgeoned and dragged to make it look like an accident or that she had been deliberately run over – murdered. The victim was a woman with numerous boyfriends, all of

A FRENCH MURDERER WENT TO THE GUILLOTINE AFTER A TEST SHOWED THE BLOOD COVERING HIM WAS NOT FROM A RABBIT

Below: ***In 1864 in India, a servant of Her Majesty's empire, William Herschel, noted that no two fingerprints were ever alike and began using the system to pay off pensioned Indian Army soldiers.***

whom were tracked down by police. One of them even turned out to be a policeman, James Robertson, who soon became the main suspect in her death. His home was searched and a large quantity of stolen property was found. Although an indication of his dishonesty, it didn't pin a deliberate murder on him.

But he broke under questioning and said that he accidentally knocked her over after dropping her off at home and that he moved the car "backwards and forwards in an attempt to free her". When this failed, he claimed, he at first tried to pull the woman free but then panicked and left the body there.

This "confession" was unmasked as the fallacy it was by the fact that the victim had no injuries to her legs. Professor John Glaister, an expert in Lacassagne's methods, had said that there would have been considerable amounts of blood on his trousers if he had indeed tried to free her. There was not a speck. So, too, another killer went to the gallows because of blood – this time because of the lack of it.

As the ways to kill a human being became more sophisticated it became necessary for police forces to equip themselves with the technology to catch murderers. The greatest challenges for lab experts have come from firearms, where the study known as ballistics has become an art unto itself. It was in Paris in May 1912, at the Congress of Legal Medicine, that ballistics was accepted as a new branch of forensic science in its own right.

The necessity for this had been the advancements in firearms, particularly cheap ones like those made by Colt in America, which took guns out of the hands of the ruling class and put them into the grip of a great mass of seething, discontented people – the proletariat. Ballistics works in much the same way as fingerprinting. Every gun has a unique signature which leaves its mark upon bullets fired into a victim. Tracing the gun is usually the first step in solving the crime.

At the Paris conference in 1912 Professor Victor Balthazard, an eminent expert, spoke of a case in which a man named Guillotin had been shot dead. Upon

examination, his body was found to contain several bullets. When the main suspect in the case, a man called Houssard, was brought into custody, Professor Balthazard was brought in to examine his weapon. Local firearms experts in the south of France were unable to detect whether or not the bullets had been fired from his gun, but Balthazard was able to point out no less than 86 similarities between his gun barrel and marks on the bullets. Houssard was guillotined and Balthazard's methods of comparing marks on projectiles to the metal tubes that expelled them laid the foundations for ballistic science.

A member of the New York State prosecutor's office called Charles Waite refined that science into the art it has become. He devoted his life to firearms investigation, spurred on by a trial in America in which a man's life was spared because of proof that a bullet which killed a man had come from a gun other than his own. For ten years, with the aid of gun manufacturers across America, he catalogued every type of weapon together with the signature that it left upon bullets. Next he began chronicling European imports and then, to refine the system even further, approached the Bausch and Lomb Optical Company to make him a microscope for comparing bullets. A man named Philip Gravelle then proceeded to invent the "comparison microscope" which could place a test bullet next to a murder scene bullet for instant comparison. A physicist called John H. Fischer then made a device called a helixometer, a slender, lighted probe for the study of gun barrels. Armed, as it were, with all this new information, Waite and Calvin Goddard, a friend and former army doctor, set up the Bureau of Forensic Ballistics in New York in 1923.

Ballistic knowledge was vigorously pursued all over the world. The greatest mass-exhumation of bodies for forensic study of the bullets that put them in the ground was carried out by Nazi Germany.

Above: ***The crime at Katyn Wood. Forensic evidence showed that the mass slaughter was by Stalin's killers.***

Opposite Top: ***James Robertson – a lack of bloodstains at the scene of Catherine McCluskey's demise pinned her murder on him.***

Opposite Below: ***The body of his victim, which he had despatched by running over her in a car.***

Above: ***Dr Hawley Harvey Crippen. Poisons found in the stomach of his wife caught the sinsister but clever physician.***

GENERALS AND LIEUTENANTS WERE BOUND AND SHOT IN THE BACK OF THE HEAD AND BURIED IN MASSIVE LIME PITS

In 1940, some 4,000 Polish officers, from generals to lieutenants, were bound and shot in the back of the head and buried in massive lime pits shrouded by the towering fir trees that made up the forest of Katyn, near Smolensk in Western Russia. The corpses were discovered during Germany's invasion of Russia in 1943 and immediate propaganda was made of it – the Germans said that they had been murdered by the NKVD, Stalin's dreaded butchers. All the victims had their hands tied to a macabre noose around their necks which tightened if they struggled, all bore the same single-entry head wound testifying to their methodical execution.

It was later learned the liquidations at the Katyn Forest began on April 3 1941 and did not end until May 13, five weeks later. In the previous week the prisoners were rounded up in their respective camps at Kozelsk, Starobelsk and Ostashkov and taken in batches of 50 to 500 to railheads to board cattlewagons for unknown destinations. It was the 4,400 prisoners of the Kozelsk camp whose final halt was to be the forest at Katyn.

Dr. Gerhard Buhtz, a professor of forensic medicine from a leading German university, was put in charge of the exhumation and examination of the grave pits which were re-opened in early March 1943. For ten weeks the stink of rotten flesh and Egyptian tobacco – the Germans smoked it to mask the smell of the dead – mingled with the scents of moss and pine sap as the murdered men were disinterred and laid out. Three separate commissions were invited by the Germans into Katyn. The first was entirely German, the second composed of scientists and forensic experts from Switzerland, Belgium, Hungary and Bulgaria and the third entirely Polish. The evidence was mightily in favour of the German viewpoint. Although the ammunition was German, records from the manufacturing plants showed it to be batches sold to Lithuania before the war which was later seized by NKVD police units. Buhtz used the tests pioneered by Waite to test the bullets and the guns from which they came – there was no doubt that the Soviets were to blame for the massacre.

THE APPLIANCE OF SCIENCE

For close to five decades the crime at Katyn Wood remained the single biggest whodunnit of World War Two. The Germans claimed that the Russians had done it, the Russians that the Germans were the perpetrators. But simple scientific facts proved that it was a Soviet crime. Stalin was able to do many things as dictator, but altering indisputable scientific facts was not one of them.

It is far from Europe and Russia, in America, where the need for ballistic science remains greatest. Among the population there are 75 million guns – and rising. Sixty three people die each day from firearms while in Britain and other European countries, firearms deaths are still minimal. Each day the FBI ballistics unit increases its knowledge to take on board details of the latest killing weapons, like machine guns and pump-action shotguns being used by the drug gangs and the mobsters. When it comes to ballistics, the Americans lead the world.

But it is probably fair to say that when it comes to stone cold corpses, Britain must take much credit for criminal pathology. In this century great criminal pathologists like Bernard Spilsbury, Francis Camps and Keith Simpson have helped to solve some of the most baffling murder cases. British medicine has always enjoyed an enviable reputation around the globe – it followed that the application of that to crime detection produced some of the most brilliant medico-legal brains of all time. What do they look for when first presented with that mass of cold flesh that was once a living, breathing human being? And how can they tell what the cause of death was when often all they are presented with is a pile of decomposing or burned flesh wrapped around a few skeletal bones?

SUREFIRE CLUES

Of course, that is their trade and what may seem the medical equivalent of looking for a needle in a haystack is often elementary. No smoke on lung tissue on a charred corpse means death before the fire – there was no inhalation. Similarly, no water in the lungs of a "drowning" victim means they were dead before they hit the water. Broken bones in the throat of a corpse found by an empty bottle of pills means the tablets were forced down instead of being swallowed voluntarily.

And what layman could have found in over 400lbs of human "sludge" – rendered down by the acid of notorious killer John George Haigh – a single gallstone and single hairpin? Professor Keith Simpson found them and they were the clues which sent Haigh to the gallows as one of the most notorious killers in British history.

Identifying a corpse from just a few particles of flesh and bone is, of course, the hardest task facing forensic pathologists, but it is one which they invariably rise to the occasion to meet. Sir Bernard Spilsbury, who became as famous as a pop star might be nowadays because of his awesome presence in court and unmatched knowledge of crime, cut his teeth on some of the most infamous murders in British history – including one that bears the name of a man known from the jungles of the Amazon to the ice floes of the Arctic: Dr. Crippen. Sir Bernard was 33 and unknighted when he became involved in the Crippen case in 1910, but his success in that most chilling of cases only served to propel him into forensic fame.

Dr. Hawley Crippen was an American-born physician working in London whose attentions wandered from his wife Belle – dominant, overbearing, cool towards the bespectacled doctor – towards a mistress called Ethel Neave, who took the fancy name Ethel LeNeve because she thought it made her more sophisticated. Although he divorced his wife she hovered on the periphery of Crippen's life with Ethel, casting a long shadow over his new, younger lover. He decided that shadow could only be lifted with her death, which he duly

WHEN IT COMES TO STONE COLD CORPSES, BRITAIN MUST TAKE MUCH CREDIT FOR CRIMINAL PATHOLOGY

Below: ***Ethel LeNeve, mistress of the wicked Dr Crippen.***

dispensed by poisoning her, dismembering her and covering what remained of the corpse with quicklime and fleeing to America to begin life afresh in the New World. Chief Inspector Walter Drew of Scotland Yard sent the famous telegraphic warning that served as the first Marconi message to arrest a murderer.

It was left to Spilsbury to examine what was left to determine what had killed her and if her death could be pinned on Crippen. Firstly, Spilsbury was able to prove the traces of hyoscine poison in her stomach – a poison which the good doctor had purchased shortly before she vanished. Brian Marriner, the respected author of *On Death's Bloody Trail*, a work on forensic science, wrote: "Then the next most important clue was a piece of flesh from the abdomen which bore an operation scar – as had Mrs. Crippen. Defence experts claimed it was just a piece of flesh from the thigh, and the scar was just a fold in the skin. Spilsbury, in his calm and patient manner, showed that it came from the abdomen, pointing out that part of the rectus muscle of the abdominal wall was still attached to the specimen in question. He had shamed his elders with superior knowledge." Spilsbury won that case and many hundreds more before his own loneliness and demons drove him to take his own life.

SILENT TESTIMONY

Forensic pathologists are also invaluable for those crimes to which there have been no witnesses. When Juliet Marion Hulme and Pauline Yvonne Parker were brought before the Crown in Christchurch, New Zealand, in 1954, the case received worldwide attention because of its morbid themes. Like the case of the Chicago thrill killers Loeb and Leopold – a couple of intellectuals who killed a small boy in the mistaken belief that they could get away with the perfect murder – psychologists were at pains to try to explain the fusion of two normal, caring minds into a single unit bent on misery and death. For that is what Juliet and Pauline descended to when they feared that their parents were bent on breaking up their friendship.

In a bid to forestall or prevent the breakup they believed was coming they plotted, and carried out, the murder of Mrs. Honora Mary Parker. Mrs. Parker, 45, Pauline's mother, was bludgeoned repeatedly to death by the vile duo who tried to cover their tracks by claiming she had fallen. It was on June 22 1954 that two hysterical girls, covered in blood, shattered the tranquility of the afternoon tea ritual at a sedate Christchurch restaurant when they burst through the doors. "Mummy's been hurt," blurted out Pauline. "She's hurt, covered with blood." Tearfully they begged the manageress of the restaurant to phone for police while they gulped down sugared tea in an apparent attempt to ease their shock.

Below: ***The wicked duo Juliet Marion Hulme and Pauline Parker after their arrest for the murder of Pauline's mother.***

Some of the customers went with the police and the girls to a beauty spot in a nearby park that was close to a small bridge over a stream. Lying in a pool of blood, with her face unrecognisable, was Mrs. Parker. She was quite dead.

There were no witnesses to what had happened and immediate sympathy was with the hysterical girls. They explained she had fallen on a rocky path and that she had banged her head and died.

It wasn't until the pathologist examined the corpse and said there was bruising around the throat consistent with her having been held down as blow after blow – he speculated as many as 49 – was rained down on her head. The girls were sent away for long periods.

POISONOUS INDIVIDUALS

Another speciality of the forensic boffins is venom. Poison has always been a form of murder that British killers have been particularly fond of. One of them, Graham Young, was of that breed who thought himself cleverer than the experts pitted against him. But he too would go down in the record books – not only for his victims, but because he was trapped due to the miracles of forensic science.

From his earliest days the boy who would grow up to become immortalised as The Broadmoor Poisoner was spellbound by potions which slowly squeezed the life out of his helpless victims. A thrill killer, it was the sensation of power which fuelled his manic desires and his intelligence which masked his wicked games.

When he was finally caught for poisoning his aunt, his father and his school chum – luckily they didn't die although he had at 14 murdered his stepmother and got away with it – he spent nine years in Broadmoor, only to be released from incarceration to murder twice more.

In April 1971, after he had been released, came the job advertisement in a local paper which would seal his fate – and that of several of his workmates. He saw an offer of employment with the John Hadland company of Bovingdon, in Hertfordshire, for a storeman's position. Hadland's was an old established family firm that manufactured high grade optical and photographic equipment.

Above: ***One of the most famous pathologists Britain has ever produced – Professor Keith Simpson.***

POISON HAS ALWAYS BEEN A FORM OF MURDER THAT BRITISH KILLERS HAVE BEEN PARTICULARLY FOND OF

He impressed managing director Godfrey Foster at his interview, and explained that his long time away from regular employment was due to a nervous breakdown he had suffered. Foster checked up with the training centre and also Broadmoor, but received such glowing references as to the young man's abilities and recovery that he offered him the job.

On Monday May 10 1971 Graham Young arrived at Hadlands. The company thought that they were getting a storeman. In reality they had hired an angel of death. With his £24-per-week wages he rented a £4-per-week bedsitter which in short order became his own little shop of horrors.

He lined his cupboards and shelves with an increasing collection of poisons, among them the antimony tartrate with which he had begun his fledgling career as a poisoner.

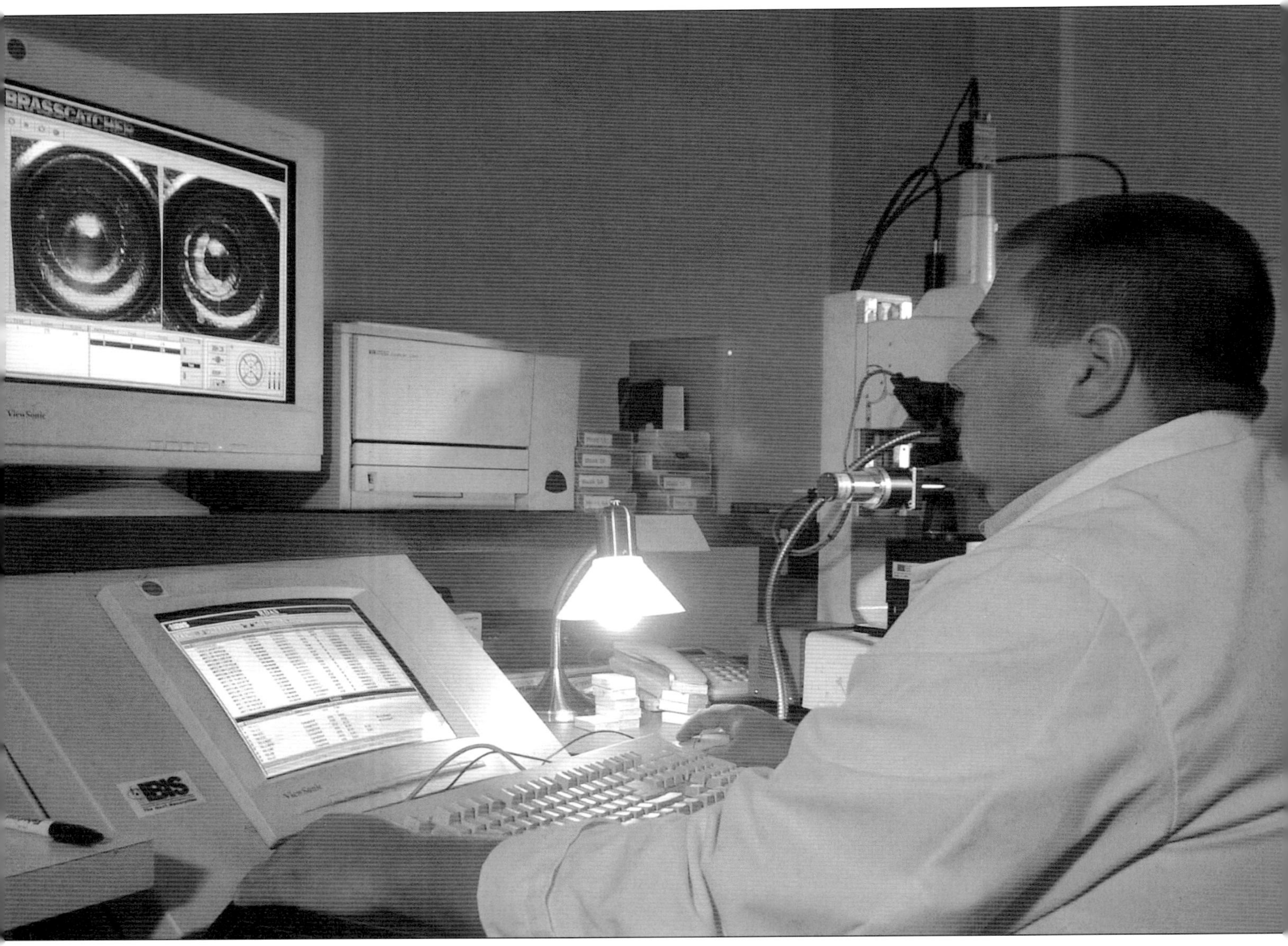

Above: *A forensic scientist examines a shell casing with the aid of a computer which greatly speeds up the matching of ballistic evidence.*

THEY WERE BEING SLOWLY POISONED BY THALLIUM, A SEVERELY RESTRICTED POISON THAT IS USED TO KILL RATS

At work he was regarded, in turns, as a quiet, often distant young man or a belligerent, persistent speaker if he touched on the subjects of politics or chemistry. His best friend at work was 41-year-old Ron Hewitt, whose job he was taking. Ron stayed on to show the new man the ropes and introduced him to the other hands in the plant. Many showed great kindness to Young, lending him money and giving him cigarettes when he had none. Young repaid their affection and warmth by being the first one at the tea trolley when it trundled in during morning breaks.

The terror had begun.

On Thursday June 3, less than a month after he started there, Bob Egle, 59, who worked as storeroom boss, was taken ill with diarrhoea, cramps and nausea. Next, Ron Hewitt fell violently ill, suffering the same symptoms accompanied by acute stomach pains and burning sensations at the back of his throat. Workers at Hadlands called the mystery pains "the bug". In fact they were being slowly poisoned by thallium, a severely restricted poison used to kill rats that is so toxic it can cause death merely by being handled. Young bought the poison from chemists in London and was putting the tasteless, odourless chemical into his workmates' teas. On Wednesday July 7 Bob Egle died. His was a horrible, painful death, caused by a paralysis which spread throughout his body before it caused his heart to fail. There was no inquest on his body because doctors misinterpreted his illness as being bronchial-pneumonia linked to polyneuritis.

In September, after a relatively quiet summer, in which Young was often away, the nightmare continued. Fred Biggs, a part-time worker, was the next target. After 20 days of agonising cramps and pains he died. Four other workers were poisoned, two of them ending up in hospital with all their hair gone and with severe cases of depression brought on by the poison that they had ingested through the tainted tea.

It wasn't until Hadlands brought in a local doctor, Iain Anderson, to talk to staff and try to track down what was poisoning the workforce, that the noose began closing around Young's neck. Anderson said he had run down numerous checks but was unable to determine the source of the "bug". Young, unable to suppress his own ego over his knowledge of poisons, soon took the meeting over.

He reeled off mind-numbing statistics about poison and its effects – so much so that Anderson became suspicious. After consulting with the company management, Scotland Yard was called in. They ran a background check on all company employees – a move that was guaranteed to shine the light on the unsavoury past activities of Graham Young.

A COLD-HEARTED KILLER

Forensic scientists from the government research station at Aldermaston were called in and it was believed that thallium had caused the deaths and the illnesses. Thallium is a metal-based poison that has no smell, is colourless and tasteless. Young was arrested at his father's house, making himself an egg sandwich. As he was being led away he said to police: "Which ones are they doing me for, then?" The authorities were concerned that they did not have enough evidence on Young, and as both the bodies of his victims had been burned they feared he would, quite literally, get away with murder once again.

But in a forensic first the ashes of one of the cremated corpses showed traces of thallium in them. A process that is called "atomic absorption spectrometry" was deployed in which five micrograms of Thallium per gram of ash were found. On December 3 he was charged with murdering Egle. Now he wanted maximum publicity – the notoriety of Crippen and others that he now felt he had rightly earned. So he pleaded not guilty.

Later he was also charged with the murder of Fred Biggs and the attempted murders of two others and of further administering poison to two others. He went into the history books and captivity at St. Albans Court in 1972.

Now the world of the forensic expert is shifting away from blood and bone, hair and tissue, into the realm of sci-fi where lasers and electron microscopes are at the forefront of the war on crime.

The forensic science laboratory of Scotland Yard is now one of the most highly advanced criminal investigation labs on earth, where great emphasis and faith is being placed on laser technology. Graham Jackson, the Met's laser expert, likes to joke that he can literally make "clues glow in the dark" with his technology. He cites the case, for instance, of an Essex policeman who had been asked to look out for a truck involved in a hit-and-run case.

IN A FORENSIC FIRST THE ASHES OF ONE OF THE CREMATED CORPSES SHOWED TRACES OF THALLIUM

Below: ***Graham Young, the Broadmoor poisoner, who sent so many innocents to their deaths.***

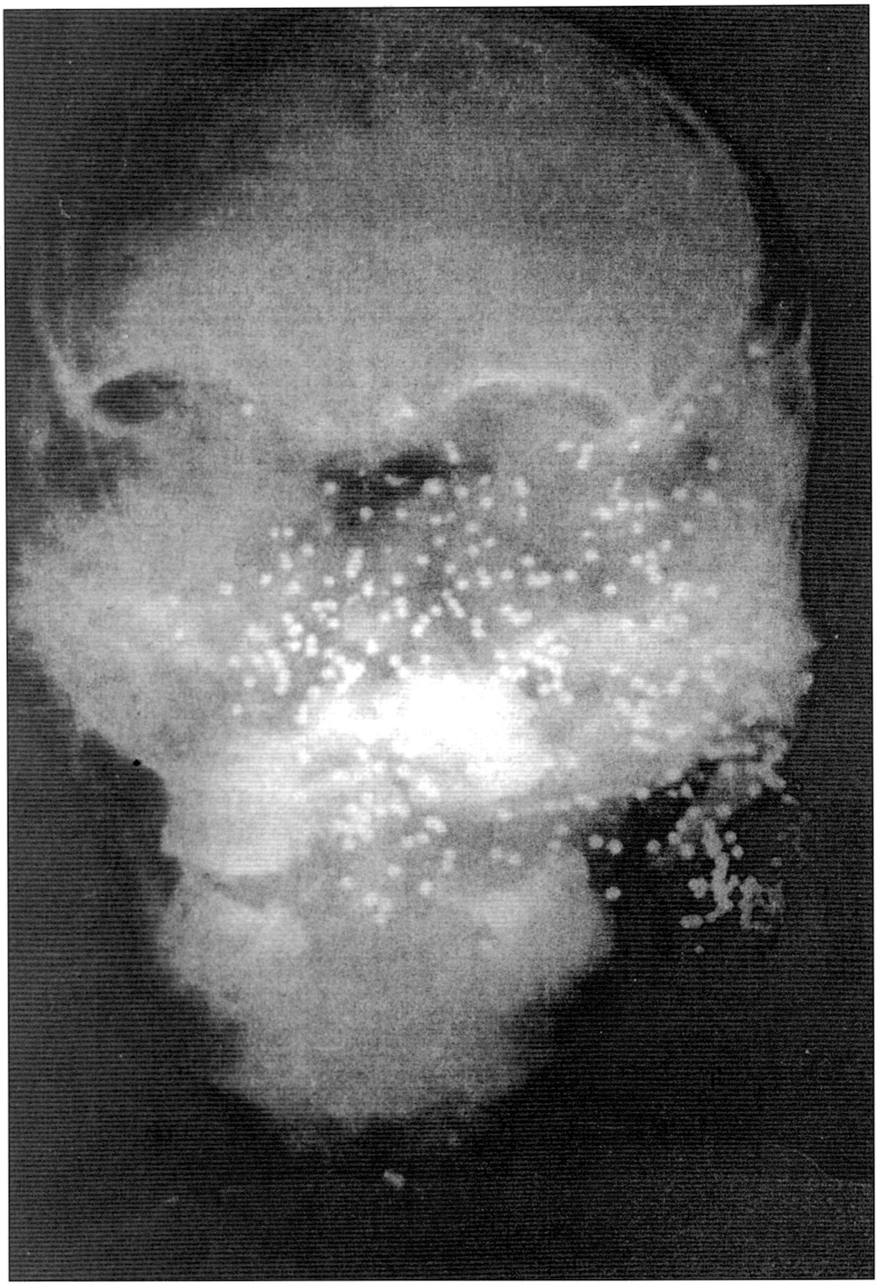

Above: ***A head x-ray showing a pattern of shotgun pellets on the victim's left side.***

The officer in question thought he had spotted the offending lorry while out on his beat, wrote the registration number down on his hand and ran to the nearest telephone box to call it in to check with the station. It was the wrong number and the marks on his hand were erased later that night in the officer's bathtub. The next day a telex came into the station where he was based from police in the north of England seeking a hijacked vehicle.

Feeling that the number of the lorry he had written down might be that of the hijacked truck he tried to recall the digits, without luck. Then he was sent to the forensic lab. According to Dr. Ray Williams, the lab's director, the number showed up on his hand after it was subjected to laser-light! "He was not so much astonished by the technology but relieved that his hand was still in one piece," said Dr. Williams.

Laser technology is now also coming into its own in the field of fingerprinting. Until recently, the standard method of gleaning fingerprints from a crime scene was to dust aluminium powder over everything and hope that it stuck. For various reasons it may not – and in the old days that would have been the end of it.

But thanks to lasers many acids found in the ordinary human fingerprint fluoresce under laser light. In a darkened room the display can be spectacular – hundreds of "dabs" showing up where ordinary aluminium powder failed to detect them. The lights can also read underneath the correction fluid pasted over a word to reveal the word that was corrected.

Jackson said: "It has improved previous methods of detection considerably. Things like shoeprints, fingerprints, fibres, marks on bodies, stains and so on. It has proved possible to recover these types of evidence on occasions when often they cannot be seen at all by the human eye."

A METICULOUS MICROSCOPE

The scanning electron microscope is another high-tech tool worth its weight in gold. This uses electron beams instead of rays of light to identify fingerprints in circumstances which, on the surface, may seem impossible. For example, gunmen often carry firearms in rolled-up newspapers, the surface of which no-one believed a fingerprint could be retrieved from. A fingerprint on a picture, for example, is made up of thousands of tiny dots which would interfere with a laser scan. But the electron microscope can get around the problem. Firstly, the forensic scientist paints the page with a liquid containing a suspension of silver. When it comes into contact with the fingerprint the silver separates. When the page is then scanned the fingerprint stands out because the heavy silver atoms bounce back the electrons fired at them by the microscope while the lighter carbon atoms of the paper and ink do not.

Dr. Williams cites the case of the assassination attempt upon the Israeli ambassador to Britain in 1982 as one of those which would have led to a conviction if it had not been for the great strides forward in forensic technology. When the accused, Hussein Said, stood in the witness box in February 1983 he was confident of an acquittal. The man he had shot, Shlomo Argov, was too ill from his wounds to give evidence, the police had discharged their own firearms at the scene and Said had said nothing under interrogation to incriminate himself. Traces of gunpowder and gun oil found on Said after the attempt could, said his lawyers, just as easily have come from the police weapons.

Dr. Williams called it a 'classic forensic conundrum'. Analysis of the guns, ammunition and residue samples taken from the suspect, the police and the victim told a remarkable story. The particle analysis showed traces of mercury on the discarded weapon, the one the prosecution said had been used to shoot the ambassador. Mercury also showed up on the suspect and on the flesh and clothing of the ambassador. The combination of residue particles, it turned out, was characteristic of ammunition from Iron Curtain countries, China and the Middle East. Europe and America hadn't used mercury in ordnance for 30 years. Analysis of police weapons and clothing showed only the trinity of barium, antimony and lead.

This information eliminated the possibility that the police, in their arrest of the man, had passed on firearms residue from their own weapons. So there was a clear-cut link between assailant, victim and weapon. The jury returned a verdict of guilty on Said – another victory that was due to the leaps and bounds made by forensic boffins.

FORENSICS AGAINST TERRORISM

The advancement of forensic science has grown at an unprecedented rate over the last decade and police have come to rely more and more on the traces of evidence found at or around the scene of the crime. Modern terrorism challenges conventional methods, with their modern and improvised weapons, especially those designed to cause mass destruction. With recent dramatic terror attacks like September 11, the Madrid bombing in 2003 and the more recent bombings in London, police worldwide are relying ever more on the assistance of the forensic scientist. After any major terror attack the immediate focus is on the victims and putting out any possible fire caused by the explosion. Then the police start putting together the details of the attack, and it is at this point that the forensic scientist and his expertise comes into play.

As in any other crime, it is vital that the forensic team move into the crime scene as soon as possible after the event has occurred, so that any evidence is still fresh and, where possible, is not destroyed or contaminated by the rescue parties. The specially trained anti-terrorist units use every method of modern forensic equipment available to them to collect and analyse samples.

With modern technology it is not always necessary to remove the samples collected to the laboratory, in certain cases the forensic scientist will use a mobile forensic laboratory so that he can analyse any suspect data on the spot. It can analyse samples such as hair, body fluids, glass, paint, drugs and explosives. All this evidence can help track down the suspects especially if they use the same *modus operandi.*

Forensic toxicologists are experts in dealing with chemicals, drugs and poisons, which is an essential service in the case of chemical warfare. Being able to analyse a chemical is paramount not only to the victims but also to the welfare of the crime-fighting personnel. Its use in anti-terrorism has a significant impact on how long a person can be exposed to a certain chemical and what damage it is likely to cause with its toxic gases and vapours.

As science and technology advance and become more sophisticated, in the relatively new field of nuclear forensics it is now possible to identify nuclear materials with high degrees of accuracy. Just as you would with a human fingerprint, nuclear material can be identified, examined and profiled. With the information gathered it is possible to trace even the most microscopic quantities accurately. These advancements in science are once again vitally important in helping our fight against terrorism and securing international safeguards.

MERCURY SHOWED UP ON THE DISCARDED WEAPON, THE SUSPECT AND ON THE FLESH AND CLOTHING OF THE AMBASSADOR.

IT IS VITAL THAT THE FORENSIC TEAM MOVE INTO THE CRIME SCENE AS SOON AS POSSIBLE AFTER THE EVENT SO THAT ANY EVIDENCE IS STILL UNCONTAMINATED.

DNA EVIDENCE
Fingering Criminals

Professor Sir Alec Jeffreys of the University of Leicester stumbled upon the miracle of DNA fingerprinting while he was researching another subject. His brilliance has taken away all hiding places for criminals and advanced the detection of crime more than any other single discovery.

It was a revolutionary request that sparked an enormous amount of controversy. It came when police hunting the maniacal killer of two young girls stepped forward to say they would be "fingerprinting" 2,000 men of a single village in a bid to trap their man. But it wasn't fingerprinting in the normal sense, an ink pad and roller to take the dabs of every male over a certain age in the community. This was "genetic fingerprinting", the technique devised by a brilliant university professor that would compare the living tissue of a person with tissue samples found on the two dead schoolgirls.

The human DNA cannot lie and if the police had a match they also had their killer. There were complaints about civil liberty violations, wrangling from a major chemical company which laid claim to the licensing rights on the process and scepticism from certain old-fashioned lawmen who doubted whether such a new-fangled system could ever replace the old tried and

THE HUMAN DNA CANNOT LIE AND IF THE POLICE HAD A MATCH THEY ALSO HAD THEIR KILLER

Opposite: ***Professor Sir Alec Jeffreys, discoverer of DNA.***

Below: ***Taking a blood sample is all that is needed to begin DNA analysis.***

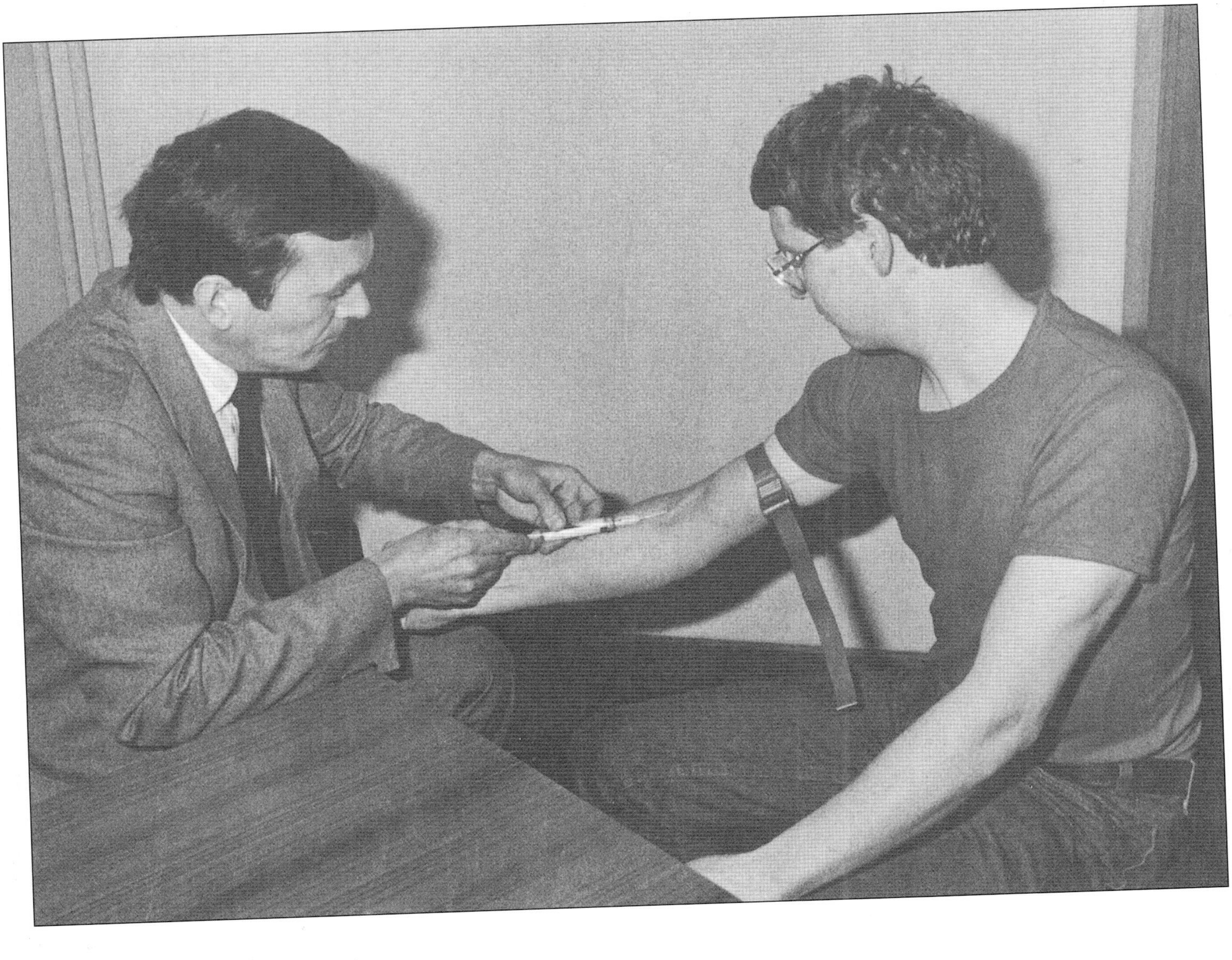

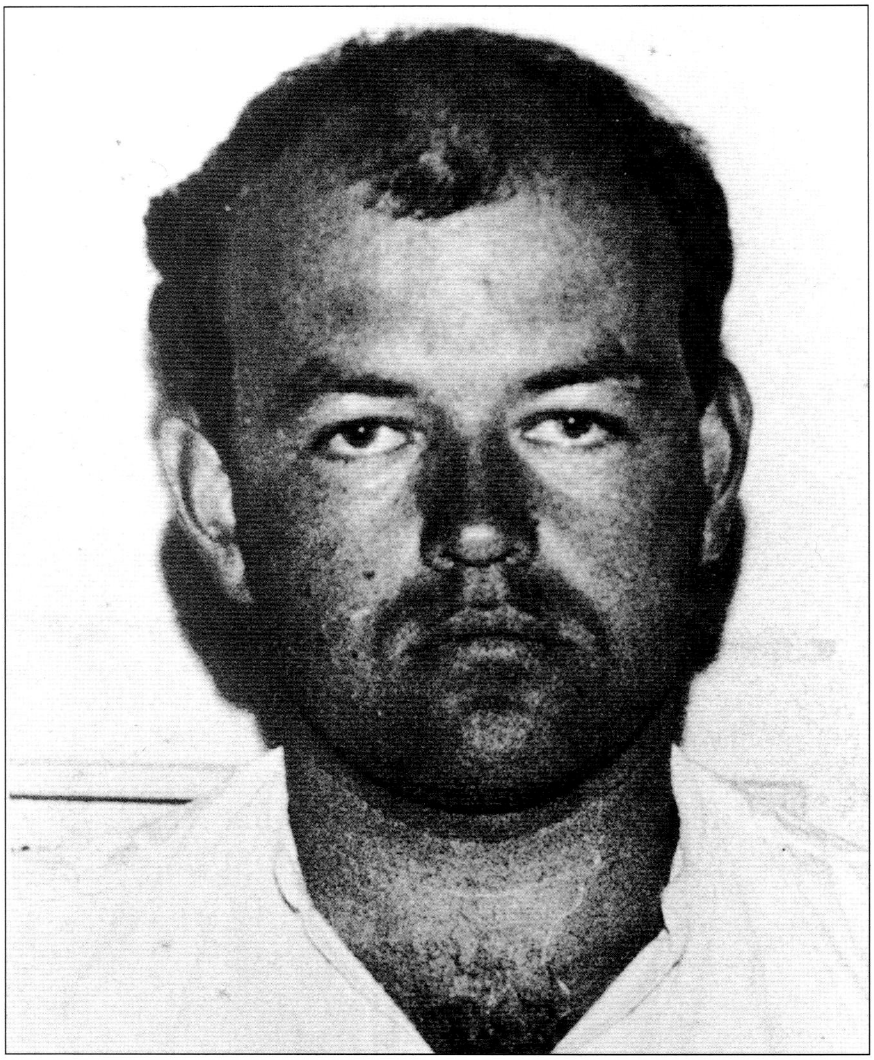

Above: ***Colin Pitchfork, the brutal sex killer who sent a man in his place to give blood when he feared that the DNA test would find him out.***

Right: ***Dawn Ashworth, one of Pitchfork's victims.***

THE MURDERS WERE OF SUCH DEPRAVITY THAT THEY MENTALLY SCARRED THE INHABITANTS OF THE REGION FOR YEARS

trusted policing methods. But the test worked 100 per-cent – sending the guilty man to prison for life and ensuring a place for DNA fingerprinting in criminal detection for decades to come.

The murders of the two girls came three years apart in Leicestershire, murders of such brutality and depravity that they mentally scarred the inhabitants of the region for years. Lynda Mann, 15, was the first to die. She set off from her home in Narborough, Leics., to see a friend in the nearby village of Enderby. It was the evening of November 21 1983 and the girls were going to spend an evening playing records and going over their schoolwork. But Lynda never arrived – her body was found the next morning near a footpath, raped and strangled with her own scarf, tied, police said, with "maniacal ferocity". There was a massive police hunt, nationwide appeals for help and the usual cross-checks through the nationwide police computer to locate sex offenders and child murderers who had been released from jail near to the time of the killing. The enquiry dragged on for months with numerous CID officers manning an emergency incident room, desperately waiting for the one phone call or lead that would set them on the killer's trail. Eventually the investigation, although never closed, was forced to wind down as police manpower was needed for everyday crimefighting.

Three years later came the second brutal killing that bore many of the hallmarks of the first. Dawn Ashworth, also 15, was walking from a friend's home in Enderby to her own on July 31 1986 when she too failed to show up. Her body was found partially covered by hay three days later, near a footpath linking Enderby and Narborough. She too had been raped, but her physical injuries were worse than Lynda's; this time the killer had inflicted much more suffering in his attack.

A post-mortem examination disclosed horrifying injuries to her face, head and private parts. Senior officers at the scene of the crime were certain that the two attacks were linked – that somewhere in their quiet community was dwelling a monster who had urges that could not be controlled.

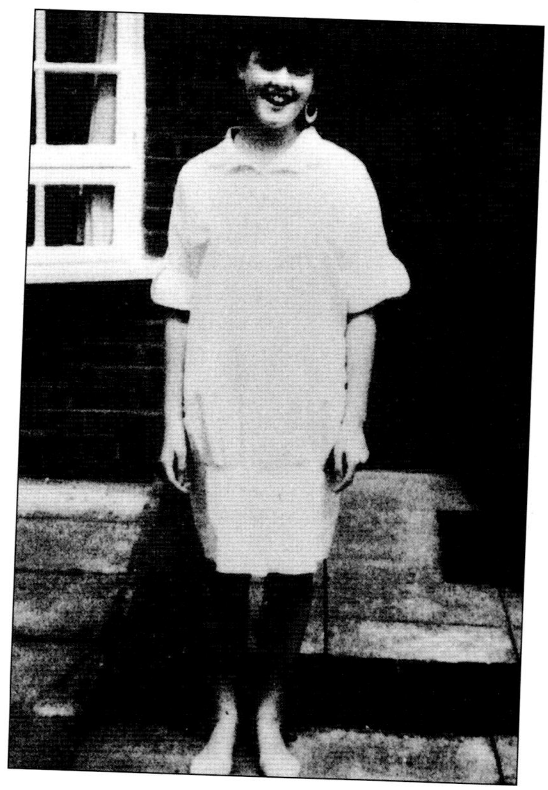

There was another huge manhunt, another mass appeal, anything that could home in on the killer who, the police were certain, was local. His knowledge of the footpaths around the village, near the M1 motorway and just five miles south-west of Leicester, led them to believe he could not be a stranger. Yet he had left no discernible clues at the crime scene... or had he? For in the years that spanned the murders a professor called Alec Jeffreys – later Sir Alec – had literally stumbled upon an astonishing new technique that would have profound consequences for crime and its detection all over the world.

AN ACCIDENTAL MIRACLE

Professor Jeffreys of the University of Leicester stumbled upon DNA fingerprinting while he was researching something else. DNA stands for deoxyribonucleic acid, found in the nuclei of all human body cells. Later Professor Jeffreys would say with characteristic understatement: "Like all good scientific breakthroughs, it was made while searching for something else and shows how important good basic university science is for Britain."

He was working on haemoglobin genes when he discovered that human DNA – the gossamer chemical strands of genetic material that determine individual body characteristics – are unique from person to person. Just as there are no two fingerprints alike, so there are no two specimens of human DNA alike. The possibilities for his discovery became limitless – in learning about the very building blocks of life, in the study of pregnancies and in the application of forensic science. By analysing these sections of DNA, called mini-satellites, a clear genetic fingerprint of a human being can be built up. "From a single drop of blood," said Dr. Jeffreys, "a bar code, unique to an individual, can be made.

"The test is highly accurate and is generally much better than present blood and other tests which often produce inconclusive results." The chiefs of police throughout Britain were not slow in recognising the fantastic potential of his discovery.

Detective Inspector Derek Pearse, leading the investigation into the two murders, first made use of Dr. Jeffrey's remarkable technique to clear a suspect. Richard Buckland, a 17-year-old youth, was wrongly accused and charged with murdering Dawn. He had been seen hanging around the murder scene and was unable to explain his wherabouts on the night to the satisfaction of police officers. He was dramatically freed when DNA tests failed to link him to the murder because the DNA found on both bodies was the same – and he didn't possess it. It led the police to put into effect plans for the biggest DNA testing ever – across three villages in the area involving 2,000 men. So convinced were they that the killer was local they believed he was bound to be flushed out. Police emphasised that the tests were "purely voluntary" – but it was clear that the finger of suspicion would hover unerringly over those individuals who did not step forward.

Thousands of letters were sent out and testing sites arranged for this unique exper-

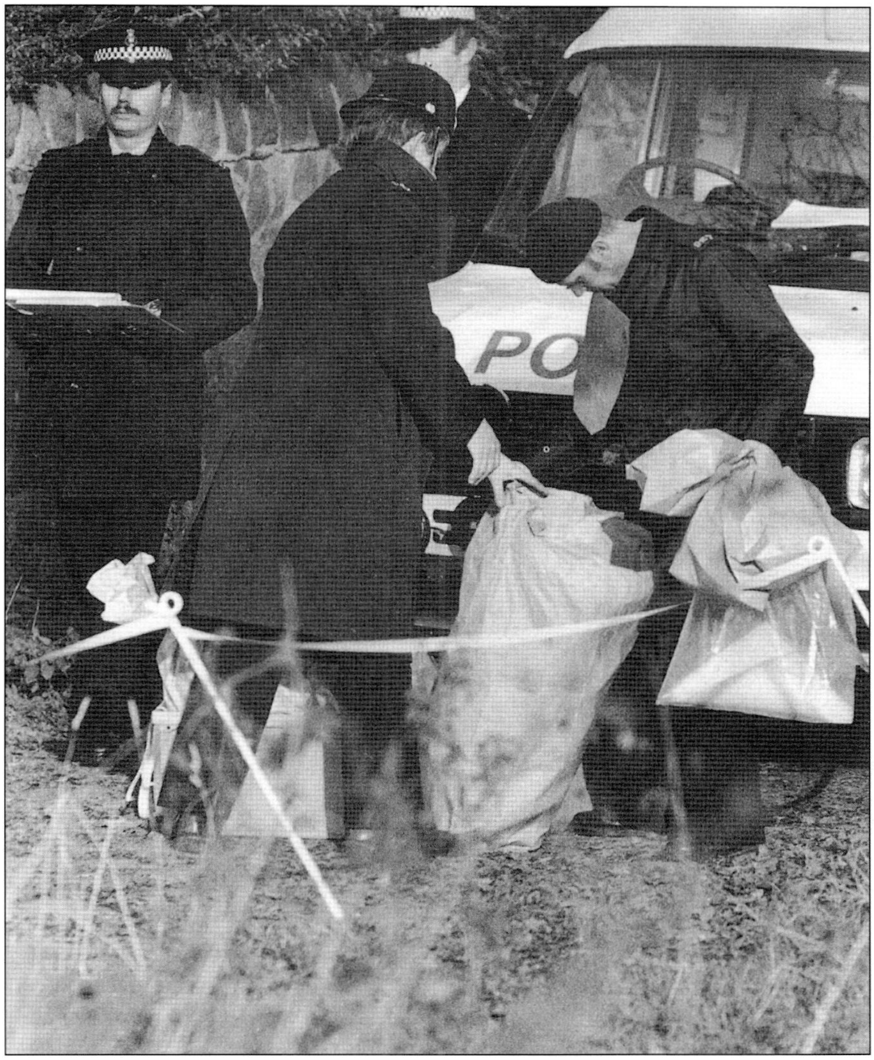

Above: ***Police at the scene of the Lynda Mann murder. It would take an operation unprecedented in the history of crime detection to finally nail her killer.***

HE HAD STUMBLED UPON A TECHNIQUE THAT WOULD HAVE PROFOUND CONSEQUENCES FOR CRIME

iment in the science of crime fighting. But before it got off the ground there were problems. The chemical giant ICI claimed it owned the exclusive rights to the test and clearly felt it had expertise to offer.

In a statement in January 1987 the company said: "We know nothing about police plans to use our test. We are very concerned about this. We are the only people who have the right and capacity to carry out wide-scale testing using genetic fingerprinting but Leicester police haven't approached us at all."

ICI had indeed bought the copyright from Professor Jeffreys. There were also disquieting rumbles from some civil liberties quarters who felt personal rights could be trampled on in the mass test. But in time the problems were smoothed over and the government labs at Aldermaston were made ready to receive the tests.

Police wrote to men in the three villages between the ages of 17 and 33. Det. Insp. Pearse said: "The public response has so

Above: ***The grieving parents of Dawn Ashworth, with Det. Chf. Supt. David Baker at their side, made a plea for the killer to give himself up.***

Right: ***A policewoman dressed in clothes similar to Dawn's strolls near to where her body was found in a bid to jog the memories of potential witnesses.***

THOUSANDS OF LETTERS WERE SENT OUT AND TESTING SITES ARRANGED FOR A UNIQUE EXPERIMENT IN CRIME FIGHTING

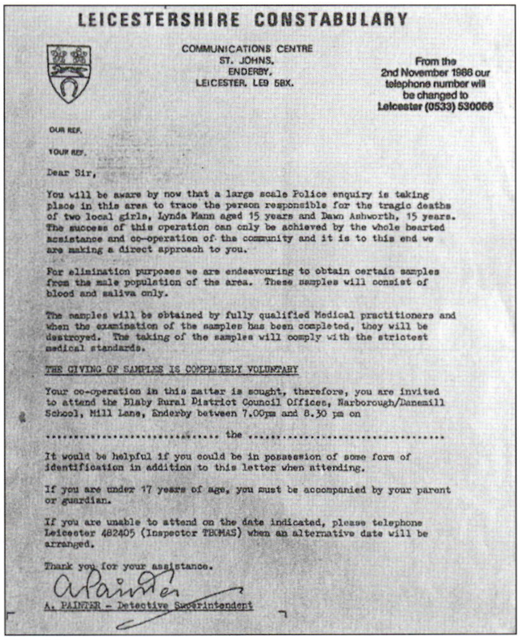

LEICESTERSHIRE CONSTABULARY

COMMUNICATIONS CENTRE
ST. JOHNS.
ENDERBY.
LEICESTER. LE9 5BX.

From the 2nd November 1986 our telephone number will be changed to Leicester (0533) 530066

OUR REF.

YOUR REF.

Dear Sir,

You will be aware by now that a large scale Police enquiry is taking place in this area to trace the person responsible for the tragic deaths of two local girls, Lynda Mann aged 15 years and Dawn Ashworth, 15 years. The success of this operation can only be achieved by the whole hearted assistance and co-operation of the community and it is to this end we are making a direct approach to you.

For elimination purposes we are endeavouring to obtain certain samples from the male population of the area. These samples will consist of blood and saliva only.

The samples will be obtained by fully qualified Medical practitioners and when the examination of the samples has been completed, they will be destroyed. The taking of the samples will comply with the strictest medical standards.

THE GIVING OF SAMPLES IS COMPLETELY VOLUNTARY

Your co-operation in this matter is sought, therefore, you are invited to attend the Blaby Rural District Council Offices, Narborough/Danemill School, Mill Lane, Enderby between 7.00pm and 8.30 pm on

.... the ....

It would be helpful if you could be in possession of some form of identification in addition to this letter when attending.

If you are under 17 years of age, you must be accompanied by your parent or guardian.

If you are unable to attend on the date indicated, please telephone Leicester 482405 (Inspector THOMAS) when an alternative date will be arranged.

Thank you for your assistance.

A. PAINTER - Detective Superintendent

Left: ***The letter sent to the male population in the area around the murder site.***

far been overwhelming. Hundreds of people have phoned the murder incident room to book a test, including students and servicemen. We haven't had one refusal so far." For some men, the tests were a great weight off their minds – they had become the target of suspicion and innuendo in a small community where neighbour was being turned against neighbour in the witch-hunt hysteria that surrounded the search for the killer. Groups of youths were among those volunteering together, so it could be seen that they were volunteering.

LIVING IN FEAR

But one man who had no intention of volunteering for anything was Colin Pitchfork. Pitchfork, of Littlethorpe – one of the villages earmarked for the test – had much to be afraid of, for it was he who had murdered the innocent schoolgirls to satisfy his perverted lust. A 27-year-old misfit with a history of exposing himself to women, he had been careful at the crimesites not to leave behind any items of clothing or other clues which might possibly lead detectives to his door. Yet he had read the newspapers; he knew that he could not possibly hope to beat the DNA test.

At the bakery where he worked Pitchfork told workmates he had previous convictions for indecent exposure before he married in 1981. He laughed them off, attributing them to high-spiritedness after drinking, saying he wasn't "a pervert" but merely someone the police were out to get for what he considered a minor crime.

Using that as his theme he began to pester his workmates to step forward in his place. He tried to persuade them that the police would never know that he was at home if they went and gave their sample. "They want to fit me up for what happened before," he told them. "I would be a prime target for the police hoping to pin this on someone." The power of the DNA test was clearly great, even though it had not been performed on him. He offered one young man £50 to go in his place, then another £200. Finally, he persuaded a workmate named Ian Kelly, 23, to go instead and even coached him after hours at the bakery in how to forge his signature and memorise

Below: ***Ian Kelly, who had his blood tested in Colin Pitchfork's place.***

"extraordinary lengths" to evade justice, but that in the end his partner in the deception had had second thoughts about it.

Judge Mr. Justice Otton had special praise for Dr. Jeffreys' breakthrough, saying: "In this case it not only led to the apprehension of the correct murderer, but also ensured that suspicion was removed from an innocent man.

"Had it not been for genetic fingerprinting, Colin Pitchfork might still be at liberty and that is too terrible a thing to contemplate." Kelly, of Leicester, admitting providing blood and saliva samples to police while pretending to be Pitchfork. He admitted conspiracy and was jailed for 18 months, suspended for two years. Pitchfork had told police that he never intended to murder the two girls – merely to achieve a sexual thrill by exposing himself to them.

certain details of his family life. On January 22 1986 Kelly stepped forward at the incident room pretending to be Colin Pitchfork. His blood sample was taken and the name of Colin Pitchfork was removed from suspects in due course when it was found that his DNA did not match that found at the murder scene.

But Kelly, essentially a decent young man who was cajoled and pressurised into taking the test, began to have his doubts. He talked it over among workmates who also thought that Pitchfork's reluctance might be based on more than a mere suspicion that the police were after him for previous convictions of exposing himself.

One of these workmates went to police and told them of the deception. A police squad swooped that night and both men were arrested. As he was being taken into custody it dawned on police that only Pitchfork and one other man, excused from giving a sample for medical reasons, were the only ones who did not respond to their appeal for help. And when a sample of Pitchfork's blood and hair was sent off for analysis it linked him to both murders, murders which he could no longer deny.

He appeared at Leicester Crown Court a year later where he was sentenced to two terms of life imprisonment and concurrent terms for the sexual assaults on the girls, plus conspiracy to pervert the course of justice. Mr. Brian Escott-Cox, QC, prosecuting, told the court that he had gone to

Both were random attacks that went wrong. He became highly aroused, raped them then killed them to prevent identification.

After Pitchfork's conviction, the potential for genetic fingerprinting leaped onwards. Police may soon have genetic "photofits" at their disposal, predicting the sex, race, hair and eye colour of suspects from forensic samples. Dr. Jeffreys said that rapid advances in molecular genetics means that semen, blood or even tiny traces of saliva from the scene of a crime could reveal their owner's characteristics. DNA profiles are anonymous at present – it is impossible to tell if samples are from a teenager or a 50-year-old.

AN IMPERFECT SOLUTION

But Dr. Jeffreys said that "decoding" a person's genetic make-up would lead to even more clues. He said: "Criminal investigations where DNA evidence is available will frequently flounder due to the lack of a suspect. The sex of an individual can already be determined by a simple method of DNA analysis, but that is about it.

"Some of the difficulties scientists face include height, which is partly due to genetic make-up but also partly due to environment. It's not as simple as saying: 'Here's a band on the DNA fingerprint so their nose will be a certain number of centimetres long.' There might be a case for keeping the profiles of previous offenders. In the end it will come down to assessing whether such a database would be cost effective." Soon, very soon, what Dr. Jeffreys calls "fantastically small" amounts of DNA could lead to full genetic profiles. It means a kidnapper who licks the stamp for his ransom demand could be caught by the minute spittle left on it. Such is the power of the discovery that Dr. Jeffreys stumbled on by accident!

Now both the Home Office and the FBI in America are considering a DNA database that would span both countries. A database of all previous sex offenders – given that a high proportion of them reoffend after release from jail – might be the logical course to pursue. Dr. Jeffreys makes the point that had there been one in effect when Pitchfork was around, "we would have caught him, the Yorkshire Ripper and every rapist and murderer when there is plenty of biological evidence but no suspect". The civil liberties arguments against such a database appear groundless when it is considered that the genetic code reveals absolutely nothing about a person.

Above: ***Colin Pitchfork, his head hidden under a blanket, is driven away from a court hearing. He was eventually sentenced to life.***

Opposite Top: ***Yorkshire Ripper, Peter Sutcliffe (extreme right), might have been caught more quickly if DNA had been in existence when he was on the loose in the 1970s.***

Opposite Below: ***A smiling killer in a morning suit – Colin Pitchfork on his wedding day in 1981.***

GIVEN THE POTENTIAL OF DNA TESTING, THE ONLY CRUCIAL QUESTION IS HOW FAR HUMAN CURIOSITY WISHES TO GO

"There is no way a bureaucrat could divine anything about you other than the fact that the material came from you – the anonymous nature of these patterns is vital," said Dr. Jeffreys.

Since the success in the murders case the number of applications for DNA tests have multiplied; in the first 18 months following the case he was besieged by immigrant families imploring him to DNA-test their families to establish relationship. "Settling immigration cases has been wonderful," said the professor. "It is wonderfully worthwhile." It has also been used to determine paternity of a baby in a number of lawsuits, which, he says, "just reveal what squalid and complicated lives some people have".

Given the untold potential of the testing, the only crucial question is how far human curiousity wishes to go. Tests can determine if a person is carrying a defective gene which at 20 could lead to the onset of a fatal disease at 40 or 50. "Do people really want to know about these time bombs inside them?" he asked.

Yet whatever the future applications, Leicestershire police and the people of that county have cause to be eternally grateful to him for putting behind bars a man who deserved no place in decent society.

FUTURE DNA FORENSIC USES

Advancements in DNA research now allow laboratory technicians to identify precise genetic marks from the smallest piece of evidence left at the scene of a crime. It could now be said that DNA testing has become one of the most important tools in solving crime since the development of fingerprinting a century ago. DNA samples recovered from the crime scene can now be used to incriminate an individual with an astounding degree of accuracy or, as in the case of Frank Lee Smith, exculpate a wrongly-accused person. For whatever reason, DNA testing has certainly revolutionised the way in which the police process their evidence and investigate certain types of crimes.

FRANK LEE SMITH IS EXONERATED

Frank Lee Smith spent 14 years on Florida's death row after being charged with the brutal murder of an eight-year-old girl that took place on April 15, 1985.

Frank Lee was by no means a model citizen, he had already spent a spell in prison for a previous crime. But when he came out in the mid-eighties he was prepared to turn over a new leaf and make a new life for himself. But this was not to be.

The evidence which convicted Frank Lee was very shaky as it relied on eyewitness descriptions from neighbours and the victim's mother. The investigation was centred on a six-foot black male, with very muscular arms, shoulders and chest, approximately 30 years old and wearing jeans and an orange coloured T-shirt. The police put together a composite sketch and Frank Lee was arrested on April 29, 1985.

The prosecution relied totally on the identification of Frank Lee by the victim's mother, who identified him as the man she had seen jumping out of her living room window on the night of the murder. They also relied on his past criminal history, but apart from this information there was very little to say that Frank Lee Smith was guilty of murdering and raping the little girl.

Frank Lee's defence team submitted an insanity plea, but this was turned down by the court and he was found guilty of murder and given the death penalty.

Although his death warrant was signed in 1989, Frank Lee managed to win a stay of execution. In 1998, the Supreme Court ordered that there was to be a hearing due to the fact that they had been presented with new evidence. At the time this new evidence had nothing to do with DNA samples, one of the eyewitnesses had changed her story having been shown a picture of another suspect. With this new evidence the judge requested that DNA forensic sampling be carried out.

Unfortunately, it was only after Frank Lee died of cancer on January 30, 2000, that he was totally exonerated of the crime. The DNA samples that were taken of his blood and of the semen found in the victim's vagina, did not match. It was 11 months after Frank Lee's death and 14 years after his initial conviction that the DNA evidence was

'FRANK WAS THE ANGRIEST MAN I'VE EVER KNOWN. HE JUST COULDN'T COMPREHEND WHAT WAS HAPPENING TO HIM.'

Below: *O. J. Simpson looks at a new pair of Aris extra-large gloves that prosecutors asked him to put on during his trial in Los Angeles on June 21, 1995.*

to prove conclusively that Frank Lee did not commit the murder. It also identified the true perpetrator, Eddie Lee Mosley, a previously convicted rapist and murderer.

O. J. SIMPSON COURT DRAMA

The O. J. Simpson case went down in history as the longest jury trial in Californian history. The ex-football star turned sports announcer captured the attention of the world media when he was charged with the murder of his ex-wife Nicole Simpson and her friend Ronald Goldman on June 12, 1994.

The defence team hired by O. J., who became nicknamed the 'Dream Team', undermined the prosecution's evidence and suggested that the key physical evidence against their client was either contaminated or planted, or perhaps both. The case not only caught the public eye but it was televised daily, in fact just like a 'soap' – 133 episodes of a real courtroom drama. The evidence at the time seemed incriminating but as the case unravelled the outcome seemed more and more uncertain.

Blood stains found at the crime scene were tested to determine blood type and to provide DNA samples. Blood stains were found in Simpson's white Bronco car, on a pair of socks in his bedroom, on a pair of gloves, at the crime scene, in his driveway and in his house. The prosecution stated that the blood evidence proved that Simpson was the murderer, while the defence challenged that the blood was either contaminated and/or planted.

Another criticial piece of evidence in the trial was a pair of gloves. The left-handed glove was found outside the residence of Nicole Brown Simpson, and the right-handed glove was recovered from Simpson's estate. During the court session the judge requested that Simpson put on the gloves and after what appeared to be a little 'play acting' announced that they were too small. The prosecution suggested that the gloves, once drenched in blood, would have shrunk. However, the defence team contended that if the gloves didn't fit, Simpson could not be the killer.

The murders were believed to have been carried out using a single-edged knife, and O.J. Simpson had purchased a single-edged knife just a few days prior to the murders. Possibly the most compelling and important fact regarding this knife is that the actual murder weapon has never been found.

FBI shoe print specialist, William Bodziak, testified that shoe prints found at the murder scene were left by size 12 Bruno Magli shoes. Although the actual shoes which left the footprints have never been recovered, comparisons showed that O.J. Simpson could have worn the shoes.

'I DEEPLY BELIEVE THAT THIS COUNTRY LOST TODAY. JUSTICE WAS NOT SERVED.'

By the end of the trial all the members of the jury, who had been isolated for the best part of a year, were showing signs of exhaustion and stress. They spent only three hours deliberating over the case and at 10.00 a.m. on October 3, 1995, the verdict was announced as the public watched:

> *We the jury in the above entitled action find the defendant, Orenthal James Simpson, not guilty of the crime of murder.*

Although DNA evidence can be used as evidence in court it is by no means foolproof, as the case of O. J. Simpson proved. Although the evidence appeared damning, the defence team managed not only to convince the jury that the DNA samples taken at the time of the murder had been corrupted during testing, but they also managed to refocus their attention on the corruption in the Los Angeles Police Department.

In interviews with the jurors after the trial, a few said that they believed Simpson probably did commit the murder, but that the prosecution bungled the case. Those jurors that mentioned the DNA evidence showed an obvious lack of understanding of its relevance in the case.

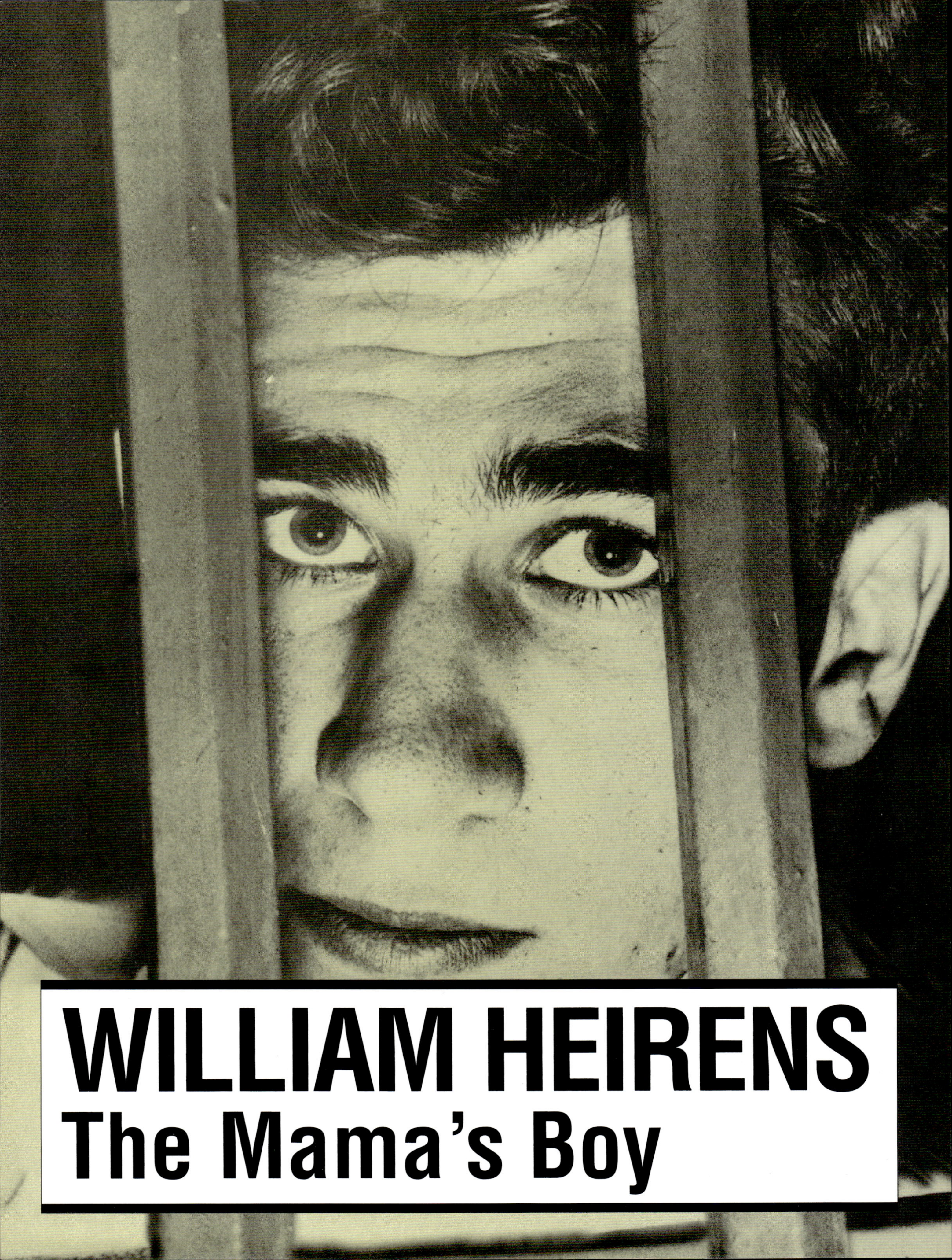
WILLIAM HEIRENS
The Mama's Boy

William Heirens pitted his evil wits against the best that law enforcement could throw at him after committing crimes against defenceless victims. He lost his perverse battle with the law, thanks to the advancements in forensic science that pinned him to his crimes like a butterfly to a board.

It was a balmy day in Chicago on June 3 1945, the breeze coming from Lake Michigan affording little relief to the residents of the huge metropolis. Many sought shelter on that afternoon in movie theatres – one of the few places, aside from the huge slaughterhouses which gave the city its nickname "Hog Town" – that had air conditioning. Attractive widow Josephine Alice Ross was thinking of going to the cinema that day too, but instead stayed at home... a decision that was to cost her her life. The nude body of the 43-year-old woman was found later on her bed, her skirt and a nylon stocking tied around her throat. But she hadn't died from strangulation – huge knife wounds covered her face and neck and it was later determined that she bled to death. The most peculiar aspect of the crime scene to detectives was the blood-soaked towels and her own pyjamas lying in a tub of water in the bathroom. Captain Frank Reynolds of the Chicago police department glanced at his men and said: "The killer washed the blood from the body. This is a new one on me."

The body of the dead woman was found at lunchtime that day by her 17-year-old daughter who had left the apartment shortly before 9.00am, so she had been murdered in a four-hour time period. There was no sexual assault on the body, no money was missing, no valuables taken. It all pointed to a frenzied, motiveless murder. The killer, police learned, would have had no trouble entering the apartment as she never kept

THE NUDE BODY OF THE WOMAN WAS FOUND LATER ON HER BED, HER SKIRT AND A NYLON STOCKING TIED AROUND HER THROAT

Opposite: ***The face of pure evil stares through the bars of a cell. There was to be no escape for William Heirens.***

Below: ***Josephine Ross (left) and Frances Brown (right), two of Heirens' victims.***

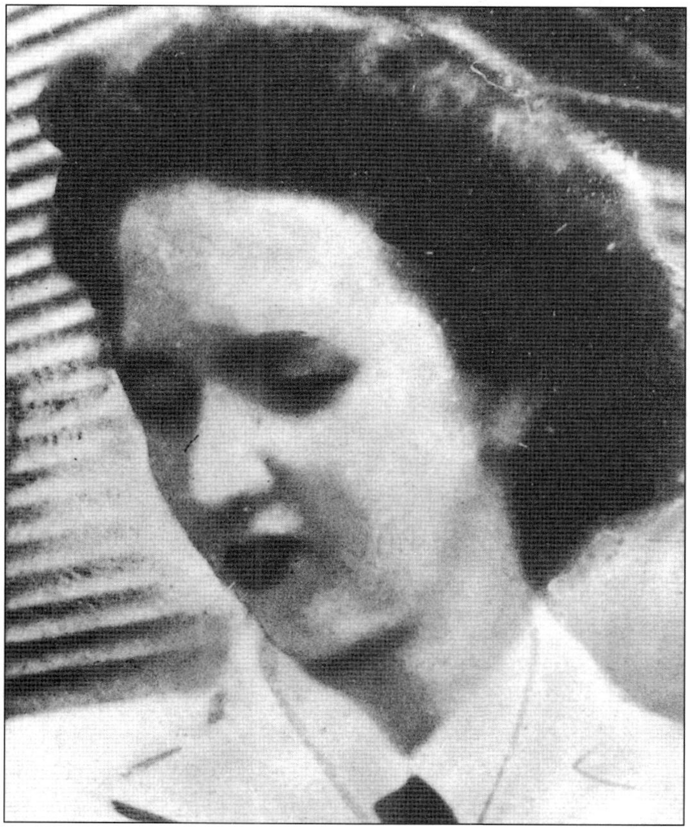

Above: ***A monster's victim, six-year-old Suzanne Degnan (left), seen here with her sister Elizabeth.***

SCRAWLED ON A WALL WAS A MESSAGE: "FOR HEAVEN'S SAKE CATCH ME BEFORE I KILL MORE. I CANNOT CONTROL MYSELF"

the door locked. And he was a methodical man – he had wiped the place clean of all fingerprints. He was so thorough the forensic experts didn't even find a print of her daughter or her sister who also lived there.

Yet on that first day they questioned two eyewitnesses, a janitor and a neighbour, who swore that they had seen a hatless young man walking into the building wearing a white sweater and dark trousers with his hair brushed back in a pompadour. One saw him enter, the other saw him leaving around two hours later – the delay was probably the result of his obsessive cleaning of the apartment.

Months went by and no suspect was turned up. The initial police theory that the man was a lover of Mrs. Ross who had lost his head in an argument could not be substantiated. Every man who knew the widow was questioned and eliminated from the investigation. But as time went on several more apparently meaningless, equally brutal attacks were made on women in the city. On October 1 Veronica Hudzinski, 19, was shot with a revolver and barely lived.

Four days later Army nurse Evelyn Peterson was beaten unconscious in her home and was in the process of being strangled with electrical flex when the man suddenly stopped and asked if he could get her a doctor. He walked calmly from the apartment as she clung to life... but not before he wiped the place clean of dabs. A second unexplained shooting happened on December 5, and again the victim managed to escape with just minor injuries.

But five days later the body of 30-year-old Frances Brown was found draped over a washtub at the residential Pine Crest Hotel. Near the body, scrawled on a wall in her bright red lipstick, was a message: "For Heaven's Sake Catch Me Before I Kill More. I Cannot Control Myself." The victim had been shot, strangled, and her face mutliated with deep knife wounds. And her body had been washed of blood and the room wiped down meticulously to remove all fingerprints. She too had not been sexually molested.

A VITAL MISTAKE

Yet this time the killer made one slight slip. He had indeed been methodical in removing the fingerprints, but not methodical enough. On the left jamb of the bathroom door was a print of one finger. It was a seemingly hopeless task matching this one print to an individual as the Chicago police department filed and classified fingerprints according to the dominant characteristics of all five fingers. Nevertheless a police sergeant named Thomas Laffey was assigned the mindbending task of sorting through 1,250,000 sets of prints. If nothing else, public opinion needed to be satisfied that everything was being done.

But four weeks later the horror of the murders and woundings receded in the public consciousness with the kidnapping of six-year-old Suzanne Degnan. Suzanne had gone to bed on the evening of January 7 1946 in her parents' home a mile from the Ross murder site – and the next morning her father James, going into her bedroom, found the window was open and the bed empty.

Two policemen cruising the area in a patrol car were there within a minute, one of them finding on the floor of her room a note that read: "Get $20,000 Ready & Wait For Word. Do Not Notify FBI or Police. Bills in 5's and 10's." On the reverse side of the note in capitals was the threat: "BURN THIS FOR HER SAFETY."

With police help, her father made a desperate and heart-rending appeal on the city radio station to return the little girl. The police didn't initially tell him, but the clues at the crime scene pointed to the fact that her abductor could be the same maniac responsible for the murders and woundings. There was a single print on the note that didn't correspond to the print found at the last murder… but did correspond with a fragment of fingerprint that a second search of the first murder scene had thrown up! Police were downcast and certain that a man of such a psychotic nature might already have murdered the little girl.

Later that night, as her father's wireless appeal was repeated over the city airwaves, two detectives lifted the lid of a storm drain. Floating in the sewer water beneath was the head of Suzanne. The rest of her body was missing.

During the next four hours Mayor Kelly had to repeatedly go on the air to assure Chicagoans of their safety. In the same period the other parts of little Suzanne's body were found in various sewers across the city. Something approaching panic gripped the usually stoical citizens of Chicago, many of whom protested outside the police department headquarters. Yet some progress was already being made in the hunt for the killer even as they shouted threats of violence.

FLOATING IN THE SEWER BENEATH WAS THE HEAD OF SUZANNE. THE REST OF HER BODY WAS MISSING

EYES OF TRUTH

A witness was found who could have seen the murderer; a former Marine had been parked in his car near the Degnan home talking to his girlfriend when he saw a young man walk by with a shopping bag. The shopping bag was later found containing parts of the little girl's dismembered body. An intensive search of the region

Below: ***Mr and Mrs James Degnan, the strain showing in their tired eyes, wait for news of their little girl.***

turned up a small piece of twisted wire on which were found three head hairs that matched Suzanne's. A handkerchief was wrapped round one end of the wire – a hanky bearing the initials 3168-S. Sherman. It was customary for soldiers at the time to mark their possessions with the last four digits of their serial numbers. A search was launched to find the owner.

Above: ***Bones sifted from the ashes of an incinerator in Chicago – the incinerator that Heirens used as his DIY crematorium for his victims.***

THE EXPERTS' ESTIMATE

As the hunt was on, forensic experts determined that Suzanne had died between 12.30 and 1.00am, strangled with the piece of wire that was found with the handkerchief. There were traces of coal dust on her feet and in her hair roots. Other than that, various parts of the body appeared to have been washed after they had been cut away. But the clue of the coal was later to prove significant in catching the killer.

Detectives believed that the coal dust indicated the girl had been dissected in a cellar. The next morning police began house-to-house searches of all cellars in the neighbourhood of Suzanne's home. In the afternoon they appeared to strike gold. In the basement of a four-storey house on Winthrop Avenue, just a block from her home, detectives found faint smears of blood in the basement and in a drain trap discovered bits of flesh and blonde hairs.

DETECTIVES BELIEVED THAT THE COAL DUST INDICATED THE GIRL HAD BEEN DISSECTED IN A CELLAR

A woman tenant in the apartment directly above said she had been disturbed at 2.30am by someone in the laundry room running water. A new shipment of coal had come that morning and when detectives moved it they discovered bloodstains from the bin on the floor.

A locker belonging to one of the tenants had been forced open. Inside it had been the shopping bag which was eventually found floating in the sewer with parts of Suzanne's body inside. The man didn't live in the building as a door was found forced. Later police would find out that the handkerchief belonged to an innocent sailor called Sherman whose home had been burgled. They now believed they were looking for a thief who had been transformed into an unstoppable, murderous beast.

Harry Gold, a man who had been on holiday in Florida when the Suzanne murder occurred, returned home to find his apartment – one that overlooked the dead girl's home – ransacked. They believed the culprit had gone to the apartment on a burglary and on an impulse had seen the little girl and decided to enter the apartment for another moneymaking scheme – except that his own berserk impulses were unable to stop him ultimately from killing her.

The guilty man's arrest, despite one of the largest police efforts in Chicago history, finally came through pure chance – even though it wasn't for some hours that they realised that the man they had could be the maniac they were seeking. A youthful burglar was caught after being chased by police. The sprightly thief was fleet-footed and gave a long chase, turning to fire on his pursuer. But an off duty police officer finally hurled three flowerpots on to his head and he offered no more resistance. Papers on the youth identified him as William Heirens, a 17-year-old student at the Chicago University.

THEY WERE LOOKING FOR A THIEF WHO HAD BEEN TRANSFORMED INTO AN UNSTOPPABLE, MURDEROUS BEAST

PREVIOUS FORM

A check on police records showed that he had been arrested in 1942, when he was 13, for carrying a pistol. Other arrests were for a string of burglaries – six homes which he torched after looting. Heirens was taken to a prison hospital for wounds sustained during his arrest. While he recovered, police seized a large arsenal of weapons at the house where he lived with his parents in a city suburb. These included a rifle, a .25 calibre pistol, two .38 revolvers and four more pistols and a rifle hidden under tarpaulin on the roof.

This seemed encouraging enough, but Heirens lay in a coma in hospital. As he remained unconscious a search of his room on the university campus turned up stolen

Below: ***A telegram from the FBI showing that Heirens' palm prints matched those on the ransom note in the Degnan child case.***

Above: ***Three detectives who did mankind a favour – the ones who caught Heirens. They are Detective Abner Cunningham (standing), Det. William Owens (left) and Det. Tiffen Constant.***

Right: ***Heirens, flanked by his mother and father and surrounded by lawmen.***

MINUTE PARTICLES OF DUST ON HIS SHOES MATCHED THE DUST IN THE CELLAR WHERE THE LITTLE GIRL WAS CUT UP

property from dozens of burglaries – including items taken from the Gold home opposite the murdered girl's house. But it didn't link him directly with the murders – not until a dirty pair of shoes was handed to the forensic department that had collated scenes-of-crime clues. An examination of minute particles of dust on the soles of his shoes matched exactly the coal dust found in the cellar where the little girl was cut up.

A police department expert, Brian Connolly, said: "There are hundreds of grades of coal, thousands of sub-grades. But using a chemical solution and a machine which span the dust particles from the shoes and the cellar we were able to determine, without question, that they had come from the same source. Whatever else he did or didn't do, those shoes and the person in them had been in that cellar. And the samples were all taken while he was unaware. There was more. Underneath the killer's fingernails were minute quantities of soap. These were removed as he slept and placed through similar testing at a laboratory which determined that it was exact-

Above: ***Carried from his hospital bed by detectives, Heirens is pictured en route to his appointment with a lie detector machine.***

ly the same kind of soap which he had used to wash the chopped-up corpse with."

For three days more, police kept this information from him, preferring a confession to relying solely on forensic evidence. Too often before it had been thrown out of court by laymen jurors who were medieval in their outlook when it came to "new fangled" devices such as acid tests, solutions and spectrographs.

When he finally came around from his "coma" – a feigned state which police think was a device to bide him some thinking time – he rambled on about another man called George Murman being responsible for the crimes. He agreed to go under sodium pentathol – truth serum – an experiment that backfired badly for the police.

AN INTERESTING DRUG

The injection of sodium pentathol induces the patient to a state of narcosynthesis, blotting out the active mind, freeing the subconscious state to answer questions. Most times the person who receives the drug cannot help himself in telling the truth. But Heirens spoke of the mystery man George with such clarity and conviction that the police and FBI thought they had blown it. The stenographic record of the polygraph machine linked up to him seemed to suggest that every answer he gave, however implausible, was the truth. Only the undisputed forensic evidence gave the police hope of proceeding with the prosecution. Detective Chief Storms said: "We could have nailed him on burglary charges no problem, but the truth test stymied us. We needed that forensic badly."

An extensive search across America, utilising police files, FBI data, servicemen's records, missing persons' records and social security numbers failed to find any record of a George Murman, the mystery man that Heirens said he befriended in a hotel in Chicago shortly before the little girl was murdered.

Police were willing to risk a prosecution on the strength of the forensic evidence alone when Heirens was forced to undergo a psychiatric examination. Mind doctors believed that Heirens had managed to sink into a deep psychotic state in which he possessed an alter ego – George – that had carried out the killings.

Above: ***A Dr Stein (left) conducts the lie detector test on the Mama's Boy.***

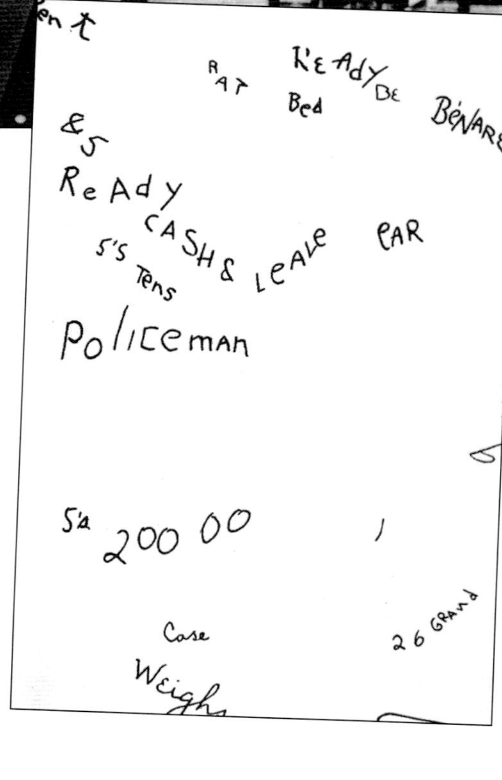

Right: *A Phoenix forensic specialist noted that Thomas's handwriting closely resembled that found on a ransom note found in the Degnan home.* Chicago Daily News *artist Frank Hamel, who was assisting the police, discovered "hidden indentation writing" which linked Heirens to the note.*

He was indicted on a total of 27 burglaries and four woundings as a means of holding him in jail while enquiries continued. There was still no proof of linking him with the murders unless he confessed. There seemed little chance of a direct confession and so the case was to hinge on the soap and coal dust.

Yet on August 6 the same impulses that had snapped to change him from a burglar to murder, snapped to turn him from innocent to guilty. He admitted killing the two women and the child, saying he derived sexual satisfaction from the deaths even though he didn't rape them or otherwise sexually molest them. "I got a real thrill," he said. "It was more the breaking in than the murders. I just lost it. But I never touched them in that way." He could not say why he had lingered for two hours each time over the deaths of his victims, nor why he had washed them.

HE ADMITTED KILLING THE TWO WOMEN AND THE CHILD, SAYING HE DERIVED SEXUAL SATISFACTION FROM THE DEATHS

REAL FANTASY

And he finally admitted that George was a figment of his own imagination. "To me he's very real," said Heirens. "He exists. You can accept George as being me but, well, it's hard to explain. A couple of times I had talks with him. I suppose I was really talking to myself. I wrote lots of notes to him which I kept."

It was during his confession that psychiatrists noted continued references to his mother, about how he always wanted to please her throughout his life and how he always seemed to fail to do so. Hence the nickname "Mama's Boy" which stuck with him through the trial and the rest of his days behind bars.

On September 7 1946 he pleaded guilty to the murders and was ordered to be held for life without any possibility of parole. Shortly after entering the Illinois State Penitentiary he became an unruly, troublesome prisoner who was often in trouble for fighting and infracting other prison rules. He was again examined by psychiatrists who deemed him insane and he was transferred to a mental institution similar to Britain's Broadmoor.

William Heirens tore up the rule book for serial killers. Men who kill mature women don't go after children. Burglars don't become serial killers. Burglars don't become snipers who shoot women. The only thread running through his crimes was the strange washing-up afterwards of the bodies which brings the police to an ironic postscript to his evil reign. For forensic scientist David Steinman said: "Had he washed the bodies in warm water instead of cold – and wiped his shoes with warm water instead of cold – he would have removed the forensic evidence. That in turn would have made police loathe to charge him and in turn he would have served some time for burglary and been on the streets of Chicago within a decade. We are lucky he didn't have warm water."

Below: ***Smiling and casual, this portrait of Heirens was snapped just after his attempted suicide.***

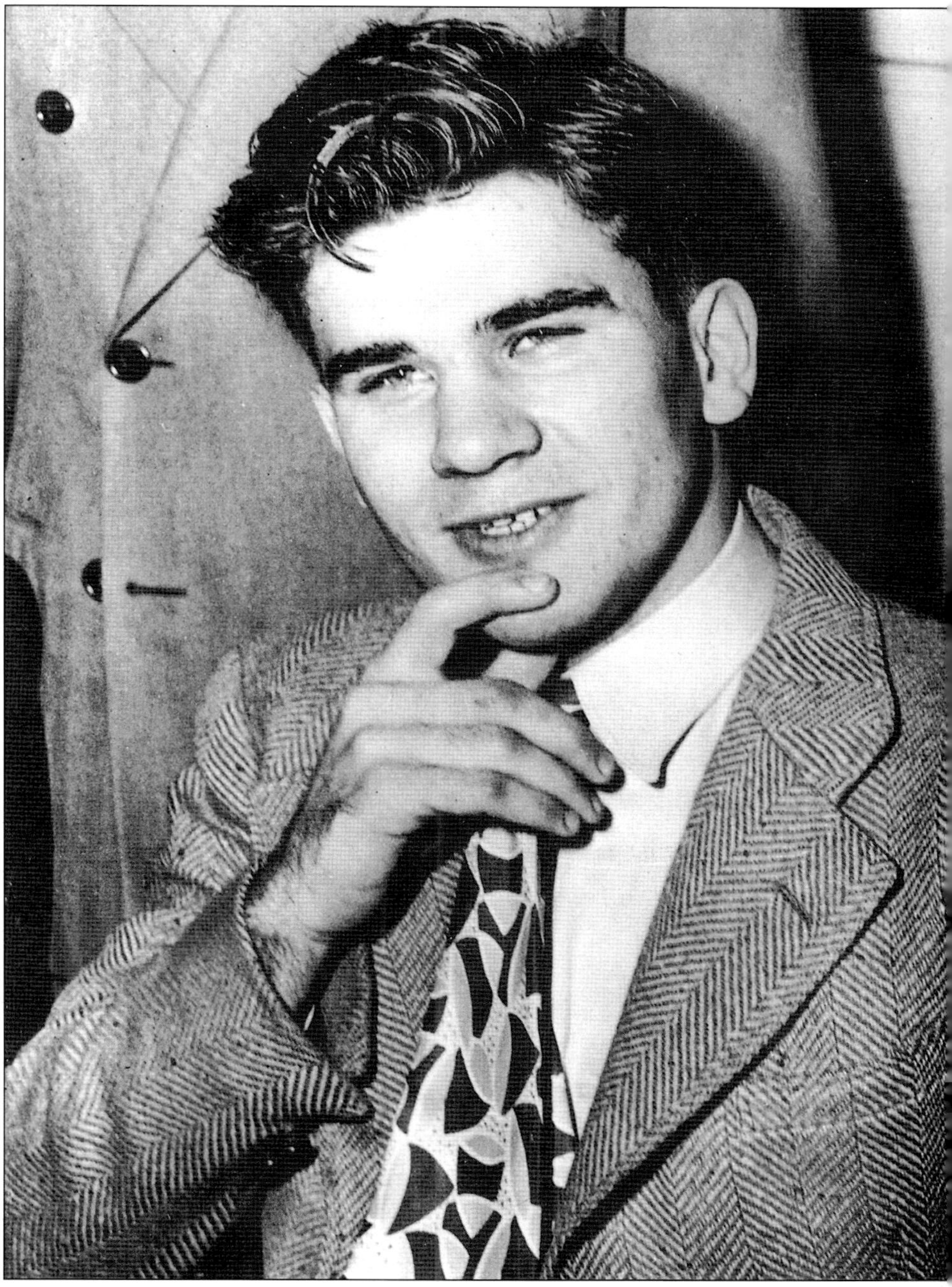

HARALD SHIPMAN
Doctor Death

Until recently Britain's worst serial killer was Victorian serial poisoner, Mary Ann Cotton, who murdered an estimated 21 people in the 1870s. Now that dubious distinction is claimed by Dr. Harold Shipman.

Dr Shipman ran a one-man practice in Hyde in the north of England. Most of Harold Shipman's patients were elderly women, living alone and vulnerable. They adored their doctor, Harold 'Fred' Shipman, and even when their contemporaries began dying in unusually high numbers, patients remained loyal to the murderous M.D. It seemed that as long as he spared them, his victims loved their doctor – to death.

A KILLER'S CHILDHOOD

Harold Frederick Shipman was born into a working class family on June 14, 1946 and was known as Fred or Freddy. His childhood, however, was far from normal. He always kept a distance between himself and his contemporaries – mainly due to the influence of his mother, Vera. The reason for this distance was to become clear in later years.

It was Vera who decided who Harold could play with, and when. For some reason she wanted to distinguish him from the other boys – he was the one who always wore a tie when the others were allowed to dress more casually. His sister Pauline was seven years older, his brother Clive, four years his junior, but in his mother's eyes, Harold was the one she held the most hope for.

'VERA WAS FRIENDLY ENOUGH, BUT SHE REALLY DID SEE HER FAMILY AS SUPERIOR TO THE REST OF US. NOT ONLY THAT, YOU COULD TELL HAROLD (FREDDY) WAS HER FAVOURITE – THE ONE SHE SAW AS THE MOST PROMISING OF HER THREE CHILDREN.'

Shipman was comparatively bright in his early school years, but rather mediocre when he reached upper school level. Nonetheless, he was a plodder determined to succeed, even down to re-sitting his entrance examinations for medical school.

Funnily enough, he had every opportunity to be part of the group – he was an accomplished athlete on the football field and the running track. In spite of this, his belief in his superiority appears to have prevented him from forming any meaningful friendships.

There was something else that isolated him from the group – his beloved mother had terminal lung cancer. As her condition deteriorated, Harold willingly played a major supportive role.

WATCHING VERA DIE

Shipman's behaviour in his mother's final months closely paralleled that of Shipman the serial killer. Every day after classes, he would hurry home, make Vera a cup of tea and chat with

Above: *Dr Shipman's surgery in Hyde, Greater Manchester*

her. She found great solace in his company and always eagerly awaited his return. This is probably where Shipman learned the endearing bedside manner he would later adopt in his practice as a family physician. Towards the end, Vera experienced severe pain, but, because pumps to self-administer painkillers did not exist at that time, Vera's sole relief from the agony of cancer came with the family physician.

No doubt young Harold watched in fascination as his mother's distress miraculously subsided whenever the family doctor injected her with morphine. Mrs Shipman grew thinner and frailer day by day, until on June 21, 1963, the cancer claimed her life. Harold felt a tremendous sense of loss following his mother's death. After all, she was the one who made him feel special, different from the rest. Her passing also left him with an indelible image – the patient with a cup of tea nearby, finding sweet relief in morphine.

This must have made a great impact on the 17-year-old, as it was a scene he would recreate hundreds of times in the future once he became a doctor – with no regard for human life or feeling.

HE WAS OFTEN UNNECESSARILY RUDE AND MADE SOME OF HIS COLLEAGUES FEEL 'STUPID' – A WORD HE FREQUENTLY USED TO DESCRIBE ANYONE HE DIDN'T LIKE. HE WAS CONFRONTATIONAL AND COMBATIVE WITH MANY PEOPLE, TO THE POINT WHERE HE BELITTLED AND EMBARRASSED THEM. NOT YET THIRTY, SHIPMAN HAD BECOME A CONTROL FREAK.

HAROLD THE STUDENT

Two years after his mother died, Harold Shipman was finally admitted to Leeds University medical school. Getting in had been a struggle – he'd had to re-write the exams he'd failed first time around. His grades, however, were sufficient enough for him to collect a degree and serve his mandatory hospital internship.

It is surprising to learn that so many of his teachers and fellow students can barely remember Shipman. Those who do remember claim that he looked down on them and seemed bemused by the way most young men behaved. 'It was as if he tolerated us. If someone told a joke he would smile patiently, but Fred never wanted to join in. It seems funny, because I later heard he'd been a good athlete, so you'd have thought he'd be more of a team player.' He was simply remembered as a loner. The one place his personality changed, however, was the football field. Here, he unleashed his aggression and his dedication to win was intense.

Shipman finally found companionship in a girl, Primrose, who was three years his junior. He married her when he was only nineteen years old.

Primrose's background was similar to Fred's, whereby her mother restricted her friendships and controlled her activities. Being rather a plain girl, Primrose was delighted to have finally found a boyfriend. Shipman married her when she was only seventeen and 5 months pregnant.

Above: *Primrose, Shipman's wife.*

By 1974 he was a father of two and had joined a medical practice in the Yorkshire town of Todmorden. At this stage in his life Fred seemed to undergo a transformation. He became an outgoing, respected member of the community in the eyes of his fellow medics and patients.

But the staff in the medical offices

where he worked saw a different side of the young practitioner. He had a way of getting things done his way – even with the more experienced doctors in the practice.

ADDICTION

His career in Todmorden came to a sudden halt when he started having blackouts. His partners were devastated when he gave them the reason – epilepsy. He used this faulty diagnosis as a cover-up. The truth soon came to the surface, when the practice receptionist Marjorie Walker came across some disturbing entries in a druggist's controlled narcotics ledger. These records showed how Shipman had been prescribing large and frequent amounts of pethidine in the names of several of his patients, when in fact the pethidine had found its way into the doctor's very own veins.

Not only that, he'd also written numerous prescriptions for the drug on behalf of the practice. Although this was not unusual because drugs were kept for emergencies, the prescribed amounts were excessive.

Following the discovery of Shipman's over-prescribing, an investigation by the practice uncovered the fact that many patients on the prescription list had neither required nor received the drug.

When confronted in a staff meeting, Shipman's way of dealing with the problem was to provide an insight into his true personality. Realizing his career was on the line, he first begged for a second chance.

When this request was denied, he became furious and stormed out, threw his medical bag to the ground and threatened to resign. The partners were dumbfounded by this violent – and seemingly uncharacteristic – behaviour.

Soon afterwards, his wife Primrose stormed into the room where his peers were discussing the best way to dismiss him. Rudely, she informed the people at the meeting that her husband would never resign, proclaiming, 'You'll have to force him out!'

And this was exactly what they had to do. They forced him out of the practice and into a drug rehabilitation centre in 1975.

Two years later, his many convictions for drug offences, prescription fraud and forgery cost him a surprisingly low fine – just over £600. Shipman's conviction for forgery is worth noting, because he was to use this skill later when faking signatures on a patently counterfeit will – that of his last victim, Katherine Grundy.

BACK TO WORK

Today, it is unlikely Harold Shipman would be allowed to handle drugs unsupervised, given his previous track record. However, within two years, he was back in business as a general practitioner in the Donneybrook Medical Centre in Hyde in the north of England. How readily he was accepted demonstrates his absolute self-confidence – and his ability to convince his peers of his sincerity. Again, he played the role of a dedicated, hardworking and community-minded doctor. He gained his patients' absolute trust and earned his colleagues' respect, but perhaps he was not watched carefully enough. In Hyde, Harold Shipman was home free – and free to kill!

A DIARY OF DEATH

Because of the nature of the Shipman case, it may never be possible to document every murder he committed, but it is estimated that he is responsible for the deaths of at least 236 patients over a 24-year period.

SHIPMAN WAS CHALLENGED IN A STAFF MEETING. THEY PUT BEFORE HIM EVIDENCE THAT HE HAD BEEN PRESCRIBING PETHIDINE TO PATIENTS, THAT THEY'D NEVER RECEIVED THE PETHIDINE, AND IN FACT THE PETHIDINE HAD FOUND ITS WAY INTO HIS VERY OWN VEINS.

MARIE WEST, 81

On March 6, 1995, Harold Shipman injected Mrs West, his first victim, with a fatal dose of diamorphine (the medical term for heroine), unaware that her friend was in the next room. Shipman first told Mrs West's son that she had died of a massive stroke, then said it was a heart attack. Mrs West ran a clothes shop in Hyde, a suburb of Manchester, where all the victims came from.

IRENE TURNER, 67

Mrs Turner was found dead fully clothed on her bed by her neighbour, after Dr Shipman had called at Mrs Turner's house on July 11, 1996. Earlier, he had asked the neighbour if she could help pack Mrs Turner's belongings for hospital, but told her to wait for a few minutes before going over. Morphine was later found in Mrs Turner's body.

JEAN LILLEY, 58

Mrs Lilley was visited by Dr Shipman on the morning of her death on April 25, 1997. A neighbour became increasingly concerned about the length of time that the GP had been with Mrs Lilley, who was suffering from a cold. She found her friend's body within moments of the doctor leaving her home. An ambulance crew later said Mrs Lilley had been dead for some time, killed by a lethal dose of morphine. She was the only one of the 15 victims to have been married at the time of her death. Shipman contacted her husband by mobile phone to tell him his wife had died.

KATHLEEN WAGSTAFF, 81

Shipman confused Mrs Wagstaff with another patient, Anne Royal, whose daughter was married to Kathleen's son Peter, and called on the wrong person on December 9, 1997 to announce she had died. Harold Shipman visited Angela Wagstaff at her workplace to tell her her mother had died, but the dead woman was in fact her mother-in-law Kathleen. After injecting Mrs Wagstaff with morphine, Shipman put her death down to heart disease.

KATHLEEN GRUNDY, 81 (right)

A former mayoress of Hyde and the last victim, Mrs Grundy died on June 24, 1998. She was found fully clothed on a settee at home. Dr Shipman killed her with a heroin overdose on a visit to take a blood sample. He has also been found guilty of forging her will and two letters to secure her £386,000 estate, as well as altering his medical records to suggest that the widow was addicted to morphine.

BIANKA POMFRET, 49

Mrs Pomfret, a German divorcee, was found dead at her home by her son William on the same day she had been visited by Shipman, on December 10, 1997. Excessive morphine levels were found in her body, but the GP claimed Mrs Pomfret had complained to him of chest pains on the day of her death. He fabricated a false medical history to cover his tracks after killing her.

LIZZIE ADAMS, 77

Mrs Adams, a retired sewing machinist, died at home on February 28, 1997. Dr Shipman stated that she had died of pneumonia and pretended to call for an ambulance, although no such call was made.

NORAH NUTTALL, 65

Mrs Nuttall, a widow, died on January 26, 1998 after visiting Shipman's surgery for cough medicine. The GP later visited Mrs Nuttall at her home, where her son Anthony found his mother slumped in a chair.

MAUREEN WARD, 57

Mrs Ward, a former college lecturer, died on February 18, 1998. Although she had been suffering from cancer, she was not ill at the time of her death. Dr Shipman claimed she died of a brain tumour.

WINIFRED MELLOR, 73

Mrs Mellor, a widow who had been Dr Shipman's patient for 18 years, was found dead on May 11 1998 in a chair at home with her left sleeve rolled up to suggest a heroin habit, following an earlier visit by Dr Shipman. He killed her with a fatal injection of morphine, and then returned to his surgery to create a false medical history to support a cause of death from coronary thrombosis.

JOAN MELIA, 73

Shipman murdered the divorcee on a visit to her home in Hyde on June 12, 1998. She was found dead by a neighbour in her living room, having earlier visited Dr Shipman at his surgery about a chest infection. Shipman issued a death certificate stating she had died from pneumonia and emphysema. Her body, later exhumed, was found to contain morphine. The GP also claimed to have phoned for an ambulance, but didn't.

IVY LOMAS, 63

Dr Shipman killed Mrs Lomas at his surgery on May 29, 1997 in Market Street, Hyde. He then saw three more patients before telling his receptionist that he had failed to resuscitate her. Morphine was later found in her body. She was such a regular there that Shipman told a police sergeant who was called after her death he thought her a nuisance. He joked that part of the seating area should be reserved for her and a plaque put up.

MURIEL GRIMSHAW, 76

Mrs Grimshaw was found dead at her home on July 14, 1997. Shipman, who was called to examine her, said there was no need for a postmortem. Morphine was later found in her body.

Above: *Bianka Pomfret*

THE SHIPMAN LETTERS WERE WRITTEN BETWEEN SEPTEMBER 1998 WHEN HE WAS FIRST ON REMAND, AND JANUARY 2000 WHEN HE KNEW HIS TRIAL DEFENCE WAS DOOMED – THESE INTIMATE LETTERS ARE THE ONLY INSIGHT TO THE TRUE THOUGHTS OF DOCTOR DEATH.

MARIE QUINN, 67

Dr Shipman injected Mrs Quinn with morphine at her home on November 24, 1997. Shipman claimed she had contacted him complaining of feeling unwell before her death. But her telephone bills showed no such call was made.

PAMELA HILLIER, 68

Shipman gave Mrs Hillier's family a confusing account of how she had died, on February 9, 1998, saying she had high blood pressure, but that it wasn't high enough to give him major concern, although she had died from high blood pressure. He had in fact given her a lethal dose of morphine.

ANGELA WOODRUFF

In this macabre and still unfinished story, Shipman's former patients are grateful indeed he was finally stopped. The feeling that they could have been next will always haunt them, and there is little doubt that some owe their lives to a determined and intelligent woman named Angela Woodruff.

This lady's dogged determination to solve a mystery helped ensure that, on Monday January 31, 2000, the jury at Preston Crown Court found Shipman guilty of murdering 15 of his patients and forging the will of Angela's beloved mother, Katherine Grundy.

Following her mother's burial Mrs Woodruff returned to her home, where she received a troubling phone call from solicitors. They claimed to have a copy of Mrs Grundy's will.

A solicitor herself, Angela's own firm had always handled her mother's affairs, in fact her firm held the original document lodged in 1986. The moment she saw the badly typed, poorly worded paper, Angela Woodruff knew it was a fake. It left £386,000 to Dr Shipman.

It was at this time that Angela went to her local police. Her investigation results ultimately reached Detective

Superintendent Bernard Postles. His own investigation convinced him Angela Woodruff's conclusions were accurate.

THE TRIAL BEGINS

To get solid proof of Kathleen Grundy's murder, a post mortem was required which, in turn, required an exhumation order from the coroner. By the time the trial had begun, Det. Supt Postles' team would be uncomfortably familiar with the process. Of the fifteen killed, nine were buried and six cremated. Katherine Grundy's was the first grave opened. Her body was the first of the ongoing post mortems. Her tissue and hair samples were sent to different labs for analysis, and the wait for results began.

At the same time, police raided the doctor's home and offices. It was timed so that Shipman had no chance of learning a body had been exhumed for a post mortem. Police had to be certain no evidence could be destroyed or concealed before their search. When the police arrived, Shipman showed no surprise; his approach was one of arrogance and contempt as the search warrant was read out.

One item crucial to police investigations was the typewriter used to type the bogus will. Shipman produced an old Brother manual portable, telling an improbable tale of how Mrs Grundy sometimes borrowed it. This unbelievable story was to go against Shipman – especially when forensic scientists confirmed it was the machine used to type the counterfeit will and other such fraudulent documents.

The search of his house also yielded medical records, some mysterious jewellery and a surprise. The Shipman home was littered with filthy clothes, old newspapers and, for a doctor's home, it was nothing short of unsanitary. But an even bigger surprise was due.

When toxicologist Julie Evans filed her report on the cause of Mrs Grundy's death, Det. Supt Postles was astounded.

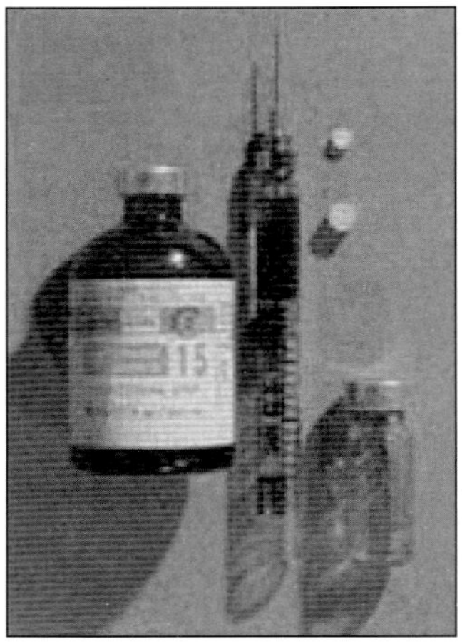

IT WAS DISCOVERED THAT THE MORPHINE LEVELS IN THE DEAD WOMAN'S BODY WOULD UNDOUBTEDLY HAVE BEEN THE CAUSE OF DEATH.

It was discovered that the morphine level in the dead woman's body would undoubtedly have been the cause of death. Not only that, her death would have occurred within three hours of having received the fatal overdose.

Shipman would claim later that the stylish and conservative old lady was a junkie. Even today psychologists speculate on the possibility that he wanted to be caught. Otherwise, why would he hand them the typewriter and use a drug so easily traced back to him? Others believe he saw himself as invincible, believing that, as a doctor, his word would never be questioned.

The detective realized the case went far beyond one death, and the scope of the investigation was broadened immediately.

THE VERDICT AND SENTENCE

The outcome of all the tests carried out was consistent. In case after case, it was proved that the victims had not died from old age or natural disease. Typically, morphine toxicity was the cause of death.

It took the judge, Mr. Justice Forbes, two weeks to meticulously dissect the evidence heard by the jury. He urged caution, noting that no witness had actually seen Shipman kill, and he also urged the jurors to use common sense in arriving at their verdict.

At 4:43 pm on Monday January 31, 2000, the foreman declared all the jury's verdicts were unanimous – they found Shipman GUILTY on 15 counts of murder and one of forgery.

The disgraced doctor stood motionless showing no sign of emotion as he heard the jurors' verdicts read. Wearing black, Shipman's wife, Primrose, also remained impassive. Her boys – one beside her and the other seated behind – looked down and seemed to visibly shrink on hearing the results.

Fifteen murders had been dealt with and the 57-day trial was over. But the extent of the killing was yet to be revealed.

AMAZING TEAMWORK

KAREN PRICE

Face Value

The case of Karen Price stands unmatched in British criminal history. It was a work of such intensive labour, painstaking forensic investigation, brilliant deduction and awesome teamwork that it deserves to stand apart from all other cases in this or any other century.

Thanks to the brilliance shown by the team in identifying murder victim Karen Price from nothing more than her fleshless skull her killers were caught and imprisoned. One prominent academic said that the case "significantly advanced forensic science in this country by 20 years". More than that, it enabled justice to be done and for the family of the missing girl to finally – more than ten years after she disappeared – place her remains in a grave where she could rest in peace and they could mourn her with respect.

Karen Price was murdered a decade earlier but the corpse of the woman who was to become so valuable in the forensic fight against crime was actually discovered on the afternoon of December 7 1989. Workmen Keith Lloyd, Syd Williams, Billy David and Paul Bodenham had been gutting a house in Fitzhamon Embankment, Cardiff, an address bordering a seedy red light area of the city. Number 29, a gothic three-storey building, was being converted into flats as was the custom with many turn-of-the-century homes in this bedsit area of the Welsh capital. On this afternoon, as dusk was falling, it became apparent to the men that the trench they had been digging in the garden for a new wastepipe was not going to be deep enough. Lloyd jumped into the excavation to dig another six inches down – but his pickaxe head hit a soft object. Closer inspection revealed it to be a carpet tied with electrical flex. When the cigar-shaped object was removed and the flex untied a human skeleton was revealed as the contents.

Within an hour the area had been sealed off as a murder site. Forensic experts collected soil samples while a police pathologist examined the remains. Most of the flesh had gone but rotting particles of clothing still draped off some of the bones. Blonde curls were visible around the skull and a pair of gilt earrings were found nearby. It became clear from the most senior officer present to the most junior rookie that identifying such a body would be a mammoth task. Detective Chief Superintendent John Williams, head of South Wales CID, viewed the body the day

WHEN THE CIGAR-SHAPED OBJECT WAS REMOVED AND THE FLEX UNTIED A HUMAN SKELETON WAS REVEALED

Opposite: ***Karen Price's body was found a decade after she went missing.***

Below: ***It was when renovations were being carried out at this house that the Woman Without a Face was discovered.***

it was found and said: "I didn't think it was possible to reconstruct a face from what I saw." In fact the medical and forensic experts set out to accomplish nothing less than the total reconstruction of a long-dead body. It was to be an extraordinary alliance of pathology, odontology – the study of teeth – forensic tests on the clothing, anthropology, entomology – the study of insects – a brilliant medical illustrator and geneticists. Each of them deserves a slice of the credit in bringing the murderers of this young girl to book.

The first stage in the investigation was the police decision to treat her death as murder. Det. Chf. Supt. Williams said he was satisfied, even before hearing from the pathologist, that a body being buried in a garden was clearly due to foul play and pledged to "call in every 'ologist in the book the solve the crime". On the evening of the day that the corpse was discovered it was laid out in the morgue at the Cardiff Royal Infirmary for inspection by Dr. Bernard Knight, professor of pathology at the Welsh Institute of Forensic Medicine. He determined that the skeleton was of a young white woman, about 5ft. 4ins. tall. The doctor said analysis of the bones suggested a girl in her mid-teens but he had not determined the cause of death.

Above: ***Richard Neave, a man who has built reconstructions of numerous historical figures.***

DET. CHF. SUPT. WILLIAMS PLEDGED "TO CALL IN EVERY 'OLOGIST IN THE BOOK TO SOLVE THE CRIME"

While the pathological team examined the corpse the soil that it had lain in was coming under the intense scrutiny of Nicholas Coles, a Welsh archaeological expert. Unfortunately, his examination of the grave site was fruitless because much of the soil had already been removed by workmen before they had jumped into the ditch to deepen it.

A MACABRE INVESTIGATION

The next cog in the machinery of identification was the Home Office forensic laboratory at Chepstow, Gwent. Most of the material had rotted, but the clay in which she had lain had preserved some remnants. Working from the material which survived the scientists were able to determine that her bra was a size 36B and had been manufactured by the Shadowline company in Liverpool and sold in Cardiff through a company called Mrs. Knickers. This was an important piece of the puzzle – as police liaised with missing persons' bureaux over the number of missing teenaged girls in Britain it seemed likely that she was local and had purchased the items there. Her sweatshirt was size 18, manufactured by the American firm Levi for the British market and sold around 1980 – placing her death at some time in the last decade.

The skull was delivered to the Natural History Museum in London where anthropologists Dr. Christopher Stringer and Theya Molleson examined it from every angle, measured it and fed the data into a computer programme used to identify 2,500 different skull types from around the world. They determined the girl's skull was from a caucasian female.

Further examination of the teeth and jaw made them speculate that she was probably not an indigenous Briton – widening the net to immigrants and visitors to the

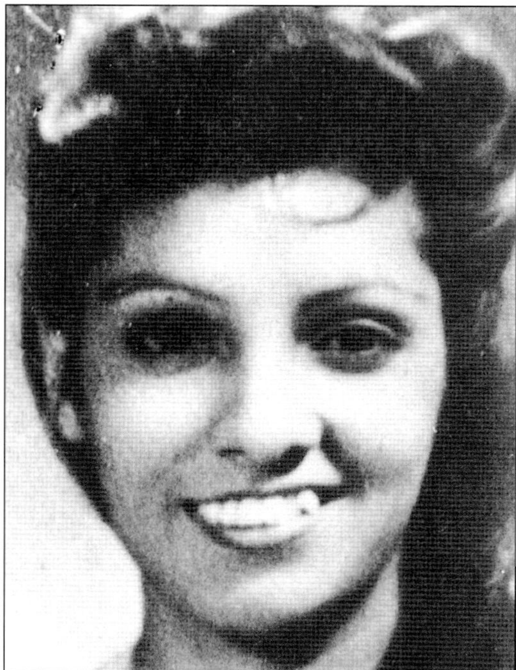

Left: ***In an American case, a girl's identity was discovered using the same techniques as those employed in the Karen Price case.***

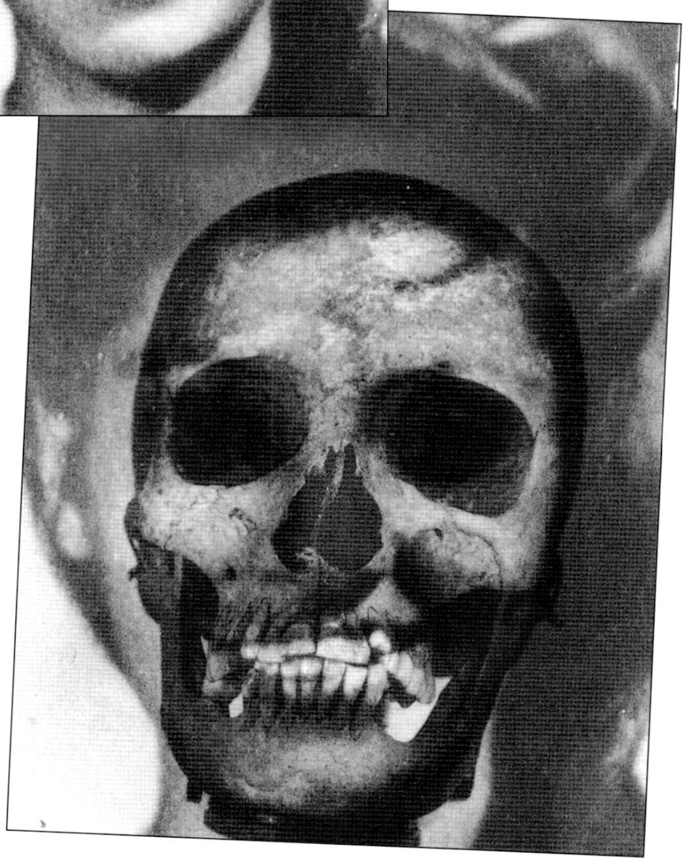

Below: ***Every minute detail of the skull was examined time and time again.***

country. The skull became the focus of the inquiry – it was undamaged and from it much more could be gleaned than from any other part of the skeleton.

Dr. David Whittaker, the forensic dental adviser to the Home Office, used a tried and trusted method to try to gauge her age from the teeth. He took a cross section of one tooth and, rather like determining the age of a tree by counting the rings of a sawed trunk, speculated "80 per-cent" certain that she was 15-and-a-half when she died. He also found traces of blood in capillaries in the skull. These tiny veins are usually empty at death, except in cases of violent death; he speculated that she had met her end at the hands of a strangler. He also remarked that the poor quality of the dental work indicated that she had spent time under the care of a foreign dentist, but he couldn't pin down a country.

HE MEASURED HOW LONG THE CADAVER HAD LAIN IN THE GROUND BY EXAMINING DEAD INSECT TISSUE FOUND WITH HER

HUMAN COMPLICATIONS

A 70-strong police team meanwhile embarked on all the routine, necessary enquiries related to such a murder. It was estimated by Williams that some 700 people had lived in the house and the adjoining one during the decade, many of them drifters who stayed for only a short while. But no-one quizzed seemed to remember a fair-haired teenager. Williams began to sense that as the case progressed he was going to have to rely more and more on the "boffins" who were methodically trying to find out who Miss X was.

The next person to be called in provided some of the most fascinating clues. In December 1989 and January the following year the skull, soil samples, skeletal remains and clothing particles were examined by Dr. Zakeria Erzincliogu, a brilliant Cambridge University professor specialising in entomology – the lives of insects.

He was able to measure how long the cadaver had lain in the ground by examining the dead insect tissue found with her. Woodlice, phorid flies – tissue-eating insects – and bluebottle larvae, the eggs of flies. The first two indicated that the girl had been buried in the ground for five years at least, placing her death before 1984, which corresponded with the clothing found on her.

More importantly, the bluebottle eggs could only have been laid on the corpse when it was exposed to air and in this he estimated that her body had been unburied for two days after her murder.

It was all leading somewhere but no-one knew quite where. That is when one of the police officers recalled reading about a renowned artist who had been helping to build a plaster-cast of a victim of the 1987 Kings Cross Underground fire who had remained unidentified since then. Williams thought it was worth contacting Richard

Neave, a 54-year-old medical illustrator who was based at Manchester University. Neave's skill came in re-constructing human faces based just on the shape, size and contours of their skulls. He started on the face of Miss X by making a plastercast of the skull and gradually built up features using modelling clay.

He was the first to admit that putting the features on a skull is the part "where art and science meet" and that mistakes can occur. But probably there is no-one in the world with his skill or attention to detail. During a lengthy career he has put the faces on long-dead Egyptian mummies, a murder victim whose killers were caught thanks to his efforts and the ancient ruler Phillip of Macedon.

He gained his expertise in human anatomy by watching surgical procedures and dissections at medical universities across Britain and has honed his skills to a finer-than-fine art. He saw the task of re-creating Miss X as a great forensic challenge and the skull was placed in a cardboard box and driven to him by police.

Below: ***All the efforts of the investigators were to prove worthwhile for the comfort they brought to Karen's family. They also made British crime history.***

PAINSTAKING CONSTRUCTION

Neave received the skull on December 18 and set to work. He used anatomical sketchbooks while he started to "build" the face, muscle by muscle, feeling with his fingers where the flesh, bone, muscle and sinew would have been on every square centimetre of her face. He uses exact measurements on muscle depth and skin type based on figures of real people and applies them to whatever age he is working to.

It is very methodical work that has to be done carefully piece by piece because, he says, "I am not a sculptor making a piece of artwork – it is a scientific construction." In the case of Miss X he said: "I used all the information that was gathered from experts. You have to remember that she was only 15-and-a-half, healthy, lots of elasticity in her face. Life won't have driven a truck over her face."

Nose and lips could be done first because the skull doesn't dictate their size or thickness. Then he continued his moulding of the eyebrows, forehead, cheeks, chin and ears until, in two days, he was satisfied with what he had in front of him.

On January 8 1990 Det. Chf. Supt. Williams called a press conference in Cardiff during which photographs of the reconstruction were handed out to representatives of TV and newspapers. The photo-

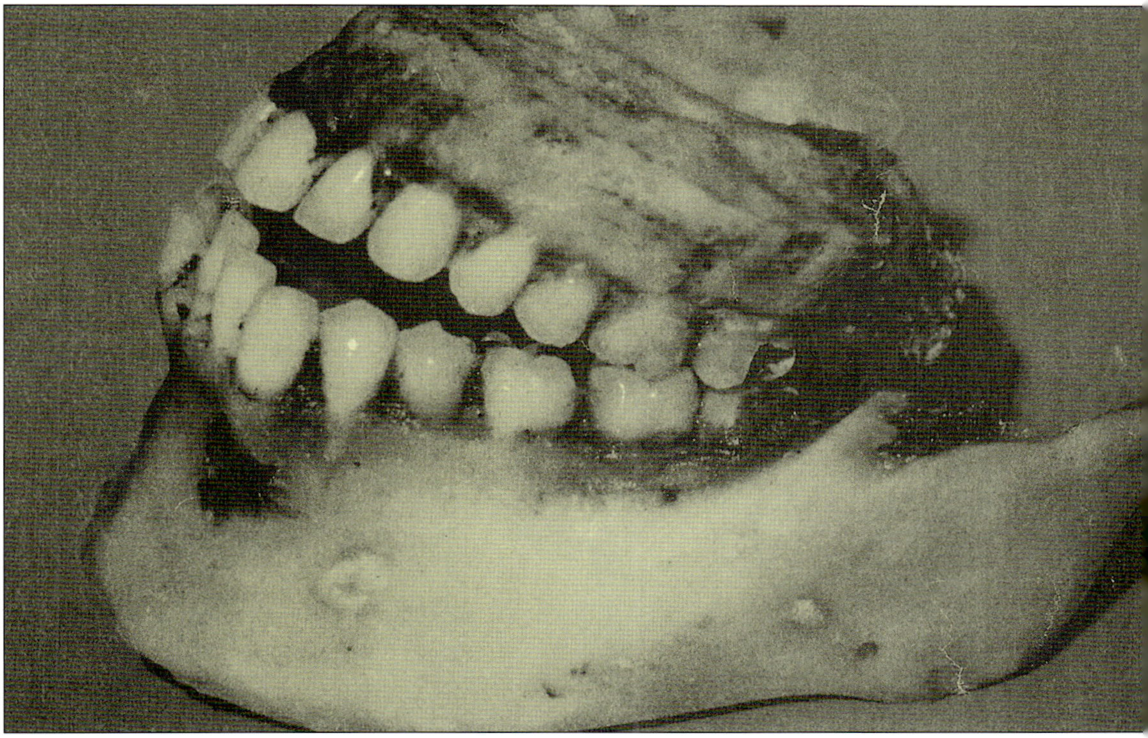

graph was also made into a "have you seen this girl?" poster which was issued to police stations all over Britain for distribution at social halls, railway and bus stations and other places where crowds congregate.

The face was of a young girl with slightly flared nose and straggly hair. But it was a complete face, a complete human being, not a shadowy artist's impression which have often proved worse than useless in tracking down criminals and missing persons.

The speed with which the girl's identity came after that press conference was truly astonishing. Forty eight hours after the nationwide appeals went out two social workers in Cardiff contacted police to say they believed the girl looked like a young runaway called Karen Price, aged 15.

She had been in care when she went missing in 1981, said the informants, and were emphatic it was her. Other names of missing girls were offered up too, but they were all traced.

FINAL CONFIRMATION

It then fell on police to find Karen Price's dental records, which turned up in a Cardiff dentist's storeroom in late January 1990 and were sent to the expert Whittaker for analysis. He said there was no doubt that the dead girl was Karen Price. Further confirmation came when Dr. Peter Vanezis, a senior lecturer in forensic medicine at the London Hospital, was sent a photo of Karen. Using the latest video-computer technology he electronically superimposed the photograph of Karen on to her skull and got an almost perfect match.

The corpse had a name and she had a family who would now be able to mourn for her properly.

Between January and July 1990, as police efforts concentrated on finding her killers, further forensic work was carried out. Police were determined to get a DNA match through genetic fingerprinting – which would prove scientifically it was her. This was obtaned by sending a bone sample from Karen's femur to Dr. Erik Hagelberg of the Institute of Molecular Medicine at Oxford University.

Her test involved chilling the bone with liquid nitrogen, then crushing it to extract the DNA. Professor Alec Jeffreys, of the department of genetics at Leicester University – the man who invented DNA fingerprinting – compared the DNA with blood samples taken from Karen's parents, who had been traced in the intervening time. Despite being used on bones of such an age and subject to decay, he was able to say better than "99.9 per-cent that these are the remains of Karen Price".

The life of Karen Price was, police discovered, an unhappy one. Her father Michael and her mother Anita Nicholaidis were divorced when she was a child and she went into the care of the Glamorgan social services when she was 10. Her mother's Greek-Cypriot roots accounted for Karen's teeth appearing "foreign". Not long before her 16th birthday she was moved to an assessment centre for troublesome children where decisions were to be made about her future. But she absconded on July 8 1981, joining the legions of missing children who make up a lost army in Britain.

Above: ***The teeth of Karen Price – although it would take far more than her dentures to identify her.***

THE CORPSE HAD A NAME AND SHE HAD A FAMILY WHO WOULD NOW BE ABLE TO MOURN FOR HER PROPERLY

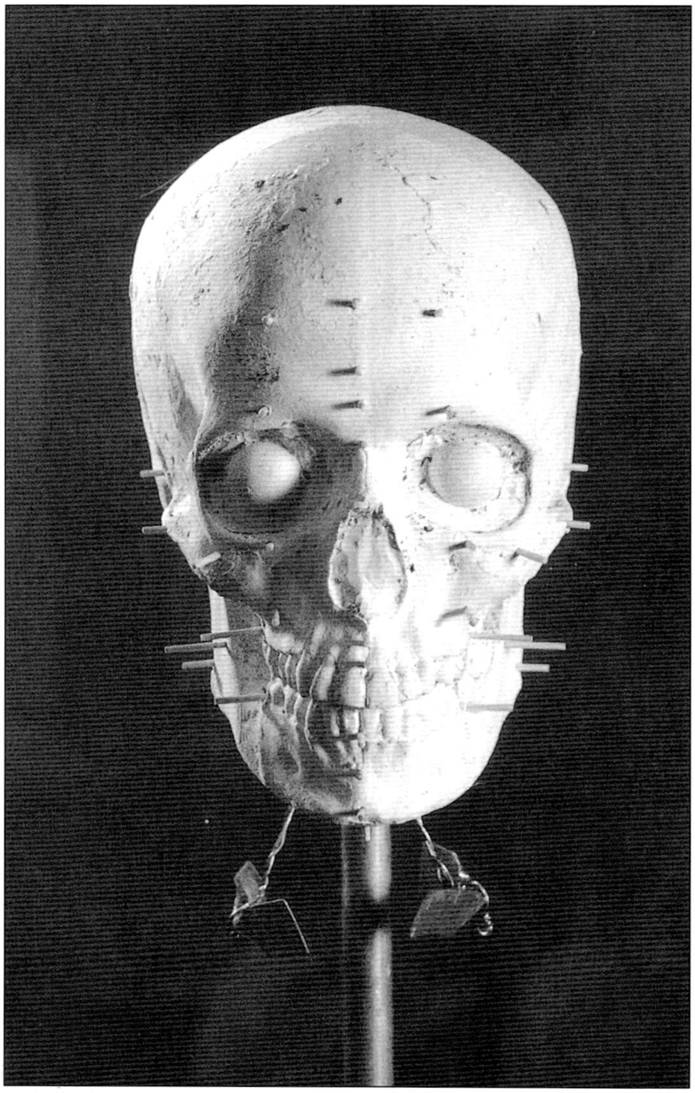

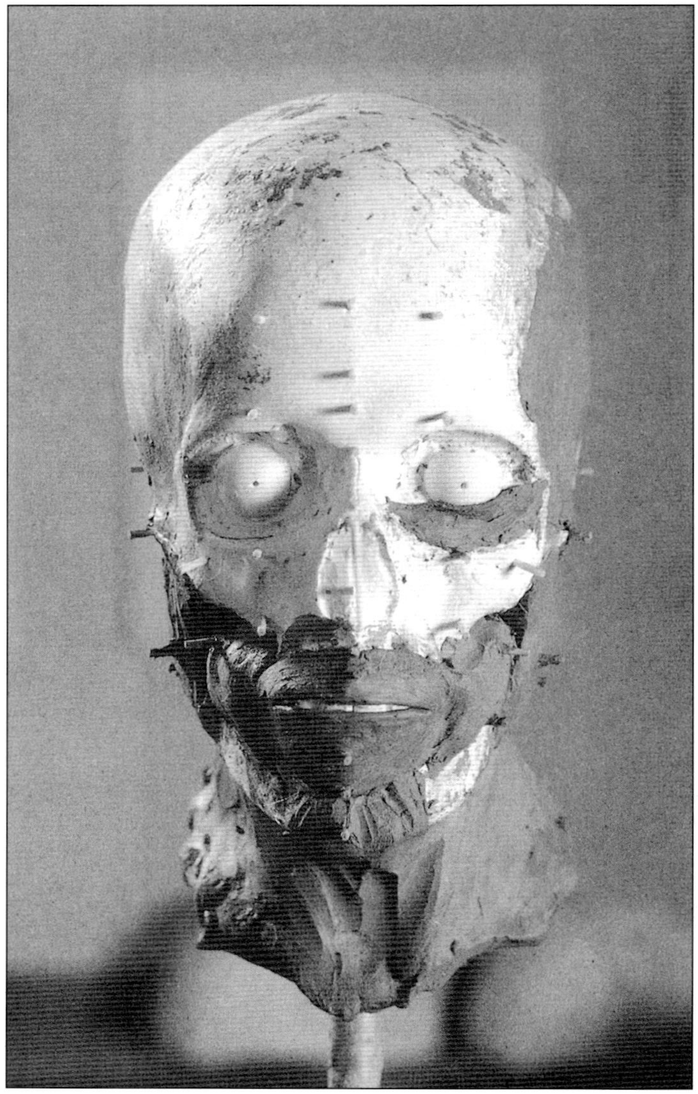

There was no police hunt for her and, apparently, no-one to weep for her. She simply became just another statistic in an ever-lengthening book.

The police issued further appeals, concentrating once more on people who had one time been resident of the house where the body was buried. Sifting through records they found that an Alan Charlton had once been resident in the bottom flat – the flat from which the off-cut of carpet came that was used to wrap Karen's body. Charlton lived in Bridgewater, Somerset, and had recently been released from a jail sentence for attempting to rape a 55-year-old woman. It was interesting to the police, but inconclusive.

But soon after he was interviewed a TV appeal went out for more information and a young girl who had been at school with Karen came forward. She said a a man called Idris Ali had boasted that he knew Karen. He was eventually interviewed and, unexpectedly during what the police considered a routine suspect-elimination session, he broke down and confessed: "I killed her. I am sorry."

Ali fingered an accomplice – the attempted rapist Charlton who had been seen by lawmen previously. He also implicated another girl, whose identity was withheld at their subsequent trial, who knew about the killing but escaped prosecution because of what she knew. She was to prove a star witness at the trial of the two men. It turned out that Ali had persuaded Karen to become a prostitute while the two were together at a school for disadvantaged children. Ali became her pimp and pimp to the other girl, simply known as Miss X at the trial. Charlton came into the scene when he said he could organise porno

Above: ***The model of the skull begins to take shape with wooden skewers inserted to determine the correct depth of flesh and skin. It was a laborious process but one that was to pay enormous dividends.***

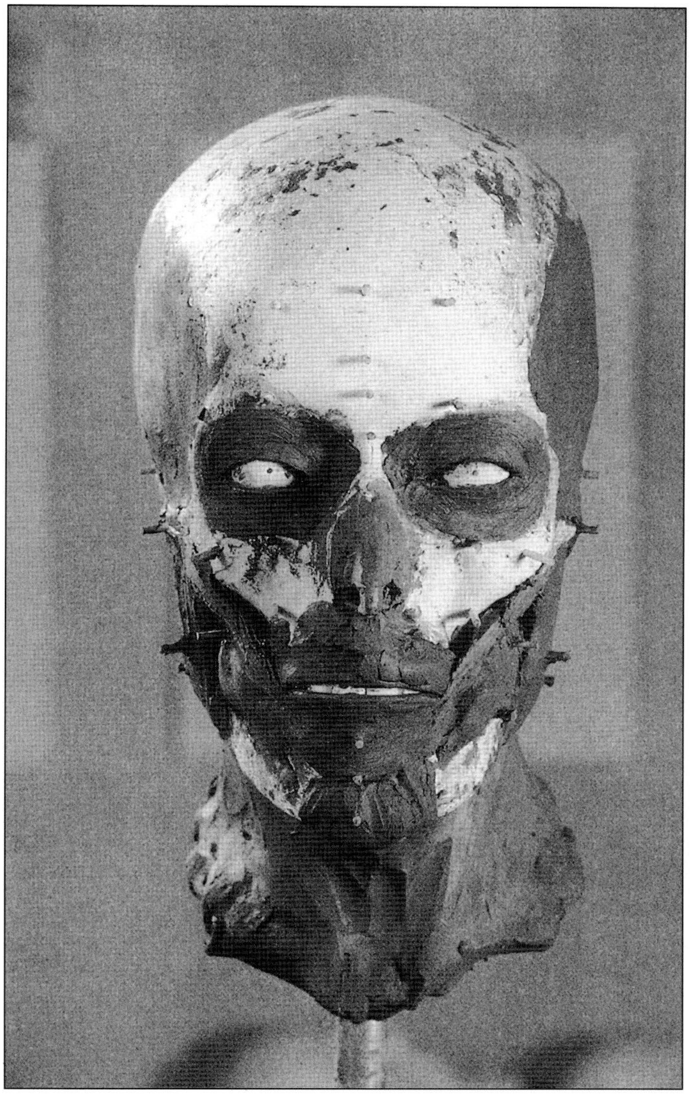

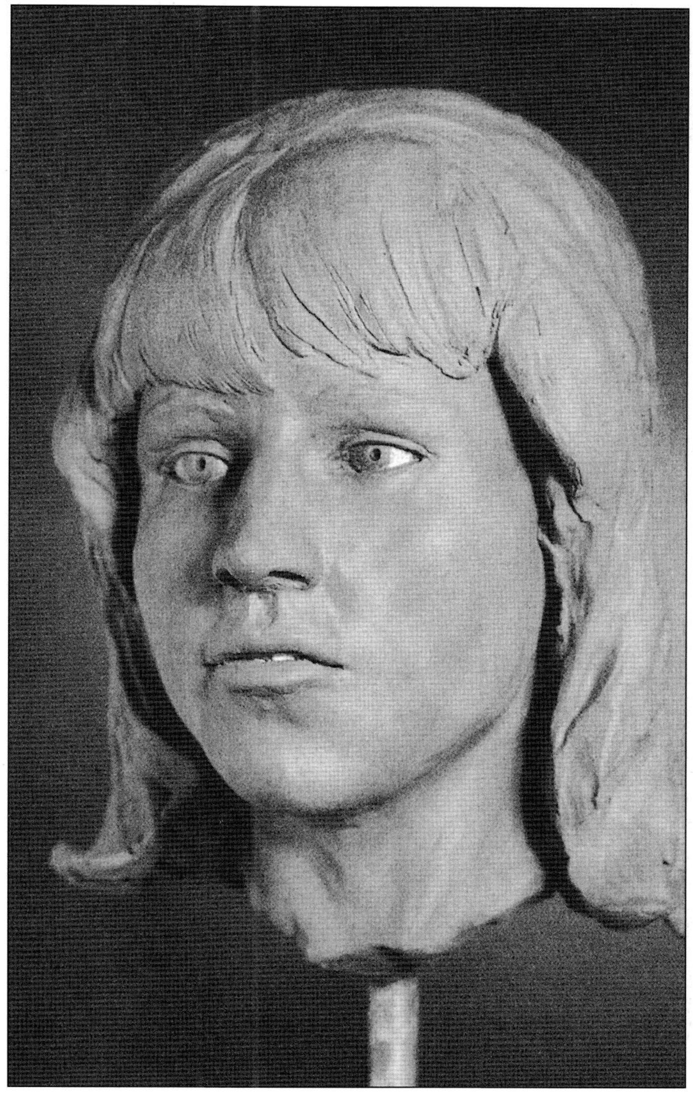

movies and drugs in his basement flat at... Fitzhamon Embankment. The girls would procure the clients and they would all share in the profits.

But something went wrong. Miss X testified that Karen refused to be photographed naked. She quarrelled with the men and Charlton exploded, beating her to death in the basement. Her body was left exposed for four days – hence the bluebottle larvae found on the skeleton – and she was later interred by Ali and Charlton in the back garden. After so many years they figured their secret was safe.

But in a five week trial which ended at Cardiff Crown Court on February 26 1991 justice finally caught up with them when they were jailed for life. After Mr. Justice Hose had sentenced the prisoners he paid special compliments to the unique alliance of law enforcement, forensic and scientific

Above: ***Slowly but surely the model began to resemble less a Hallowe'en caricature and more the face of a beautiful girl whose life was brutally and cruelly snuffed out. Finally, this sculpture was unveiled to the world, and the girl who had no dignity in death was finally accorded the full rights of a Christian burial.***

people who had collaborated so unselfishly in the process of finding out the identity of the corpse. Det. Chf. Supt. Williams, who has since left the force, paid particular tribute to Neave, whose masterful reconstruction of Karen's face was, in his opinion, integral in finding out who she was. He said: "I don't know whether we would have done it without him.

"It was of the utmost importance that the identity of the girl was corroborated beyond doubt. That was the first objective. It was a bonus that we were able to charge two people with murder. Co-operation between the police and the forensic experts reached new heights and in my 33 years as a police officer this case was unique."

Karen Price was given a decent, Christian burial. It was, perhaps, one of the few times in her short, sad life that she was truly recognised by society.

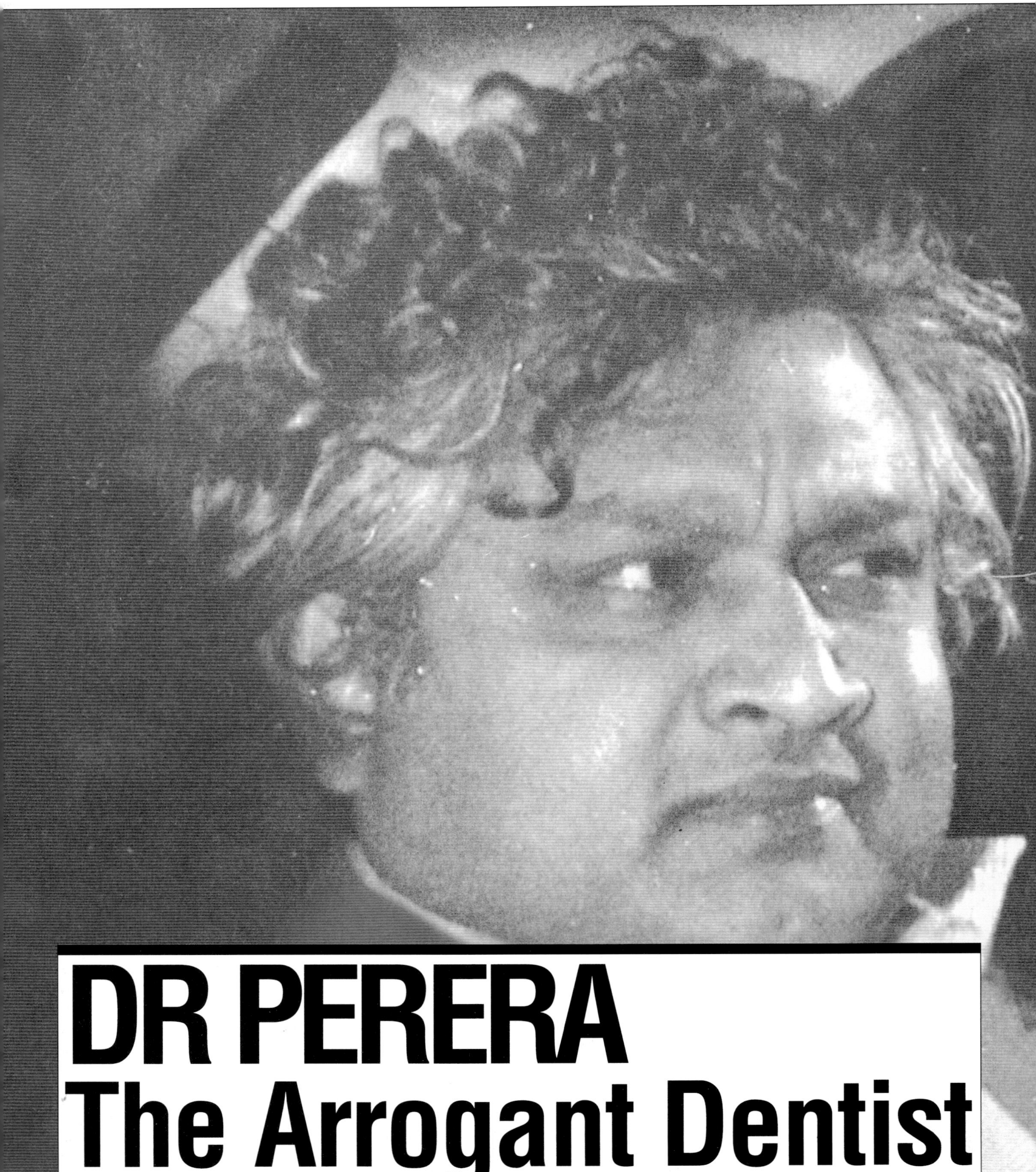

DR PERERA
The Arrogant Dentist

A smooth and well-educated murderer thought he could outwit a simple Yorkshire detective. But he had not bargained for police perseverance and expert assistance in putting together the gruesome evidence that eventually convicted him

In 1935 Bukhtyar Hakim, a Parsee doctor who had changed his name to Buck Ruxton when he settled in the northern English town of Lancaster, strangled his wife Isabella in a fit of jealous rage. The sound of the struggle brought her maid, Mary Rogerson, to the scene. Ruxton killed her too.

He took the bodies upstairs and cut them into small pieces in the bath before wrapping them in newspapers and strips of cotton sheet. Then he drove north and scattered the packages along the side of the Edinburgh–Moffat road.

Ruxton was eventually arrested and brought to the gallows at Lancaster Gaol.

At some time during the early winter of 1983 history, in the person of Dr Samuel Perera, repeated itself almost detail for detail when Perera killed and cut to pieces his adopted daughter.

Above: ***DI Tom Hodgson, who spent a year gradually building up a case against Dr Perera.***

Opposite: ***Dr Perera is taken away by the police.***

Below: ***Perera's house in Sitwell Close, in the Wakefield suburb of Sandal.***

Like Ruxton, Perera was a native of the Indian subcontinent, having been born in Sri Lanka, at that time the British colony of Ceylon. He too was a doctor, a specialist in oral biology at Leeds University School of Medicine. He lived near Wakefield, West Yorkshire, just fifty miles from Lancaster. And, like Ruxton, he was astonishingly arrogant.

As one detective who worked on the case was to put it: 'He must have known of Ruxton from his medical studies. All doctors do a course in forensic medicine, and Ruxton is a standard text. You'd have thought that he would have learned from Ruxton's mistakes.'

Perera was born in 1943. After graduating from Colombo University he travelled to England to take up a three-year research scholarship at Newcastle University dental school. There he met and married his Hindu wife Dammika, converting her to Roman Catholicism.

In the early seventies he successfully applied for a post as lecturer in oral biology in the Dental Department of the Leeds School of Medicine, and travelled to England to settle in the middle-class suburb of Sandal, near Wakefield.

Above: ***Nilanthe 'Philomena Perera', the Sri Lankan girl adopted by Dr Perera.***

PERERA, WHO HAD PAID MONEY TO HER FATHER, MAY HAVE INTENDED TO USE HIS ADOPTED DAUGHTER AS A HOUSEHOLD SLAVE

JUNGLE GIRL

Mrs Perera gave birth to two daughters during the latter part of the 1970s. But in December 1981, for reasons which were never satisfactorily explained, her husband decided he wanted to adopt a further child. He and his wife went back to Sri Lanka and returned with a ten-year-old girl named Nilanthe, giving her the adoptive name of Philomena. Perera may have had long-term plans to use Philomena as a sort of household slave. He had paid money to her natural father and, as he was later to tell police dismissively, 'in any case she was only a jungle girl'.

Over the next couple of years the little 'jungle girl' became known and liked by the other residents of Sitwell Close. Her lack of English gave her a somewhat forlorn attitude, but her waif-like figure, large doe eyes and long, glossy hair held the promise of great beauty.

In November 1983, Nilanthe 'Philomena' Perera disappeared. 'My husband is very strict,' Mrs Perera told a neighbour. 'He has banned her from going out because she would make eyes at the men.'

But Christmas came and went, winter gave way to spring and there was still no sign of little Philomena.

The neighbours' curiosity began to stir again and finally, in April 1984, Mrs Perera told them: 'She's gone home. She grew very homesick and my husband decided it was kindest to send her back to her father in Sri Lanka.'

LETTER TO THE LAW

But the neighbours were not satisfied, and so they did a rather un-English thing. They called a meeting and, after discussing the matter, decided to send a letter laying out the facts to the authorities. The letter was opened at Wood Street Police Station in Wakefield, by a fifty-one-year-old detective inspector named Tom Hodgson.

Hodgson was a burly, snub-nosed man with a stubborn, cleft chin. His receding hairline and the bags under his amiable eyes bespoke years of police service, mostly as a detective officer.

It was a warm summer morning in July 1984 when Detective Inspector Hodgson drove up to 16 Sitwell Close, at the beginning of what was to be a year-long investigation – and Hodgson's last case.

From that first meeting, the detective later claimed, he was struck by the smooth doctor's exaggerated sense of his own importance. As he ushered his visitor through the front door, Perera snapped at his wife: 'Get upstairs with the children.'

'She's only a wife, after all,' he told Hodgson. Seated in Perera's front room, the policeman told him that he was

Above: ***Philomena's home in Sri Lanka.***

Left: ***Philomena's mother.***

making routine enquiries about the missing girl Nilanthe Philomena. Dr Perera was easy in his reply. Philomena, he said, had failed to settle, growing more and more homesick as the months passed. 'After all she was only a jungle girl.'

In April, he said, he had decided to take her home. He had taken her with him on a weekend trip to Catania in Sicily, where his brother lived. From there, the brother was to have put her on a flight to Sri Lanka.

Tom Hodgson returned to his desk at Wood Street to set in motion a long and careful series of checks, first with the airport authorities and then with Interpol.

First, the airport authorities: had Dr Perera booked a flight to Sicily with his adopted daughter from any British airport at any time in the early months of the year? No.

Next, Interpol came back to Hodgson with the result of their enquiries in Sicily and Sri Lanka. The girl had not turned up there. It seemed likely, therefore, that she must still be in the British Isles.

Meanwhile, Hodgson had paid several surreptitious visits to the Dental Department of Leeds Medical School, winkling out details of Dr Perera and his ways. 'Arrogant' was the word repeatedly used by his colleagues of Perera.

FROM THEIR FIRST MEETING DETECTIVE INSPECTOR HODGSON WAS STRUCK BY PERERA'S ARROGANT SELF-ASSURANCE

SEARCH FOR THE BODY

By now, Hodgson had no doubt in his own mind that Perera was a murderer. But where was the body? Hodgson's best course of action seemed to lie in shaking Perera into making some kind of a move – perhaps shifting the body to a safer hiding-place. To this end the tenacious

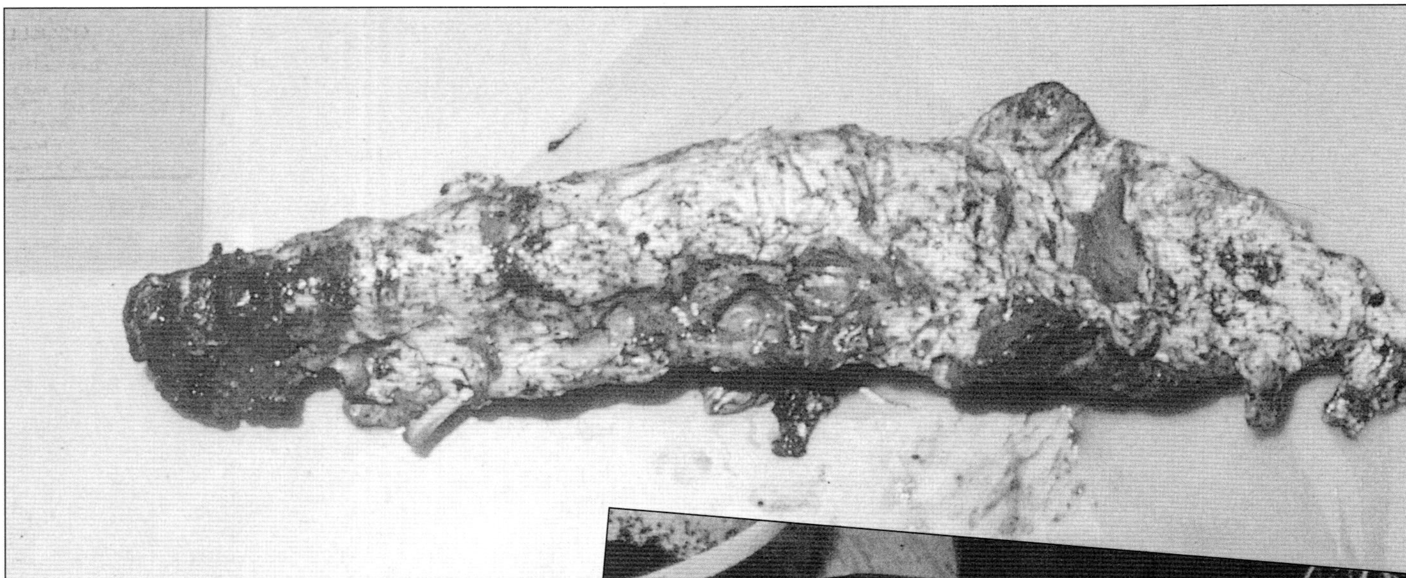

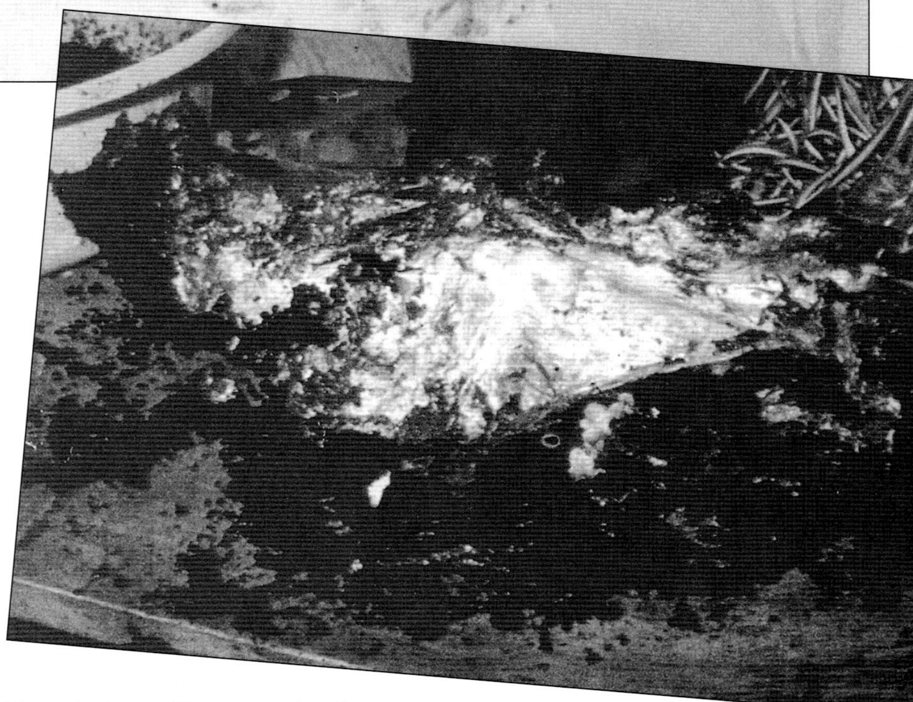

Yorkshireman began to play a cat and mouse game with the doctor, making it clear to him that he was being watched – 'showing out', in police parlance – and making several personal calls at his home to interview him on small points.

Just before Christmas 1984, Inspector Hodgson decided to give his quarry a good shake-up. 'I knew by this time that something was seriously wrong, so I started to put pressure on him. I told him I was coming to see him at the university on the first day of the new term in January 1985. Perera started blustering, saying I was making assertions I could not prove.'

And then, on 4 February 1985, came dramatic evidence to justify Hodgson's pressure tactics. A colleague of Perera's who shared a desk and cupboards with him noticed a large brown envelope in one of the desk drawers. It contained a human jawbone with several teeth present, and a number of pieces of human skull. Aware of the police interest in Dr Perera, the lecturer made a rapid search of other drawers and cupboards used by the Sri Lankan. He found a five-litre glass beaker, a coffee jar with a screw-top lid, and a shallow, stainless steel tray. Each of these contained small bones and bone fragments, immersed in a bluish liquid which later proved to be a decalcifying fluid which would ultimately have dissolved the bones completely. None of these bones appeared to have anything to do with orthodox dental research.

Top: ***A piece of human spine found in a plant pot in Perera's house.***

Above: ***Pieces of human flesh were found under geranium plants in two other pots.***

A UNIVERSITY COLLEAGUE NOTICED AMONG PERERA'S BELONGINGS A BROWN ENVELOPE CONTAINING HUMAN BONES

The lecturer telephoned Wood Street Police Station, and Hodgson arranged for the remains to be transferred to Wakefield. He also arranged for Dr Perera to come to the station to assist the police with their enquiries.

Early the next morning, Mrs Perera and her two children were taken into care from the house in Sitwell Close. Overall-clad policemen arrived at their home with spades, trowels and gardener's riddles.

THE SEARCH FOR EVIDENCE

The police eventually turned to the Department of Forensic Medicine at Sheffield University. Head of the department and holder of the chair of forensic pathology at the university was Professor Alan Usher, whose active career spanned over thirty years.

Several identical 'murder bags' containing equipment for on-site investigation were always kept packed and ready in Professor Usher's office. On receiving Hodgson's call he picked one up, loaded it into his car, and set off on the hour-long drive to Wakefield and the suburb of Sandal.

When he arrived, the police were already digging in the garden at Sitwell Close. Between the rear of the garage and the garden fence they had excavated an oblong hole about five feet by three feet, and were sieving the earth through large garden riddles. On a plastic sheet by the hole lay a tooth, a small bone and a long hank of dark, earth-clotted hair.

A brief examination convinced Usher that the bone and tooth were human. They were docketed and placed in samples envelopes for later scrutiny.

As the police continued their digging outside, Usher and the two senior detectives entered the hallway of the house. The first objects to confront them were three large plastic plant pots. The central one was raised, and contained a narrow leaved plant. The other two, containing geraniums, stood on the floor on either side.

'The plants seemed very small for such large pots,' recalled Professor Usher, 'and they didn't seem to be doing terribly well. They were wilting somewhat.' When the professor bent to examine them further he caught a distinct whiff of the sickly-sweet stench of decaying flesh.

Ouside the door stood a plastic dustbin. Usher placed its upturned lid on the ground and very carefully decanted the contents of the central plant pot on to this ad hoc examination table.

What met their eyes gave Chief Superintendent Walter Cowman, at least, one of the more unpleasant frissons of his long career. 'I don't think I shall ever forget,' he said later, 'the sight of a virtually complete human spine curled around the roots of the plant.'

The two geranium pots were emptied in turn. Plant, earth and roots slid out in a solid lump, revealing that the geraniums were embedded in some browning, slimy material. It was rotting human flesh.

Eventually Professor Usher's team were to identify a total of 106 bony fragments which, in their opinion, came from 77 individual bones or parts of bones. They had been gathered from eight different sites – four at home, four in the Leeds lab – accessible to Samuel Perera.

FROM THE POTTED GERANIUMS IN THE SUBURBAN HALLWAY CAME THE SICKLY-SWEET STENCH OF DECAYING FLESH

PIECING TOGETHER A HUMAN JIGSAW

But that was in the future. In that second week of February 1985, Usher was faced with the long and tedious task of 'defatting' the bones. This meant stripping them of their remaining fat and flesh, and then with infinite care attaching numbers to them so that each tiny piece of the jigsaw could be identified, and the source not be lost, as attempts were made to rearticulate them into the semblance of a skeleton.

It was a colossal project, and one of the most complex ever undertaken. Over a period of time Usher assembled a

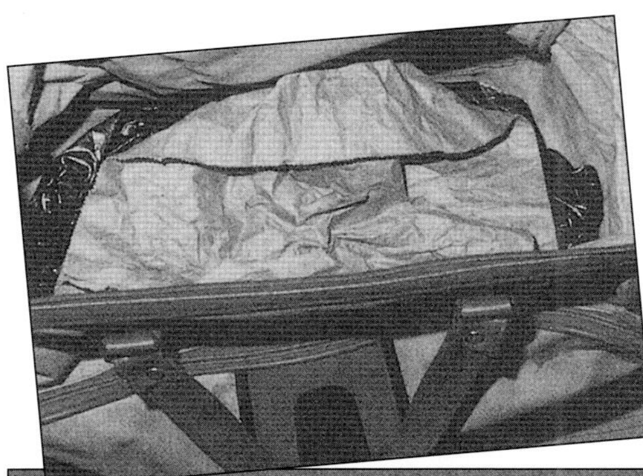

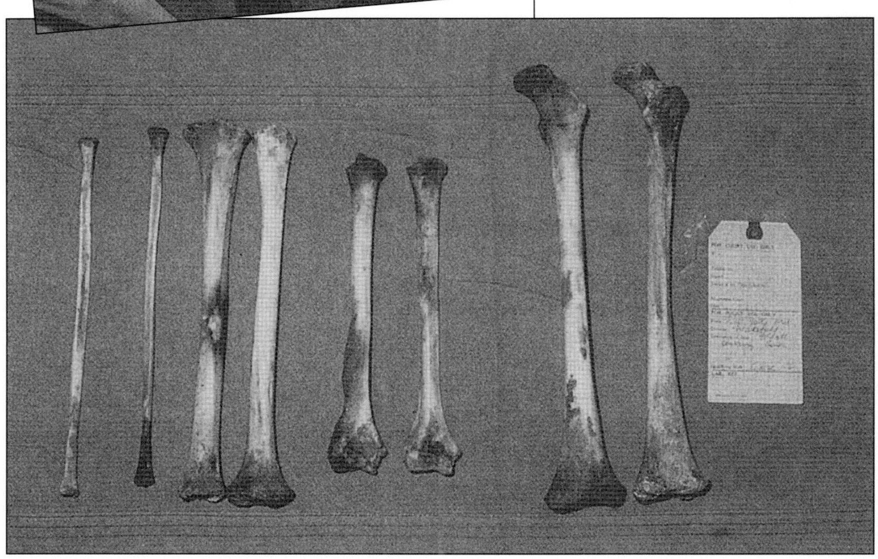

Left and below: ***A holdall was found containing a collection of human bones.***

seven-man team of distinguished experts, headed by himself.

The anatomist's role was filled by Professor G.N.C. Crawford. Then there were Professor R.D. Grainger, Professor of Radiodiagnosis at Sheffield Medical School; Dr G.T. Craig, senior lecturer in oral pathology at Sheffield University and an expert in forensic dentistry; Dr Y.Z. Erzinclioglu, an entomologist from Cambridge University – brought in to study organisms in the soil; Dr P.J. Tarff, a postgraduate student, and Mr D.R. Jarvis, Usher's senior medical scientific officer.

SCIENTIFIC KNOW-HOW

The deliberations of the seven experts took several months, for they had several vital points to establish: points which should eventually satisfy a court of law.

First, were the bones human, and were they the bones of one person only? The answers to both questions were affirmative. Second, what of sex? In general the bones were gracile and slender, with little evidence of any strong muscular markings: 'Though not conclusive in themselves, the delicacy of the bones and the lack of muscular development are predominantly female characteristics,' said Professor Usher, 'and these facts, coupled with the pelvic angles and Professor Grainger's radiological studies, satisfied us that these were the bones of a female.'

Like sex, the determination of age was difficult from the incomplete remains. In the end, Usher took data from previous enquiries in conjunction with independent assessments made by Professor Grainger, radiologically, and Dr Craig, using dental methods, and came to the firm conclusion that the remains were those of a person 'certainly not seventeen years old and most probably between twelve and fifteen years old at the time of death'.

The establishment of the exact race of the dead person proved, in the end, impossible. Again the bones were so fragmented that little significance could be made of, for instance, skull shape. However, Dr Craig found certain deposits on the front upper and lower molar to be so unusual as to suggest that the skeleton was not Caucasian.

As this complicated work was being carried out at the Sheffield Medico-Legal Centre, a team from the University's Department of Television and Graphics was preparing a series of charts showing the bones recovered in relation to the average human skeleton. These charts would later prove invaluable in court.

For it was towards the criminal courts, of course, that these enquiries were inexorably heading.

The entomological studies performed by Dr Erzinclioglu were in themselves proving quite damning to Dr Perera. Tiny insect pupae on many of the bones showed that they had first been buried at an outdoor site – and soil samples matched those of the Sitwell Close garden – before being transferred indoors, first beneath the house floor and then into the oral biology laboratories at Leeds University.

The degree of putrefaction found in the

Above: ***A tray of bone fragments in decalcifying fluid was found in the laboratory where Perera worked.***

Below: ***Police digging up Perera's garden in the search for evidence.***

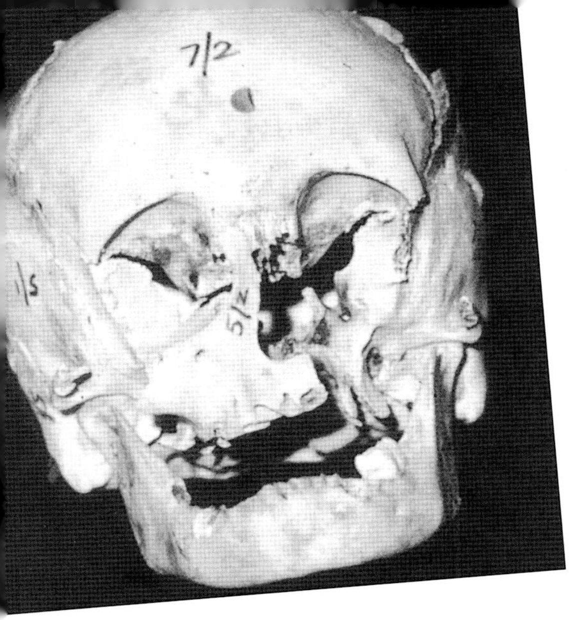

Left: ***The reconstructed skull of the victim.***

THE SUSPECT CLAIMED THAT THE FLESH IN THE FLOWER POTS WAS PORK, WHICH HE WAS EXPERIMENTING WITH AS A FERTILIZER

mass of flesh in the central plant pot meant that death had occurred at least six months prior to discovery and possibly a great deal earlier than that. 'What it all came down to,' remarked Professor Usher dryly, 'was that I could conceive of no legitimate purpose for what was literally half a human torso being concealed in a domestic flower pot.'

By now Perera was, as one detective put it, 'losing some of his cool'. First, he claimed that the flesh in the flower pots had been pork, which he was trying as a new kind of fertilizer. Analysis of the flesh proved this to be palpable nonsense.

Then he claimed that the partial destruction of bones in his laboratory was necessary to his research work. While it is true that decalcification of bone does play a part in dental pathology, the samples used are invariably small – usually no bigger than a postage stamp. And the study of ribs, pelvises and long bones is hardly relevant to dental medicine.

'It simply wasn't possible, due to the fragmentary nature of the remains, to come to any firm conclusion as to the cause of the young girl's death,' admitted Professor Usher.

'But from the systematic attempts made to destroy and dispose of her body, I would strongly deduce that she died of foul play. All indications were that this was the body of Nilanthe Philomena Perera.'

In desperation, Perera tried one last ploy. His new story was that he had

Below: ***Professor Usher sifting through the contents of the plant pots.***

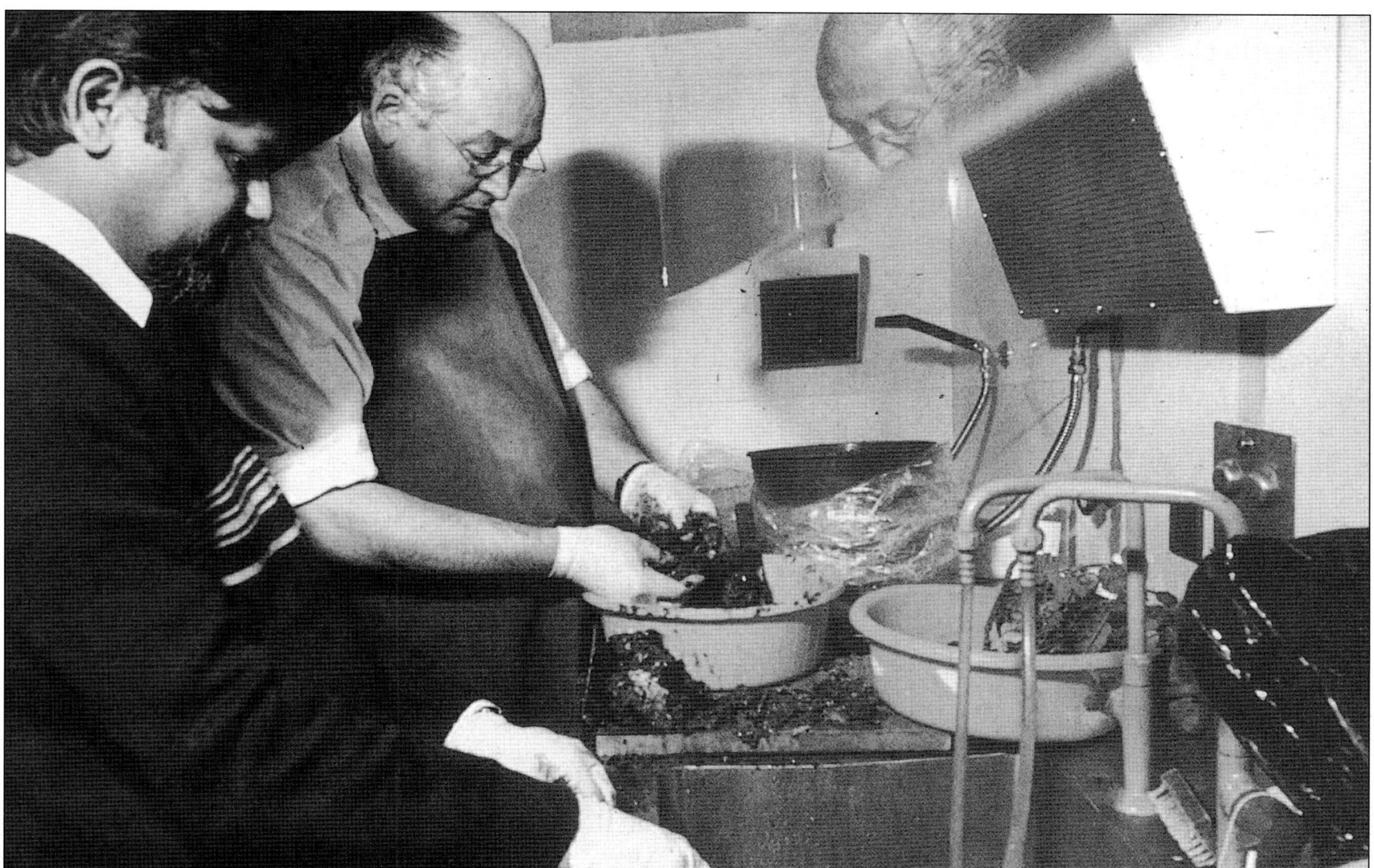

obtained the corpse of a young girl legitimately from a Sri Lankan university for medical purposes and had brought it to England in his suitcase, knowing that open importation would be prohibited.

'Again,' said Usher, 'the idea that someone would voluntarily carry such a huge mass of mouldering flesh and bone about, in hand luggage, was to my mind quite preposterous.'

Nevertheless, Cowman and Hodgson decided to check out this latest tale and travelled to Sri Lanka to interview the university authorities. They discovered that Perera had never been given a body for research, for export or otherwise.

'In many ways,' said Cowman, 'Sri Lankan society is living under Victorian standards, but their ledgers were a policeman's dream. Everything was written out in copperplate longhand.'

The two West Yorkshire policemen also met Nilanthe's grieving father, who confirmed that she had left for England with the Pereras and had never returned.

So what were Perera's motives for killing his adopted 'jungle girl'? Some sort of sex angle seemed likely, in view of Mrs Perera's earlier comments to the neighbours when Nilanthe first vanished. In any case, a jury at Leeds Crown Court found him guilty of unlawfully killing the girl, and on 11 March 1986 Dr Samuel Perera was gaoled for life.

In every way it had been a classic murder investigation, an immaculate piece of scientific and lay detection. Walter Cowman, who became head of Lincolnshire CID after the trial, commented: 'If Tom Hodgson had not been determined, had not refused to accept explanations which others may have accepted, who knows how things may have turned out?'

For Tom Hodgson, it set the seal on his police career. He retired soon afterwards. For Professor Usher the scientific side of the investigation was a personal triumph, but he is quick to point up Hodgson's part in the affair. 'To me, the abiding delight of the case was that this arrogant intellectual murderer obviously thought he was vastly superior to the hick Yorkshire copper who came to question him. But the final score was a resounding game, set and match to Tom.'

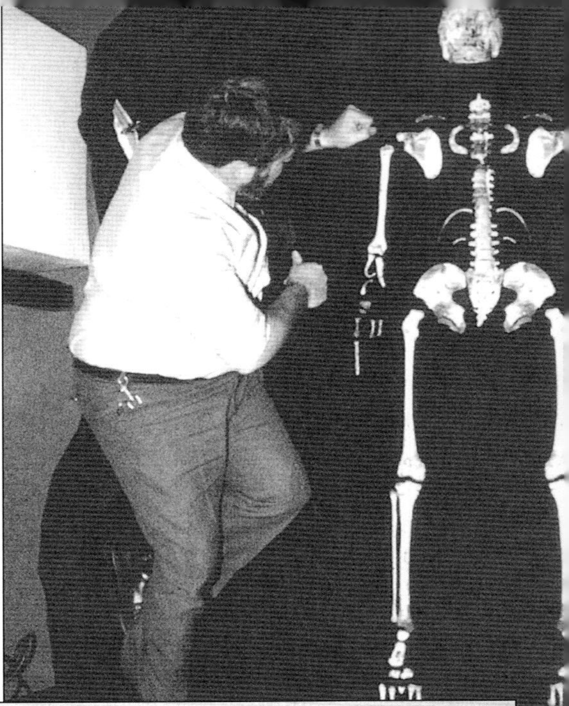

Right: ***A team of experts spent several months reconstructing the victim's skeleton.***

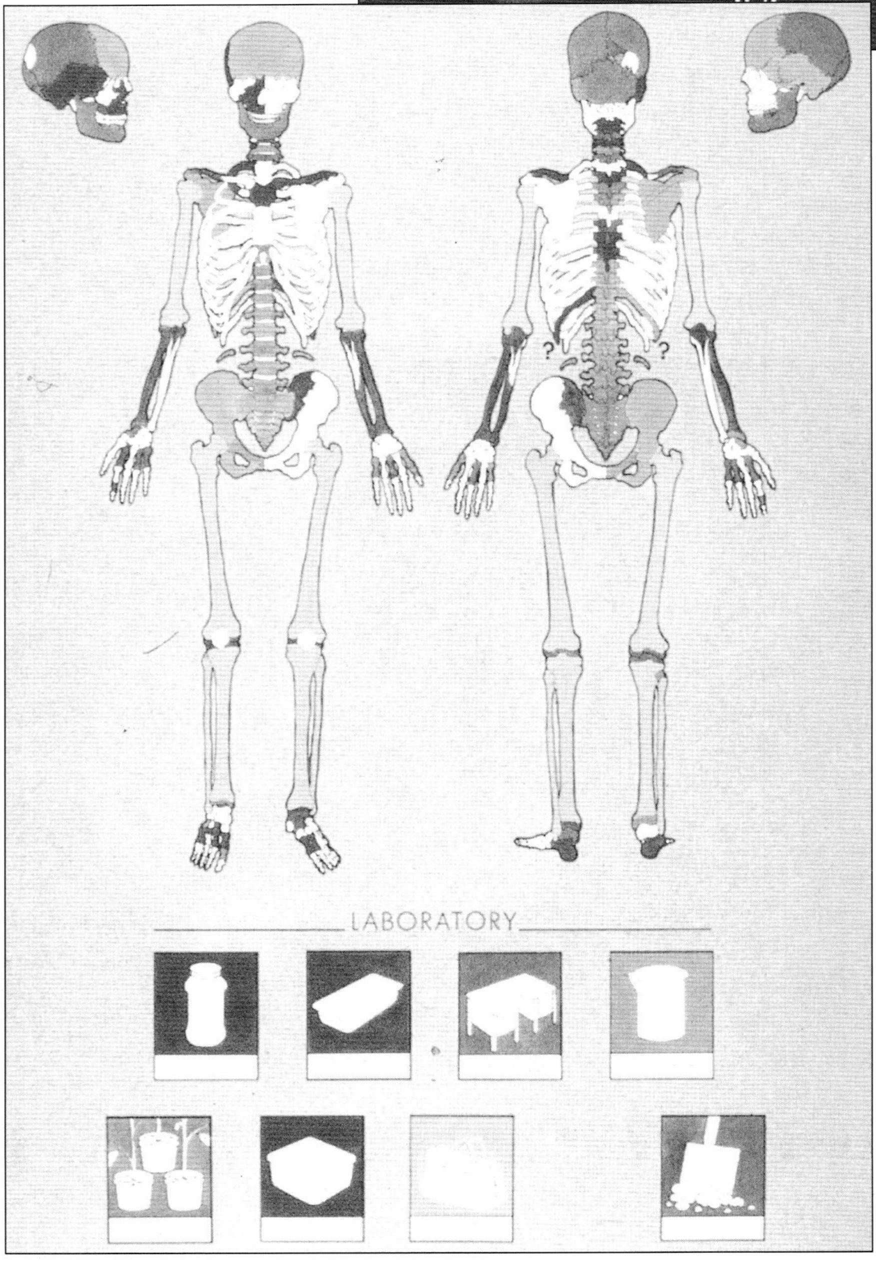

Below: ***The diagram shows which bones were found in Perera's laboratory and which in his house.***

PETER FALCONIO
Outback Ambush

The disappearance of the British tourist Peter Falconio resulted in controversy as several years later the body has still not been discovered.

The disappearance of backpacker Peter Falconio has become one of Australia's most notorious unresolved crimes and led to much panic, shock, horror and controversy.

Twenty-eight-year-old Peter Falconio from Huddersfield, West Yorkshire, had a dream when he graduated from Brighton University of travelling the world. In 2001 this dream was realised when he embarked on a round-the-world trip with his 27-year-old girlfriend, Joanne Lees.

Peter and Joanne set off on their travels on November 15, 2000, planning to make stops at Nepal, Thailand, Cambodia, Australia, New Zealand, Fiji and America. They arrived in Sydney, Australia, in January 2001 where they spent a few months working to earn enough money to fund the remainder of their trip.

In June the couple bought an old orange camper van which they used to travel around the country, sleeping either in the back of the van or in lay-bys on the side of the road. On their travels they made friends with several Canadian backpackers and offered them a lift to Watarrka National Park. At Alice Springs they separated and all went their separate ways.

On the morning of Saturday, July 14, Peter Falconio went to see an accountant by the name of Maureen Laracy, who informed him that he owed money to the tax office for the time he had been working in Sydney. Later that day he bought a ticket for a flight to Papua New Guinea.

While Peter had been with the accountant, Joanne had gone to the local library in Alice Springs to check her emails. When they had both finished their relevant business they met for breakfast at the Green Frog café.

Left: *Joanne Lees (left) and boyfriend Peter Falconio as they sit in their van, taken shortly before they were allegedly ambushed by a man near Barrow Creek in July 2001.*

The couple spent the rest of the day at the Camel Cup races, had a meal at the Red Rooster restaurant, and then, with Joanne driving, they headed off towards Barrow Creek in the Northern Territory. Little did they know when they started this leg of their adventures that it was to be where Peter's journey ended.

THE AMBUSH

On the night of July 14, 2001, the couple stopped to buy fuel at the Ti Tree Roadhouse and afterwards sat and shared a 'joint' of cannabis as they watched the sun go down. Peter Falconio took over the driving at this point and they headed north along the Stuart highway. It was an extremely remote stretch of road which led to Barrow Creek, and it was not unusual to travel miles without meeting another vehicle. Allegedly, Peter and Joanne were flagged down by a man at the side of the road indicating that they had problems with their exhaust. Joanne was nervous about stopping in the middle of nowhere, but Peter, perhaps the more confident of the two, got out of the camper and went to see what the man was talking about. Joanne could hear the two men talking about sparks coming out of the back of the camper and then heard Peter say, 'Cheers mate.' While they were talking she noticed that there was an Australian cattle dog sitting on the passenger seat of the man's truck. A few minutes later Peter returned to the window of the camper and asked her to rev the engine, took out his cigarettes and then returned to the back of the camper. Minutes later Joanne heard a bang, thinking initially that it was probably the van backfiring, but realised that something was definitely amiss when the man who had stopped them appeared at the window of the van.

There are many inconsistencies in this part of Joanne's story, as she later stated to the police that the truck had been behind them and it eventually pulled up alongside the camper and signalled for the couple to stop.

Above: The scrub where Peter Falconio and Joanne Lees were allegedly assaulted, which was part of the evidence presented to the jury during the Falconio murder trial on October 31, 2005, in Darwin, Australia.

The man threatened Joanne by holding a gun to her head, and then tied her hands behind her and bundled her into the back of his truck. This was another point in dispute, because when she was found by a passer-by, Joanne had her hands bound at the front of her body. During the struggle with her assailant, Joanne's T-shirt became soiled with his blood, from an injury he received whilst trying to get her into the back of his truck. Joanne reported that at no time did she see Peter's body or in fact any

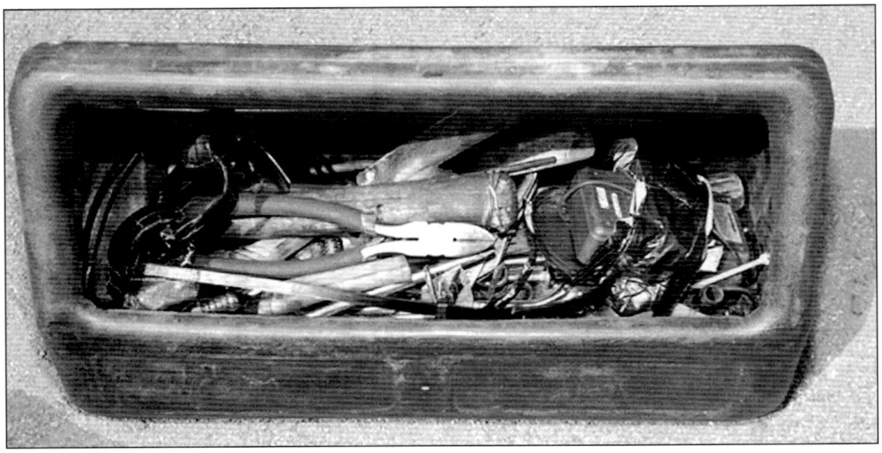

blood, which was later to be found all over the road.

Somehow, Joanne managed to escape from her attacker and with her hands still tied, ran into the surrounding bushes and hid for several hours while the man searched the area with his dog. According to Joanne he eventually gave up and drove away. Joanne was extremely lucky to have survived not only the attack but also not to have been bitten by one of the many snakes, spiders or scorpions that lived in the Australian outback.

The attack had taken place at about 8.00 p.m., and at about 12.38 a.m. on the Saturday, a man had been spotted on the CCTV camera at the Shell truck stop in Alice springs, where he bought fuel, ice and an iced coffee.

Joanne hid until about 1 a.m. when she heard a vehicle approaching. She jumped out of the scrub and flagged down a truck being driven by a man called Vince Millar. She told him what had happened and asked if he could help her look for her boyfriend, as she was scared that he had been shot. Millar said that as her attacker could still be in the area and was carrying a gun it would be better if they went off for help. He drove her to the Barrow Creek roadhouse, where they telephoned the police.

LARGEST EVER MANHUNT

Garry Moseley, of the Alice Springs police force arranged for a series of road blocks covering all the main routes. They contacted every single roadhouse and cattle station in the area, asking them to be on the lookout for anyone suspicious. Officers from the Northern Territory police started to scour the Australian outback in one of the largest ever manhunts recorded. They utilised the extraordinary skills of Aborigine trackers but the evidence they found at the alleged site of the attack only added to the confusion. The only tracks they could find were those of Joanne Lees and if, as Joanne said, the assailant spent several hours searching the area with his dog, there would surely be other clues. It was argued that rain had destroyed the tracks, and yet if this were the case why were the footprints of Joanne not destroyed as well?

Above: *The toolbox containing cable ties and tape which was used as evidence.*

Below: *The accused, Bradley John Murdoch.*

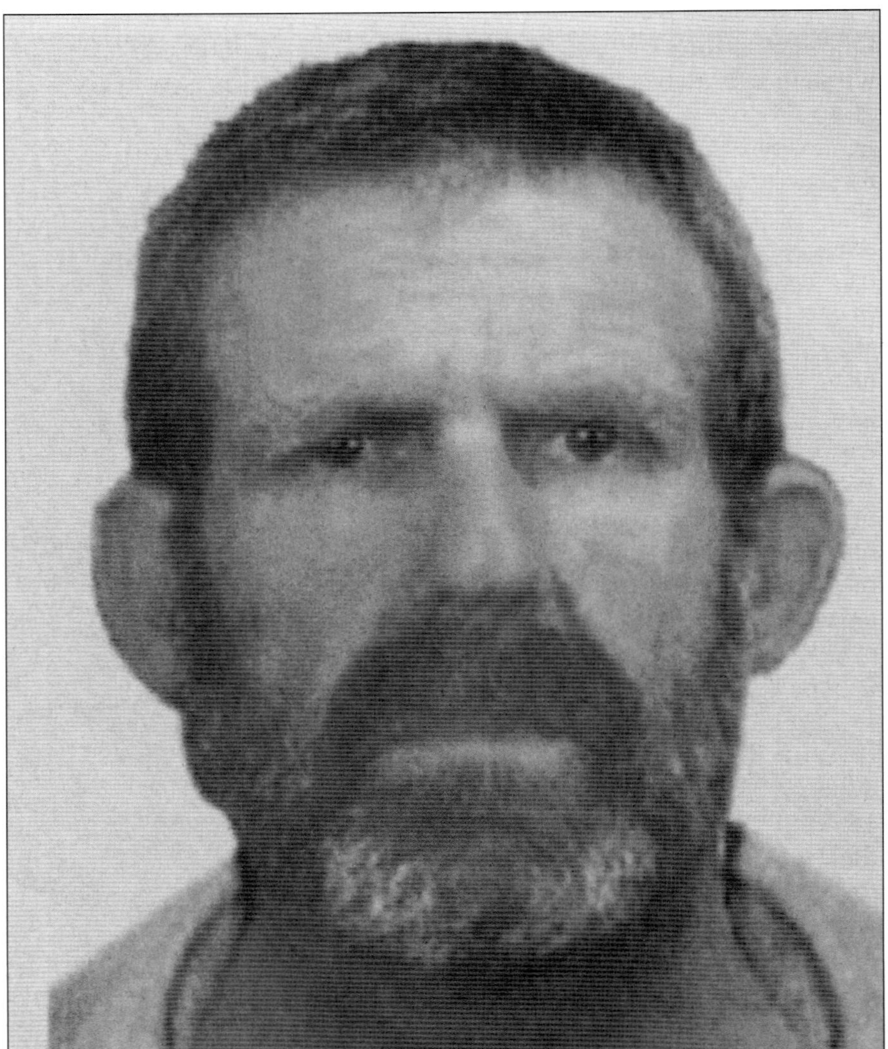

Another piece of information that came to the fore during the investigation was the fact that Joanne Lees was having an affair with a man who has never been named, but who has been referred to as 'Nick'. Joanne vehemently denied that she was seeing anyone else but when confronted with documentary evidence had to admit that there was another man. She has always refused to disclose his identity.

Despite the scale of the investigation the police failed to turn up any convicting evidence until approximately two years later.

BRADLEY MURDOCH

When a man called Bradley Murdoch was arrested in November 2003 in connection with a rape case, it is alleged that the police found an article in his room about the backpacker Peter Falconio. Murdoch had a violent past with a morbid obession for guns and he claimed that the police had tried to frame him on a number of occasions for crimes that he had not committed. The arresting officers found a huge amount of weapons in the back of his truck, about 800 rounds of ammunition, and a number of chains and shackles similar to the ones Joanne had described. Time and time again he tried to resist samples being taken so that the forensics team could test his DNA. When they did manage to get a sample of his DNA, it matched positive to the bloodstains found on Joanne's T-shirt, on the tape used to bind her and also to a smear on the gearstick of the couple's camper van.

THE TRIAL – THE PROSECUTION

When the trial by jury began on October 18, 2005, the prosecution had to rely on the forensic evidence against Murdoch to fight their case. However, a suspect cannot be found guilty on the evidence of DNA alone and so they knew they had a hard fight ahead of them.

The forensic team found no blood on Murdoch's truck which meant it would have been very hard for him to transport the body without leaving some sort of a trace, and so the mystery surrounding the whereabouts of the body was still unsolved. Even if Murdoch had cleaned his truck thoroughly, it would have been very hard to remove any traces of blood completely. There were, however, several eyewitnesses who claimed that Murdoch, a mechanic by trade, had made major alterations to his truck just a few weeks after the offence, which meant that he could have destroyed any vital clues.

Another weak part of the prosecution was Murdoch's motive – rape. It would seem very unlikely that a man who

Below: *Joanne Lees, girlfriend of Peter Falconio, on day 38 of the murder trial at Northern Territory Supreme Court.*

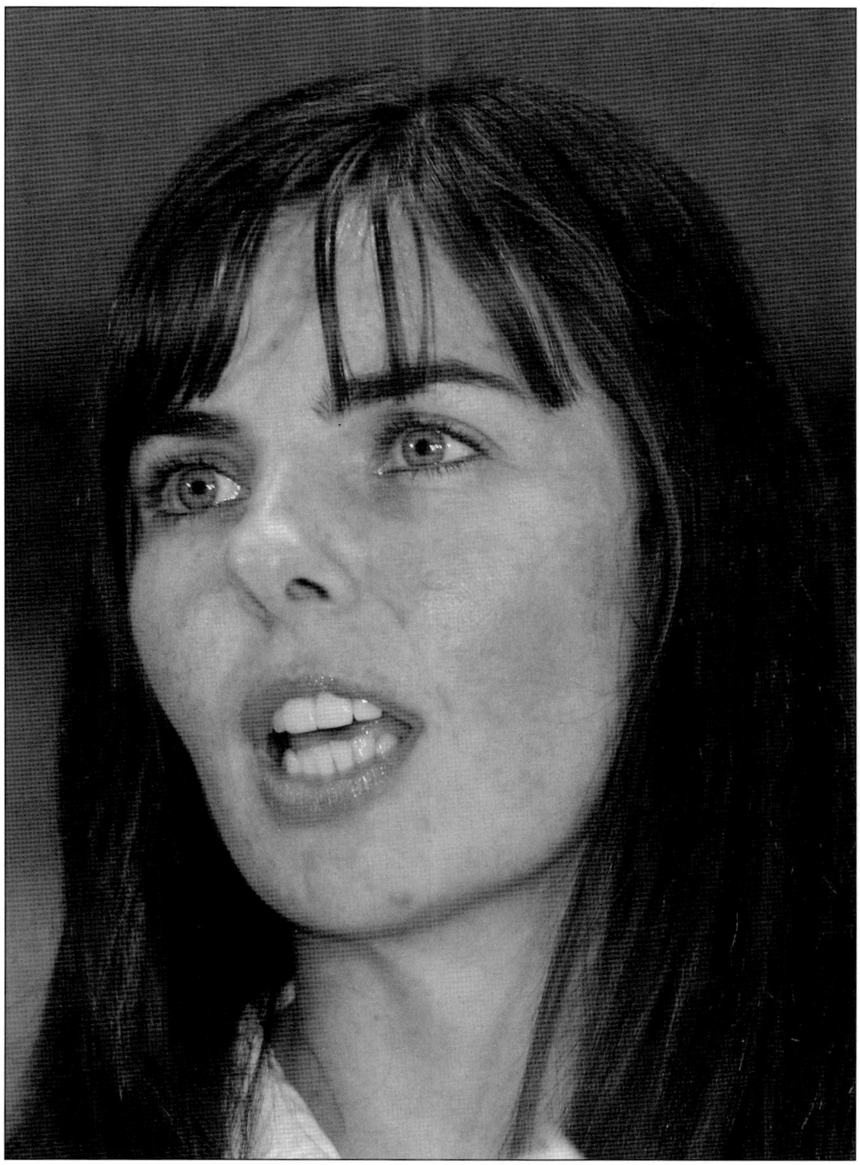

already had a history of rape and knew the area, would stand on an isolated stretch of road on the offchance of a car passing by, let alone one containing a woman. If this motive were true, he could have been standing there for days, not really the action of a man with a desire to rape.

The prosecution also made a strong point that Murdoch had been spotted in a service station near Alice Springs on the night of the alleged murder. Alice Springs, however, is well over one hundred miles away from Barrow Creek and so his presence at the service station could not be used to implicate him in the alleged attack. However, the defence used the evidence of a narcotics expert, who said that a person who regularly uses speed, a stimulant drug, would be quite capable of driving up to 36 hours keeping a high level of concentration.

Joanne Lees had positively identified Murdoch as her attacker from a photograph shown to her by the police. Murdoch was known to be a drug dealer and at the time of the offence was in the middle of a deal which involved carrying dope from South to West Australia.

The blood found on the road at the site of the alleged attack, was confirmed by the forensics team to be that of Peter Falconio.

One witness, an Aboriginal woman, said she saw a car speed away from Barrow Creek shortly after the alleged time of the attack, but she was the only person to actually witness the presence of another vehicle.

Even after a thorough search of the area, forensics were unable to find a trace of any bullets having been fired either in the van or on the ground beneath it. But the prosecution argued that any traces of gunfire could have been wiped away when the police were dusting for fingerprints. They also pointed out that it was quite plausible for a bullet to enter a skull and leave no exit wound, especially if it was fired from close range.

THE TRIAL – THE DEFENCE

The defence team used many tactics during the trial in an effort to win the jury over. Although Joanne Lees openly admitted to having cable ties in the back of the camper van she denied that she had ever used them to bind herself. They also argued that as both Peter and Joanne were heavy users of marijuana and occasional users of ecstasy, it is possible that Joanne was stoned at the time of the attack and was not clear about exactly what had happened.

Murdoch, Falconio and Lees were all positively identified as having been in a café in Alice Springs on the night of the alleged murder. This, the defence argued, could have accounted for the blood stains on Joanne's T-shirt saying that she could have accidentally bumped into Murdoch.

The times given by Joanne Lees didn't quite tally because the speedometer in the van showed that its maximum speed was 80 km per hour, and yet if the evidence she gave to the police was correct, she would have had to drive at 176 km per hour.

Lees eventually admitted to police that she was having an affair behind Peter's back, and yet she was not prepared to give his name beyond the name 'Nick' and that he was from Sydney.

Below: *A stick of lip salve found in the bush, which was allegedly used by Joanne Lees to free herself of handcuffs, was offered to the jury as evidence on day two of the trial.*

the police, Joanne completely denied ever having been there.

Peter Falconio, who had been working in Australia on a legitimate work visa, had been wrongly taxed by his employers meaning that he owed approximately $3,000–$5,000 to the tax office. On the day that he disappeared there is a record of him making enquiries as to how he could get out of paying the money back, also asking what would be the best way of faking his own death. This information was given to the police from an anonymous source, and the evidence was dismissed as inconclusive.

All of the DNA samples tested at the forensic laboratory were deemed inadmissible due to the fact that the laboratory did not come up to the required standards. The prosecution argued that the laboratory was only just below the required standards and that it would be virtually impossible for any contamination to have occurred.

The DNA evidence that was uncovered from the hand ties became contaminated due to poor police procedure and therefore could not be submitted as evidence. Several other pieces of evidence including a lip salve and some black tape were not found until three months after the alleged attack. The defence claimed that this pointed to the fact that it could have been planted, but prosecution argued that due to the thickness of the shrub it could have just been difficult to find.

As to the evidence against Murdoch himself, he did not remotely match the description originally given to the police by Joanne, but the prosecution simply argued that he had put on a disguise to carry out the alleged attack. Also the description of his vehicle was nothing like the truck that Murdoch owned and on top of that he had never owned a cattle dog, his was a dalmatian cross which was not even similar in appearance.

Although Peter and Joanne were positively identified as having been in a road house between Alice Springs and Barrow Creek just a few hours before the alleged crime, which made a mockery of the times she had given to

Above: *The Kombi camper van belonging to Joanne Lees and Peter Falconio is impounded as evidence at the Northern Territory Supreme Court.*

CLOSING ARGUMENTS

The defence closed their case by saying that Peter Falconio had faked his own death in an effort to get out of paying back taxes and that when the couple stopped on the road near Barrow Creek it was to meet a third person, who simply drove Peter away alive.

They stated that the police had simply planted evidence to implicate the known drug-runner Bradley John Murdoch. They also pointed to the absence of blood at the alleged crime scene, the contamination of the DNA samples, the lack of a body, and also the sightings of Peter Falconio in the days after the supposed attack. They said that in view of the inconsistency in Joanne Lees's statement, the poor police procedures and the lack of a positive ID on Murdoch, that there was no way he could be found guilty of murder.

The prosecution, on the other hand, told the jury that this is what really happened. Bradley Murdoch noticed Peter and Joanne in Alice Springs and thought that they were following him in connection with his drug run. He decided to follow them along the Stuart Highway and then stopped in an effort to get rid of them. However, after they stopped Murdoch panicked and killed Peter Falconio, making sure that he left no traces by shooting him at close range directly into the skull. He then abducted Joanne Lees by tying her up with cable ties and placing her in the back of his pick-up. Whilst Murdoch was attempting to get rid of the body, Joanne managed to escape but, despite searching with the aid of his dog and a torch, was unable to find her and after several hours gave her up as lost.

Murdoch then buried the body of Peter Falconio in an unknown site, using Joanne's denim jacket round his head to prevent any blood from going on his truck. After this Murdoch, still in a state of panic, drove back to Alice Springs where he was spotted on CCTV buying supplies.

Following the alleged attack Murdoch not only changed his own appearance but also modified his truck to avoid detection. They concluded by saying that the jury should ignore any coincidental evidence that would suggest that Murdoch did not murder Peter Falconio and find him guilty.

Chief Justice Brian Ross Martin tried his best to instruct the jury:

> *How you approach the evidence is a matter entirely for you. There are many issues that have been raised for your consideration. You may or may not find it necessary to resolve all the issues. You may or may not be able to resolve all of the issues. You must put aside the flamboyant suggestions of counsel that we do not need experts from the mother country to teach us colonials a thing or two . . . Please put aside all the hyperbole and concentrate on the evidence before you. That's why you look at all the evidence, not just the experts . . .*

FOUND GUILTY

On December 14, 2005, 47-year-old Bradley Murdoch was found guilty of murdering the British backpacker, Peter Falconio and abducting and assaulting Miss Joanne Lees. Joanne Lees who has been under suspicion since the day Peter disappeared, pleaded with Murdoch to tell them where he had buried the body. However, this is unlikely to happen as Murdoch has instructed his lawyer to appeal against the sentence.

Below: *Luciano and Joan Falconio (front), parents of Peter Falconio and brothers Paul (rear left) and Nick leave the Northern Territory Supreme Court after day two of the murder trial in Darwin, Australia.*

CASE COMPARISON

The Peter Falconio case has been compared to that of the 'Backpack Murderer' Ivan Milat, and at one point in their investigations the police were concerned that they were once again looking for a serial killer.

In March 1996, following a trial in Campbelltown Local Court, Ivan Milat was sentenced to life imprisonment for the murder of several backpackers in New South Wales.

His murder spree started in 1992 when Caroline Clarke and Joanne Walters, two British travellers, left a backpackers' hotel in Sydney and headed for the south-east area of New South Wales. Their bodies were found in September of that year buried in an area which was known as 'Executioner's drop'. Two more bodies were found in 1993 in the same remote area of Belanglo Forest. The bodies were later identified as those of James Gibson and Deborah Everist, both 19-year-olds. Police decided to do an intensive search of the area and in November uncovered two skeletons. Using forensic technology they were able to identify their DNA and they proved to be the remains of two German tourists, 21-year-old Gabor Kurt Neugebauer and his 20-year-old girlfriend, Anja Susanne Habschied. They had been on the missing persons register for two years, and when they found the remains of Anja not only had she been stabbed several times but she had also been decapitated.

Thorough forensic examinations carried out at the scene where the bodies were found uncovered gun cartridges which matched those taken from a farmhouse just outside Sydney. A witness came forward saying that she had been offered a lift by a man who had started to strange behavely, so she asked to be dropped off in the Belanglo Forest area. As she got out of the car the man fired at her, but luckily she managed to escape unharmed. She was later able to identify the man who had given her the lift as Ivan Milat.

It is thought that Ivan Milat could be linked to a possible further six unsolved murders, but Milat still continues to claim his innocence.

MILAT WAS A KNOWN GUN FANATIC WHO USED THE NAME 'TEXAS'. THIS NICKNAME HAD BEEN ENGRAVED ON ONE OF THE GUNS USED IN AN ATTEMPTED MURDER.

Below: *A 'Crime Stoppers' sticker on the back of Milat's car.*

TOO FEW CLUES

SILENT WITNESSES
The Maggot Murder

A bleached skull and some rotting bones... nothing to give a clue to detectives with regard to who might have killed the victim whose gravesite they were now gathered around. But an honest army of silent witnesses, in the shape of loathsome, writhing maggots, would finally capture the killer.

A pathologist must have a strong stomach as well as steady nerves when it comes to carrying out his or her extraordinary duties. Corpses are rarely in a pristine state – decomposition makes them stink to high-heaven, as well as providing a feeding ground for insects of every kind. This very "unpleasantness" is used now in certain crime-prevention programmes in America. In Columbus, Georgia, for example, first-time drug offenders have to sit through full-blown criminal autopsies. Many of them can cope with the dissection of the body – the removal of the heart, liver, brain for examination – but those who faint invariably do so because of the stench of decomposition, or at the sight of creepy-crawlies that have wormed their way into the cadaver.

But to trained experts these parasites seeking food and refuge in a corpse are sometimes a welcome sight. Their very presence can render up a wealth of clues as

TO TRAINED EXPERTS, PARASITES SEEKING FOOD AND REFUGE IN A CORPSE ARE SOMETIMES A WELCOME SIGHT

Opposite: ***Maggots feasting on a human skull.***

Below: ***Police search Bracknell Woods for clues to the corpse in The Maggot Murder.***

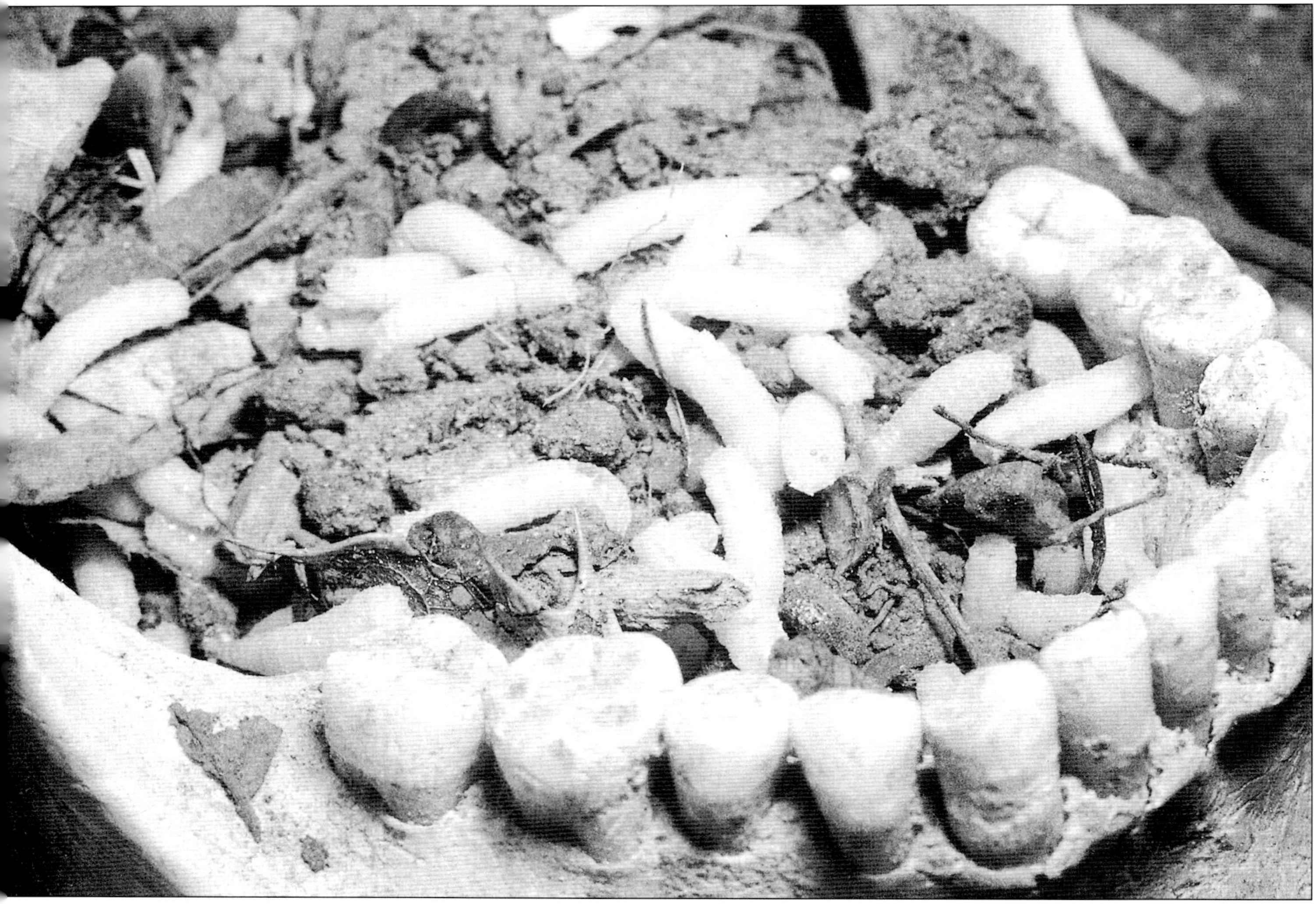

Above: ***Maggots writhe between the teeth of the victim's skull. They would hold the key to solving the otherwise baffling case.***

THOSE WRIGGLING, WHITE, FAT BODIES LIVING WITHIN THE CORPSE WOULD PROVIDE THE KEY TO THE KILLER

to when the person died, how long they had been exposed to air before death and even provide clues as to where the murder may have taken place. In June 1964 Britain's foremost Home Office pathologist Professor Keith Simpson began his examination of a maggot-infested corpse. The stench was terrible, the state of the body lamentable. But never was an expert more glad to see those wriggling, white, fat bodies living within the corpse... visitors who would provide the key to the killer.

Two 13-year-old boys out for a day's fishing near Bracknell Woods in Berkshire on June 28 of that year paused before going to the riverbank to look for a small, dead animal that might be maggot-infested. Paul Fay and Tony King had done this countless times before, seeking out a pigeon or a rabbit, maybe a starling, that had been long dead and ripe for larvae. As they cut through the dry undergrowth they saw an unusual sight – maggots writhing on a mound of grass when usually they had to sweep aside leaves or undergrowth to get to the object which they fed off.

It was quite a find and would save the boys plenty of time in their quest for live bait. Yet as they started to collect the maggots, they pulled away the turf to reveal a semi-rotted human arm with a hand still attached to it that suddenly flopped out of the hole. Running out of fear and shock the boys bolted to the nearest police station. Their fishing trip abandoned, the maggot site became a murder investigation within 30 minutes.

Detective Chief Superintendent Arthur Lawson was disturbed at his home shortly after his Sunday lunch that day. The chief of the Berkshire CID, he supervised the careful removal of the corpse from its shallow grave. The body was that of a fully-grown man, fully clothed, lying on his back, the head wrapped in towelling. Scenes-of-crime officers – SOCOS in police parlance – were unable to garner much evidence from the actual gravesite. There were no tyre tracks visible through the vegetation on the soft earth to indicate how the body was brought there; no weapons, glasses or other pieces of clothing that might have belonged to the unfortunate victim's murderer were found either.

Lawson speculated from the state of the body that it might have been several weeks old, but Professor Simpson – who had also been disturbed from a post-lunch snooze in his garden – surprised him by deducing that the body was no more than 12 days old at the most. "It is astonishing how quickly maggots will eat up the flesh," he said. "I have seen a body reduced to this state in as little as ten days."

THE EXPERT'S VIEW

It became clear that the forensic evidence offered up by the cadaver would be of supreme importance – both in identification and in any prosection of the perpetrator of the crime. Professor Simpson described the maggots in his autobiography *Forty Years of Murder*.

"I thought it safe to assume the maggots were larvae of the bluebottle Calliphora erythocephalus, but I preserved samples because the maggots of other flies of the calliphorine type, with slightly different hatching times, are not dissimilar to the naked eye. The ordinary life history of the bluebottle is quite simple: the eggs are laid in daylight, usually sunlight, and in warm weather they hatch on the first day.

"The tiny 'first instar' maggot sheds its skin after eight to 14 hours, and the second instar after a further two to three days. The third instar, the fisherman's maggot, feeds voraciously for five or six days before going into a pupa case. The larvae I was looking at were mature, indeed elderly, fat, indolent, third-stage maggots, but they were not in pupa cases. Therefore I estimated that the eggs had been laid nine or ten days earlier. Adding a little more time to allow for the bluebottles getting to the dead body, I reckon death had occurred on the 16th or the 17th of June.' The maggots were to play a vital role in the case.

Due to the extreme fragility of the corpse, Professor Simpson decided to do some of his autopsy at the site, fearing that the body might break up in transit. Tell-tale small pools of blood either side of the head and a similar pool inside the voice box – coupled with the detection of crushed bones in the larynx – told him that the man had died with a vicious blow to the windpipe, perhaps more than one.

Back in the laboratory the remains yielded other data: he had broken his left arm when he was young and the fracture had not set properly and the skeleton measured 5ft 3ins. Now it was a question of matching the remains to a person – which was where Professor Simpson left off and the police came into their own again.

Below: ***The decomposing body of Peter Thomas, a man who found justice through the maggots which feasted on his remains.***

As with all murders the immediate checks are with missing persons. Chief Supt. Lawson checked with the central office for such information – then, as now, Scotland Yard. The missing persons bureau highlighted the fact that a Peter Thomas had vanished from his home in Lydney, Gloucestershire, on June 16.

A Scotland Yard "heavyweight" detective, Superintendent Horace Faber, had been down to the countryside at the request of the local constabulary to help out on the disappearance. When he learned that there might be a link between the missing person and the corpse that had turned up in the woods 100 miles away he attached himself to the crime squad.

Thomas matched the characteristics of the corpse. He was listed as being the same height as the cadaver, he had broken his left arm in childhood and, more importantly, he had a criminal record. Simpson was telegraphed to take fngerprints off of the decaying flesh of the corpse. They established beyond doubt that the corpse which had become a feast for maggots was indeed that of the man from Lydney. The police now had identity and cause of death – it was time to concentrate on the killer and the motive for the violent end.

Above: ***The bluebottle fly, whose larvae hatched on the body of Thomas, thereby providing the forensic expert with invaluable clues as to his death.***

Opposite Top: ***Dr Keith Simpson, the undisputed genius of British forensic science. His expertise would crack the mystery of The Maggot Murder.***

Opposite Bottom: ***Dr Simpson in his usual pose, crouching down at a crime scene – this one is the infamous Haigh 'acid bath' murders.***

Enquiries soon discovered that Thomas had been living a life on the edge of poverty in a wooden bungalow. The scene at his home was one of bachelor untidiness writ large – half-eaten meals, uncleaned plates, empty soup tins everywhere. He was receiving unemployment benefit, although a police search of the unkempt property revealed that, some years earlier, he had been in receipt of the not-insubstantial sum of £5,000 in an inheritance, left to him by his father in his will when he died three years earlier. The money was loaned to a Thomas Brittle, a heating-radiator salesman of Hook, Hampshire.

More significantly, paperwork revealed that "this debt shall be repaid no later than the 30th of June 1964". The instinct of hardened policemen was aroused by the coincidence that the due date of the loan repayment fell in the same month that the man was murdered. Suspicion fell upon the Thomas Brittle to whom the money had been loaned – loaned, it later turned out, against the advice of Thomas' lawyer who said it was a "bad prospect".

Detectives learned that Brittle had advertised in a newspaper seeking investors for an agricultural project – namely that he would pay 12-and-a-half per-cent for six months to anyone willing to offer up the cash. Thomas did – and it was to cost him his life. Brittle was questioned, cautioned, and arrested for the murder – despite the lack of evidence against him.

LIES AND ALIBIS

In custody he admitted that he had gone to Lydney on June 16 – the day of the dead man's disappearance. He said that he had repaid the money – although, of course, it was not to be found in Thomas' modest bungalow, nor at the crime scene. He said he had won the repayment cash on the horses at Epsom, although could not give to police the names of the winning steeds. There was no forensic on his clothes, on his car or on any of his possessions to link him to the murder. And he produced a hitch-hiker to swear that he had picked him up en route to pay back the money. "I ask you, would I have given a lift to someone if I was on my way to kill him?" he asked police with a look of wide-eyed innocence.

Police had expected to find at least a trace of evidence in the car. Crimes of violence are always about an exchange

between parties, whether of bodily fluids, blood or tissue. The criminal and the victim tend to leave traces – however microscopic – of their presence. Yet on Thomas' body there was nothing connected to Brittle. The case dragged on for months – then there came a break. A Dennis Roberts, who lived in Gloucester, stepped forward to say he had seen Thomas at Gloucester bus station on June 20 – a date he was certain of because he was on strike for the first time in his life from the fabrics factory where he worked. This information seemed to clear Brittle – he had the testimony of the hitch-hiker to back him up that he had been going to see him four days previously. If he was still alive four days later, how could he be the culprit?

PROFESSOR SIMPSON WAS PREPARED TO SWEAR ON THE WRITHING LARVAE OF THE BLUEBOTTLE FLY

In the end, it came down to the workings of the maggots – those silent but ravenous guardians of the corpse – which would determine guilt or innocence.

Professor Simpson was working in his laboratory when Faber of the Yard came to see him about the testimony of Roberts. "Is it possible he was killed on the 20th and was only dead for eight days?" Faber asked Simpson. "No it isn't," answered the expert. "And I am ready to stand up to severe cross-examination on the point if it comes to trial."

IN THE END THE JURY DECIDED THAT THE MAGGOTS WERE MORE RELIABLE THAN THE DEFENCE WITNESS

To back up his verbal assurance Professor Simpson attached a note to the Director of Public Prosecutions, on whom the decision rested as to whether to bring Brittle to trial. It read: "I have today been shown a copy of a statement by Dennis John Roberts to the effect that on Saturday, 20th June, he saw a man whom he recognised as Peter Thomas at a bus station.

"The condition of the body when examined in the wood suggested in the first instance, while still at the scene – 'some nine or ten days, possibly more' – was a minimum period. Nothing in the post-mortem state of the body suggested any special conditions likely to have accelerated the ordinary process of maggot infestation and disintegration of the body. I have had considerable experience in the timing of death and would regard Dennis Roberts' statement as being wholly inconsistent with my findings." Professor Simpson was prepared to swear on the writhing larvae of the bluebottle fly against the word of a defence witness.

"NOTHING IN THE STATE OF THE BODY SUGGESTED CONDITIONS LIKELY TO HAVE ACCELERATED MAGGOT INFESTATION"

The DPP passed on the prosecution – he felt there was not enough evidence to convict Brittle. However, a jury at the inquest returned an extraordinary verdict – "that Thomas had been murdered by a person around about the 17th of June". And in a rider they named that person as Brittle. The Coroner then had no choice but to commit Brittle into custody while a reluctant DPP pressed ahead with his prosecution – a prosecution in which he hoped writhing maggots would make the star witnesses!

The counsel for the defence in the case was the redoubtable Quintin Hogg, later to become Lord Hailsham, the Lord Chancellor. Professor Simpson knew he

would be given a hard time in the witness box by this courtroom expert, but he was convinced that the maggots had to have been there before the time Roberts swore he saw the victim alive at the bus station.

Above: ***The counsel for the defence in the case was the redoubtable Quintin Hogg, later to become Lord Hailsham, the Lord Chancellor.***

CLEAR EVIDENCE

In his autobiography he recounted: "When I was examined by the crown counsel, Ralph Cusack, I set out as clearly and as briefly as I could the nature of the fat, third instar maggot, not yet pupated, yet plainly having passed the growing-up stages from the day the eggs hatched. I further set out the several periods of time that it took eggs to hatch, and the three stages of maggot instar to develop before pupation.

I added up the times and in court said, as deliberately and as purposefully as I knew how: 'I had no doubt that this man had been dead some ten days.' Nine or ten was a minimum." He also supplied expert testimony on the blow or blows which killed the dead man – in his opinion karate-chop type strikes to the throat, such as might be administered by someone who was an expert in unarmed combat. And the defendant, it turned out, had taken Commando training in the British Army and had learned such manoeuvres...

Professor Simpson was too much of an expert to doubt – even for Quintin Hogg, who asked no further questions of him. He tried to shake the prosecution evidence about the maggots from Professor McKenny-Hughes, a specialist in insects. He hoped this eminent entomologist would be able to refute the testimony about the maggots, but he only reinforced the pathologist's opinion. When asked if the flies might have been laying their eggs at midnight rather than midday the academic replied: "Oh dear me no. No self-respecting bluebottle lays eggs at midnight. At midday, perhaps, but not at midnight."

The trial took place nine months after Brittle was arrested. The prosecution made much of the fact that time had blurred the memory of the man who had allegedly seen the dead man at the bus stop. But Dennis Roberts was not to be dissuaded from his initial testimony and the jury, after a five day trial, had to decide upon the unreliable sighting or the expert testimony of Professor Simpson. They decided the maggots were more reliable and Brittle was given a life sentence for murder.

Professor Simpson said: "The case was particularly satisfying to me. My insistence on the timing of death has become pretty well known, to the police, to the Director of Public Prosecutions, the lawyers – and the Press, who would have scented a public disgrace for me if I had been wrong."

Legal expert James Staniford added this postscript: "It was an extraordinary victory for forensic expertise, indeed a landmark case, presented in such a way so as not to baffle the jury and allow them to come to the right conclusion about a particularly cold-blooded murderer."

GORDON HAY
Marks of Death

From the horrifying condition of her dead body, it was obvious that 15-year-old schoolgirl Linda Peacock had fallen prey to a savage beast. There were few clues left at the murder scene to aid police... but, thanks to teethmarks that had been left on the corpse, justice was eventually done.

They found the girl in a cemetery, her violated body lying between two graves and beneath the shadow of a fully grown yew tree. The little town of Biggar, midway between Edinburgh and Glasgow, was not used to such depraved murder. The girl, later identified as 15-year-old Linda Peacock, had not been raped during the frenzied assault on her on the night of August 6 1967, but her clothing was pushed up to expose her breasts. When police were called to the murder scene the next morning they began the usual hunt for clues – the search for minutiae which even the cleverest criminal must leave behind at the site of a crime.

There was little to make the scene of crime officer and the pathologist happy about the possibility of finding who had done this to the poor victim. But then a veteran police sergeant noticed the strange bruising around the right breast and took photographs of it. Detective Sgt. John Paton had attended dozens of murder scenes, arsons, rapes and break-ins during his 20 years on the force. There was something about the bruising which made him convinced that it was a human bite, although it did not have the usual teeth outline. It was he alone who had grasped the significance of the wound – and a good job he did. For in doing so the case of Linda Peacock went into the criminal history books because her killer was the first ever to be caught by his teeth.

Criminal odontology – the study of teeth in relation to crimes and criminals – was a relatively murky area to British experts in the 1950s. The Scandinavians seemed to lead the world in research and the application of the new science in relation to crime solving. Teeth, it was learned, largely thanks to the expertise of Swedish expert Gosta Gustavson – have many of the properties of fingerprints when it comes to individual characteristics. Together with his wife Anna Greta he had also discovered it was possible to divine the age of a corpse by careful microscopic investigation of molars. Yet there had never been a conviction in a British court based solely on teeth identification the way there had been with

SOMETHING ABOUT THE BRUISING CONVINCED DETECTIVE SGT. JOHN PATON THAT IT WAS A HUMAN BITE

Opposite: ***Linda Peacock's body, covered by tarpaulin in the graveyard where it was discovered.***

Below: ***Bitemarks would lead to the killer of innocent schoolgirl Linda.***

Above: *Police at the Peacock murder scene undertaking the usual hunt for clues. But clues were in short supply in this case.*

WHEN LINDA PEACOCK'S BITEMARKS WERE ANALYSED FURTHER IT SET IN MOTION A BRILLIANT CRIMINAL INVESTIGATION

Daily Mirror

FRI MAR. 4 1949

ONE PENNY

FORWARD WITH THE PEOPLE

No. 14,095

Registered at G.P.O. as a Newspaper.

VAMPIRE—A MAN HELD

THE Vampire Killer will never strike again. He is safely behind bars, powerless to lure victims to a hideous death.

This is the assurance which the *Daily Mirror* can give today. It is the considered conclusion of the finest detective brains in the country.

The full tally of the Vampire's crimes is still not known.

It may take squads of police many weeks yet to piece together full details of the murderer and his ghastly practices.

So far five murders are attributed to him. They are:—

Dr. Archibald Henderson;

Mrs. Rosalie Mercy Henderson, his wife;

Mr. Donald McSwan;

Mrs. Amy McSwan, his wife; and

Mr. Donald John McSwan, their son.

The police believe that Donald McSwan, junior, was the first of the Vampire's victims—in 1945—followed two months later by his parents.

Dr. and Mrs. Henderson are known to have disappeared in February of last year.

Genteel

Hour after hour, before relays of detectives and shorthand writers crowded into the buff-painted interrogation room of a London police station, the Vampire has been questioned.

Drinking mug after mug of strong police tea—but never forgetting to crook his little finger genteelly away from the coarse china—the Vampire has shown himself a man ... easy manners.

He wears a quiet suit of immaculate cut, with a discreet tie. His hair is sleekly brushed, his nails well-kept.

Made to sign alibi notes, says brother

AFTER killing Dr. Henderson, the Vampire is believed to have kept Mrs. Henderson alive for at least a month writing letters—and signing typewritten letters—to relatives and friends.

When the Vampire thought himself safe, Rosalie Mercy Henderson followed her husband to a ghastly death.

This theory is held by her brother, Mr. Arnold Henry Burlin, 35, hotelier, of Arnfield-road, Withington, Manchester.

"I am convinced," he told the *Daily Mirror* last night, "that my sister was kept under duress for at least a month before she was shot and her body disposed of.

"During that time I believe she was forced to sign typewritten letters posted in different parts of the country to allay any suspicions of mine."

Dr. and Mrs. Archibald Henderson disappeared on February 16, 1948.

But on February 27 Mr. Burlin received a letter from his sister, saying they were going to Glasgow.

He continued to receive letters until March 21.

A letter followed every phone call Mr. Burlin made to one of his sis-

Held captive for a month?

Mrs. Rosalie Henderson

No. 79—room of horror

In tins, bags and little parcels, detectives bring specimens from the back-basement of 79, Gloucester-road, London, S.W., in which the McSwans are believed to have been slain. Police digging found false teeth in the floor.

Right: *Twenty years before the Hay case, a vampire killer had spread terror across London, claiming five victims.*

fingerprints and blood groups. When Linda Peacock's bitemarks were analysed further it set in motion a brilliant criminal investigation which would change that.

Dr. Warren Harvey, Scotland's leading expert in forensic odontology and lecturer to the Scottish Detective Training School, was the first to inspect Sgt. Paton's photographs. He concurred that the marks on her breast were indeed of teeth and human ones at that. Yet there was a troublesome aspect to their location; it seemed from examination of the corpse – she had been strangled and the bite was inflicted just moments after death – that the bite had come from behind. It would have taken an act of some considerable contortion, but was not impossible. The only formidable task was finding a man whose teeth matched the indentations of the bite.

INITIAL SUSPICIONS

Chief Superintendent William Muncie of the Lanarkshire CID handled the police investigation while Dr. Harvey enlisted specialist help from further afield. The crime bore all the classic hallmarks of an attempted sexual assault that had gone wrong. He believed that the girl had been approached for sex, she had resisted and in doing so had sealed her fate. Such crimes are in the category of "opportunist" and are rarely planned; Muncie was certain, therefore, that he was looking for a local man with a knowledge of the area and, obviously, the girl. He and his officers spent ten days interviewing all 3,000 men in the locality and, to a man, they all had alibis and were eliminated from the enquiry.

The only place he hadn't been to was a nearby borstal for young offenders where 29 apprentices-in-crime were undergoing incarceration and training in the hope that they would go straight. Dr. Harvey said to Muncie: "It seems as if your enquiries are now winding down in regards to local males on the outside – perhaps it would be prudent for me to ask you to check the teeth of those inside. I think that dental casts should be made of all the inmates." Each boy inside signed a form which read: "I have been told that this is in relation to the investigation into the death

Below: ***Police chiefs William Muncie (left) and Det. Insp. Weir pore over maps of the murder area in their hunt for the killer.***

Left: ***Professor Keith Simpson, Britain's most eminent criminal pathologist, played a key role in the investigation.***

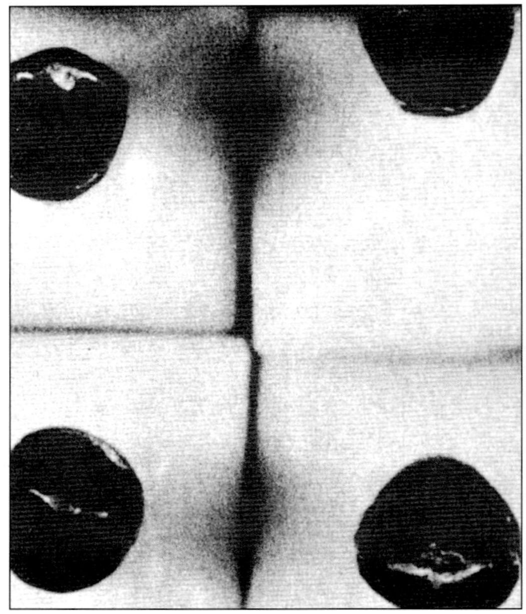

Right: ***Copper plate models of Gordon Hay's teeth, clearly illustrating the pits which would trap him.***

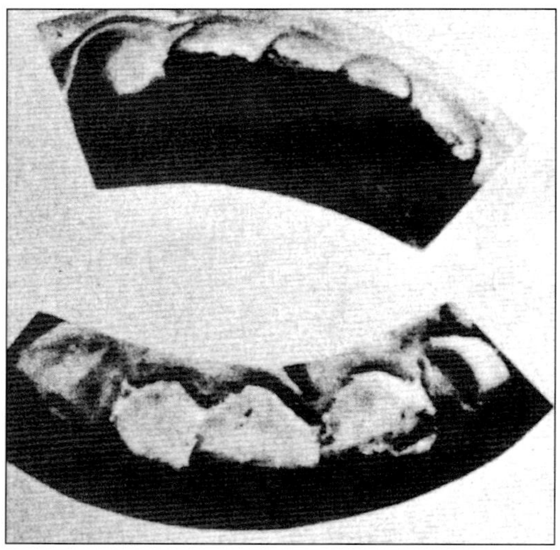

Left: ***Casts of Hay's upper and lower teeth, vital links in the chain of evidence that led to him being fingered as the girl's killer.***

of Linda Peacock. It has been made clear to me that I can refuse to comply with the test. It has also been made clear to me that should my dental impressions be linked with other evidence in the case they may be produced as evidence."

The boys in the borstal, aged between 14 and 17 – none of whom possessed a particularly high IQ – all volunteered for the project which, if nothing else, gave them a day out from their drab surroundings. At Glasgow's Dental Hospital, plaster casts were made of each one's teeth. Experiments then began trying to match individual teeth to the marks found on the girl's breast. The largest mark was a very dark oval, about 13mm by 7mm, and there were four smaller ones.

Dr. Harvey later said: "I examined the casts with Detective Inspector Osborne Butler of the Identification Bureau of Glasgow Police. Several were instantly recognisable as being useless to the case because they possessed no jagged teeth capable of inflicting the marks. I decided to call in the aid of another expert."

The expert he called upon was Britain's most eminent criminal pathologist and forensic expert – Professor Keith Simpson – who listed the notorious Haigh acid bath

EXPERIMENTS THEN BEGAN, TRYING TO MATCH INDIVIDUAL TEETH TO THE MARKS FOUND ON THE GIRL'S BREAST

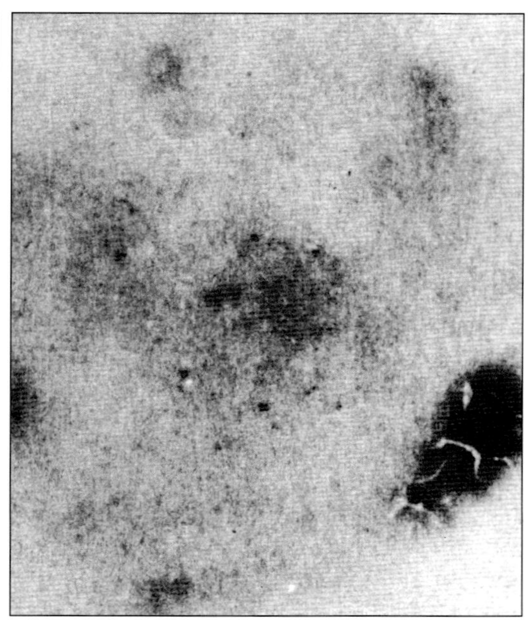

Right: ***The bitemarks that were found on Hay's victim, Linda Peacock.***

murders as one of his celebrated cases. Increasingly, Professor Simpson had been at the forefront of advancing the scientific application of forensic odontology into crime solving. He was a great friend of the Swedish expert Gustavson and had given evidence on the importance of teeth and their value as a source of clues at a number of trials and inquests.

At his base in Guys Hospital, London, Professor Simpson and Dr. Harvey made new casts of resin, which were tougher, and whittled the 29 boys down to five major suspects. From the resin casts they made models capable of "occlusal" movements – that is, capable of biting in much the same way as a living human. A female body was brought from the morgue and tests were begun. Initially, Simpson had concurred with Harvey that one particular cast labelled No.14 – the experts were not provided with names – was the prime suspect, but tests ruled him out completely. Starting from the beginning again, all 29 casts were examined under the most stringent scientific conditions. Attention focussed on two curiously shaped abrasions – abrasions which no-one believed could have been made by teeth; there was certainly no such mention of them in Gustavson's "Bible" *Forensic Odontology*.

But later, re-examination of the teeth of suspect No.11 turned up something definite. Dr. Harvey pressed the upper and lower right canines of the cast into his thumbnail for several seconds and with considerable pressure; when he released them, left on the base of the nail were

Above: ***Guys Hospital, London, where expert analysis led to the teeth which belonged to the killer of Linda Peacock.***

LEFT ON THE PROFESSOR'S NAIL WERE MARKS IDENTICAL TO THOSE THAT HAD BEEN FOUND ON THE DEAD GIRL

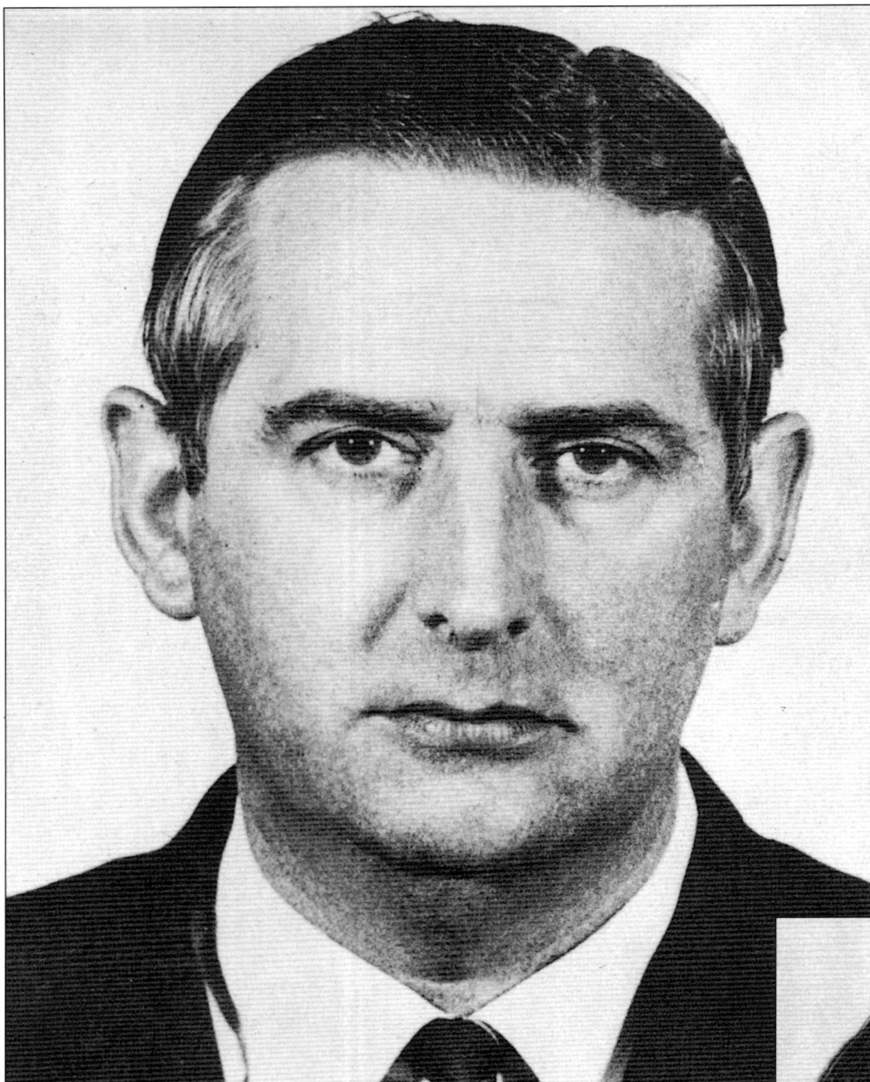

was not so far fetched as it might seem. The mark of the ligature round her neck was most pronounced in the front and least at the back, showing she had been strangled from behind. Blood in front of her left ear, from one of her head wounds, had clotted while she was vertical. Her left wrist had been tied with a piece of string – burned off after death, leaving a scorch-mark and a blister – and her arm had probably been held behind her. And, although Harvey and Butler did not yet know it, mud had been observed on the knees of No.11's jeans that night, suggesting he had been kneeling on the ground."

It was five weeks after the murder by the time the final tests had been done and all three members of the scientific team were convinced that Number 11 was their suspect. That coincided with Chf. Supt. Muncie's theories too because he had spent time interviewing the boys and the only one whose alibi he didn't feel comfortable with was his. No. 11 was a callow 17-year-old called Gordon Hay, a hardened petty thief, car stealer and general bad boy who had been in trouble with the law since he

Above: ***Det. Supt. Osborne Butler of the identification bureau of the Glasgow police co-operated closely with odontologists on the case.***

Right: ***Gordon Hay's teeth-marks condemned him as the killer.***

"THE MAN WHO HAD KILLED HER HAD COME OVER THE GIRL'S SHOULDER WHILE SHE WAS SITTING... HE HAD EXTREME DEXTERITY"

marks identical to those that were found on the dead girl.

Harvey was still concerned about the angle at which the bite marks appeared to have been made. Later, in a scientific paper about the case, he wrote: "Since, to put it mildly, this orientation seemed strange a further attempt was made with the other four models. But apart from the already-discredited No.14, none of the others fitted at all. It was my opinion that the attacker, the man who had killed her, had come over the girl's right shoulder while she was sitting and that he had extreme dexterity."

Professor Simpson, writing of the case years later, said: "The medical evidence showed this

was nine. He was also a compulsive liar, coupled with a feral cunning which alerted him when danger was around. There were no clues to link him to the murder other than the statement of one other boy and Muncie's own hunch. As far as the authorities were concerned, all the boys were tucked up in their beds in the barrack-style dorms when Linda Peacock met her untimely and violent end.

KEY EVIDENCE

The other lad in the dormitory, who remained anonymous due to his age, told Muncie: "On August 6 one of our masters saw Hay in the dining room at about 10.00pm and another one saw him at 10.30pm lying in bed in his pyjamas. But I saw him come through the window. His hair was blown about and he was dirty and sweaty and out of breath. We had heard some screaming from the direction of the cemetery and I couldn't help thinking that he had had something to do with it. The day before he had been allowed out on a good conduct pass and had gone to a local fair where he met a girl. He couldn't stop bragging about her when he came back – said she was a 'nice bit of stuff' and that he would like to have sex with her."

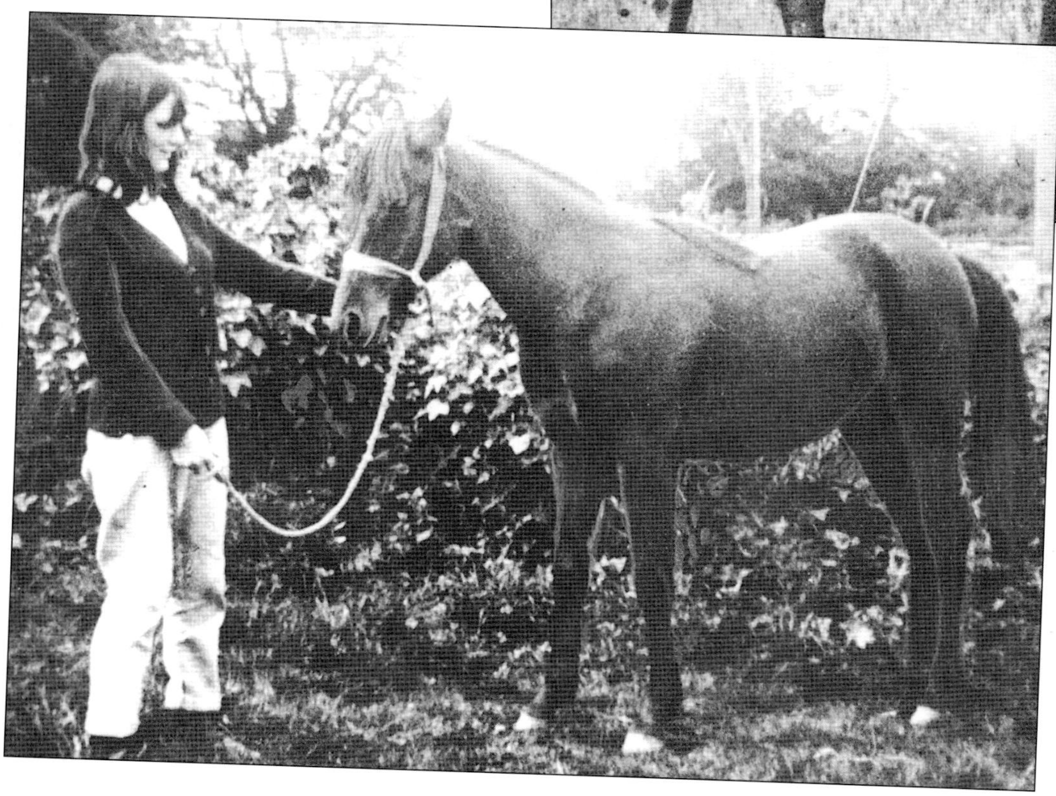

Above and Left: ***Linda Peacock – a life of promise lay ahead until she was brutally murdered by a deranged borstal boy. Linda was a gentle soul who loved animals as much as she loved people.***

Above: ***Linda's pretty home, a home from which she went missing forever on that fateful night in 1967.***

"CIRCUMSTANTIAL EVIDENCE WAS CLEARLY INSUFFICIENT AND, THEREFORE, THE DENTAL EVIDENCE WAS CRUCIAL"

Muncie's detectives interviewed Hay again but kept back from him the evidence of the youth who had seen him come in the window. He even volunteered to them that he had indeed met the dead girl, but that he was sound asleep when she was killed. There was no hard evidence, just circumstantial, to link him to the crime. Police even made a healthy P.C. run from the crime scene to the borstal to see if it could be done in a couple of minutes; it could.

DISMAL RUMOURS

Yet there was consternation among senior officers, shared by the Procurator Fiscal, that a prosecution would fail without more tangible evidence. Professor Simpson said: "Circumstantial evidence was clearly insufficient and, therefore, the dental evidence was crucial. Harvey and Butler came back to London and showed me the latest results of their work. I encouraged them to make a more detailed study of Hay's teeth and to prepare scaled 'overlay' transparencies. They fitted the scale bitemark print perfectly – of that there was no doubt."

Dr. Harvey researched deeper and found that minute pits on Hay's teeth could have been caused by drinking water without fluoride added when he was a child. This was significant because in previous criminal cases abroad, bitemark identifications had usually required the identification of five teeth – the team had identified just two. But an examination of government records in Scotland showed that no-one else had more than one pitted-tooth. Professor Simpson felt that all the evidence of his teeth put together would be enough to gain a conviction, adding: "A jury should have no difficulty in understanding this evidence and appreciating its simple strength. It is akin to tool-marking evidence or fingerprints."

The Procurator Fiscal decided to let the prosecution proceed. Hay was arrested and charged with murder and pleaded not guilty when he came before Lord Justice Grant at the High Court of Justice in Edinburgh. His trial lasted nine days, during which Hay vehemently denied having anything to do with the crime. The evidence – medical evidence on the teeth alone amounting to 400 pages of manuscript – would have to speak for itself with the aid of testimony from Dr. Harvey and Professor Simpson.

COOL DEFENCE

It was Professor Simpson who would face the cool, challenging questions from Hay's defence counsel William Stewart, Q.C., who attempted to call up the expertise of Gustavson in defending his client – a case of trying to rescue him by using the evidence of those who would seek to damn him. Professor Simpson later wrote in his autobiography: "When I was in the witness box the defence counsel, as I had expected, quoted from the Swedish expert Gustavson's book, to which I had written a foreword published in an English translation. 'Do you agree with the view expressed inside the book'," asked Stewart, "'that at least four or five teeth, and they say they are adjacent teeth, should correspond exactly before a positive identification can be made?'

"'I think it is a sound view,' I answered, 'but I think probably a better attitude is a general one; that is to say that the more points of comparison that can be pointed to, the more points of proof and the fewer the less certain.'"

Hay sat impassive throughout his trial, paying no heed to the massive press attention or the sketch artists who drew him while he was in the dock. He understood that, on the surface, everything rested on those tooth marks and whether or not a jury would accept such evidence to condemn him to imprisonment. The trial lasted nine days and at the end of it observers thought that the accused man had a singularly smug look on his face, as if he expected to be out that evening.

After deliberating less than three hours the jury returned a verdict of guilty. Hay was attempting to shout at the judge when he was hurried to the cells to begin his detention "at Her Majesty's pleasure". Police commented later that friends of Linda had told them of the borstal boy she had met at the fair, but that she had not been attracted to him. Hay, for his part, was inflamed with lust, particularly at the sight of her well-developed breasts. She had resisted him. In his frenzy and with his agile body, he had lunged at her from behind to leave the signature that would commit him to jail for years.

As part of his summing up, Lord Justice Grant paid special praise to the work of the forensic experts. "Forensic odontology," he said, "as it is called, is a relatively new science. But of course there must be a first time for everything."

Because of Hay's insatiable lust, a lassie had died… and a young man who was supposed to be salvaged from crime had gone into the record books.

IN HIS FRENZY HE HAD LUNGED AT HER TO LEAVE THE SIGNATURE THAT WOULD COMMIT HIM TO JAIL FOR YEARS

Below: ***William Muncie, Chief Superintendent of the Lanarkshire CID, handled the police investigation. It was of great comfort to him and Linda's family to know that justice had been done.***

EMMETT-DUNNE
A Deadly Affair

Frederick Emmett-Dunne brought shame upon his British Army uniform. He dallied with the wife of another soldier and when his passion was inflamed, killed his rival. It was almost the perfect murder, but forensic science was to unearth the evil sergeant and ensure a long prison sentence for him.

Above: ***Sergeant Reginald Ernie Watters and his German bride Mia. She later found solace in the arms of another sergeant.***

Opposite: ***Military police escort Frederick Emmett-Dunne (centre), as he faces charges of murdering a fellow soldier.***

Post-war Germany for British Army garrison troops was a dismal billet. Rationing was still enforced, the local population was often resentful and the bombed-out towns and cities offered little in the way of entertaining diversions. Life, for the most part, centred on the base itself where the wives of married men became as bored as their husbands in the tiresome duty of policing a defeated nation.

The boredom of one such wife, and the interest shown in her by a sergeant named Frederick Emmett-Dunne, was to lead to murder... a murder the sergeant nearly got clean away with. But 15 months after the lid was closed on the coffin of his rival the body still yielded vital clues – clues a second forensic expert would detect... and finally send Emmett-Dunne to jail for life.

It was early in the morning of December 1 1953 that the body of Sgt. Ernie Watters was found hanging in a barrack block at the Glamorgan Barracks in Duisberg, “discovered” by Sgt. Emmett-Dunne and another man. It seemed from the scene that it was a suicide; on the ground was a bucket which had been turned on its side, indicating that the dead man had stood on it as a makeshift gallows and kicked it aside to allow the rope to tighten around his neck.

There was an Army enquiry followed by an Army inquest which judged that the unfortunate sergeant had taken his own life due to depression – even though all who knew him testified that he was a cheerful man with seemingly little to worry about. He had no money problems, no skeletons in his closet and was an efficient and well-liked soldier.

But Dr. Alan Womack, the pathologist who carried out the post-mortem, added his expert testimony to ensure that a suicide verdict was recorded. Dr. Womack testified that death had come from hanging because of the broken cricoid bone – a bone in the throat just below the thyroid – in his neck. He was wrong, and because of it a murderer walked scot-free.

NO SECRETS

Sgt. Emmett-Dunne had killed him, and even before the ink was dry on the inquest report the rumours began circulating about him. Emmett-Dunne had taken a fancy to Watters' German-born wife Mia some time before and his attentions had not been unrequited. There were snatched brief encounters while her husband was on duty and he was not; excursions to the local cinema and picnics in the rolling countryside.

At dances and other social functions the other members of this insular community tut-tutted at the apparent closeness with which they danced, the glances that lingered too long over the mess table. None of this was presented at the inquest, of course, but six months after the body of Sgt. Watters

AN ARMY INQUIRY FOLLOWED BY AN ARMY INQUEST JUDGED THAT THE UNFORTUNATE SERGEANT HAD TAKEN HIS OWN LIFE

Above and Below: ***The killer and his black widow – Sergeant Emmett-Dunne acts as escort to the former Mrs Mia Watters.***

had been laid to rest Sgt. Emmett-Dunne married the widow. There were stage whispers of "I told you so" sweeping the camp, and soon they were to come to the ears of the top brass.

The Army decided that perhaps the inquest first time around had been too hasty. Anonymous letters were sent to them informing on the marriage between the widow and Emmett-Dunne. After consultations with the War Office and the Home Office, the Army was informed that it had no choice but to call in Scotland Yard.

By the time Dr. Francis Camps, a distinguished Home Office pathologist arrived in Germany accompanied by two detectives from Scotland Yard, Emmett-Dunne and his new bride were back in Britain, the murder now having happened a full 15 months previously.

Of course, what the police needed was evidence of murder – no rumour in the world would stand up to scrutiny in a court of law, be it martial or civilian, without the foundations of truth to underpin it.

FURTHER INVESTIGATIONS

As the body was disinterred in Germany, Emmett–Dunne was questioned at his new home in Somerset, England, about his relationship with Mrs. Watters before she married him. He sensed the direction the conversation was going in and stormed: "My only crime was marrying before the proper lapse of time prescribed by Victorian morality!" Indeed, there was little the police could do without hard evidence – it was his word against a lot of people who smelled something fishy, but could offer nothing by way of hard fact.

The task facing Dr. Camps from the decomposing remains of Watters was to find evidence of murder. Dr. Womack, who had carried out the first post mortem was a skilled and dedicated pathologist, but it turned out that he was mistaken in deciding that the cause of death was strangulation. Dr. Camps laboured intensively in the Army morgue until he came up with the real cause of Watters' demise.

Where the unfortunate man's voice box had been remained evidence of blood. The small bones of the larynx were crushed and he was able to pick them out one by one like small chicken bones. Such bones would not be broken by a rope's pressure but by the sudden, swift, blow of a hand or blunt object. Perhaps, and most probably, surmised the eminent forensic expert, by a man trained in unarmed combat, like a commando or other armed forces specialist. Bleeding in the windpipe had caused death within minutes. John Rowland, who made a study of the case in his 1958 book *More Criminal Files*, said: "Mr. Mervyn Griffith-Jones was the prosecutor at Emmett-Dunne's trial. He pointed out that Dr. Womack, though his post-mortem had been carefully and meticulously carried out, had been a comparatively inexperienced pathologist, and had made an error in his interpretation of the facts.

Dr. Camps, who had superintended the exhumation of the body, and had carried out a further and more detailed examination of the remains, was satisfied that death was not due to strangulation followed upon hanging, but to a sudden and severe blow, delivered by the hand of a murderer on the front of Watters' throat."

In April 1955 the police felt they had enough – thanks to the forensic examination of the corpse – to charge Emmett-Dunne with murder, and build a case in which the circumstantial evidence was interwoven with the undeniable expert testimony of Dr. Camps, then probably the most eminent man in his field. Emmett-Dunne was flown back to Germany and charged there on April 15 by a military court. The trial eventually opened in Dusseldorf on June 27 with Mr. Griffith Jones outlining the affair which led to murder. He said that the trysting between the two had started at the end of 1952 and had carried on right up until the time of Watters' death.

He centred his case on the behaviour of the accused towards Mrs. Watters while she was still married; how he stayed on the base while Watters took part in an exercise

Above: ***Witnesses arrive at Emmett-Dunne's court martial in Dusseldorf to give evidence of his infatuation with Mrs Watters.***

"DEATH WAS DUE TO A SUDDEN, SEVERE BLOW, DELIVERED BY THE HAND OF A MURDERER ON THE FRONT OF WATTERS' THROAT"

Left: ***Mr Griffith-Jones, who led the prosecution against Emmett-Dunne, leaves the courtroom in Germany after the suspect was found guilty of murder.***

Above: ***The beautiful Mia Watters, later to become Mrs Emmett-Dunne.***

that he should have been on; how he had enjoyed picnics with her in the countryside; how telephone records at the base showed numerous phone calls to her married quarters whenever duty rosters showed that her husband was away on duty elsewhere. "Shortly before Watters' death," Mr. Griffith-Jones said, "Emmett-Dunne had said to Sergeant Browne that there was a certain person in the barracks who would be committing suicide if his wife did not learn to behave herself. The court might feel that this statement was made to pave the way for the faked suicide which Emmett-Dunne was already planning."

"EMMETT-DUNNE SAID... THERE WAS A CERTAIN PERSON IN THE BARRACKS WHO WOULD BE COMMITTING SUICIDE"

DEMONSTRATIVE EVIDENCE

Dr. Camps called into court several officers trained in the use of unarmed combat, the kind of combat that taught men how to kill with their bare hands. Dr. Camps said: "It is my contention that he actually killed Watters as he was sitting beside him, perhaps in a chair, perhaps in a car." After the soldiers had presented this in court Mr. Derek Curtis-Brown, Q.C., defending Emmett-Dunne, said: "I quite understand your theory.' Dr. Camps shot back at him, rather curtly: "It is not a theory; it is straightforward mechanics."

His description of how the blow had been delivered, how he had discovered it due to the exhumation of the body, made it impossible for Emmett-Dunne to plead innocence any longer. Instead of just "finding" the body he now said that he had killed him only after Watters had threatened him with a revolver.

Mr. Curtis-Brown told the court: "Watters had threatened the accused with a .38 pistol, saying: 'You are too big and too cocky in barracks.' Emmett-Dunne, thinking that Watters was about to shoot, had struck the blow that killed him. Then he had panicked and faked the suicide."

Three days into the court martial trial – it was held under Army regulations – 34-year-old Emmett-Dunne took the stand. He said: "Watters had accused me of living with his wife in Cologne when he had been absent on military exercises. I told him that he was talking out of the side of his hat. There was no love affair between me and Mia – that happened later when we met in England.

Right: ***Emmett-Dunne maintained throughout that he was innocent but overwhelming forensic testimony sealed his fate.***

We had been good friends who liked to dance together, that is all.

"There is not a word of truth to what the prosecution has had to say."

But he had not reckoned on the damning testimony of a half-brother, Ronald Emmett, who was living in another part of the barracks. He came forward at the last minute to say that the accused had sent for him at 8.00pm on the night of the murder to say that he had killed a man in an argument. He wanted Emmett to give him an alibi, to say that they had been together all evening. He then led his half-brother over to the entrance to the barrack block where he showed him the corpse of Sgt. Watters hidden under a cape. "He said if we could lift him up," said Ronald Emmett in court, "we could make it look like suicide.

"I refused. I went to bed, but I didn't tell anybody, not until now." Ronald Emmett said he had come forward because of the expertise of the Home Office pathologist. "Once he said that it was a blow to throat," he said, "and not some kind of accident, like the fellow had hit his head like I was led to believe, then I felt I had no choice but to speak up." Emmett-Dunne was indeed back home living in Cheshire when the story of the exhumation and discovery was carried out. He added: "In view of the way events moved I knew I had to come forward with the whole story."

The Army tribunal found Frederick Emmett-Dunne guilty in Germany – which was just as well for him. The death penalty was still in force in Britain, but not there. He was therefore sentenced to life imprisonment. Immediately after sentencing he was sent back to Britain to serve time in a maximum security jail among other murderers, robbers and rapists. Mia stood by him, claiming she believed in his innocence and that she was certain he had been in a fight that had gone wrong. But there was too much evidence in the trial for her not to be left with some nagging doubts.

Above and Below: ***Scenes outside the court martial in Dusseldorf where Emmett-Dunne was found guilty of murder.***

FRUITLESS PLEAS

Back home in England he tried his best to get his sentence altered with petitions to the government of the day and even the Queen. All decided that it was best for him to remain behind bars. The case itself is something of a textbook one for criminal pathologists and forensic experts. Crime writer George Crossen said: "If they had been more discreet in their affair the body of the dead man would never have been dug up. If he had not been dug up Dr. Camps would never have detected the clues of the single killing blow.

"If he had not detected the evidence of the single killing blow Emmett-Dunne would have gotten away with that rare thing – the perfect murder. In the end, he was defeated by a medical science that was far, far more precise than him."

GEORGI MARKOV
Murder by Umbrella

Bulgarian writer Georgi Markov's sensitivites could not cope with the brutal Bulgarian regime he and his countrymen had to endure under communism. He escaped to Britain, to voice his protests to greater effect. But his life was to end in one of the modern era's most notorious assassinations.

Georgi Markov's murder in London is probably the most intriguing and original assassination of this century. Individuals have certainly been killed in numerous and monstrous ways down the years of this turbulent century – shot, stabbed, garroted, hanged, drowned and poisoned – but none reached the heights of Ian Fleming-esque originality and cunning as the fate which befell Bulgarian defector Markov. He was poisoned as he walked down a London street in broad daylight, his fate sealed by a small poisoned capsule delivered into his leg by – an umbrella! The story of his diabolical end is one that continues to fascinate and mesmerise, long after the communist chieftans who plotted his end have themselves passed into history.

A STRIDENT VOICE

Markov, 49 when he died, was a dissident from the orthodox communist regime in Bulgaria who had managed to defect to the West and settle in London. An educated, urbane individual, he had first angered the totalitarian rulers of his homeland in the late 1960s when he still lived there. Before then, he had towed the party line, written the saccharine-sweet prose that praised the glories of communism.

For his efforts he was rewarded with a BMW car, an opulent home and an account with foreign currency that allowed him to buy the best in luxuries that his countrymen could only dream of. Yet Markov was a sensitive, caring individual who eventually woke up to the blind injustices of the regime and decided to take a stand against them. Then he penned a play about a plot to

Opposite: ***Georgi Markov, victim of one of the most cunning assassinations of the Cold War.***

NO ASSASSINATION REACHED THE HEIGHTS OF IAN FLEMING-ESQUE ORIGINALITY AS THAT WHICH BEFELL MARKOV

HE WAS A SENSITIVE, CARING INDIVIDUAL WHO EVENTUALLY WOKE UP TO THE BLIND INJUSTICES OF THE REGIME

Below: ***London, where Markov began a new life in the early 1970s.***

murder a general – a work clearly anti-government and perceived by the dictator-in-residence, Todor Zhivkov, as an incitement to civil unrest.

VICIOUS PERSECUTION

Markov suffered the usual state harassment – loss of privileges, surveillance, warnings – before he escaped to Italy and from there to London, where he was granted political asylum. But if Zhivkov and his minions thought they had heard the last of him they were very much mistaken. Markov got a job with the Bulgarian section of the BBC foreign service. From his office at Bush House in the Aldwych, he transmitted messages back to his enslaved homeland that riled the communist chieftains even more. Soon Markov became the magnificent obsession for Zhivkov, who was determined to silence him... one way or another.

MARKOV BECAME THE MAGNIFICENT OBSESSION OF ZHIVKOV WHO WAS DETERMINED TO SILENCE HIM... ONE WAY OR ANOTHER

On the morning of September 7 1978, Markov drove from his home in Clapham to Bush House, but the London traffic was appalling. Markov could not get his car parked anywhere near his office and so ended up putting it in a vacant spot near Waterloo Bridge. He walked to his office, completed a day's work and went back around 6.00pm to retrieve his vehicle to move it nearer to Bush House. After parking it near the Strand he once more set off back towards his office when he felt a sharp stab of pain in the back of his right thigh. He thought it had come from the accidental prod of an umbrella, the wielder of the offending instrument being a man in a bus queue. When Markov turned to face the man he mumbled profuse apologies in a thick, Eastern European accent, and then slipped out of the bus queue to jump into a cab.

Just four days later Georgi Markov would be dead.

Upon getting back to the office his leg had already begun to stiffen up. He showed a colleague what had happened and said: "Look at that! Some fool stabbed me with

Below: ***Bush House, where Georgi Markov found employment with the BBC in the 1970s.***

an umbrella!" He showed off a wound like a pimple, with purple and red widening out from the centre to the flesh around. But Markov had been mistaken in believing he had been stabbed by the umbrella tip itself. In fact, the brolly contained a highly sophisticated spring-loaded device in the tip which actually shot poison into his leg, like a silent dart gun. Markov stayed on at the BBC to read news and current affairs bulletins at 11.00pm, but he felt increasingly feverish – a condition he put down to flu. But he was too ill to work the following day and his wife Annabella drove him to St. James Hospital in Balham when his temperature soared over 100 degrees.

A STRANGE INJURY

Doctors were puzzled by the puncture wound on his thigh – too big to have come from either a hypodermic syringe or an insect bite – but they did not at first perceive its true significance. His condition continued to worsen as the hours wore on. By the third day he was given massive antibiotic injections to try to counter an alarming rise in the white corpuscle count in his bloodstream. Doctors who registered his white corpuscle count upon entry to the hospital listed it as 10,600. Soon it raced to an "unbelievable" 26,300. But Markov still failed to respond to treatment and on the fourth day he died of a massive heart attack.

It was only because of the suddenness and mysteriousness of his death that a post-mortem was needed to determine what had actually killed him. When traces of the poison ricin were discovered the telephones rang in Whitehall's corridors of power. Forensic scientist Dr. Robert Keeley found the tiny metal ball in Markov's leg which had been used to deliver the poison while Dr. David Gaul, of the top secret Chemical Defence Establishment at Porton Down, provided all the information on poisons and antidotes. Scotland Yard's Anti-Terrorist Squad and MI5 were also informed of the findings of the autopsy.

Dr. Keeley found the tiny metal ball only after X-rays had been taken around the area of the puncture wound on the deaceased's right thigh. It measured 1.52mm in diameter and was made from an alloy of platinum and iridium, a compound noted for its resistance to corrosion and one which can only be worked in a high-temperature furnace. The minute sphere was drilled through with two holes that met in a centre well where the poison rested. Dr. Keeley had examined a similar ball sent from Paris once the European intelligence agencies of NATO began co-operating over the disturbing death of Markov. This ball too had been recovered from the body of a Bulgarian defector, Vladimir Kostov, but he had been lucky enough to survive the experience.

Above: President Khikov, Bulgarian ruler at the time of the Markov killing.

THE BROLLY CONTAINED A HIGHLY SOPHISTICATED SPRING-LOADED DEVICE IN THE TIP WHICH ACTUALLY SHOT POISON INTO HIS LEG

A RECIPE FOR DEATH

Dr. Gaul later testified at Markov's inquest in London in January 1979 about the ricin poison. Dr. Gaul said: "Tests have ruled out that he died from any other kind of venom, be it from snakes, scorpions, spiders or marine life. Ricin tests were carried out on a live pig and the symptoms it developed before death were almost identical to those suffered by Mr. Markov before his death."

The ricin poison, he told the inquest, came from the seeds of the castor oil plant which, incidentally, grows in abundance in Bulgaria. "There is no legitimate use for ricin," said Dr. Gaul. "And there is no known antidote."

Mrs. Markov said at the inquest that it was her strong belief that her husband had died at the hands of a foreign assassin

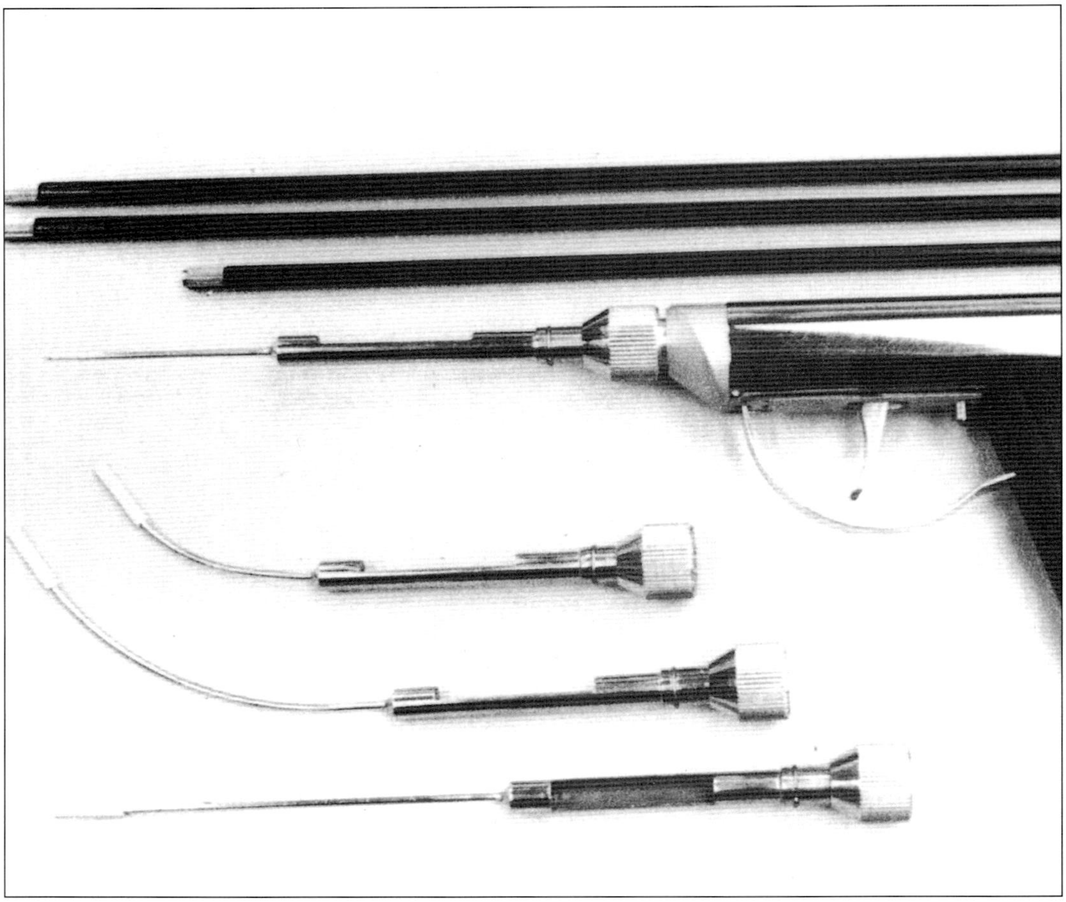

Right: ***The assassin's "umberella" contained a sophisticated weapon which was used to inject the poison.***

IT STOKED UP THE OLD FEARS OF THE SOVIET COLOSSUS WAITING BEYOND THE HORIZON TO CRUSH ALL OPPONENTS

working on the orders of the Bulgarian secret police. But Cold War or not, diplomatic niceties had to be maintained. Besides, the operation had been so swift and so well carried out that there was nothing to connect the government of a sovereign country with the murder of a single defector. Whatever Whitehall and MI5 spycatchers privately thought, in public there was little that could be said or done and, consequently, Markov was recorded by West London Coroner Dr. Gavin Thurston as having been "unlawfully killed".

WHEN THE TRUTH DID COME OUT IT WAS EVERY BIT AS FANTASTIC AS THE THEORIES WOVEN AT THE TIME

The papers, however, had a field day. No-one could recall such an audacious murder of an exile in a Western capital. It stoked up the old fears of the Soviet collossus waiting beyond the horizon to crush all opponents and provided endless fodder for polticians, spy writers and right-wingers who spoke menacingly of the Soviet bear waiting to devour us all. Yet it would be many years before the real truth of what happened to Georgi Markov was made public. It would take the collapse of communism in Russia and her satellite states itself. But when the truth did come out it was every bit as fantastic as the theories woven at the time. The mission to eliminate Markov was sanctioned by the head of the KGB himself in Moscow after a request from the paranoid dictator Zhivkov and involved tests on animals and a condemned man.

Details of the assassination were finally revealed by Oleg Kalugin, a Major General in the KGB who was given the task of preparing it by the KGB chairman Yuri Andropov himself. Kalugin, once head of the KGB's counter intelligence branch, was a devoted disciple of the Soviet state. He says he found the task onerous, but that duty meant it was Markov's life… or his.

PRESIDENTIAL HATRED

Kalugin said: "The problem with Markov was raised by the Bulgarians in 1977. Members of their security organisation visited Moscow and told us they had difficulties. Markov was greatly disliked by the Bulgarian president Zhivkov. The president wanted to get rid of him because he was upset by Markov's broadcasts on the BBC's foreign service. They were vehemently anti-communist and anti-Zhivkov. The president felt that Markov's activities were undermining the very foundations of his regime.

"My counterpart in Bulgaria was Vladid Todorov, who regularly came to Moscow to discuss many problems, but he would always end up touching on Markov. At that stage we just listened politely and he went away. But then one day in the spring of 1978 I attended one of our regular meetings with the KGB chairman Yuri Andropov in his office in Moscow. Also there was Vladimir Kyryuchkov, then chief of the intelligence service and later the boss of the KGB, and Vice Admiral Usatov, another senior intelligence official. As the meeting was about to end Kryuchkov said on his own initiative: "We have a request from the Bulgarian interior minister Stoyanov to physically eliminate one of their dissidents, a Mr. Markov. They want us to help them."

A STUNNING REQUEST

"I recall vividly that Andropov was somewhat taken aback. He did not answer straight away. He sat pensively for a while, then he got up and started walking up and down. Then he said: 'You know what? I am against political assassinations. This is not the way to solve our political problems. Let the Bulgarians do it themselves if they wish to. Why should we be involved?' Still walking up and down he ended emphatically: 'I am against it.'

"Kryuchkov, clearly surprised by this negative answer, started cajoling the chairman. 'Mr. Andropov, it is Mr. Zhivkov's request. If we decline to co-operate with the Bulgarians then Mr. Zhivkov might think the Bulgarians are out of favour with the KGB or maybe Mr. Zhivkov is out of favour with the Soviet leadership.

"It is a political problem and we must face it. We cannot simply turn down the Bulgarians' request.'

"Comrade Andropov, who later became president of the USSR, continued walking up and down saying: 'I'm against it.' But he was obviously convinced by the political expediency, and finally he said: 'OK, OK, but I want no direct participation. You provide the weapons, whatever is needed, and give the Bulgarians all the instructions. But then to hell with them. Let them do the final job themselves.' Since I was present and my role covered dealing with the problems of primarily Soviet traitors I was called on to handle this, even though a Bulgarian was involved. I was given the job of preparing the ground for the execution of the man.

Left: ***Yuri Andropov, head of the KGB, gave the order for Markov's assassination to go ahead.***

THE PRESIDENT FELT THAT MARKOV WAS UNDERMINING THE VERY FOUNDATIONS OF THE REGIME

Below: ***Dr Bernard Riley arrives to give evidence at the inquest into the defector's death.***

Right: ***The dissident's proud widow Annabella has tears still glistening in her eyes as she arrives to give evidence at the inquest into his death.***

THREE TYPES OF POISON, AND THE MEANS OF DELIVERING IT INTO MARKOV'S BODY, WERE DISCUSSED

"IT PROPELLED A SMALL PELLET FILLED WITH POISON WHICH PENETRATED THE SKIN AND DISSOLVED QUICKLY"

Chairman Andropov told me: 'Kalugin, you take charge of this. You do it.'"

Kalugin summoned Colonel Sergei Golobev, who ran "wet" operations for the KGB – wet being the in-house term for assassinations – and told him to report to the agency's Directorate of Science and Technology which dealt with everything from wiretaps to chemical weapons. Three types of poison, and the means of delivering it into Markov's body, were discussed before it was settled that the umbrella would be used.

He went on: "The Bulgarians had designed a small gadget like a fountain pen, about five inches long, which could be fired from a distance of a metre and-a-half. It propelled a small pellet filled with poison which penetrated the skin and dissolved quickly, leaving no trace. The device was fitted into an umbrella and operated from the handle. But the Bulgarians, wary of earlier failures and the fury of Zhivkov, insisted on testing it first. They tested it on a horse and the horse died within hours. They then tested it on a man who was under sentence of death."

AN INHUMAN TEST

"The man was taken out of his condemned cell for a walk and the guards shot at him with this pellet from the distance of about a metre. The man was startled as he felt the pain in the back of his knee, and started shouting and crying. He thought the moment of execution had arrived without anyone telling him. Then he calmed down, recovered and actually survived the attack. Moscow was informed and the scientists started working again to try to enhance the poison. In the end they came up with more effective pellets.

"After Markov was executed I was given a small token of the Bulgarians' appreciation – a Browning hunting rifle with a bronze plaque inscribed by their interior minister. I did not feel happy about such things but I was a loyal servant of the state myself. I had to obey orders too, orders given to me by Mr. Andropov. To refuse the chairman of the KGB would have been suicide for me."

Later, as a result of this interview, which he gave to a British newspaper, Kalugin was arrested by Scotland Yard and held for 24 hours while the Director of Public Prosecutions pondered his case. He decided that there was not enough evidence to proceed on a charge of conspiracy to commit murder. After his brush with British justice Kalugin said: "My participation in his death was precisely zero."

THE MYSTERY ASSASSIN

As to the assassin and the poisoned umbrella – they have vanished into history along with the regime that made them. Books since published in post-communist Sofia suggest that the assassin may be a retired Bulgarian diplomat living in his nation's capital, but Markov's friends dismiss this. Scotland Yard enquiries in his country as well as exhaustive checks in Britain after the attack have failed to turn up a culprit.

The death of Markov has gone unavenged long after the dictator who ordered his demise has himself fallen. The file on his death disappeared from Bulgarian secret service offices just after the collapse of the regime in 1990 and there is little hope now of anyone being brought to book for the murder.

His widow Annabella took some solace from a visit to Bulgaria after the fall of communism when she stood in a crowd of 100,000 people in freezing temperatures and heard them reel off the names of those murdered under Zhivkov's regime – with the cry of "killer!" to Zhivkov after every name. When it came to the name of Georgi Markov there was the biggest cheer of them all. He was loved by the Bulgarian people because he managed to make them laugh at their rulers – and there is nothing that a dictator fears quite so much as being laughed at; it means he is no longer feared.

But perhaps there is one epitaph to his memory that the writer – a humanitarian figure who believed in the ultimate good of man – would be pleased with. Early tests of a "magic bullet" treatment for cancer, based on the poison used to kill him, have shown remarkable results. Professor Philip Thorpe of the University of Texas South West Medical Centre says the first trials on patients have been "uncommonly good".

The therapy uses a monoclonal antibody linked to ricin. The ricin antibody recognises molecules exclusive to a certain type of blood cell. Once it finds them it sticks and delivers the fatal ricin to the cell. Fifteen patients with a cancer called B-Cell lymphoma, or non-Hodgkin's lymphoma, which causes more than 3,000 deaths each year in Britain, took part in the trial in 1993. Professor Thorpe reported that six of them had the size of their tumour reduced by more than half within a week of therapy.

If nothing else came from his death, Markov would surely smile at such lifesaving progress coming from the very venom that killed him.

Above: ***A grown-up Sasha, Markov's daughter, poses with her widowed mother in London in 1991, two years after the hated communist regime that killed a loving husband and father had been consigned to the scrapheap of history.***

THE ASSASSIN AND THE POISONED UMBRELLA HAVE VANISHED INTO HISTORY ALONG WITH THE REGIME THAT MADE THEM

WHEN IT CAME TO THE NAME OF MARKOV THERE WAS THE BIGGEST CHEER OF ALL. HE WAS LOVED BY THE BULGARIAN PEOPLE

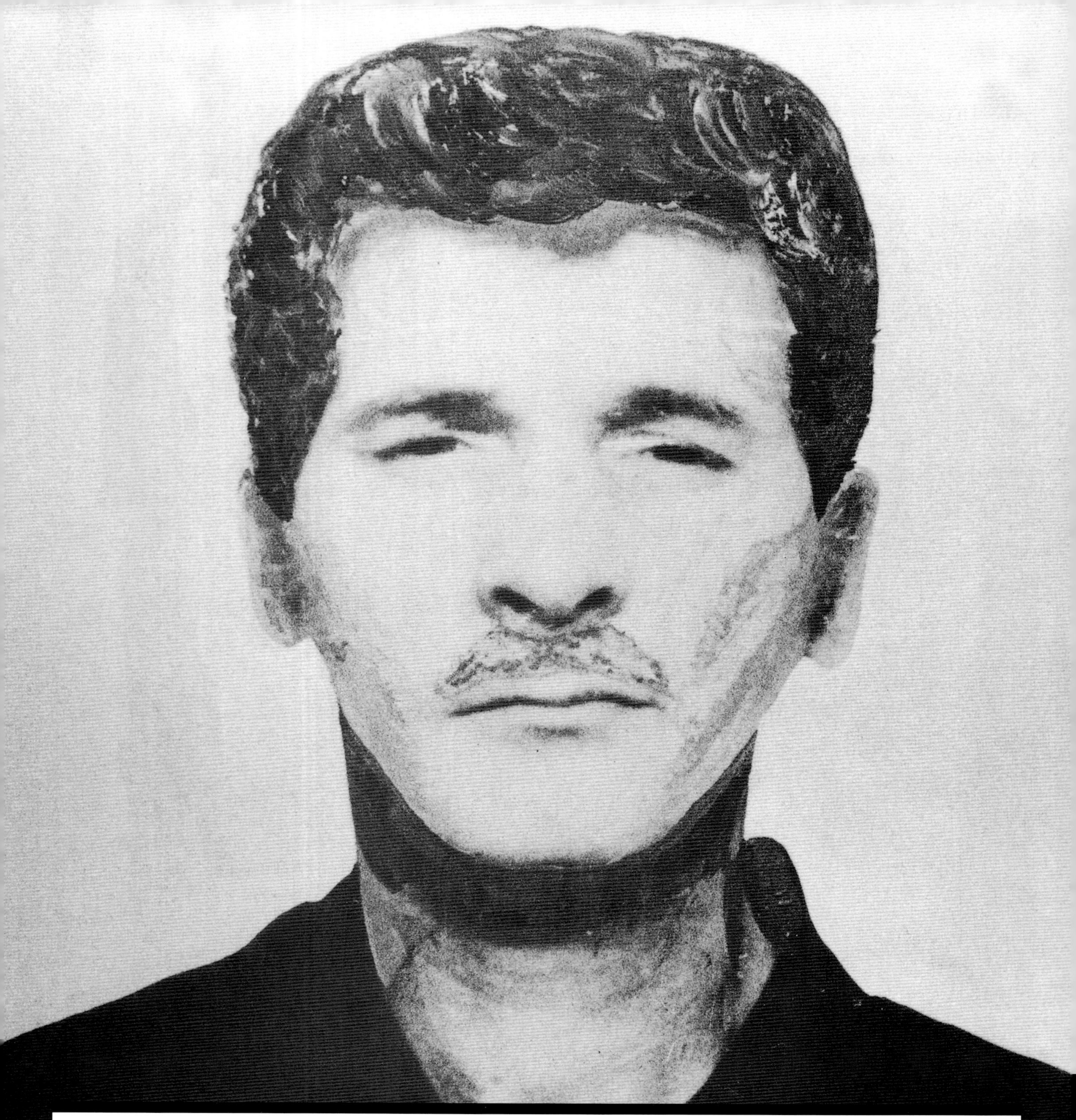

MURDER INC.
Cheapskate Killers

An innocuous block of flats in East London hid behind its walls scenes of medieval horror. There, the killing company known as Murder Inc. burned their victims in a tiny grate, later sprinkling their ashes from car windows. If ever criminals deserved to be found guilty, it was the perpetrators of these crimes.

He was one of the most formidable figures ever to stand in the dock of Number One Court at the Old Bailey; a small space that has seen some of history's most infamous individuals grace its confines. He made no speeches during his time in court, preferring that the prosecution did all the talking while he left his "not guilty" plea to speak for him. Harry "Big H" MacKenny hoped that the jury would believe the unbelievable – that he was not a mass murderer, but a lifesaver who had been framed.

At the end of his trial he leapt to his feet and screamed abuse and invective as the jury returned, beyond reasonable doubt, with guilty verdicts. Listening to the appalling catalogue of evidence stacked against him, it is inconceivable to believe that MacKenny could have conned himself into thinking that it could have gone any other way for him.

HE LEAPT TO HIS FEET AND SCREAMED ABUSE AND INVECTIVE AS THE JURY RETURNED GUILTY VERDICTS

Opposite: ***John Henry Childs, the killer who cracked and turned Queen's Evidence against the comrades in crime.***

Below: ***The flat where victims were turned from corpses to ashes.***

The macabre story began in a small fireplace in a small flat in a grimy part of East London, barely enough for more than one or two logs at a time. Outside, washing strung on the walkway of the flats fluttered in the breeze while dirty kids kicked a ball and tin cans around in the concrete play area outside the entrances. Inside flat 13 in Dolphin House, High Street, Poplar, the coals burned down to red hot embers. John Childs, the tenant of the overheated apartment, slugged whisky straight from a bottle. He handed it to Harry "Big H" MacKenny, who drank a deep draught, savouring the hot liquid as it burned on the way down before spreading a warm, mellow feeling throughout him. It was not a social drink. The men needed this liquor to steel themselves for the night's work ahead.

The fire, which was boosted with a gas burner to increase the heat, cast flickering, ominous shadows over the paraphernalia on the walls. Four knives, a pump-action shotgun, a shield, four axes, a crossbow, a

pump-action air rifle, a compressed-air spear gun, Chinese flails and a fencing mask testified that the resident of this flat was a man who clearly dabbled in violence and violent things.

Childs, dressed in a weird black outfit that made him resemble a Victorian undertaker, put more smokeless fuel on to the grate as Big H went out to the back room. There Childs had installed an industrial mincing machine – bought for £25 from a wholesale butcher who advertised in Exchange and Mart magazine – a butcher's block, knives and hooks.

Hanging from the hooks were various human body parts. They had been dismembered earlier by Childs as he waited for Big H to come around and help him with the disposal of the corpse.

CALLOUS KILLERS

Piece by piece, as if carting home a joint for Sunday lunch, Big H carried through the human remains to Childs in the sitting room. The fire reached maximum heat and, for the next eighteen hours, the flames were fed with flesh and bone, fat drained off, the bones broken with mallets, the ash put into plastic bags to be finally scattered to the four winds by MacKenny as Childs drove them along the Barking by-pass in East London. The whisky blotted out the awful reality of what they were doing… the contract killings they specialised in for £25 down payment and easy instalments for the balance. They called themselves Murder Inc., and before they were caught half-a-dozen people were murdered for the paltry sum of a few thousand pounds.

Murder Inc. actually went on to become a triumvirate of misfits, although it was Childs and MacKenny who did all the killing. The third villain, who would eventually join Big H and Childs in the dock at the Old Bailey, in November 1980, was Terence Pinfold, a petty criminal and failed bank robber. An outsider in the terrible alliance of MacKenny and Childs, he was a hypocritical, weak man with the failing of most paranoid power lovers; he thought himself a cut above the other two and would become enraged if he thought they were laughing at him behind his back. Together they killed, for discount prices, using guns, a swordstick and an axe, dismembering the corpses at Childs' flat or at a disused factory in Chadwell Heath, Essex, that had once been used for manufacturing teddy bears.

Above: ***A Teddy Bear of the sort manufactured by Terence Eve.***

Opposite top: ***The unprepossessing base where Murder Inc. committed their crimes.***

Opposite bottom: ***The farm that was once owned by George Brett before he and 10-year-old son Terry were sten-gunned to death by Big H.***

The founding of this vile business came about when Pinfold and MacKenny became friends in the early 1970s. In 1972, at a factory in Chadwell Heath, they began making teddy bears with another man, Terence 'Teddy Bear' Eve. A secondary line at the factory was lifejackets. Although MacKenny was a psychotic killer, he was also an enigma, a talented, self-taught man who was a first class diver and qualified pilot. He once invented a unique diver's valve that was hailed in the trade press as a breakthrough and a life-jacket which incorporated the best points of six other types of

Above: ***The interior of the Teddy Bear factory where George Brett and his 10-year-old son Terry were murdered.***

A SEEDY, SMALL-TIME CROOK, PINFOLD BUNGLED EVERYTHING HE DID, FROM BURGLARY TO ARMED ROBBERY

life preserver. He drastically cut the weight of the existing systems by converting the diver's oxygen cylinder so that it would also inflate the life-jacket. The old method used a separate cylinder for the job.

At the factory the men grandly called themselves 'directors' and dressed in snazzy suits. But MacKenny was extremely lazy, refusing to rise much before midday each day, and soon the life-jacket business began, slowly but surely, to slide. The stuffed toys business, however, under the direction of Eve, continued to thrive with orders from all over the country. It was his success which would eventually lead him to becoming a victim.

It's clear at which point MacKenny turned the corner from legitimate businessman to murderer; it occurred in 1974 with the release from jail of John Childs.

Childs had known MacKenny in East London for several years, and had been friendly in the late 1960s in prison with Pinfold who was serving time for a robbery. A seedy, small-time crook, he had been in court on no less than 17 occasions and had served three jail sentences. From burglary to armed robbery, he bungled everything he did, but he always harboured the ambition to become a kingpin of crime in the East End, just like the Kray twins Reg and Ron whose reputation he admired so much. He also pulled a bank robbery once with Pinfold in south Woodford, Essex, saving Pinfold from capture when he was attacked by two bank staff after he failed to draw out his Walther .38 automatic in time to threaten them. They fled empty handed from that botched affair.

Childs was not even his real name. He was born Martin Jones, but took on the pseudonym when he rented the £6 per-week flat which he planned to turn into the human abattoir. A deeply unhinged psychopath, he liked to pull his own toenails out with a pair of pliers when dark moods overcame him. His greatest fantasy was – and still is, by all accounts – to have a waxwork model of himself repose in Madame Tussaud's in Baker Street.

The two of them formed their macabre new business. Each had contacts in the underworld on both sides of the Thames; each knew that they were all capable of going ahead. For discount prices – £25 to £50 down and easy repayments on the balance – they would take human life. Pinfold, reluctantly, was drawn in.

Before the first contract killing, Childs murdered Terence Eve, the man whose soft toy business was thriving. Early in 1975 he shot him dead with an automatic pistol, took MacKenny with him to the Poplar flat, and spent 14 hours burning Eve's corpse in a grate as the pair of them drank a litre of whisky. Pinfold, who never murdered, was later found guilty at the Old Bailey of ordering the killing and jailed for life. The jury were convinced that his greed harnessed Childs' macabre talents for the job.

SMALL-FRY

In February of that same year they received their first contract for £1,800 – a pathetically small sum compared to the fees charged by international, professional hitmen. The target was George Brett, a haulage contractor who lived on a farm in Upminster, Essex. Brett was on the fringes of the underworld – a dodgy deal here, a suspect load there – but was not a big-time criminal. But somewhere along the line, George Brett had crossed the line when his enemies learned that he had started 'grassing' them up to police as a paid informer. He was marked for death and the bargain-basement killing team were the perfect instrument to use.

Childs, a man obsessed with weapons and with a theatrical air about him, donned a wig, heavy eyebrows and dyed his straggly beard with black boot polish when he went to meet Brett to propose a lucrative business deal. Within a mile of his farmhouse he parked his car, stripped down to a tracksuit and ran along the roadside, pretending to be a jogger. When he "accidentally" bumped into Mrs. Brett, he got chatting and told her he was a engineer whose firm needed transport. She arranged a meeting with her husband who was "just the man you're looking for".

A killing zone was arranged at the factory. Tarpaulin sheets lined with plastic, to collect blood, were laid out in an area at the back of the site. Childs went back to the farm the following day dressed as a city gent to bring Brett to the factory. At the very last minute, just as he was manoeuvring his car out of the yard, Brett's young son Terence, aged 10, ran across. "Dad, can I come along for the ride?" he said, pleadingly. The boy climbed into the car for the last journey of his short life.

A DEEPLY UNHINGED PSYCHOPATH, HE LIKED TO PULL HIS OWN TOENAILS OUT WITH A PAIR OF PLIERS IN HIS DARK MOODS

Below: ***The police hunt at Beredens Farm for George and Terry Brett.***

Above: ***At Beredens Farm a large section of the farmyard was dug up as police looked for the bodies.***

into smaller pieces and once again burned in the 18-inch-wide grate. It is still not known how much they charged for that particular contract killing.

A chilling insight into the menace they generated was provided by Mike Fielder, a veteran crime reporter for *The Sun*, who visited the death factory for a story about the disappearance of Eve. He said: "I came face to face with the killers in their factory of death. Pinfold told me that Eve had vanished with £600 in takings and had got 'a bit of woman trouble'.

"As we talked both MacKenny, 6 ft 5 ins tall and an unmistakeable figure, and Childs hovered nearby without joining in the conversation.

"Pinfold stonewalled every question. I got a guided tour of the factory from Pinfold.

AT THE FACTORY THE BOY WAS HELD BY CHILDS WHILE WATCHING HIS FATHER'S HEAD BEING BLOWN OFF

MACKENNY TOOK ONE OF GEORGE BRETT'S EYES FROM HIS CORPSE WITH THE INTENTION OF PRESERVING IT IN VINEGAR

At the factory he was held by Childs while watching his father's head blown off with a silenced Sten gun by Big H. Then the boy was cut in half by bullets fired from the same gun. As he looked at the boy's corpse MacKenny said: "It don't matter – he's only a grass's son." They were cut up, taken in plastic bin liners to Child's flat and burned. Then their ashes were thrown from the moving car. They had simply vanished from the face of the earth. Except for one of 35-year-old George Brett's eyes... MacKenny took it from his corpse with the intention of preserving it in vinegar.

The rubicon had been crossed. Killing for cash, they thought, was this simple.

The next to die was Frederick Sherwood, proprietor of a nursing home in Herne Bay, Kent. Sherwood, 48, was wanted out of the way by a business rival keen on muscling in on his lucrative enterprise. MacKenny discovered his car was for sale and lured him there on the pretext of being interested in buying it for £480. When Sherwood arrived the same killing zone had been prepared and he was shot through the head by MacKenny at the same time as Childs smashed a sledge-hammer over him. At the factory his legs were sawn off, the body complete with dismembered limbs taken to Childs' flat where it was sawed and hacked

"He showed me the teddy bear production line and how the toys were stuffed with foam rubber. Then he cheekily asked for my help in trying to prove that he had been 'framed' by the police on a £20,000 bank raid charge. At the time he said he had just been granted bail while awaiting trial. I said I would make a few enquiries on his behalf. But I felt in my bones that Pinfold was an evil and dangerous man. I never returned to the factory. And if I had known then what the world knows now, I would not have slept easy in my bed that night. A prying newspaperman would have made a tempting target for murder."

ANOTHER BRUTAL KILLING

Robert Brown, 36, an escaped prisoner who ended up working at the factory, was the next victim. He was killed with an axe by Childs because he "irritated him", and, like the others, disposed of in the grate.

While they touted for murders, MacKenny and Childs also drew up a lurid "shopping list" among the underworld of the kind of "services" that their organisation was offering. For £50 they would break someone's nose. For £500 they would blow kneecaps off with a shotgun. And for two grand – £2,000 – they would kill. They offered to help slum landlords deal with bothersome tenants by slipping diseased rats through letterboxes and they touted their talents to the right-wing National Front party – promising to deal with "troublesome Pakis" if they so wished. They even hit on the hare-brained idea that Lord Lucan, the runaway peer wanted for the murder of his nanny in Belgravia, was still alive, so they offered his relatives bargain-basement contracts on anyone who showed "malevolence" towards the Earl! The offer was never taken seriously. Another person they approached was the self-confessed racialist Robert Relf, the 56-year-old white supremacist who had gone to jail in Leamington for refusing to take down a sign which offered his house for sale to a white person only. Relf would later tell police: "MacKenny thought I would be a good customer. They thought I had a lot of black enemies that I wanted to dispose of. MacKenny put it to me that if I had any bother with coloureds he would get them 'seen to'. He said they could either get rid of them altogether or just frighten them off like break their arms and legs – for a price. I told him I wasn't interested. I know I'm a racialist but I'm not going for things like that – not with any violence."

A VICIOUS FRIEND

The next, and last, victim was Ronald Andrews – a man killed over MacKenny's lust for his wife. Andrews, 35, a roofing contractor, was MacKenny's best friend, a man he had known since his childhood days in Camberwell. But twice-married MacKenny, always a lady's man, did not let friendship stand in the way of what he wanted. He had been carrying on an affair for some time with his wife, Gwen, deciding, with the aid of Childs to murder him in the autumn of 1978.

MacKenny lured him to the DIY crematorium in Poplar on the pretext of introducing him to a private detective who alleged-

THEY SLIPPED DISEASED RATS THROUGH LETTERBOXES AND OFFERED THEIR SERVICES TO THE NATIONAL FRONT

Below: ***The farm was pulled apart as the police conducted the most thorough of searches.***

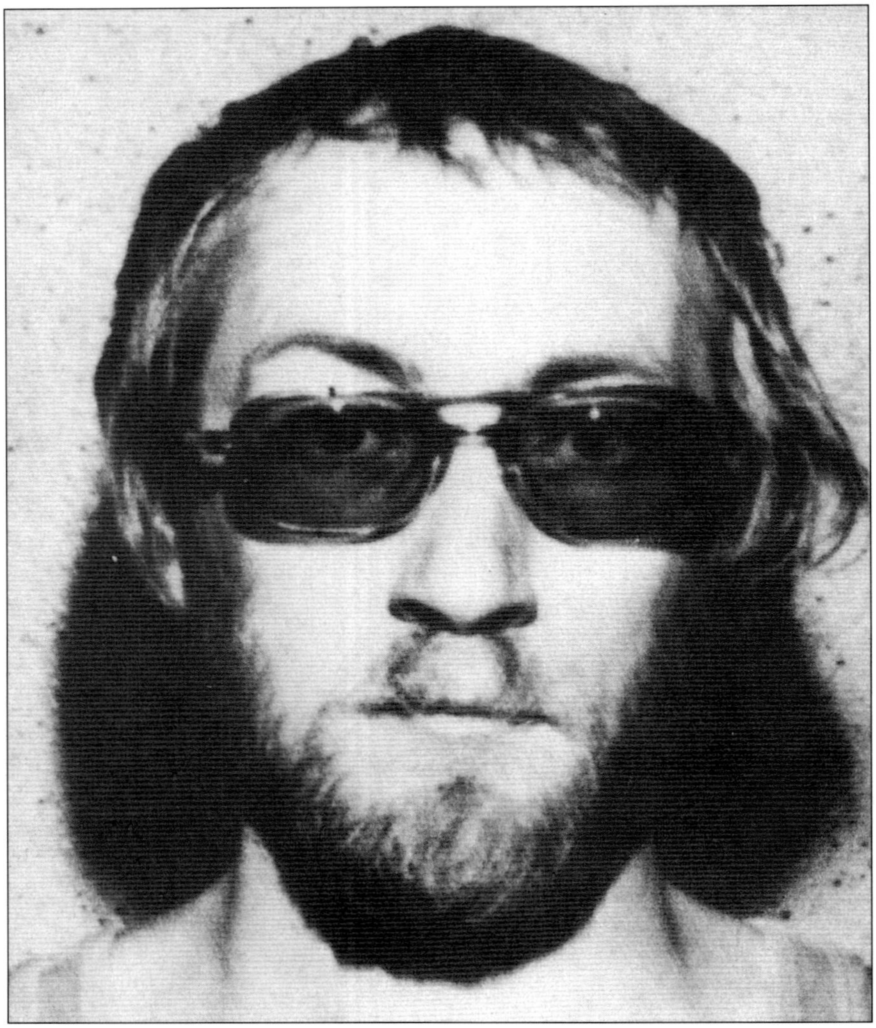

ly had information on affairs his wife was having with other men. The private detective turned out to be Childs. Andrews was lulled into a false sense of security, being offered tea by MacKenny who then went out into the kitchen, pretending to have a conversation with "Mrs. Childs", although in reality there was no-one else there.

Concealing a .38 revolver under a tea-towel he came back in, ripped the towel away, and shot him point blank through the back of the skull. Then his body was sawed up into log-size pieces, parts of it grated down in the industrial mincer and the flesh burned in the grate. Childs had to drink two bottles of whisky… his nerves were close to cracking.

To cover up the killing Childs had got his ex-wife to write a loving postcard to "Dear Ron", which was posted from Wisbech, Cambridgeshire, to his wife – MacKenny wanted it to appear to her that her husband was the cheat. He drove Andrews' car to the River Nene and dumped it in the black waters. Wearing frogman's gear, he waited until the car completely filled up with water before breaking out and swimming to the surface. He hoped that police would think that the body had been swept away by the current. Days later, when Ron Andrews was already ashes, MacKenny stood with Gwendoline on the banks of the river and comforted her as the car was dragged up from the depths.

Above: ***The defendants were desperate men.***

Right: ***Henry 'Big H' MacKenny, one of the vilest killers ever to stand trial for multiple murder.***

HIS BODY WAS SAWED INTO LOG-SIZE PIECES, PARTS OF IT GRATED DOWN IN THE INDUSTRIAL MINCER. FLESH BURNED IN THE GRATE

PAYING THE PRICE FOR EVIL

By this time, Childs' nerves were almost completely shot. He had grown sleepless, wracked by nightmares about the terrible things he had done. He was now drinking at least one bottle, sometimes two, of whisky each night, merely to blot out the memories to get some sleep. He would later tell police that he had, in his paranoia, become convinced that MacKenny was out to kill him. He wanted to get the first shot in and began practising with pictures of MacKenny tied to a tree in Epping Forest that he took pot-shots at with a crossbow.

MacKenny, too, began to question some of the murders, particularly the killing of Andrews. In one moment of remorse he

said to Childs: "I shouldn't have done that. He was my best mate." But he was nowhere near as close-to-the-edge as his partner... although time was rapidly running out for them both.

Police had been probing the disappearances of all the victims, but had nothing to tie them in – until the end of 1978 when a suspect wanted for a string of armed robberies in the home counties began talking of an underworld hit team. Villains all over knew of the gruesome speciality of Childs and MacKenny, but true to their criminal code, they stayed silent.

This particular suspect named Childs and MacKenny, although to police it seemed almost impossible to prove. For if what the crook was saying, there would be no bodies, no forensic evidence, to ever link them with the crimes.

The squad assigned to cracking the case was led by Det. Chief Supt. Frank Cater, later Commander Cater, a lawman with an outstanding record of success against organised crime in the capital. His second-in-command was Det. Insp. Geoffrey Foxall, responsible for co-ordinating operations and all relevant information in the murder squad incident room. With information from a further two informers, a 20-strong task force called Cater's Company began the task of seeking hard evidence to back up the uncorroborated statements of criminals.

Above: ***The Volkswagen which led police on a high-speed chase and the capture of Big H.***
Below: ***The Barking by-pass, resting place for many of Big H's murder victims.***

CRIMINAL LINKS

Childs was arrested for questioning over a £500,000 security van robbery in Hertfordshire in the summer of 1979. But he soon realised he had been offered up by a "squealer" for something far more damaging than mere armed robberies or grievous bodily harm. With his nerve completely broken, he turned supergrass, confessing to six killings, detailing every single gruesome episode. The hardened detectives could simply not believe that human beings could be so thoroughly disposed of in an 18-inch-grate in a council flat. So to test the theory two officers were assigned the task of burning an 11-and-a-half-stone pig in the flat. They had reduced the animal to ashes in 13 hours, pulverised its bones and disposed of the ashes from a car on the Barking by-pass – just like Childs and MacKenny had done. Childs hoped that his full confession would be enough to earn him a pardon. He was sadly mistaken.

With detectives sent to interview all the associates of the missing people, tracking down the places where they drank and where they placed their bets, forensic evi-

dence proved more difficult. A search of the teddy bear factory showed an area where large amounts of concentrated acid had been poured to remove bloodstains. But there was one mark in the floor which corresponded to the tip of a bullet that had been disguised with the aid of polish and wax. It was the first small, but significant, clue that would eventually lead to the downfall of Murder Inc.

THE BIG SEARCH

In July 1979 a massive dragnet was set up by police to find MacKenny. But he too had his underworld contacts. He realised that he had been sold out by Childs and had gone to ground, and managed to elude capture despite a massive poster campaign combined with radio and TV appeals. He was eventually found to be staying at a house in Morse Close, Plaistow, East London, the home of his friends William and Pauline Woodcraft.

A large team of armed officers, wearing bullet-proof vests, ringed the house, evacuating some neighbours while telling others to keep quiet and stay indoors. Shortly after 1.00 a.m. on September 21, police telephoned the house, spoke to Mrs. Woodcraft, and told her that the place was surrounded. MacKenny, realising the hopelessness of the situation, came out without a shot being fired.

They came to trial at the Old Bailey in October 1980 – the largest mass murder case ever to be brought where no victims had ever been discovered. For close to two months the jury listened to what judge Mr. Justice May called 'a story I have seldom heard even in these violent times.'

MacKenny and Pinfold were in the dock, their erstwhile business partner and cohort in crime John Childs paraded before them as their chief prosecution witness. Childs left nothing out. He detailed every gory move that he made. Pinfold was made to look weak and pathetic; even though he wanted Terence Eve dead, Childs had to confess that he did not take part in the killing. He told the court: 'I live in fear of my life now. I was a professional criminal and I have broken the code.'

For their part, the police revealed how two detectives who were on the squad which cracked the case were under constant fear of their lives from another underworld contract, put out on them by acquaintances of MacKenny while they delved into their murders.

THE TRIAL AT THE OLD BAILEY WAS THE LARGEST MASS MURDER CASE WHERE NO VICTIMS HAD EVER BEEN DISCOVERED

TWO DETECTIVES ON THE SQUAD WERE UNDER CONSTANT FEAR OF THEIR LIVES FROM ANOTHER UNDERWORLD CONTRACT

Big H, defiant to the end, insisted he was a life-saver, the inventor of the life-jacket and breathing apparatus at the factory, not a cold-blooded killer. But John Childs' description of his callous remark over the dead body of 10-year-old Terry Brett virtually froze the courtroom.

He was convicted of murdering the Bretts, Eve and Frederick Sherwood and jailed for four life terms, concurrently, with Mr. Justice May recommending that he serve not less than 25 years. The pitiful Pinfold, the outsider in the drama who just got greedy over wanting the teddy bear factory for himself, was sentenced to life imprisonment for ordering Eve's murder.

DRAMATIC SCENES

There were scenes of high drama in the heavily guarded courtroom on Friday November 28, 1980, as the judge came to sentence MacKenny. He told him: 'The public needs to be protected from your criminal and totally unjustified activities.' MacKenny, tall, greying, dressed in a cream suit, shouted back: 'Straight people need to be protected from you.' The judge, ignoring this outburst as prison officers restrained him, said: This is one of the most macabre cases ever heard, even in this famous building.' Again MacKenny interrupted: 'I think you are a hypocrite. Bring this farce to a close. Do your worst. I killed nobody. I have saved lives!'

Psychopath Childs was sentenced to life with little hope of ever seeing the world outside of an institution ever again. But even from behind bars the hot breath of his menace can still be felt. In August 1983 he attempted, from his cell at Hull maximum security prison, to write the memoirs of Murder Inc. He wrote to Redbridge council, the local authority which gave planning permission for the teddy bear factory. He asked for the council to send him the plans of the factory for one of his chapters. The council had to treat the request 'like any other'. But an official said: 'We feel like telling him to get lost. He certainly has a nerve.'

DRAWN OUT CASES

JOHN LIST
The Murderous Dad

It was a horrific case but, at the same time, it should have been an easy one for the police to solve. A family had been wiped out except for the father, who automatically became the chief suspect. Yet it was to be two decades before the forces of law and order caught up with killer and arch-hypocrite John List.

John Emil List was a modest man with much to be modest about. He looked like the humdrum, churchgoing accountant that he was. He neither smoked nor drank, had no interest in women or gambling and rarely took a vacation. He was parsimonious to the nth degree – turning the heat in the family's rambling mansion home so low in winter that all were forced to wear boiler suits to stay warm. German was the language spoken in the home in New Jersey, even though the furthest List had gotten to the land of his forefathers was a brochure from a travel agency. It was a miserable life for his wife Helen, their three children and his elderly mother – made more miserable by his dire financial straits and insistence on Bible-bashing at every given opportunity.

List, a man troubled by demons we can only guess at, decided to end what he saw as his family's "suffering" in this world. On a cold, foggy night in November 1971 – plagued by his children's apparent ungodliness, distraught at the looming spectre of financial ruin clouding his ordered life – John List took two handguns and wiped out his wife, three children and mother. The Friday before the massacre his daughter Patricia, 16, had told her high school drama teacher in the bucolic town of Westfield, New Jersey, that she was afraid her father was going to kill her – acting, in his eyes, was akin to prostitution. The teacher thought her prophesy nothing more than teenaged histrionics although she had told him: "He called us around the table and said he would have to kill us because he could no longer support us. He said he could not look after us the way he wanted to."

Her drama teacher never acted on her pleas and on Tuesday, November 9 1971, John List set about his macabre plan. He cancelled newspaper, milk and mail deliveries, informed the schools his children attended that the family would be visiting a sick relative out of town and told his bosses at a local bank that he was taking the day off sick.

LIST, A MAN TROUBLED BY DEMONS WE CAN ONLY GUESS AT, DECIDED TO END WHAT HE SAW AS HIS FAMILY'S "SUFFERING"

Opposite: ***The seemingly timid John List murdered his family.***

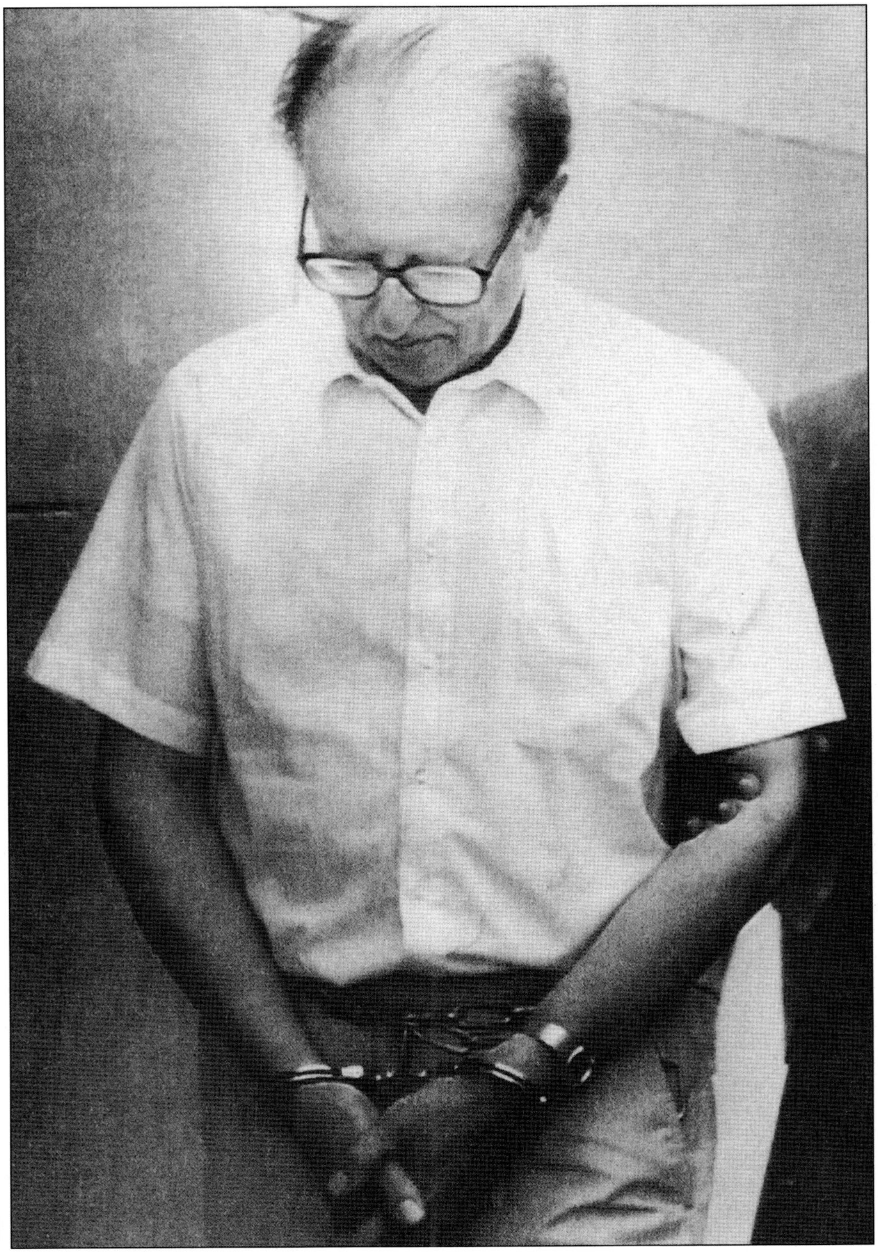

Below: ***John List after a brilliant piece of forensic modelling had led to his capture.***

Behind the locked doors of the rambling, run-down mansion that was the unhappy family home, List executed his loved ones one by one. It was not until a month later, the house still brightly lit, that police broke into 431 Hillside Avenue with Edward Illiano, the drama teacher who had heard Patricia's fears first hand. Inside they saw a vision of hell. Laid out on the floor of the mansion's old ballroom were Helen List, aged 46, next to children John Frederick, 15, Frederick Michael, 13, and Patricia. John's body alone was riddled with ten bullets, although autopsies showed that death was brought about for all of them with a single bullet in the back of the head.

DEATH WAS BROUGHT ABOUT FOR ALL OF LIST'S FAMILY WITH A SINGLE BULLET IN THE BACK OF THE HEAD

List's 84-year-old mother Alma was found on the third floor underneath a sloping roof near a bathtub. List had attempted to drag her body downstairs but was unable to do so. Police found a filing cabinet in the house with the murder weapons along with five letters – one to his employer, one to his wife's mother, one to his mother's sister, one to his wife's sister and one to his local pastor – a rambling five page self-justification in which List tried to explain what led him to such a gruesome act. He wrote: "I know that what has been done is wrong from all that I have been taught and that any reasons I might give will not make it right. But you will at least possibly understand why I felt I had to do this."

DESPERATE TIMES

"I wasn't earning anywhere near enough to support us. Everything I tried seemed to fall to pieces. True, we could have gone bankrupt and maybe gone on welfare. But... knowing the type of location that one would have to live in, plus the environment for the children, plus the effect on them knowing they were on welfare was just more than I thought they could or should endure...

"With Pat being so determined to get into acting I was also fearful about what that might do to her continuing to be a Christian. Also with Helen, not going to

Below: ***John List pictured with the family he massacred. Daughter Patricia stands behind, next to him is his wife Helen and sons John and Frederick.***

church. The whole family seems to be slipping from Christianity. I knew this would harm the family eventually. At least I am certain all have gone to heaven now. If this had gone on who knows if this would be the case. I am sure many will say 'How could anyone do such a horrible thing?' My only answer is it isn't easy…

"It may seem cowardly to have always shot from behind but I didn't want any of them to know even at the last second that I had to do this… I am only concerned with making my peace with God and of this I am assured because of Christ dying even for me. P.S. Mother is in the hallway in the attic, 3rd floor. She was too heavy to move." He also said he had got down on his hands and knees and prayed after every killing – comfort for his soul that did little good for his innocent victims.

A QUICK GETAWAY

John Emil List, however, had vanished by the time police trawled through the scene of indescribable horror. List, 46, left behind everything that identified him – his wallet, his driver's licence, his college class ring, even his overcoat and boots. He had methodically wiped up the blood from the executions with a towel – and eerily left classical music playing on an intercom system that stretched throughout the rambling 19-room mansion – before vanishing into the great expanse of North America. His first trip was to a bank where he withdrew $2,100 in bonds belonging to his mother. Then he drove to New York's Kennedy Airport where his Chevy car was found by authorities two days after the discovery of the bodies on December 7. James Moran, the Westfield Police Chief who was among the first of the lawmen to witness the rotting bodies in that room, made a vow to himself to track List down until the day he died. In the end he didn't succeed – but he did nevertheless live to see justice done.

For the next 18 years John List lived as a phantom in America. James Moran knew he was alive, knew he had adopted a new identity somewhere, but every lead drew a blank. In the first days and weeks after the discovery of the bodies the publicity was intense; America, brutalised as it is by violent crime, was sickened to its core by a man capable of such a monstrous act.

Above: ***Robert Clark, otherwise known as John List, arrives at court to answer for his savage murders.***

Tip-off lines to the FBI and police burned with information – policemen logged thousands of man hours following up leads that proved to be false. The insignificant List, who served as a private in World War Two and a reservist in the Korean War, had vanished off the face of the earth.

In Westfield in the weeks following the murder the List house became a kind of gruesome tourist attraction with people driving by to stare at the turn-of-the-century structure. Local children nicknamed it the "Norman Bates Motel" after the grisly murder site in the Hitchcock thriller *Psycho*. The attraction lasted little more than a year – it was mysteriously destroyed by fire in 1972. By then, a full 12 months after the killings, the trail had gone colder than an Arctic night. While frustrated FBI agents trawled across America, South America and Europe, John Emil List was living in a small town near Denver, Colorado. And for his new life he had taken out a new name – Robert P. Clark. The insignificant accountant with an obsession for orderliness and religion was working at his profession and attending the same kind of Lutheran church that he had left behind in New Jersey.

HE SAID HE HAD GOT DOWN ON HIS HANDS AND KNEES AND PRAYED AFTER EVERY KILLING – COMFORT FOR HIS SOUL

On November 22 1971, 12 days after the killings, he had applied for a new Social Security number – in America the key to a new identity. Anyone under 50 can get a number without question and his was taken out in the name of Robert Peter Clark, residing at Motel Deville, 650 W. Paltax St., Denver, Colorado.

On the application he listed his parents as dead and his year of birth as being 1931. He did what so many on the run from justice failed to do – camouflaged himself by hiding in plain sight. His first job was as a night cook in a roadside diner, but he soon plucked up enough courage to list himself in the phone book as an accountant. He was back at his old trade… and he had managed to get away with murder.

Above: ***FBI posters cry out for information on List.***
Below: ***Finally List is caught.***

In 1977, so confident of life in his new identity, he courted a divorcee called Delores Miller whom he had met through a church singles group. Delores had many of the qualities of his murdered wife – before she strayed from the path of righteousness – and soon they were a couple in all but marriage. He put that right in 1985 when she became the second Mrs. List – and, in many respects, the sixth victim of the unfeeling monster.

A WILD GOOSE CHASE

Throughout these years the hunt continued for him without success. The only things that brought it into the public mind were occasional newspaper articles about the murders on anniversary dates. "Police Still Pursue Mass Killer", "14 Years And No List", "Police Still Baffled", they screamed with monotonous regularity. List lived a life of monotony and regularity, scrupulously avoiding any trouble, anything that might lay a trail to his new life in a new town 2,000 miles from the murders. Chief Moran laboured ceaselessly, checking out the leads and calls that flooded in each time a newspaper resurrected the murders, but each time there was no luck. Moran, however, remained optimistic, saying: "So he was careful, so he was keeping a low profile. So he was a nondescript kind of guy, so he never did one single thing to draw attention to himself. Nonetheless, I knew that one day he would make a mistake and that someone would be waiting to snap the cuffs on him. I hoped so much it would be me."

In the latter half of the 1980s List moved with his wife to Richmond, Virginia – now less than 500 miles from the murder scene. Still wimpy, still churchgoing, he nevertheless enjoyed watching TV on a regular basis and one of his favourite programmes was *America's Most Wanted*, a weekly expose of the killers, conmen, rapists, robbers and bad guys who were wanted by the FBI. It was the programme that would eventually lead to his capture.

America's Most Wanted was approached by an officer on the murder squad and

Left: ***Commercial photographer and forensic sculptor Frank Bender specialised in creating busts of fugitives for law enforcement authorities across America.***

asked if it could broadcast an appeal about List. Margaret Roberts, the show's managing editor, was keen to help, but hampered by the lack of recent photos of him. Michael Lindner, an executive producer of the show which had an impressive track record of catching fugitives, thought he could solve the problem with the aid of a 47-year-old commercial photographer and forensic sculptor called Frank Bender. Bender had specialised in recent years in creating busts of fugitives for law enforcement authorities across America. In the case of List, all he had to work with was a 1971 photo, a computerised update on his image and a police description. "It was a challenge," said Bender, adding: "But I think I had worked on harder projects."

Bender's journey into forensic sculpture had begun in 1977 by accident. Accompanying a friend on a tour of the Philadelphia morgue he had been shown the corpse of a woman shot three times through the head at point-blank range. Because of wounds and advanced decomposition, identification of the body was impossible. As an artistic experiment he rebuilt her face – and the woman was identified two days after he completed the cast in clay. Since then his work as a "physiognomic reconstructionist" had continued unabated and he was regarded as the foremost expert in the field.

THE FORENSIC SCULPTOR TACKED UP ENLARGED PHOTOS OF LIST IN THE KITCHEN OF HIS HOME AND STUDIED THEM INTENSELY

A PSYCHOLOGICAL PROFILE

Bender turned to a friend, criminal psychologist Richard Walter from Michigan, for help in fleshing out details about List and what made him tick. Walter speculated that he would be the kind of guy who wouldn't be a health freak, that he was a worrier whose age would show. He would probably wear the same kind of eyeglasses, show the same nervous strain in his face, that his hair would have receded further, leaving a very high forehead and a partially bald cranium. He would have sagging jowls and a downturned, saddened look. Bender was convinced the psychological profile was right and set to work making the clay bust of the fugitive.

Day after day he moulded the face. He tacked up enlarged photos of List in the kitchen of his home and studied them intensely. He glued rubber erases to a fibreglass skull to attain the right thickness and then filled in the gaps with the clay. He kept reminding himself of what Walter had

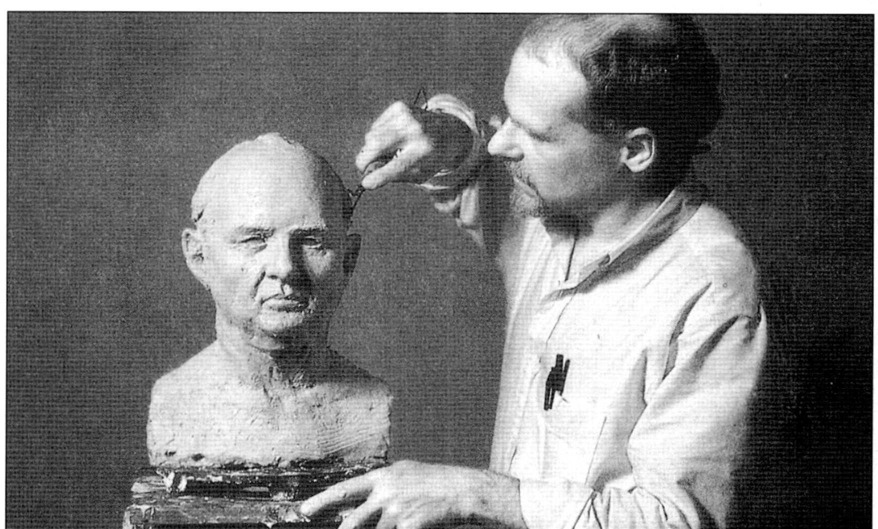

Below: ***All Bender had to work on to create the bust of List was a 1971 photo, a computerised update on his image and a police description. "It was a challenge," said Bender. "But I think I had worked on harder projects."***

Above: ***On May 1 1990, John List was sentenced to life imprisonment without the possibility of parole.***

said about him ageing, about how he would look aged 63 and not 46. Finally, satisfied with what he saw, he made a plaster mould that he then filled in with fibreglass. Afterwards he painted the model with flesh tones and handed it over to the producers of *America's Most Wanted.*

On Sunday May 21 1989 the show aired… and luck was on the side of justice. Robert Clark, nee John List, had travelled to a church social and so missed his favourite show, one that chronicled in depth his crimes, culminating with the sculpture and description of him as a pen-pusher, quiet, a nonentity. Afterwards there were 300 phone calls within minutes, all from people who claimed to know the wherabouts and new identity of John List. But only one of them proved to be correct and that came from Wanda Flannery, a friend of his wife Dolores back in Denver. "That's Bob!" she screamed when the image of the bust played on her TV screen. She rang the hotline and gave the operator the name, address and phone number of Bob Clark in Virginia.

Tracing down the hundreds of leads took time, but on June 1 1989, at 10.00 am, FBI agent Kevin August from Richmond, together with three colleagues, knocked at the door of the Clark home in Midlothian, near Richmond. Delores answered the door and mumbled the address of the small-town law firm where her husband was working. There, a little over one hour later, August confronted the fugitive and asked him: "Are you John List?" "No I am not," he lied, but August was convinced.

Three agents pinned him to the wall while August read him his rights. "My name is Robert Clark," said List, trying to bluff it out. But two hours later a fingerprint test proved him to be John List – fingerprints on file at the police station where he had applied for a firearms permit for the weapons to slaughter his family. The game was up after 18 years.

"HIS ACTS STAND AS A PERMANENT, PATHETIC AND PROFANE EXAMPLE OF MAN'S INHUMANITY TO MAN"

Former police chief Moran was one of the first to hear the news. "It's him?" was his first reaction, stunned that he had been caught by a clever model of his features when every method of modern detection had failed to find him in close to two decades of searching. "Then I said it was the best thing that had ever happened to me. That bum should never get away with what he did." List was charged with five counts of murder and caged pending a trial – the outcome of which was a foregone conclusion, even though at his arraignment on July 10 he pleaded not guilty, and insisted he was Robert Clark, not John Emil List.

A SENSIBLE PLEA

In February 1990 his attorney made him see sense and admit to being the fugitive, yet he pleaded not guilty to first degree murder at his full trial in April, claiming he had acted out of love for his family and that it was not a premeditated massacre. Clearly, with the letters left behind and his escape route planned, this was a nonsense. List's confessions to a psychiatrist were read out which showed him to be the ultimate, sneering criminal who believed himself above both God's law and that of man. In the end the jury, nine days after the trial began, found him guilty of all five counts of wilful murder. John List had been brought to book by a lump of clay fashioned by the skilful hands of a man who had never ever seen him.

When he was sentenced on May 1 1990 to life imprisonment without the possibility of parole, John List told the court: "I wish to inform the court that I remain truly sorry for the tragedy which happened in 1971. I feel that due to my mental state at the time I was unaccountable for what happened. I ask all those who were affected by this for their forgiveness, their understanding and their prayers. Thank You."

Judge Wertheimer lashed him from the bench: "His acts stand as a permanent, pathetic and profane example to the potential of man's inhumanity to man. They will not be soon or easily forgotten, and the name of John Emil List will be eternally synonymous with the concepts of selfishness, horror and evil."

John List rots in jail – and finally his family can rest in peace.

HIS MEMORY CAPTURED

In the years since his arrest the character of John List has been captured in several films and books. In the 1987 film *The Stepfather*, the main character, Jerry Blake, was based on the character of John List.

Timothy Benford and James Johnson wrote a book called *Righteous Carnage: The List Murders* and Joe Sharkey wrote *Death Sentence: The Inside Story of the John List Murders*, both books give an indepth insight into List's life of crime.

In 1993 a television movie was produced about John List entitled, *Judgement Day*. The part of List was played by Robert Blake who, incidentally, was born in Nutley, New Jersey, just 17 miles from Westfield which is where List murdered his family. In 2001 Blake's own wife was murdered, by being shot once in the head and no one has ever been charged with the crime.

In 1995 in the film *The Usual Suspects*, the elusive character, Keyser Soze, was also based on John List.

Shortly after the murders, the original scene of the crime, List's mansion, burned to the ground under very mysterious circumstances. Ironically, the glass ceiling in the ballroom was an original signed Tiffany & Co., which was worth enough money to have possibly paid off all of John List's debts.

DE LA BECKWITH
Third Time Unlucky

Byron De La Beckwith was a man who was born with hate in his heart and racist mumbo-jumbo in his mind. For more than 30 years he had managed to get away with the murder of a rising civil rights leader in the deep south but changing times and new attitudes brought him to justice... and jail.

Byron De La Beckwith was a man born with hate in his heart and bigotry burned deep in his soul. In America's old south he was raised a "Klucker" – the slang term among non-disciples for the Knights of the Ku Klux Klan, the white supremacists who strayed far beyond fancy dress in bedsheets and pointy hats to wreak their own brand of evil.

As organised terrorists who believed only in the supremacy of the white race they were – sometimes still are – responsible for bombings, lynchings and other murders. Not that they ever saw it as murder. Negroes to them – particularly back in the 1960s when the civil rights movement was "interfering" in the way the Dixieland states did things – were the lesser race, a breed for whom there could be no human compassion or decency.

They saw their extermination as the next best thing to where they once had them – under the heel of their boots. And nowhere was the stifling heat of oppression, the cruel vindictiveness of America's own brand of apartheid, more virulent and more apparent than in the city of Jackson, Mississippi, in 1963.

On a sultry June night Byron De La Beckwith murdered a young civil rights worker whose only calling was to bring basic human dignities to blacks denied them long after the last bugles had blown across the battlefields of the civil war. Byron De La Beckwith walked free from court where he was tried for the young man's murder – and walked free a second time months later. But the shot that snuffed out Medgar Evers' life was destined to be heard down three decades. And finally its ricochet got the murderer who is now serving life behind bars after scoffing at justice for 30 long years.

It was hot in Jackson on that June night as bugs danced around the humming street lights and creaking air conditioners across town struggled to keep ahead in the fight against the high temperature and humidity.

THE SHOT THAT SNUFFED OUT MEDGAR EVERS' LIFE WAS DESTINED TO BE HEARD DOWN THREE DECADES

Opposite: ***Byron de la Beckwith, racist murderer.***

Below: ***Beckwith in 1963, six years after the 'good ole boy' network of racist police, judges and jurors had saved his hide.***

Medgar Evers was in his second floor office overooking Lynch Street, clearing up paperwork in his job as the field secretary of the Mississippi branch of the National Association for the Advancement of Coloured People. These may have been Camelot days in Washington with the Kennedy administration working fast and furiously to dismantle the bureacracy of discrimination which existed across the deep south, but Evers was a front line warrior in the battle; it was he who protested at the separate lunch counters in restaurants and stores for blacks and whites, the "no blacks" signs at hotels, the signs which forbade humans of different colour from drinking from the same water fountain.

As an officer in this war he was used to harassment and threats, and often without joking said that the most valuable weapon in his arsenal was his Oldsmobile which he often used to escape from hostile towns where the local good ol' boys didn't take kindly to uppity niggers like him. Before his death he said: "Someone's been following me wherever I go. And I am getting plenty of calls. They say I am going to end up dead soon. One man who called was obviously holding a pistol. He spun the cylinder so I could hear it was a revolver. Then he said: 'This is for you.' I said to him: 'Well, when my time comes I am ready.' And I am. If I die it will be in a

Above and Below: ***Beckwith relied on the racism of his fellow white men to get him off the hook. Here the all-white jury enters the courtroom on the first day of the original trial.***

good cause." It was just eight nights later that his prophesy came true. After he finished up his paperwork he drove to his home in the still night, looking forward to seeing his wife and three small children who were waiting up for him. As he walked to the front door of his home a hunting rifle used usually to shoot deer cracked in the still night and he fell before he had got the key into the lock. At 37, he had become one of the martyrs in the war against racism, dead in the heat of the night on June 12 1963.

"You have got to understand," said Robert Moses, a former leader of the black action group The Student Nonviolent Coordinating Committee, in attempting to explain away why there was no justice for him following his death, "that Mississippi in 1963 was a police state. It was a state where its elected officals promoted racism and all the terror that went along with it. Medgar worked right in the middle of this terror, surrounded by all the violence used by the state to keep people in line."

A BORN FIGHTER

Yet Medgar was born to lead his people in the fight for justice. One of the defining moments of his life came when, as a nine-year-old boy in his hometown of Decatur in the same state, he witnessed the KKK lynching of a black man wrongly accused of raping a white woman. He recalled: "He was a friend of my daddy's and we saw him strung up. The man's clothing remained in the field where it stayed a very long time. For ages his clothes were still there, slowly rotting in the wind and the rain, long after he had been cut down and buried. I used to see them whenever I went hunting and I always remembered.

"I made a pact to myself then that I would grow up and try my best to stop this ever happening again." After a spell in the U.S. Army he returned to Civvy Street. He attended a black agricultural college but was denied entry to the University of Mississippi law school because of his colour. Ironically he was instrumental in dismantling the college's system of apartheid the year before he was killed.

It was in 1954 that he first joined the NAACP and his first job was persuading scared negroes to go to city halls to register to vote – bastions of white supremacy that most feared to go near, let alone enter. He braved mobs who spat on him, bullies with billy clubs at the crossroads into town who smashed his car up and then smashed his face up; he endured the taunts and the threats and the abuse with only his dignity and his sense of right intact. He recalled picking up an elderly black hitch-hiker who kept his eyes down on the floor of the car for the whole journey as he kept repeating over and over in a mantra fashion: "Yessir, the best friend a negro man ever had was a southern white gentleman. Yessir." Medgar said: "I had to tell him it was not a view I shared. And I said I aimed to make it my life's work to prove him wrong."

Above: ***This was the lot of many blacks in the deep south – no trial, no jury, no judges. Just a lynching.***

HE BRAVED MOBS WHO SPAT ON HIM AND BULLIES WITH BILLY CLUBS AT THE CROSSROADS INTO TOWN WHO SMASHED HIS CAR UP

That dream died on that hot still night because Medgar Evers, visionary, had col-

Above: ***The Ku Klux Klan, racists who continued to haunt, persecute and murder blacks in the deep south long after the Civil War was over.***

lided with the philosophy of Byron De La Beckwith, bigot. A self confessed white supremacist, working as a fertilizer salesman, De La Beckwith was a decorated World War Two veteran who served in the bloody battle for the Japanese-held island of Tarawa as a trained sniper. Hunting in the woods around Jackson, he kept his eye in and boasted to friends that he was able to hit a running deer at 1,000 yards. Picking off a member of the race he despised at a distance of 30 feet would have been no problem at all.

De La Beckwith harboured fantasy notions of being an heir to a great Confederate general and his home in Greenwood, 90 miles from Jackson, was cluttered with the self-glorifying paraphenalia of the obsessive. He had Dixieland stars-and-bars flags, a field-grey kepi and a musket rifle as used by an infantryman at the watershed battle of Gettysburg. He also stockpiled the literature of hate – pamphlets that he handed out at shopping centres warning against the perils of "race mixing". On one occcasion he wrote to his local newspaper: "When you get to heaven you will find me in the part that has a sign saying 'for whites only'. And, if I go to Hades, I am going to raise all hell over Hades until I get to the white section. I do believe in race segregation like I believe in God. I shall make every effort to rid the United States of America of race integrationists until the day I die. There can be no place for the mongrel negroid races defiling and diluting the blood of American whites."

DE LA BECKWITH HARBOURED FANTASY NOTIONS OF BEING AN HEIR TO A GREAT CONFEDERATE GENERAL

Such a diatribe in a newspaper in any "normal" town would have instantly brought the author to the attention of the local police department with a strong warning to officers to keep a close watch on the person responsible. But in the twisted atmosphere of Jackson, De La Beckwith was a friend of many policemen, many of

Left: ***Medgar Evers, a devoted family man and a rising star of the civil rights movement that sought to bring equality and liberty to all negroes in America.***

whom shared his not-unique outlook about black people. That is why the investigation into the death of the most prominent civil rights worker in the state of Mississippi was not pursued with anything that could be termed vigour.

PRESIDENTIAL BACKING

Four days after his death, as the JFK administration pledged the full weight of federal law to pursue his killer, Evers was laid to rest in Arlington National Cemetery, the final resting place for American heroes which would later that year receive the body of the president, himself a victim of another sniper with another rifle.

The local police were slow to act but a federal investigation team was soon on the scene and all clues pointed to the man who couldn't bear blacks in his world. The bullet found in the victim matched his rifle, he was seen in Jackson that day, the gun disappeared shortly afterwards and De La Beckwith's car tyre marks were found in town near to where Evers was slain. He was charged with murder but the first trial turned into a celebration of racism.

An indication of how things were going to go came on day one of the trial when the prosecutor, William Waller, asked prospective jurors: "Do you think it is a crime to kill a nigger in the state of Mississippi?" Anyone who seemed to hesitate, or to think it an unreasonable question, was immediately excluded, but there can be no doubt that most of the 12 good men and true who were to sit in judgement on De La Beckwith were just as bigoted as he was. De La Beckwith denied he had killed Evers, but used the dock as a pulpit to preach his gospel of hatred.

THE JFK ADMINISTRATION PLEDGED THE FULL WEIGHT OF FEDERAL LAW TO PURSUE MEDGAR EVERS' KILLER

He said that he was at home 90 miles away when the killing occurred – and produced three upstanding police officers to testify that they had seen him in Greenwood just like he said. The first trial in 1964 ended in a hung jury and a mistrial was declared. There was a second trial the same year with the same result.

At the end of the second courtroom hearing De La Beckwith had practially become a folk hero to the white racists of Mississippi. He was even greeted outside court by the Governor of the state, Ross Barnett, who shook his hand and wished him well!

Such endorsement of his actions later encouraged De La Beckwith to run for the position of Lieutenant Governor, but the majority of voters had the good sense to reject him and his rantings.

Below: ***Evers, with the 'End Brutality' sign around his neck, is arrested in Jackson, Mississippi, shortly before his murder.***

The verdicts were, of course, of little surprise to Evers' widow Myrlie and his three small children. They had been taught by Medgar to lie on the floor if they heard gunfire at their home – once the target of a firebomb attack and all had lain prostrate with fear in their house the night he died at midnight on the doorstep.

"I wanted justice," said Myrlie, "but I was pragmatic enough to realise that it would probably never come. He grinned in court, gesticulated, used the word nigger like a hammer to bash us with.

"He was disgusting, and lining up on his side were all the forces of the state. I thought that I will die and my children would die without ever seeing justice done for him."

Above: ***John F. Kennedy, president, right, speaks with brother Robert at the White House about bringing down the deep-rooted racism that infected so much of America.***

"HE GRINNED IN COURT, USED THE WORD NIGGER LIKE A HAMMER TO BASH US WITH. HE WAS DISGUSTING"

Byron De La Beckwith went back to his salesman job and married twice more in his lifetime. He was always unrepentant to the last about his racist ways, declaring that God would ultimately justify his segregationist views. But he couldn't leave it all to God. In 1979 he was arrested with bomb-making equipment and maps marking the home of a prominent Jewish leader in New Orleans – Jews, in the twisted philosophy of Byron De La Beckwith, having as little right to life as negroes. During his time in jail he couldn't resist talking to anyone who would listen about his twisted feelings on the "lesser races"... and about how he had gotten away with murder back in 1964.

SPECIAL RESEARCH

While he was doing his boasting a man who was nine-years-old at the time of Medgar Evers death was doing his research. Bobby DeLaughter had never even heard of the name of the dead man until he finished law school 13 years later. And then he became engrossed by the case, by the searing injustice of it all which he thought blemished all Mississippians and all southerners as being violent, racist rednecks. When he graduated he swore to himself that he would do everything in his power to re-open the case – and he did. "The big problem," he said, "was evidence 30 years after the fact. The murder weapon had disappeared, for instance, and I was keen to get it back.

"One day I recalled that my father-in-law, a Mississippi judge named Russell Moore III, had once shown me a rifle he kept in a closet. 'This is from one of the old civil rights cases,' said Judge Moore, unaware at what a trophy he really had, and indicating that he had taken the rifle home as a souvenir. By the time I remembered that he had shown it to me he was dead, so I went around to my mother-in-law's, checked the same gun and found that it matched the one on the records for De La Beckwith. Everthing was starting to fall into place. Police ballistic records were intact so it was a valuable piece of evidence to have." By now the boy who was nine when it happened was a man burning for justice on the staff of the district attorney's office. It was in his power to bring a new case and he intended to.

The key to getting trial number three came in 1990 when six new witnesses stepped forward to say that De La Beckwith had boasted to them during the years since the killing of how he was the hitman – of how he waited in bushes outside his home until he showed up and pulled the trigger.

The most compelling testimony came from Mark Reilly, a 36-year-old prison hospital guard in Baton Rouge, Louisiana, who guarded the suspect in 1979. Mr. Reilly, in a sworn affadavit which he later repeated at De La Beckwith's February 1994 trial, said: "He boasted of having killed 'that uppity nigger', and said that he had influence in Mississippi that protected him from ever being found guilty or of being prosecuted again."

As well as this damning testimony came even more concrete proof – De La Beckwith's fingerprints on the telescopic sights of the hunting rifle that had turned up again after so many "lost" years.

De La Beckwith was a man living in a timewarp, an anachronism in the modern age who believed that the juries who judged him in the heat and dust of 1963 would be around to listen to his bilge in 1994. He relied on the testimony of the three police officers – two of them now dead, one who turned up in person – to again place him 90 miles from the murder scene when the killing was carried out. Such evidence was seen as suspect to say the least in the enlightened 1990s, especially given the ballistic evidence. The only thing which marked this trial out as different from the others was De La Beckwith's silence in the dock. Although an unrepentant racist still, he acquiesced to his lawyer's demands to stay silent throughout the week-long trial.

THE FINAL VERDICT

At 10.33am on February 5 1994 the Civil War which had started in 1861 finally ended in Mississippi when jurors filed back into the courthouse from which Byron De La Beckwith had twice mocked justice and declared him guilty of murder. Eight blacks and four whites had judged him this time and there was no return to the "good ol'boy" days of the 1960s. The six witnesses, said the jurors afterwards, who told of his boasting, had sealed it for them. In six and-a-half hours they found the twisted old man guilty "beyond reasonable doubt'.

DE LA BECKWITH BOASTED OF HOW HE WAS THE HITMAN – OF HOW HE WAITED IN BUSHES AND PULLED THE TRIGGER

Two women in the front of the court were most affected by the verdict. One was the widow of Medgar Evers, one the third wife of Byron De La Beckwith. "He didn't do it, he's innocent," said Thelma Beckwith, tears streaming down her face for the man who had cheated justice – and the death penalty – for so long. Now, because of a change in the law, he couldn't be sentenced to die, just a life sentence instead. "Yes! Yes!" screamed the widow who has heard the shot that claimed her husband's life for 30 long years. "It's been a long journey," said Myrlie Evers, looking to the sky. Then she addressed a long-dead hero with the words: "I've gone the last mile, Medgar – but it was worth it. This will send a message to all racists who hide behind sheets and hoods.

"It won't bring you back, honey. But I hope it makes you rest in heaven a little easier."

Below: ***Mrs Evers weeps at the graveside of her slain husband during his funeral.***

SAM SHEPPARD
A Travesty of Justice

A well-respected citizen is arrested for the brutal murder of his pregnant wife. Vital forensic evidence is ignored and the trial is a travesty of justice. In this, as in so many murder cases, there are no winners, only losers

Saturday, 3 July 1954 – the eve of Independence Day – was a busy one for Dr Sam Sheppard, though his wife, four-and-a-half-months pregnant Marilyn, took things rather more easily. Dr Sheppard was on call at his father's Bay View Hospital in Bay Village, Cleveland, Ohio and split his day between work and socializing with their close neighbours, Don and Nancy Ahern.

THE FATAL EVENING

The Aherns' two young sons and seven-year-old Chip Sheppard ate first, while their parents sat on the porch overlooking the lake and sipped drinks. Later the Ahern boys were sent home and Chip went to bed, after which the four adults spent a relaxed evening.

By midnight Marilyn and Sam were drowsing. The Aherns decided to go home to bed. Before leaving, Nancy Ahern locked the lakeside door of the house for Marilyn. Then she and her husband went out by the main door on to the road. Marilyn had gone upstairs to the bedroom, Sam was snoring on the sofa.

At 5.45a.m. John Spencer Houk, a businessman friend of Sheppard's who

Above: ***The Sheppards' clapboard house in Bay Village, Cleveland, Ohio.***

Opposite: ***Dr Sam Sheppard on his way to court.***

Below: ***A detailed diagram of the Sheppard house shows the scene of the crime.***

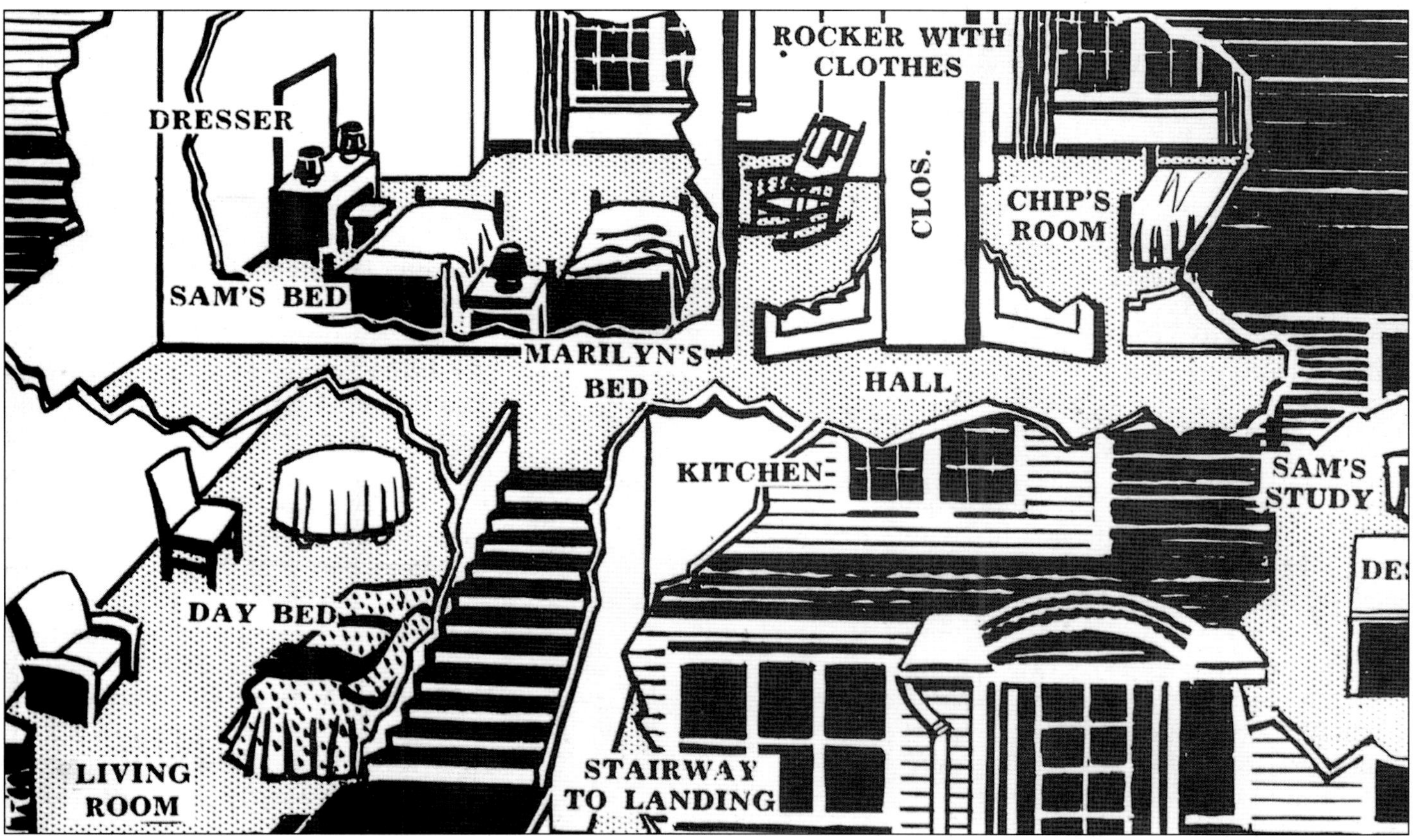

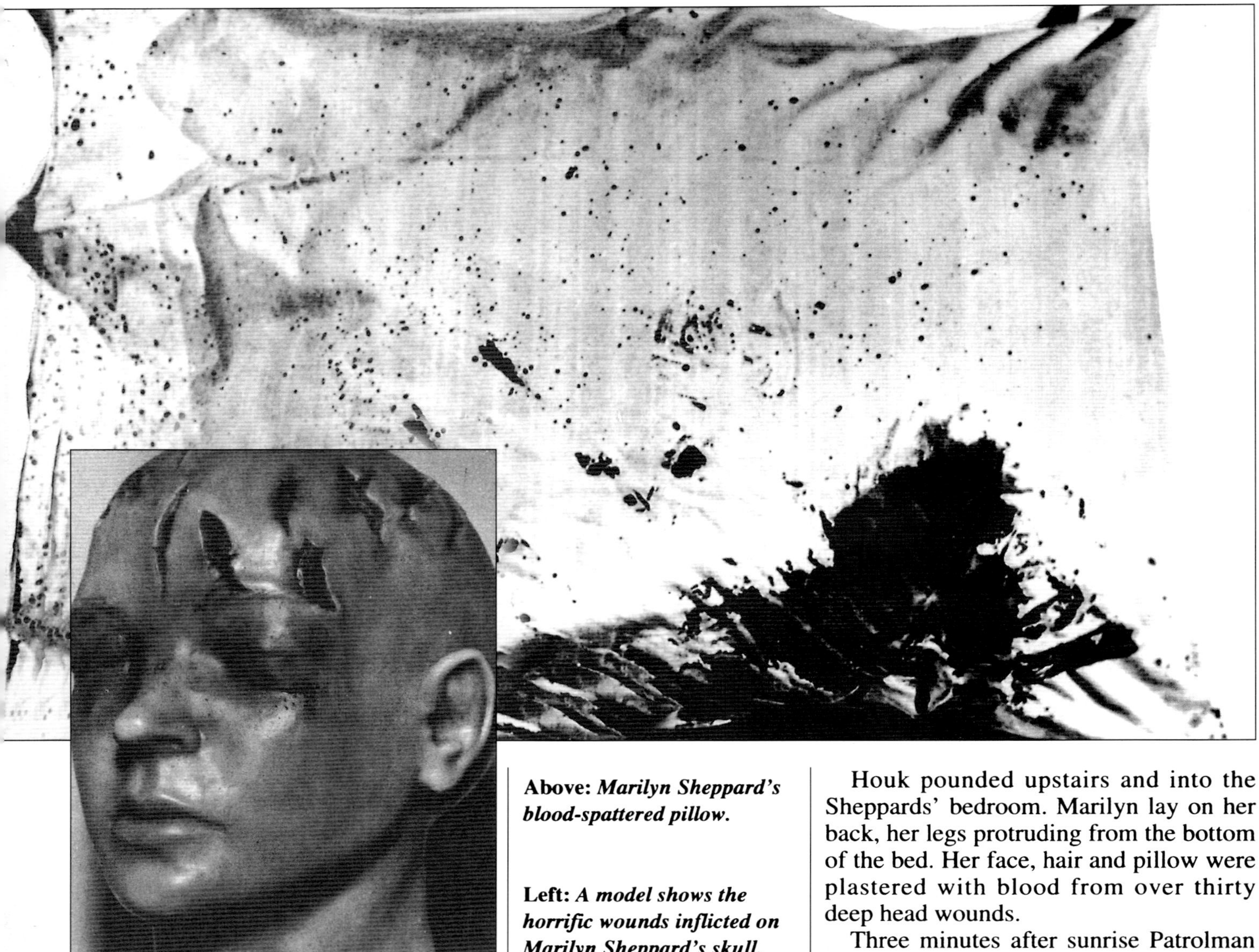

Above: ***Marilyn Sheppard's blood-spattered pillow.***

Left: ***A model shows the horrific wounds inflicted on Marilyn Sheppard's skull.***

was also mayor of Bay Village, was awakened by the shrilling noise of his bedside telephone. Sleepily he picked it up and heard the voice of Sam Sheppard: 'For God's sake, Spen, come quick! I think they've killed Marilyn!'

SCENES OF VIOLENCE

Houk's house was just 100 yards from that of the Sheppards. He and his wife arrived at 5.55 to a scene of chaos. The roadside door was open and Sheppard's medical bag lay inside, its contents scattered around. A desk drawer hung open, and the immediate impression was of a burglary. Sam Sheppard sat, stripped to the waist, in his den. His trousers were wet and his face was bruised. His neck was contorted with agony.

IT WAS A COSY, RELAXED, EVE-OF-INDEPENDENCE-DAY SUPPER WITH A COUPLE OF CLOSE NEIGHBOURS

Houk pounded upstairs and into the Sheppards' bedroom. Marilyn lay on her back, her legs protruding from the bottom of the bed. Her face, hair and pillow were plastered with blood from over thirty deep head wounds.

Three minutes after sunrise Patrolman Fred Drenham arrived. He was closely followed by Richard Sheppard, one of Sam's elder brothers, and his wife, and by the other brother Stephen and the local Chief of Police, John Eaton. At 6.30a.m., as police began their systematic work at the murder scene, Sam was driven by Stephen and John Eaton to Bay View Hospital for a check-up. Nurses who tended Sam were later to testify that his lips were badly cut and swollen, and his front teeth were loose.

By 9a.m. Sam had been fitted with a neck brace and was heavily sedated. He was, however, able to answer questions from the coroner of Cuyahoga County, Dr Samuel Gerber, who had already made a brief visit to the house. At 11a.m., Detectives Robert Schottke and Patrick Gareau of Cleveland Police took over the questioning.

The two detectives had already noted that there had been no signs of forced entry into the Sheppard house, and the only fingerprint was a thumb-mark which subsequently turned out to be Chip's. Sam's corduroy jacket, which the Aherns had seen him wearing the night before, was neatly folded and lying on the sofa. No bloodstained weapon had been found, and, despite the confusion, the detectives were pretty sure that the motive had not been burglary.

They were not happy that Sheppard had been taken to his family-run hospital, and they were certainly not happy with his uncorroborated story. As Schottke was to tell him: 'The evidence points very strongly at you. I don't know what my partner thinks, but I think you killed your wife.'

By that evening the murder was headline news, not merely because of its bloody drama but because it involved the Sheppards, one of Ohio's most prominent and controversial medical families.

PROMINENT MEDICAL FAMILY

Samuel Holmes Shepherd was born in Cleveland on 29 December 1923, the youngest of Dr Richard and Ethel Sheppard's three boys. Richard Sheppard was a general surgeon who was beginning to gain a reputation as an osteopath, at a time when this holistic form of medicine was little known in the United States.

Academically Sam was not particularly bright, but he had an ability for hard work which got him through his exams. In 1943, as an alternative to military service, he began to study medicine at the Western Reserve University in Cleveland, at Hanover College, Indiana, and finally at the Osteopathic School of Physicians and Surgeons in Los Angeles.

In the meantime he had met and fallen in love with Marilyn Reese, and in November 1945, when she was nineteen, the couple were married at the First Hollywood Methodist Church in Los Angeles.

In 1948 Sam graduated as a doctor of medicine, and he and his wife intended to stay in California. Sam's father, however, had that same year founded the Bay View Hospital back in Cleveland, and Sam, with his two brothers, was pressured into joining the family 'firm'.

Within months, business was booming. By 1954 Bay View was one of the most prestigious hospitals in the state.

Now, despite their suspicions, the police were reluctant to arrest one of the Dr Sheppards of Bay View. As his attorney, William Corrigan, told him: 'The only way to convict yourself, Sam, is by opening your mouth.'

'I DON'T KNOW WHAT MY PARTNER THINKS, BUT I THINK YOU KILLED YOUR WIFE'

PRESS CAMPAIGN

There was one man, however, who was unimpressed by Sheppard's status in the community. He was Louis Benson Seltzer, editor of the *Cleveland Press*, and well known for his hard-hitting campaigns against crooked politicians and 'soft' police departments.

On 21 July, seventeen days after the killing, the *Cleveland Press* ran a splash headline: 'Why No Inquest? Do It Now, Dr Gerber.'

Dr Gerber, the fifty-seven-year-old coroner for Cuyahoga County, had felt Seltzer's righteous wrath before. The next day he called an inquest. Gerber refused witnesses the right to counsel, and when William Corrigan protested he had him thrown out to tumultuous cheers.

Below: ***Newsmen pack the courtroom during the trial.***

Above: ***Police search Dr Sheppard's medical bag after the murder.***

Sam Sheppard waived his right not to give evidence, and was questioned for eight hours by Gerber. Among other things, Sheppard denied having committed adultery with a mystery woman in California named only as 'Miss X'. Finally, on 30 July, he was arrested, even before Gerber recorded his verdict that Marilyn had been murdered.

Sheppard's statement at the time of his arrest was essentially the same as he had made shortly after the crime was committed. He said that he had been awakened, as he lay on the sofa, by his wife's screams from upstairs. He refused to guess what time it might have been.

'I charged into our room and saw a form with a light garment,' he said. 'It was grappling with something or someone....'

He and this person had wrestled, until Sheppard was knocked out from behind. When he regained his senses he saw on the floor his own police surgeon's badge – he was unpaid police surgeon for the Bay Valley force – which he normally kept in his wallet. He took Marilyn's pulse 'and felt that she was gone'.

After checking that his son Chip was still asleep and safe, Sheppard had heard a noise, ran downstairs and saw 'a form rapidly progressing somewhere'. Sheppard had chased the figure down from the porch to the lake, where he had grappled with a large man with bushy hair. The man had caught his neck in an armlock, and he had passed out.

When he came to he had woken up on his face by the water's edge. His T-shirt was missing, though he could not recollect what had happened to it.

Also missing from his wrist was his gold watch, which was later found, spattered with Marilyn's blood, in a duffle bag in the Sheppards' boat-house by the lake. This watch was to be the centre of vigorous controversy later. Sheppard had then staggered back to the house.

TRIED FOR FIRST DEGREE MURDER

The trial of Sam Sheppard on the charge of first degree murder began in the Court of Common Pleas, Cleveland, on Monday 18 October 1954. But because of delay in jury selection – many admitted that they had firm ideas on the case – it did not properly get under way until 4 November. The judge was Edward Blythin, and Sheppard pleaded Not Guilty.

The main thrust of the case against Sheppard was indicated by prosecuting counsel John Mahon in his opening address: 'The state will prove that Sheppard and Miss X talked together about divorce and marriage. No one was in that house that morning on 4 July attempting to commit a burglary. No evidence has been found that any burglar or marauder was there.'

The Aherns were called early in the trial. Don said that he had never seen the placid Sam Sheppard lose his temper, though Nancy introduced a hesitant note when she said that, though she was sure

Marilyn was very much in love with her husband, she had never been sure of Sam's feelings towards Marilyn.

Dr Samuel Gerber, the coroner, caused a sensation when he spoke of a 'blood signature' on the yellow pillowcase under Marilyn's battered head. 'In this bloodstain I could make out the impression of a surgical instrument,' he said. The instrument, he suggested, 'had two blades, each about three inches long, with serrated edges'.

No weapon of any kind had been found at the house, but, said Gerber, 'the impression could only have been made by an instrument similar to the type of surgical instrument I had in mind'. Curiously, he was not asked to specify just what the mysterious instrument was.

On 1 December came another sensation, when Miss X entered the witness box. She identified herself as Susan Hayes, a twenty-four-year-old laboratory technician who had worked at the Bay View Hospital and met Sam there in 1951.

They had begun their affair in California, after she had left Bay View to work in Los Angeles in 1954. She admitted that they had slept together, as well as making love in cars. 'He said that he loved his wife very much but not as a wife, and was thinking of getting a divorce,' she testified.

This evidence meant that Sam was not only a perjurer – he had denied adultery at the inquest – but guilty of the then criminal offence, under Ohio law, of adultery.

On the stand, Sam now admitted lying at the inquest, saying that he had done so to protect Susan Hayes rather than himself. In any case, he went on, he had never truly been in love with her, and had never discussed divorce with either her or his wife. He admitted that he had committed adultery with women other than Susan Hayes, but refused to name them.

Summing up for the prosecution, Thomas Parrino, an assistant prosecutor, said: 'If the defendant would lie under oath to protect a lady, how many lies would he utter to protect his own life?'

Corrigan's defence was, on the face of it, poor. He made no mention of one or two curious pieces of evidence which might have helped Sam.

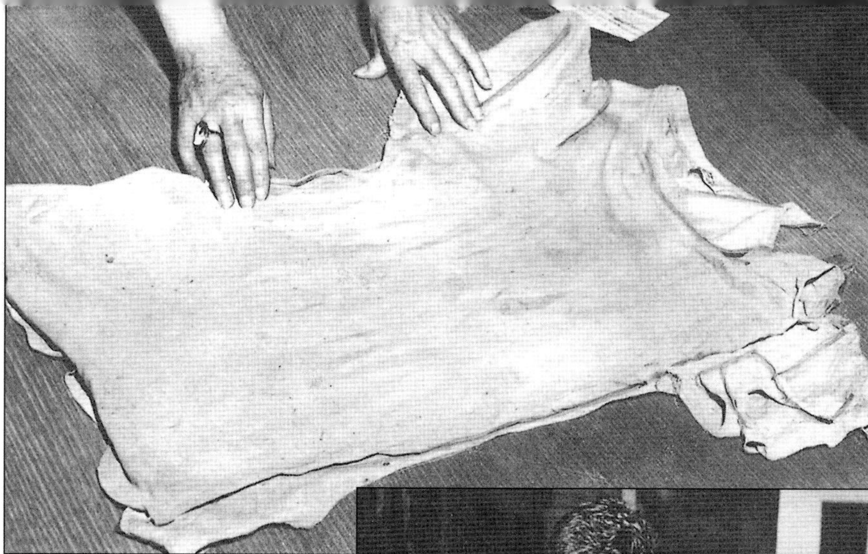

Above and right: ***Police examine evidence during the investigation of the case.***

THE CORONER CAUSED A SENSATION WHEN HE SPOKE OF A 'BLOOD SIGNATURE' ON THE PILLOWCASE UNDER MARILYN'S BATTERED HEAD

IF THE DEFENDANT WOULD LIE UNDER OATH TO PROTECT A LADY, HOW MANY LIES WOULD HE UTTER TO PROTECT HIS OWN LIFE?

Tooth chippings had been found on the bedroom floor which belonged neither to Sam nor to Marilyn. There was firm evidence that Marilyn had bitten her attacker savagely, though Sheppard bore no bite marks. There was the business of the mysterious surgical instrument. And there were wool threads, found under Marilyn's nails, which matched no clothing in the house – not hers, not Sam's, not Chip's. Above all, there was the blood-spattered watch.

Instead, Corrigan took up the prosecution's sex theme and made a negative mess of it. 'Is sex the only thing in a marriage?' he asked. 'Sheppard

> CURIOUSLY, SHEPPARD'S LAWYER IGNORED EVIDENCE WHICH WOULD HAVE POINTED THE FINGER FIRMLY AWAY FROM HIS CLIENT

wandered from the path of rectitude. That didn't prove he didn't love his wife, his home, or his family.'

After a briefing from Judge Blythin on the laws governing circumstantial evidence, and the difference between first and second degree murder, the jury retired. They returned on Tuesday, 21 December after over four days' deliberation. Their decision was that Sam Sheppard was guilty of second degree murder, and Judge Blythin sentenced him to life imprisonment.

After what must have been a melancholy Christmas for the Sheppard family, William Corrigan retrieved the keys of Sam's house from the police and handed them over to Dr Paul Leland Kirk. One of the country's leading forensic scientists, he had undertaken to do independent tests.

EXHAUSTIVE FORENSIC WORK

Dr Kirk began work in the Sheppards' house in January 1955, and after studying the results in his California headquarters produced a 10,000-word report three and a half months later.

Among the detailed facts examined in the report the most important was Dr Kirk's emphatic assertion that a fourth person, other than Sam, Marilyn or Chip, had been in the house on the night of the murder. Blood on the wardrobe door demonstrably did not match that of any of the Sheppards. And teeth fragments on the carpet showed that Marilyn had bitten her attacker very deeply, though, as had been shown at the trial, Sheppard bore no such scars.

Dr Kirk was able to show that whoever delivered the death blows to Marilyn would have been covered in her flying blood, but the only stain on Sam's clothing was a spot on the knee of his trousers – gained, he claimed, when he had knelt to take his wife's pulse.

> NO ACTUAL PROOF OF A TECHNICAL NATURE WAS EVER OFFERED INDICATING THE GUILT OF THE DEFENDANT

Furthermore, bloodstains on the walls showed that the killer had struck with his left hand, while Sam was right-handed. The blows had undoubtedly been made with a blunt instrument such as a piece of piping, which made nonsense of the coroner's 'surgical instrument' theory.

'No actual proof of a technical nature was ever offered indicating the guilt of the defendant,' he concluded.

Despite what seemed to be Kirk's irrefutable report, Judge Blythin refused, on 10 May 1955, to grant a retrial. Six weeks later the Ohio Court of Appeals praised 'the originality and imagination' of Dr Kirk, but nevertheless turned down an appeal for a new trial.

The following summer, on 31 May 1956, the Ohio Supreme Court upheld Sheppard's conviction by five votes to two. Hope was raised, however, by the two dissenting judges, who expressed the view that there had been little real evidence to prove Sheppard guilty, and that Judge Blythin had accepted gossip as evidence.

But on 19 December the highest judicial body in the land, the United States Supreme Court, refused to review the case on technical grounds. Again, however, doubts were expressed about the conduct of the Ohio judiciary.

A CONVICT'S CONFESSION

Sheppard's hopes were raised once more six months later, when, in June 1957 a convict named Donald Wedler, who was serving a ten-year sentence for a Florida hold-up, confessed to the murder. He claimed that he had been in Cleveland, Ohio on the day of Marilyn's killing, and after taking heroin had stolen a car and driven around looking for a house to burgle.

He had found a suitable one, a large white house on a lake front, had broken in, crept past a man asleep on a settee and gone upstairs.

A woman in an upstairs bedroom had awakened as he was preparing to rifle her dressing table, and he had beaten her repeatedly with an iron pipe. Then, as he fled downstairs, he had encountered a man, whom he had struck down with the pipe, before flinging the impromptu weapon into the lake and driving away.

The coroner was quick to point out discrepancies in the story. Sheppard had said that he was struck down from behind in the bedroom, not on the stairs, and Wedler had made no mention of a struggle in the garden by the lake. Nor was Wedler a burly man with the 'bushy' hair mentioned by Sheppard – he was slight, though he did have unruly, curly hair.

What interested Sheppard's lawyers most was the fact that a lie-detector expert who tested Wedler was quite certain that he was telling the truth, 'or what he believed to be the truth'.

Unfortunately, there were many imponderables about the Wedler story. As a heroin user, he might have been telling the truth and have confused the details, but equally he might have invented the whole thing after reading newspaper accounts of the case, and convinced his drug-addled mind that he was the murderer.

In the end, it was the plethora of newspaper speculation surrounding the original event which led to a successful appeal – but only after Sheppard had served ten years in jail. In 1961 William Corrigan died, and in his place Sheppard hired a smart, fast-talking young attorney from Boston named F. Lee Bailey.

> 'THE ANSWER TO THE SHEPPARD CASE RIDDLE,' WROTE A PRIVATE DETECTIVE, 'LIES IN BAY VILLAGE'

RETRIAL AT LAST

In April 1963, after a series of legal moves, Bailey lodged a petition with the US District Court, a federal rather than state body, that the case be reopened. This time he was successful. After almost a year's deliberation, Judge Carl Weinman delivered his verdict on 15 July, 1964. The original trial, he said, had been a 'mockery of justice'. He ordered Sheppard to be released pending a retrial.

Lawyer F. Lee Bailey immediately swept into the attack. Quoting the exhaustive inquiry undertaken by Dr Kirk, he compared it with the muddled and pathetic attempts of the Cleveland police, whose search for clues, he forced them to admit, had been perfunctory to a degree. Their check for fingerprints had been particularly casual. They had not even tried to get prints from the bloodstained watch found in the duffle bag, and had also ignored a key-ring and chain which accompanied it.

Bailey produced a photograph of the watch, which had blood speckles across the face such as could have been caused had Sheppard been wearing it when he battered his wife to death. But, as Bailey pointed out, there were also speckles of blood on the back of the watch and the inside of the wristband, which certainly could not have got there if he really had been wearing it under such conditions.

On 6 June, 1966, the United States Supreme Court overturned Sheppard's conviction, and he walked free.

UNANSWERED QUESTIONS

There were, of course, still questions which remained unanswered. One was the old Sherlock Holmesian puzzle of the dog that did nothing in the night.

For if an unknown intruder had indeed broken in, why had the family dog Koko not barked a warning? Although neither police nor defendants thought fit to bring their suspicions into the open, privately they admitted that, if Sam did not kill his wife Marilyn, then it was someone who knew her, and the house, well.

As Harold Bretnall, a New York private detective hired by the Sheppard family, wrote in a report dated 1955: 'The answer to the Sheppard case riddle lies in Bay Village.' At the first trial, the jury had heard part of a statement made by Sam to detectives, in which he had said that Marilyn had 'spurned lovers – potential lovers . . . three that I know of and I am pretty sure more'.

Although not named at the trial, the men had, it was claimed, been identified to the investigating officers. Bretnall also claimed that a pair of Marilyn's bedroom slippers bore evidence that she had left the house during the night of 4 July, 1954, while she was wearing them. 'Marilyn Sheppard was murdered by someone who was a frequent visitor to the Sheppard home,' wrote Bretnall.

The blood-speckled watch, too, posed unanswered questions. For if it had been splashed with Marilyn's blood, it must surely have been lying on the bedside table when she was killed – when it should have been downstairs on her husband's wrist. Did he come to bed, leaving his corduroy jacket downstairs, place his watch on the beside table and batter his wife to death?

Or did he come to bed, take off his watch, hear an intruder, put on his trousers to investigate, get himself laid out – and then inexplicably lie to the police about his movements?

BILLIE-JO JENKINS
Blood Spatter Clues

Sion Jenkins was jailed in 1997 for the murder of his 13-year-old foster daughter, Billie-Jo. By no means a straightforward murder case, it went to trial three times before blood spatter testimony led to his acquittal.

Sion David Charles Jenkins was born in 1957 in south-east London and is the former deputy headmaster of William Parker School. At the age of 23 he met 19-year-old Lois Ball, a student nurse at Whitechapel Hospital. In 1982 they married and their first child, Annie was born two years later. Lottie, their second child, was born in 1986 and it was about this time that the couple became interested in the Baptist Church. They had two more children after they moved to Waltham Forest, Esther in 1988 and Maya in 1989. After the birth of their last child, Sion's wife started work as a social worker helping children with special needs.

FOSTER CHILD

In 1992 the couple noticed an advert in a local newspaper asking people if they would be prepared to foster a child. One of the children that needed a home was a schoolfriend of his daughter, Annie, a girl called Billie-Jo who oddly enough had the same surname, Jenkins. The social workers explained that Billie-Jo had been having a hard time in care, suffering in her early years in a natural family life that had been blighted by alcohol abuse. After much discussion it was decided to place her with the Jenkins family.

In 1992 Sion Jenkins was offered the post of deputy head at the William Parker School in Hastings, East Sussex. Although Billie-Jo had reservations about moving away from London, she agreed to move with the family and Lois and Sion applied for a residence order which meant they would have parental responsibility for their foster daughter.

The new house was quite large and comfortable, with an area of overgrown woodland directly behind. It was February and the weather had been damp and miserable for most of the

Above: *Sion Jenkins, Billie-Jo's foster father*

children's half-term break, so when the sun started to shine on the Saturday, the three older girls asked if there was any way they could earn some extra pocket money so that they could go shopping. Sion said that they could paint the patio doors, clean out the utility room and wash the family cars for which they would be rewarded. Billie-Jo said she would make a start on the patio doors until one of the others was free to help, but they were not very enthusiastic and their chores were going slowly. Billie-Jo had taken a break to film their dog with a camcorder, while Annie continued to clean the utility room. Lottie had gone to a clarinet class, while Lois had taken the two younger children shopping.

'I WOULDN'T HAVE MADE MAJOR CHANGES TO HER BODY POSITION BECAUSE I THINK IN PART THE WHOLE SCENE FRIGHTENED ME.'

At about three o'clock Sion called to Billie-Jo and Annie that he had to go and pick up Lottie from music class and asked if either of them wanted to go with him. Billie-Jo decided she would carry on with her painting while Annie accompanied her father. Sion and Annie picked up Lottie and a friend of hers who was also at the music class, and after dropping her off at home at about 3.20 p.m. Sion, Annie and Lottie then returned home, but almost immediately were seen to leave the house. Apparently Sion had remembered they needed some white spirit from the DIY store. Rather than negotiate a three-point turn in a busy road, Sion headed off in the opposite direction which meant they had to take a route which went round the park. However, Sion decided that it would be too late anyway for Annie to take over the painting of the patio doors and decided to go back home. Annie made a fuss and said she wanted to have her turn, so Sion once again turned round and drove via the park. When they eventually arrived at the store he realised that he had forgotten to bring any money with him and so they returned home without having made any purchases.

When they arrived back at the house the girls ran ahead of Sion. Suddenly

Above*: Lois, Sion Jenkins's first wife.*

he heard Lottie screaming, 'Dad, Billie's hurt!' Sion ran into the garden to find Billie-Jo lying in a pool of blood on the patio, with an 18-inch metal tent peg covered in her blood, lying next to her head.

Sion panicked at the sight of his injured foster daughter and he did not know how to handle the two girls who were crying hysterically. His first phone call to the emergency services was made around 3.30 p.m., but for some reason Sion failed to carry out the necessary steps that could have saved Billie-Jo's life. Even though the 999 operator talked him through how to place her in the recovery position, he failed to move her body.

Later when he was interviewed he explained to the police:

> *I did my best, I tried, and I don't think it was good enough but at that moment when I found her it was too much for me . . . I wouldn't have made major changes to her body position because I think in part the whole scene frightened me.*

Sion panicked, not knowing what to do and at about 3.45 p.m. he phoned one of his neighbours, a woman called Denise Franklin, to ask for her help. He made a second 999 call, but as he was on the phone his children called out that an ambulance had just driven past the house. Sion put down the phone and ran down the road after the ambulance. The ambulance men tried desperately to save Billie-Jo's life, but she was too seriously injured and was pronounced dead at 4.50 p.m.

Strangely, while all this was going on Sion had left the house, leaving his two distraught daughters inside, and sat in his car until the police arrived. The first policeman on the scene was so horrified by what he saw that he had to leave and was later given trauma counselling.

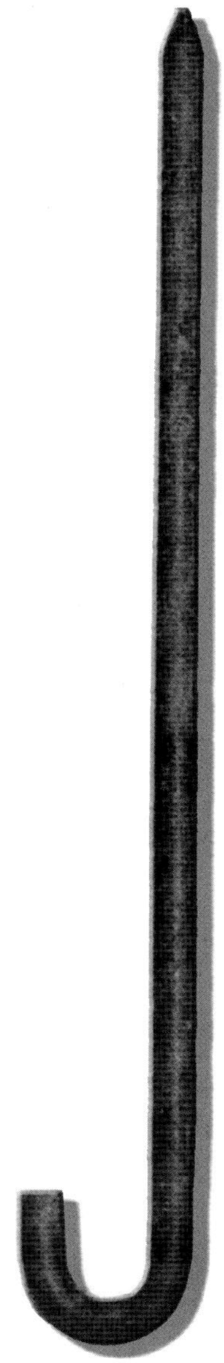

Right: *An 18-inch metal tent peg similar to the one used to kill Billie-Jo Jenkins, with which she was hit repeatedly.*

STARTING THEIR INTERVIEWS

The next day the police started interviewing the family and neighbours. The two daughters, Annie and Lottie, gave video interviews in which Annie said she clearly remembered talking to Billie-Jo just before she left the house with her father and that the gate that led to the garden down a side passage was shut at that time. At the end of this passage was a coal bunker, on top of which lay three metal tent pegs which Annie had put there after clearing out the utility room. She also remembered that when they returned to the house after picking up her sister, the gate to the garden had been left open. If someone had entered the garden by this route, the pegs would have been one of the first things they would have noticed.

'THERE ARE MANY THINGS I ACTUALLY DID AT THAT PARTICULAR TIME THAT NOW I DON'T FULLY UNDERSTAND.'

Many people in the street said they witnessed a man behaving strangely around the time of Billie-Jo's murder. He was immediately identified and was found to be a man who had a long history of mental illness. The police had already received reports from a family that their daughter had been threatened by this man, and social services had planned to section him the previous day but had been unable to trace his whereabouts. Following the murder, police called at his house, but his father said that his son wasn't at home and when they asked the father if he thought his son was capable of murder, his reply was that 'he regretted his son may have been responsible'.

FORENSICS MOVE IN

The forensics team were called in to make a thorough search of both the house, garden and surrounding area and the Jenkins's Hastings home immediately became a crime scene. The family went to stay with friends while the police carried out their investigations. They removed articles of clothing worn by Sion, Annie and Lottie on the day of Billie-Jo's murder to see if they showed any vital clues.

Adrian Wain was a forensic scientist who worked at the Lambeth Laboratory and, on Friday, February 21, he made a discovery that he felt was vital evidence. Under a microscope he had discovered spots of blood on the clothing that Sion Jenkins had been wearing on the day of the murder. In his report, Wain stated:

> *. . . these spots are typical of those I would expect to find following an impact on to a surface wet with blood. The size of the spots also indicates that the force of the impact was considerable and that the wearer was close to it.*

Sion Jenkins was arrested on Monday, February 24 and taken back to the police station for further questioning. This questioning lasted for over two days before he was finally released on bail. Sion, who had always been a respected teacher and family man, was now told that if he attempted to return to his home his children would have to be taken into care.

Dazed and completely bewildered, Sion had no idea what to do next or even where to go. He had no money with him, he was being treated like a social outcast, he felt that he was in the middle of the worst kind of nightmare from which he was unable to wake. He decided to go and stay with his parents who lived in Aberystwyth until he could get his head round what was happening to him and his family.

Right: *Bill Jenkins, natural father of Billie-Jo Jenkins. He spat at Sion Jenkins, verbally abused him and attempted to push him as the teacher was hurried into the court at Lewes Crown Court in East Sussex.*

Sion didn't return to Hastings until March of that year and was immediately taken back into custody. He was still professing his total innocence, but the police were disinclined to believe his story. To make matters worse, during their investigations, they had discovered that he had falsified his CV in his effort to get the job at the William Parker School by saying that he was a former pupil of Gordonstoun and that he had received a degree from the University of Kent.

Sion Jenkins was granted bail as long as he left the Sussex area and once again he went to stay with his parents in Wales. During the 15 months he had to wait before his case went to trial, Sion became a regular church-goer and returned to his old hobby of sculpture.

THE FIRST TRIAL

The case set by the prosecution was that Sion Jenkins had lost his temper with his foster daughter, Billie-Jo, and had bludgeoned her to death with a metal tent peg after returning home with his two daughters Annie and Lottie. They said his pretence of going to the local DIY store to buy white spirit was just a ploy, to give him time to make up a story that an intruder had entered the garden and killed Billie-Jo while they were out on an errand. They also stated that there was already a half-empty bottle of white spirit on the back of a shelf in a store cupboard, and although this could have been easily overlooked if it had been there for a long time, they felt it was positive evidence that his story was just a charade.

When Lois was cross-examined she told the court that her husband was prone to outbursts of violent anger and that on several occasions she had been slapped around the face when he got upset. However, the judge dismissed the evidence saying that it was inadmissible due to the fact that it had no direct bearing on the murder of Billie-Jo.

During the trial the jury were forced to see a video of Billie-Jo's battered body. Billie-Jo's natural mother, Debbie, fled the court in tears after watching the police video. There were cries of horror from the public gallery and the jury physically wept.

However, the decisive point in the case was the forensic evidence – the almost invisible spots of blood found on Sion's blue fleece jacket. In his defence, his lawyers disputed the fact that these spots of blood were the result of a direct attack. They insisted that

Below: *Billie-Jo's natural aunt, Margaret Coster (left) and sister, also Margaret (right) as they attend an appeal hearing to overturn Sion Jenkins's conviction at the High Court, July 13, 2004 in London.*

Billie-Jo had breathed the blood onto her foster father's jacket as he tried to help her as she lay dying. They stated that if he had in fact committed the attack, the blood spatters would be far more obvious and would cover a greater area of clothing due to the ferocity of the attack.

Technical disputes carried on throughout the trial in which forensic experts gave evidence of lung capacity and the speed and volume with which the blood would have been expired. This evidence which, to the layman would have been very confusing, would definitely have left the jury in a state of perplexity.

The jury deliberated through the night, but on Thursday, July 2, returned with a unanimous verdict of 'guilty' and Sion Jenkins was sentenced to life imprisonment.

As if the guilty verdict were not enough, Sion's wife and four children all ostracised him. Following their divorce, Lois moved her family to Tasmania and has done her utmost to shelter her daughters from the damage that has been done by Billie-Jo's murder.

SION MARRIES HEIRESS

Christina Ferneyhough was an art dealer who started to write to Sion while he was serving his sentence for murder. In her letters she expressed grave concern and doubts about his conviction and felt that he had been unfairly tried.

Sion, never stopped proclaiming his innocence or gave up his fight for a retrial, and eventually his perseverance paid off. Even though his first appeal failed in 1999, after further investigation by the Criminal Cases Review Commission, his case was referred back to the Court of Appeal. Sion was released on bail in 2004 on the condition that he reside with his parents in Aberystwyth.

Following his release Sion arranged to meet Christina and that was to be the start of a whirlwind romance. Without even telling Sion's parents, the couple got married in a discreet ceremony at St Peter's Church in Eaton Square, London, near Christina's £1.5 million home in Belgrave, in February 2005.

Sion's parents only heard about the news when a newspaper phoned his father to ask him his views on the marriage. This led to an argument between Mr Jenkins and his son, saying that he should have been told that the relationship was that serious.

Post-wedding celebrations took place in a country house hotel in Wales, where the couple drank champagne and, following a luxury dinner, retired to their room for about two hours. Sion then had to return to his parents' house under the conditions of his bail, where he spent the night alone.

Christina Ferneyhough, a divorcee with a 13-year-old son, is said to have inherited a fortune from her parents' estate in Hampshire. She was fully supportive throughout the retrial and Sion said of his new wife, 'I could not have made it without her. I am eternally grateful for her selfless support.'

'I COULD NOT HAVE MADE IT WITHOUT HER. I AM ETERNALLY GRATEFUL FOR HER SELFLESS SUPPORT.'

'I WANT TO ASSURE MY CHILDREN OF MY TOTAL LOVE FOR THEM. ALTHOUGH THEY ARE ON THE OTHER SIDE OF THE WORLD, NOT A DAY HAS PASSED WITHOUT ME THINKING OF THEM ALL.'

RETRIAL ON NEW EVIDENCE

New scientific evidence was submitted at the second appeal to Lord Justice Rose and Mr Justice Wakerley which severely undermined the original opinions given by experts at Sion's first trial. This time the report stated quite categorically that the blood spots on Sion's clothing could have been caused by exhalation, due to the fact that, after further examination, it was found that Billie-Jo's upper airway was blocked and that pressure had built up in her lungs causing a blockage. This meant that when the body was moved, even slightly, by her foster father, it could have caused the blockage to clear causing her to exhale 'passively' expelling the built-up blood. The report also said that if the original jury had heard this evidence, he felt sure they would have come to a different decision.

Lord Justice Rose agreed that the new evidence justified a retrial and said:

The offence of murder here alleged is of the gravest and, in our judgement, the public interest requires that a jury should decide the matter on the basis of all evidence now available, to the extent that it is called at retrial by the prosecution or defence.

Jeremy Paine of the Sussex Police said that it was a difficult case to prove and always had been, but pointed out that 'there is a case to answer and this court clearly thinks so'.

On February 10, 2006, Sion Jenkins's nine-year ordeal ended as the jury acquitted him of the murder of his foster daughter. He stepped out of court seven at the Old Bailey at around mid-day, realising that as the jury had failed to reach a verdict in his retrial, at last his nightmare was over.

Following the announcement, two women threw themselves at him, hitting him and leaving blood dripping down his chin. They turned out to be relatives of Billie-Jo.

COMPARE THE EVIDENCE

There will always be controversy surrounding the case of Sion Jenkins and perhaps the true murderer will never be revealed. Below is a brief description of the evidence that incriminated Sion Jenkins in his first trial, and the new evidence that forced the case to go to retrial.

EVIDENCE SUBMITTED AT FIRST TRIAL

1. On only one man's opinion, there were more than 150 minute drops of Billie-Jo's blood found on Sion's jacket that were consistent only with Jenkins being the murderer.

2. Jenkins had up to three minutes alone in the house with Billie-Jo when he could possibly have killed her.

3. The trip to the local DIY store was a ploy, taking the long way round to give himself an alibi.

4. There was already a half bottle of white spirit in the house.

NEW EVIDENCE SUBMITTED AT SECOND TRIAL

1. This time obtaining a second opinion, two forensic scientists argue the point that the blood on Jenkins's jacket could have come from air trapped in Billie-Jo's body.

2. Sion's two daughters, Annie and Lottie could provide an alibi showing that their father could not possibly have had enough time to kill Billie-Jo.

3. According to several witnesses a mentally sick man, who had been seen only minutes away from the murder scene, possibly with a fixation with plastic bags, was often seen stuffing pieces of plastic up his nose. A piece of a plastic bag was found up the victim's nose.

4. Evidence proved that Billie-Jo had been attacked from behind, if it had been as a result of a row with a family member the attack would surely have come from the front.

Below: *Sion Jenkins and his second wife, Christina, arrive at court on June 20, 2005.*

DAMILOLA TAYLOR
Too Scared to Talk

The killing of a 10-year-old boy in south London should alert British society to the fact that we need to address the matter of thuggery, bullying and violence.

Damilola Taylor was born on December 7, 1989 in Nigeria and grew up to be an exuberant young boy who loved life. Everyone that knew him said that he had a really infectious sense of humour and was a popular boy with many friends. He loved sport, especially football, and was an avid Manchester United supporter.

His sister, Gbemi, suffered from a severe form of epilepsy and in the summer of 2000 the family moved to England so that she could receive the necessary treatment. His father, Richard Taylor, who worked for the Civil Service, remained in Nigeria to support the rest of the family.

Damilola knew what he wanted to do when he grew up – he wanted to work in medical research to find a cure for epilepsy. At the age of ten he wrote:

> *I will travel far and wide to choose my destiny to remould the world. I know it is my destiny to defend the world which I hope to achieve in my lifetime.*

Damilola settled in Peckham, London with his mother and sister and was enrolled at the Oliver Goldsmith School in Camberwell. He made good progress in his classes and was popular with all of his teachers. However, it wasn't long before Damilola started to complain to his mother about bullying he was receiving from some of the kids in the area. He loved anything to do with computers and enrolled in an after-school computer club at the Peckham library, and would attend most afternoons when school was finished.

On November 27, 2000, Damilola Taylor set out from home to go to the

Left: *The parents of murdered schoolboy Damilola Taylor, Gloria (left) and Richard (right) with Damilola's older brother Tunde in the centre.*

Above: *Gloria Taylor (left) with a friend at All Saints Church in Plumstead, south-east London, for the funeral of her son.*

local library for his computer class, but he was never to return home again.

A BODY IS FOUND

The police were called out following the report that someone had found the body of a young boy on a stairwell at the North Peckham Estate. He was bleeding heavily, but despite the efforts of several passers-by and the ambulance team, they were unable to save his life. The young boy, Damilola Taylor, died shortly afterwards at King's College Hospital.

The man who found Damilola was Guillermo Casal, who told the police he had followed a trail of blood up the stairwell. He found a young schoolboy leaning up against the wall, but when he approached the boy, he told Guillermo, 'I'm ok.' But the boy then collapsed and Guillermo described how he held him in his arms realising that he was far from 'ok'.

There was a trail of blood from the wound in his leg, which led the police to Blakes Road, where they believed he had been stabbed with a broken bottle. From there he must have staggered to the stairwell, where he collapsed.

When the police studied the footage of a CCTV camera filmed just one hour before he was killed, it showed Damilola making his way to the library in Cronin Street, Peckham. He was dressed in a very distinguishing silver padded jacket and could be seen happily running along the pavement near the library. The footage started at 3.44 p.m. just one hour before the police found him bleeding to death.

When Damilola arrived at the library he was on his own, but there were quite a lot of other people in the area around the library. The police asked people to come forward if they were in the area at the time, but this did not produce any conclusive evidence.

It was known that gangs of youths on the Peckham Estate where Damilola died, made it a miserable place for people to live. Many of the gang members were violent and used to carry weapons such as knives. Some already had police records having been arrested for drugs, stealing or assault. However, it is very hard to solve the problem because the majority of the gang members were too young to take to court. It appeared that a lot of the people that were questioned from the Peckham Estate were just too frightened to give evidence against them for fear of incrimination.

At this stage in the investigation the police had two theories as to how Damilola received his fatal wounds. The one accepted by the Metropolitan police was that he was attacked and stabbed with a broken bottle. The alternative was that he had fallen on broken glass in an unfortunate accident.

In December several youths were arrested and questioned, but all were released without charge.

THE FUNERAL

Deeply shocked by the death of Damilola, hundreds of mourners attended his funeral on January 19, 2001. Among the mourners were several government officials and football stars including former Wimbledon player, John Fashanu and Nigerian player Kanu. The Nigerian High Commissioner, Prince Bola Ajibola, read out a message from the Nigerian Federal Government saying that the people of his country had been greatly touched by the death of Damilola.

In April 2001, more than 500 people marched through the streets of Peckham in a tribute to Damilola. The march was organised by several churches in the south London area and went from the Mountains of Fire and Miracles ministries in the Old Kent Road to Peckham Square, the last place that Damilola was seen alive. The march was also an appeal for people to come forward with information to help the police catch his killers.

Among the marchers was the local MP, Harriet Harman, who said:

> *The aim is to pray and then appeal to the consciences of people to cooperate with the police. We are walking together to create awareness.*

THE FIRST TRIAL

It wasn't until January 30, 2002, that four youths were brought to trial at the Old Bailey. The prosecution's main witness was a 14-year-old girl named as Bromley, who said she had seen Damilola being attacked. However, under cross-examination she was accused of being a liar and an attention-seeker and it was later revealed that she ran up a £4,000 hotel bill when she was being held under the witness protection programme. That led to the police

Below: *The grave of ten-year-old Damilola Taylor in Plumstead, south London.*

being accused of bribing the girl for information. The judge, Mr Justice Hooper, ruled that the girl was lying and therefore not a reliable witness and the whole case fell apart. The four youths were released after the defence suggested that Damilola's injuries were not those of an attack, but that they were consistent with him falling on broken glass.

Damilola's family were devastated that no one had been brought to justice for the killing of their son but the police, despite the setback, stated they were determined to keep the investigation open. Later that year the police said that they were reviewing all the evidence on the case, and that they were now using forensic techniques that were not available to them during the first trial.

NEW FORENSIC LINK

After the acquittal of the four youths for the murder of Damilola, spots of blood and fibres were discovered which linked three youths to the killing. These drops of blood, which were missed at the first enquiry, were found on a trainer and sweatshirt.

This led directly to the arrest of 19-year-old Hassan Jihad and two brothers who could not be named due to their age. The blood found on the trainer, which is believed to have belonged to one of the brothers, belonged to Damilola and there was also some evidence of blood that belonged to one of the brothers.

The second trial took place on January 24, 2006, when the three defendants appeared at the Old Bailey to face charges of Damilola's murder, manslaughter and assault with intent to rob. The trial lasted until March 29, when the jury finally retired to consider its verdict.

Once again the trial ended without any convictions as the jury returned a verdict of not guilty on all counts on Jihad. However, the jury was unable to reach a unanimous verdict on the manslaughter charge against the two brothers, so they were found not guilty. One female member of the jury physically wept as the spokesman read out the verdict.

On April 6, 2006, the Crown Prosecution Service announced that the two brothers would have to face a retrial

Above: *Britain's tabloid and broadsheet newspapers on April 26, 2002, with the story about Damilola Taylor, and asking questions about police investigations in the wake of another murder, that of 18-year-old Stephen Lawrence.*

'EVIDENCE NOW AVAILABLE POINTS WITH CERTAINTY TO THE CRIMINAL INVOLVEMENT OF THESE THREE DEFENDANTS.'

and while the older of the two has been remanded in custody, the younger has been granted conditional bail.

Damilola's parents were said to be in a state of deep shock when the verdict was once again returned as not guilty. Once again they had had to sit and listen to the distressing details of their son's death. To hear about it once was harrowing enough, but to have to sit through it all again with no end result is going to take them a long time to get over.

THE DAMILOLA TRUST

On the first anniversary of their son's death, Richard and Gloria Taylor formed the Damilola Trust at the suggestion of Peckham-born footballer Rio Ferdinand. They said they would like the Trust to help heal some of the ills that are faced by today's youth and help young victims of crime.

The Trust is trying its hardest to highlight the dangers of carrying knives through the use of music and fashion. The campaign motto is 'Respect your life – NOT a knife' and their aim is to convince youths that it is neither fashionable nor a tool to gain self-respect. It is hoping that their efforts along with those of the government will be able to tackle some of the anti-social behaviour that has been so prevalent in and around the North Peckham Estate and the nearby Five Estates.

RESPECT YOUR LIFE – NOT A KNIFE

NORTH PECKHAM ESTATE TODAY

The stairwell where Damilola Taylor bled to death still stands today, but it has been boarded up. It is not possible to demolish the stairwell until the trial of his murder is over as it is possible that there still might be some vital piece of evidence that has been overlooked.

Thousands of people still live on the North Peckham Estate and Five Estates, but over the past year more than 500 of the worst flats have been demolished by the local council in a redevelopment plan. This plan is an effort to tackle the lack of security and poor quality of housing conditions which came to light through the death of Damilola Taylor.

Below: *A memorial sculpture to murdered schoolboy Damilola Taylor is put up outside the Oliver Goldsmith Primary School on January 7, 2005, in London.*

CRIMES OF HORROR

CONSTANZO
Voodoo Murders

In 1989 a Texan student's end-of-term spree 'down Mexico way' ended with his nightmarish execution. He had run into members of a maniacal voodoo cult, as devoted to diabolic ritual as they were to criminal profit

The air of the American southwest is already warm in the middle of March, when the University of Texas at Austin takes its spring break. Students pile into cars and head to the border to revel in the bars of Brownsville, its beach suburb South Padre on the banks of the Rio Grande, and the cantinas of Matamoros, across the Gateway International Bridge in Mexico.

Mark Kilroy, Bill Huddleston, Brent Martin and Bradley Moore drove south on 11 March 1989. Five days later the four friends, all in their twenty-first year, all from the same hometown, Santa Fe near Houston in Texas, were still staggering around the hot spot in a collective euphoric haze.

Above: ***Constanzo as a young man in Florida. He was the child of Cuban immigrants who brought their Santeria religion with them.***

Opposite: ***Adolfo de Jesus Constanzo, handsome, charismatic and totally evil.***

Left: ***Mark Kilroy, a student at the University of Texas. A day trip to Mexico with friends had a horrific ending for him.***

VANISHED

At about two o'clock on the morning of 15 March, the boys joined the crowds of young Americans filtering back up the main street of Matamoros towards the border bridge. Martin and Moore had wandered ahead, and Bill Huddleston paused in an alley to urinate. While doing so he glimpsed Mark Kilroy talking to some Mexicans. When he came out of the alley Mark had vanished.

Rejoining his two friends at the bridge, Bill urged them to hang around in the hope that Mark would join them. When he did not, the trio walked back into Matamoros and searched the bars until dawn. Then they returned to their hotel in South Padre, before filing a missing persons report with the local police.

In fact, Mark Kilroy was in desperate trouble. Like most of his fellow American students, Kilroy shunned the company of the hard, streetwise Mexicans of his own age who drove around Matamoros in their battered pick-

Above: ***The shack on the Santa Elena ranch contained a bloodstained altar. The building was later destroyed on police orders.***

IN HIS DRUNKEN AND TIRED STATE, MARK KILROY WAS UNABLE TO RESIST THE MEXICANS WHO BUNDLED HIM INTO THEIR TRUCK

up trucks. But on the night of his disappearance, Mark was approached by a couple of young Mexicans, who asked him if he wanted a ride.

Slowed by alcohol and fatigue, Kilroy barely had time to reply before he was bundled into a pick-up truck between the two men and driven off down the still busy main street. Kilroy realized that he was in some kind of peril. When the driver got out to relieve himself, he summoned all his wits and ran.

But two other Mexicans were following in a Chevrolet Suburban station wagon. The American was dragged in and driven off once more, this time with a knife at his throat.

The leader of the kidnap team was a twenty-seven-year-old drug smuggler named Serafin Hernandez Garcia, who had turned to the profitable world of crime under the patronage of a Cuban Padrino – 'Godfather' – thirty-seven-year-old Adolfo de Jesus Constanzo.

Constanzo, his underlings believed, was a powerful black magician. He used the spells of Palo Mayombe, the darker side of Santeria, which was the old slave religion of Cuba, to confer on his illegal operations an air of invulnerability from police and rival gangs. He needed a blond-haired, blue-eyed 'Anglo' such as Mark Kilroy as a human sacrifice.

The two battered vehicles drove to a derelict smallholding named the Rancho Santa Elena, about twenty miles south of the border; it was the headquarters of the Constanzo outfit. Kilroy was tied up and bundled into a barn in which the gang stored marijuana. Meanwhile Garcia rang Constanzo, who was at a Brownsville hotel, to say that his sacrifice was ready.

What happened next was described later to the police by David Serna Valdez, one of the kidnappers. Set up inside a shack on the ranch was an altar, on which stood cheap images of Catholic saints, lighted candles, a chalice and seven strips of coloured cloth to represent the seven principal African gods.

LET THE CEREMONY BEGIN

At midday Mark Kilroy was given a meal of bread and scrambled eggs. Then, at two o'clock in the afternoon, he was dragged into the 'temple'. Constanzo was dressed in a white robe, with coloured glass beads around his neck. He was attended by Elio Hernandez Rivera, known in the underground world of drug smugglers as 'Little Elio'. Elio was also known as 'The Executioner' and bore brand marks on his arms, made with the tip of a red hot knife, to mark him for this role. The third man present was Alvaro de Leon Valdez, another of Constanzo's criminal lieutenants.

Mark Kilroy was brought in and forced to kneel over an orange-coloured tarpaulin, while Constanzo lit a cigar. The 'high priest' blew cigar smoke over the bound captive. Next he raised a rum bottle, took a swig and blew the rum out in a fine spray over Mark's head. The victim was thus 'purified'.

Then, as Mark knelt, Constanzo swung a heavy machete and cut off the back of his skull 'with a sound,' David Valdez

Left: ***The weapons with which Mark Kilroy was killed and butchered.***

Below: ***Titled 'La Padrona' (the Godmother) by Constanzo, Sara Maria Aldrete was once a straight-A student in Texas.***

later recalled, 'like a ripe coconut being split open'.

Constanzo then scooped out the brain and threw it into a cauldron which bubbled over an open fire. The cauldron, already containing a potion of blood, chickens' feet, feathers and a goat's head, was called a *n'ganga* – simply an African cooking pot. For a while, the 'priest' chanted over the sickening stew. Then he encouraged his followers to mutilate Kilroy's body, cutting off facial features, fingers and genitals.

Some three weeks after the terrible events at Santa Elena ranch, David Serna Valdez, who had taken part in the kidnapping of Kilroy and was known as 'El Coqueto' – 'the Flirt' – by his homosexual friends, was driving his Chevrolet Silverado when he came across a police roadblock, manned by members of the Mexican Army and the Federal Judicial Police – the Federales.

El Coqueto's reaction was to slam his foot on the accelerator and crash his way through, roaring off in his powerful car with the lawmen in hot pursuit.

CAPTURE OF THE UNCATCHABLE

Valdez drove like a demon, but the Federales were dogged in their pursuit and they were helped by the fact that Valdez was high on more than mere drugs. Since the sacrificial ceremony he was convinced, like the rest of the Constanzo gang, that he was under demonic protection and thus invulnerable to arrest and capture. He led the police straight to the Santa Elena ranch.

Above: ***Texas Attorney General Jim Mattox looks down at the blood-stained* n'ganga *which contained Mark Kilroy's brain.***

Above right: ***The shack at Santa Elena where Mark Kilroy spent his last horrific hours.***

There, Valdez was arrested, and in the ramshackle buildings of the ranch the police found a sizeable reward for their persistence. In addition to large quantities of marijuana and cocaine, they found an arsenal of firearms and ammunition and eleven brand new cars.

Also at the farm was an old caretaker; when the police routinely showed him a photograph of the missing Mark Kilroy, the old man nodded recognition. Yes, he said, the boy had been brought here some weeks ago. The old man had made him a meal of eggs and bread.

A computer search yielded the names and addresses of what appeared to be a large and powerful gang. Within days the police were making arrests. Among others hauled in were Sergio Martinez, known as 'La Mariposa' – 'the Butterfly' – along with Serafin Hernandez Jnr and Elio Hernandez Rivera – Little Elio – who was one of the most prominent names on the Federales' wanted list.

THE BODIES IN THE GRAVES HAD HAD THEIR FINGERS, LIMBS AND GENITALS SEVERED AND THEIR BRAINS SCOOPED FROM THEIR SKULLS

On Tuesday 11 April the Federal Judicial Police took the principal arrested gang members out to the ranch and demanded a guided tour. They found the evil-smelling shack with its breeze-block altar and orange tarpaulin, and noted the paraphernalia of Santeria.

They also found the cast iron *n'ganga* containing the now congealed and decaying lumps of vegetable and animal and human flesh in a soup of black blood.

Eventually thirteen bodies were discovered in nine graves. Mark Kilroy lay three feet under the ground and was identified only through dental records of his lower jaw. Most of the other bodies had been mutilated in a similar fashion to Mark's. Fingers, limbs and genitals were severed, faces obliterated, brains scooped from skulls.

The thirteenth grave was exhumed for the benefit of TV cameras and press photographers. The police made a gang member, Sergio Martinez, do the digging. The grave contained the corpse of a fourteen-year-old whose rib cage had been hacked open. The heart was missing.

With the grim secrets of the Santa Elena ranch laid bare, the police began an intensive search for Adolfo de Jesus Constanzo and his high priestess, Sara Maria Aldrete.

VOODOO CHILD

Constanzo had been born on 1 November 1962 in Miami, Florida, to Delia Gonzales Del Valle and her lover, both of whom had fled Castro's Cuba. Adolfo's father abandoned Delia and the baby soon after the child's birth, and his mother married a Puerto Rican, who brought the boy up as a devout Catholic.

When he was ten, his stepfather died and his mother reverted to old habits to make money. She was the daughter of a priestess of Palo Mayombe back in Cuba, from whom she had learned her craft. Now she began to practise as a magician again, casting spells and charms for the expatriate Cuban community.

As he grew up, his mother taught Adolfo the family magical secrets. But Adolfo also had natural charm and film-star good looks. By the time he was fourteen he had attracted a bevy of women to him.

In 1983, when he was twenty-one, Adolfo moved with his mother to Mexico City, where he became a male model. Soon he was a familiar figure in the city's fashionable circles. As a bisexual, he cultivated links with homosexuals in government and legal circles, and he began to work his way into the lucrative world of drug-dealing. At the same time, according to his mother, he was studying the black arts under a major 'santero' known as 'The Great One', apparently the most powerful magician in Central America. From him, Adolfo learned the use of human sacrifice.

Sara Maria Aldrete had been born in Matamoros on 6 September 1964 and grew up there. She married at eighteen, divorced at twenty and a year later, in 1985, was accepted into Texas Southernmost College in Brownsville on a two-year physical education course. The tall brunette was extremely attractive and soon caught the attention of Serafin Hernandez Jnr, a smart young man who made his money from the family trade of drug smuggling.

Above: ***Mexican federal policeman, Martin Solozar, examines human remains in one of several shallow graves at the ranch.***

Below: ***Police unearth dismembered human remains.***

The Hernandez family operated in two 'divisions'. Serafin Snr handled the USA side, until his arrest in February 1987. Serafin Jnr worked out of Matamoros for his young uncle, the feared 'Little Elio' Hernandez Rivera.

Sara Aldrete and Serafin Jnr saw each other at weekends, when Sara came home across the Gateway International Bridge to Matamoros. But one weekend in the autumn of 1986, a Mercedez cut in front of her car, and the handsome Constanzo got out. Using his easy charm instead of the usual Mexican macho approach, Constanzo invited Sara to a café and read her fortune from tarot cards. He told her that someone close to her would come to her with a 'terrible problem'.

Sure enough, two weeks later Serafin Jnr told her how the Hernandez family business was in danger of collapse. Sara was impressed by this demonstration of Constanzo's 'powers', while he saw an opportunity of worming into the confidence of the drugs barons of Mexico City. Soon he was Sara's lover.

Sara was now completely under

Left: ***Martin Quintana was one of Constanzo's many homosexual lovers.***

Below: ***Constanzo and Quintana lie together in death after their suicide pact.***

Constanzo's spell. During the coming months he took her to his Mexico City home, where he had already begun to dabble in human sacrifice.

SLAUGHTER: A WAY OF LIFE – AND DEATH

In the early part of 1988, acting on Constanzo's instructions, Sara seduced Little Elio. Before long she was convincing him that what he needed was the help of a powerful sorcerer to help him with his family problems. The drugs boss, as superstitious as most of his countrymen, needed little persuasion to meet Constanzo. And, like his nephew and his new mistress, he was instantly impressed.

Constanzo initiated him into the dark rituals of Palo Mayombe, branding him on the shoulders, back and chest with a hot knife to denote his new rank of executioner. Now, Constanzo and Little Elio became joint ceremonial killers, using one of Elio's gang hideouts – the Santa Elena ranch.

Gradually, true to Constanzo's predictions, the Mexican side of the drug business began to improve. Now they needed to place the US side on a solid footing once more. To do this, Constanzo ordered the kidnapping of an 'Anglo' for sacrifice, his white blood being deemed to have better protective powers over Anglo policemen than the Mexican variety. And so Mark Kilroy met his savage end.

No one knows exactly how many ritual sacrifices were made by Constanzo and his cult, but one informed estimate was that the total was nearer thirty than the thirteen discovered at the ranch. In any case, time was now running out for the black magician and his depraved coterie.

Commandante Benitez Ayala of the Federales led a posse of policemen to Sara's house in Matamoros even before the last of the Santa Elena bodies had been exhumed. Her father showed them her apartment and they burst in. Inside

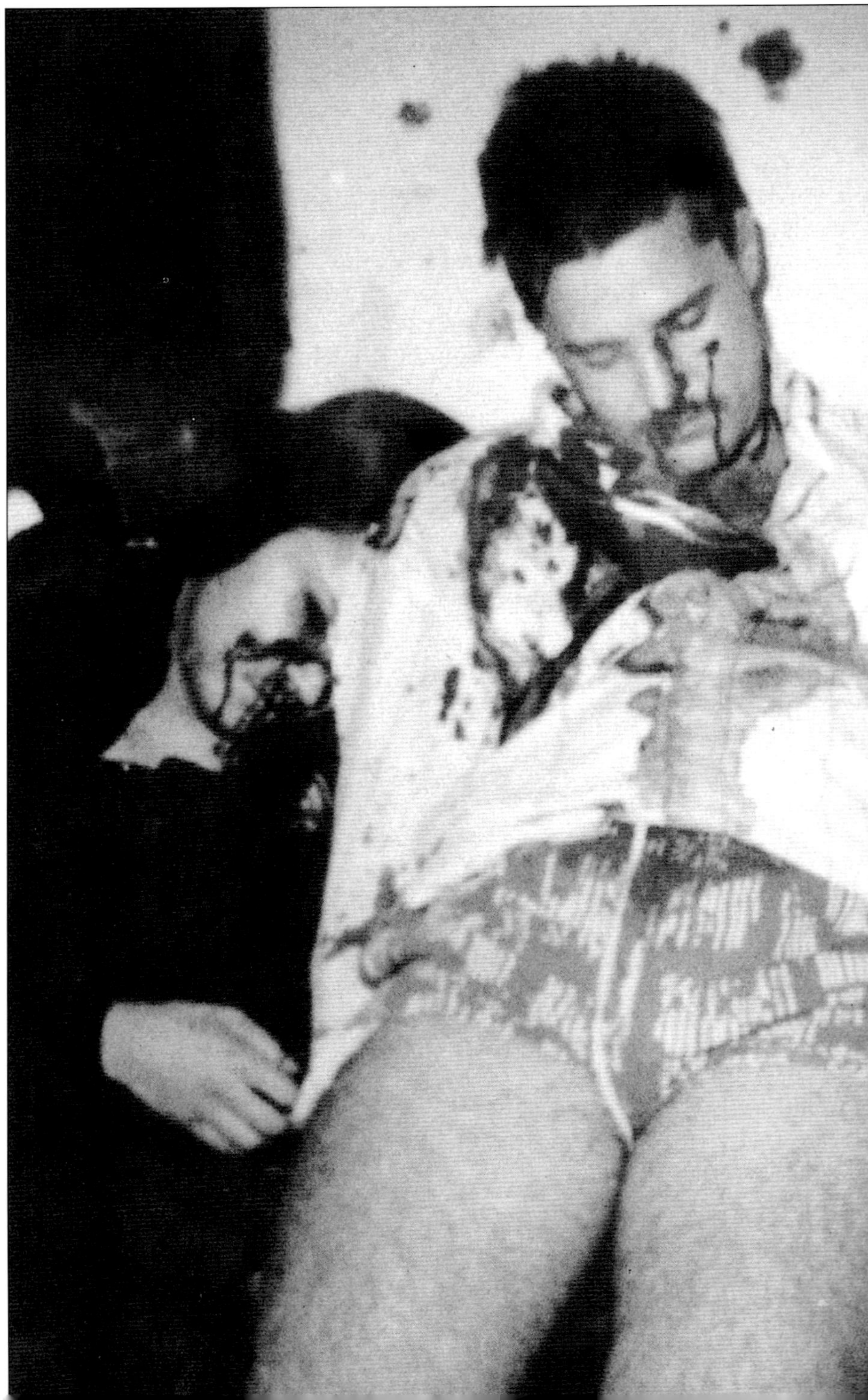

was an altar with candles, blood and bloodstained clothing – but no sign of the sorceress.

That afternoon Commandante Ayala, who himself kept 'white' Santeria charms on his desk at headquarters, summoned a 'curandero' – a Santeria priest. They went out to the ranch, and Ayala called an end to the digging. The curandero sprinkled holy water around the shack which contained the altar and chanted spells. Then he poured petrol over the red tarpaper of the walls, and set fire to the place, burning it to the ground.

As his black magic headquarters burned, Constanzo was on the run with his high priestess. Sara met him at Brownsville, where they boarded an aeroplane for Mexico City. When they arrived there, however, the Federales had already raided his flat, picked up notebooks which named important clients and laid a trap for him.

Constanzo, Sara, Alvaro de Leon Valdez and a number of others collected money at gunpoint from criminal associates, then drove in a convoy to the resort of Cuernavaca, fifty miles south of Mexico City. For three weeks they kept on the move, eluding police and police informers and finally returning to Mexico City by a circuitous route. There they holed up in a friend's apartment.

There is evidence that by this time Sara regretted any connection she had with the gang, and may have made an effort to contact the police. In any case, on 5 May 1989 the police became aware of a woman answering Sara's description, buying a large amount of groceries from various food stores. Gradually the police's net tightened.

On the morning of 6 May a lookout spotted a known police officer in plain clothes. Constanzo joined the lookout at the window and was able to pick out a number of officers moving into strategic positions. Suddenly Constanzo went berserk. 'They're here! Why run? Don't hide!' screamed the Godfather. He began to run around the flat, gathering up piles of coins and sheaves of US $20, $50 and $100 bills, flinging them through the window into the street.

Then, as passers-by ran forward to get at the money, he thrust an AK-47 out and began firing wildly, chipping chunks of masonry from the walls opposite and reducing a tamale cart to matchwood.

There followed an intense forty-five minute gunbattle, with Alvaro de Leon Valdez taking over Constanzo's gun while the Godfather himself continued to panic, burning wads of money on the gas stove and screaming, 'Let's all die!'

Finally Constanzo grabbed his homosexual lover, Martin Quintana, and hustled him into a cupboard, where the two men embraced before Constanzo ordered Valdez to kill them both.

After some persuasion, Valdez turned the AK-47 on to his chief, and sprayed the two men with bullets, killing them instantly. Valdez, Sara and the rest surrendered shortly afterwards.

In the early 1990s, the trials arising from the bizarre Constanzo affair were still proceeding. In August 1990 Alvaro de Leon Valdez was sentenced to 30 years for killing Constanzo and Quintana. Sara Maria Aldrete was acquitted on these charges but given six years for criminal association. Most of the other gang members remained in jail, awaiting their final sentence.

The reaction of Helen Kilroy, Mark's mother, to the horrors of the Santa Elena ranch was almost superhumanly charitable. 'I think they must be possessed by the devil,' said the Catholic Irishwoman. 'That is the only explanation for what they did. I pray for all of them.'

COMMANDANTE AYALA TURNED WHITE MAGIC AGAINST BLACK TO DESTROY THE VOODOO TEMPLE

'LET'S ALL DIE!' SCREAMED THE HYSTERICAL CONSTANZO AS HE BURNED WADS OF MONEY ON A GAS STOVE

Below: ***El Dubi is arrested in Mexico City following a shoot-out between police and Constanzo's cult members.***

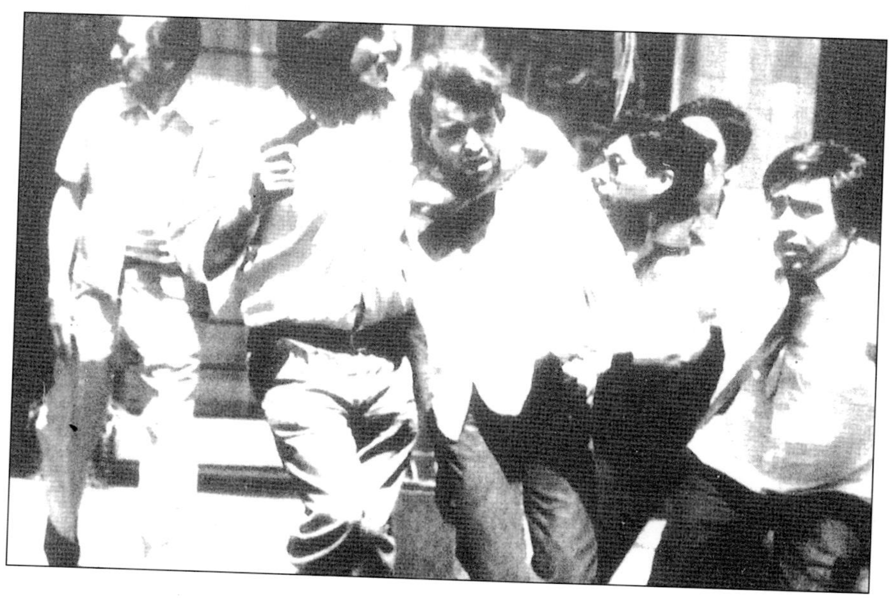

JOHN CHRISTIE
10 Rillington Place

Ridiculed for sexual inadequacy, the warped John Christie developed into a necrophiliac murderer, walling up his victims in a squalid London flat. In the process, he was a part in one of Britain's worst-ever miscarriages of justice

Right: ***The scene of the crimes. 10 Rillington Place is an address which will live in infamy.***

Opposite: ***John Reginald Halliday Christie found a horrific way to compensate for his feelings of inadequacy.***

In March 1953 a Jamaican couple, Mr Beresford Brown and his wife, received good news from their landlord. For some years the Browns had rented cramped rooms on the third floor of 10 Rillington Place, a decaying property in the Ladbroke Grove area of North Kensington in west London.

Would the Browns like to move to the ground floor? Mr and Mrs Brown were delighted. The ground-floor flat had a front room, a bedroom and a kitchen as well as a wash house, and the single lavatory shared by all the tenants was on the ground floor too. There was even a small garden out at the back.

THE NEW FLAT, THOUGHT THE BROWNS, WOULD BE FINE WITH A BIT OF REDECORATION. EVENTS WERE TO PROVE THEM WRONG

Below: ***The back room of 10 Rillington Place, where a body was found by police.***

The only slight misgiving was felt by Mrs Brown. She had often seen John Christie sprinkling strong disinfectant around the flat and along the corridor which connected the front door with the back yard.

There was also the reputation of 10 Rillington Place. Five years previously the second-floor tenant, Timothy Evans, had been charged with killing his wife and infant daughter in the house. He had been hanged for the murders in 1949.

For some days Beresford Brown worked hard, removing piles of old clothes, decaying furniture and general rubbish from the kitchen and heaping it in the back garden. Finally, on 24 March, the room was stripped to its bare walls. Brown began tapping the plaster of the rear wall, but it sounded strangely hollow. He stripped off a piece of mouldering wallpaper and found that it covered a cupboard door. Behind the wooden door was an alcove, and Brown's torch shone on the bare back and buttocks of a woman. She was hunched forward, and wore only a bra, a white cotton coat, stockings and suspender belt. The unnatural colour of her flesh, and the stench, clearly indicated that she had occupied her impromptu tomb for some time.

Right: ***The body of Mrs Ethel Christie was found under the floorboards in the living-room of 10 Rillington Place.***

The police came around quickly to continue the search. Behind the first body they found a second corpse, wrapped in a blanket, and beyond that a third, also wrapped in a blanket which had been tied with electric flex.

The search went on into the night, and in the early hours of the following day a fourth body was found wrapped in a blanket and stuffed beneath the floorboards of the front room. She was identified as Mrs Ethel Christie, and like the rest of the corpses she had been strangled.

As forensic experts were called in, the police called a press conference. They had uncovered, they said, the 'most brutal mass killing known in London', and they were looking for a 'vital witness'. His name was John Reginald Halliday Christie, aged fifty-four. He and his wife had lived at 10 Rillington Place since 1938.

> THEY HAD UNCOVERED, SAID THE POLICE, 'THE MOST BRUTAL MASS KILLING KNOWN IN LONDON'

Digging in the garden revealed two more female skeletons. The skull of one was missing, and the thigh bone of another had been used to prop up a fence. Meanwhile, undetected, John Christie wandered around London.

On 31 March, Police Constable V100 Thomas Ledger made himself the most famous copper in the land. On his beat near Putney Bridge he saw a short, middle-aged man in a trilby hat leaning over the embankment railings by the Star and Garter Hotel.

'Can you tell me who you are?' asked PC Ledger.

'John Waddington, 35 Westbourne Grove,' said the man.

PC Ledger asked him to remove his hat. The bald head thus revealed confirmed the officer's suspicions, and John Christie was under arrest.

YORKSHIRE ORIGINS

Christie was born on 8 April 1898 in Halifax, West Yorkshire, where his father Ernest was a designer for one of the town's leading firms, Crossley Carpets. Ernest Christie was an upright, no-nonsense Victorian figure, a founder of the Halifax Conservative Party.

Not surprisingly John, one of seven children, lived in mortal fear of his father. On the other hand his mother enveloped her children with affection. Four of Christie's siblings were sisters, three of them older than himself. They, too, tended to suffocate young John with perhaps misguided kindness.

John Christie went to Sunday School, sang in the choir and became a Boy Scout, rising to the rank of assistant

scoutmaster. At secondary school he was good at arithmetic and algebra and meticulously neat in his work. He was also good with his hands, making toys and repairing watches.

After he left school at fourteen, Christie's early facade of respectability seemed to crumble. One day, working in the Gem Cinema in Halifax, he was picked up by an older, sexually experienced girl and taken to an alley known locally as the Monkey Run. Christie failed to get an erection, and the girl spread the word; overnight he was known as 'Reggie-No-Dick' or 'Can't-Do-It-Reggie'.

There is no doubt that this incident had a direct bearing on the direction of his feelings towards women. 'Women who give you the come-on look,' he told a psychiatrist while in Brixton, 'wouldn't look nearly so saucy if they were helpless and dead.'

FROM PETTY CRIME TO MURDER

Sex was only the first of a line of disasters. At seventeen he got a job as civilian clerk with the West Riding Constabulary, but was sacked for fiddling the petty cash.

For the next few months he drifted from job to job, mainly as a clerk, until in 1916, during the First World War, he was called up and sent to France. In June 1918 he was gassed and invalided out of the army.

Marriage in May 1920 to a plump, amiable girl from Leeds named Edith Waddington seemed to do little to curb Christie's petty criminal ways. A job as postman ended when he was caught stealing money from packets and imprisoned for nine months. Two years later he was bound over for violence and in 1924, having drifted south, he was jailed for a further nine months for larceny at Uxbridge Petty Sessions.

For the next ten years, Christie's life continued its aimless course. Ethel left him, and for a while he lived with a prostitute until he beat her up so badly that he was sentenced to six months' hard labour. Magistrates called it a 'murderous attack'. It was not to be the last.

The placid Ethel returned to him, however, and seems to have kept him at least outwardly respectable as they settled at Rillington Place.

Despite his criminal record, Christie spent the Second World War in the Emergency Reserve as a special constable at Harrow Road police station in west London.

It was in the early summer of 1943, looking for a man wanted for theft, among the low-life cafés and pubs of Notting Hill, that John Christie met his first victim. Her name was Ruth Fuerst and she was a tall, dark-haired Austrian, a refugee from Hitler.

Curiously enough, Christie had a knack for drawing out confidences from women. He sat with Ruth in a café and listened sympathetically to her problems, even lending her ten shillings.

They continued to meet for several months. And then one hot afternoon in August, when Ethel was safely away visiting relatives in Sheffield, he invited Ruth back to 10 Rillington Place.

Above: ***Rillington Place in Notting Hill, an address made famous by Ludovic Kennedy in his book of the same name.***

IN SPITE OF HIS RECORD OF THEFT AND VIOLENCE, DURING THE SECOND WORLD WAR CHRISTIE WAS TAKEN ON AS A SPECIAL CONSTABLE

'I was rather backward and shy about the act of lovemaking on this occasion,' he was to admit, 'but she was encouraging.' The couple went to the Christies' matrimonial bed, and there, during intercourse, he strangled her with a piece of rope.

As Christie struggled to clean up the evidence of his act, the doorbell rang. It was a telegraph boy with a message announcing that Ethel was coming back.

Christie hastily prised up the floorboards of the front room and hid the body and clothes there.

Ethel returned with her brother Henry. That night Henry slept in the front room, inches above the stiffening corpse of Ruth Fuerst, while Ethel and Christie lay together in the murder bed.

The next day Christie removed the body to the wash house, and spent the afternoon digging a grave in the garden. Neighbours, he recalled, waved to him at his labours. Under cover of darkness he buried Ruth.

THE SECOND VICTIM

At the end of 1943 Christie, perhaps uneasy about what he had done, applied for a release from the police force. In January 1944 he took a civilian job at the Ultra Radio Works in Park Royal, Acton.

There he befriended a girl from the despatch department named Muriel Amelia Eady.

Muriel was thirty-one and a highly respectable spinster who lived with her aunt in Putney. She often sat next to Christie in the canteen, and soon, with his knack of inspiring confidences, he learned that her father was in the Royal Navy and she had a boyfriend.

The boyfriend gave Christie cover – an excuse to invite them both to tea at Rillington Place to meet Ethel. He had already decided that plump and homely Muriel was to go the way of Ruth Fuerst.

First, however, he had to find a method of getting her alone and subduing her without violence. In the autumn, he saw a solution to both problems. Muriel suffered from chronic catarrh, and Christie was able to convince her, with his knowledge of first aid, that he had a remedy.

In October Ethel went off to Sheffield again, and Christie seized his opportunity. He had rigged up a screw-top jar with two rubber tubes leading from it, one to a face mask and the other, secretly, to a gas tap.

Christie invited Muriel round, and, over a cup of tea, persuaded her that the apparatus would help her catarrh.

IN THEIR CRAMPED QUARTERS MARRIED BLISS COULD NOT LAST, AND SOON TIMOTHY AND BERYL WERE HAVING VIOLENT QUARRELS

Below: ***Chief Inspector Griffin and Inspector Kelly leaving 10 Rillington Place after the discovery of the bodies.***

Obediently, Muriel inhaled – the jar was filled with Friar's Balsam, to mask the smell of gas – and when she lapsed into unconsciousness, he carried her into the bedroom and strangled her during the sexual act. Afterwards he buried her alongside Ruth Fuerst.

At Easter 1948 a young couple named Timothy and Beryl Evans rented the top flat at Rillington Place. Beryl was pregnant, and the pair were eager to settle anywhere.

In October 1948 Beryl gave birth to a baby daughter. She was named Geraldine, and both Timothy and Beryl adored her.

For a while the trio were happy at Rillington Place. Unfortunately, it was not to last. The Evans, like other married couples in cramped quarters, had their quarrels, sometimes violent.

On one occasion, Beryl invited a girlfriend to stay. The two women slept in the bed, which meant that Timothy had to rough it on the floor. The following day a flurry of blows were struck. To make matters worse, Beryl began to neglect the housework, and the tiny flat became untidy and dirty.

THE ABORTION THAT WENT WRONG

In the summer of 1949 Beryl, to her horror, became pregnant again. She wanted an abortion, but Timothy and his mother, both Catholics, were against it. In desperation Beryl told Christie. He persuaded her that, with his 'medical training', he could do the operation.

Evans was furious when Beryl told him, but was somewhat mollified when Christie showed him one of his 'medical books' – an old St John Ambulance Brigade manual. Timothy, who was almost totally illiterate, was impressed by the pictures and reluctantly agreed to Christie 'taking care of' Beryl.

On either 6 or 7 November 1949, Evans came home to find Christie waiting for him. The operation had gone wrong, and Beryl was dead.

Without giving the bewildered Timothy time for grief or remonstrance, Christie told him that if he went to the police he, Christie, would be charged with manslaughter or possibly murder, as

Above: ***The house where Christie lived as a child.***

Left: ***Christie in his uniform. He served as a special constable during the Second World War.***

abortion was illegal. Slyly he got Evans to help him move Beryl's body to the second floor flat whose occupant was in hospital. Now Timothy Evans was an accessory to murder.

Christie promised that he and Ethel would find someone to look after Evans' baby daughter. He also promised to help Evans by putting Beryl's body down a drainage shaft in the street outside.

During the next few days, Evans sold the furniture – which was still on hire purchase – for £40, and destroyed the bloodstained sheets on which his wife had died. He then told Christie he was going to Bristol, but instead went to South Wales, where he stayed with his aunt and uncle.

CHRISTIE GOT EVANS TO HELP HIM MOVE BERYL'S BODY TO AN EMPTY FLAT - NOW EVANS WAS AN ACCESSORY TO MURDER

If Evans naively expected to leave his troubles behind and find peace in his native valleys, he was mistaken. He told his family that Beryl had walked out.

Finally, on 30 November 1949, he decided to go to Merthyr Vale police station. There, his habitual lying got him into an inextricable mess.

First, he told a detective constable that he had disposed of his wife. Then he said that it had been an accident, that, to procure a miscarriage, he had bought a bottle of chemicals from a man in a transport café in East Anglia.

He had told his wife not to drink the contents of the bottle, but she had done so. When he got home he had found her dead and had thrust her body, under cover of darkness, down a drainage manhole in the road outside the house.

The Merthyr Vale police contacted the Metropolitan Police, and men from Notting Hill station went to Rillington Place. The drain was empty. Faced with this weighty contradiction, Evans made another statement, implicating Christie in the abortion.

FRAMED FOR MURDER

When interviewed, Christie skilfully used his knowledge of the police mind to slip Evans into trouble while extricating himself. He told of the couple's rows and the exchange of blows. He said that Beryl had accused her husband of trying to throttle her.

A search of the premises revealed Beryl's body in the wash house, wrapped in a green tablecloth behind a stack of wood. The body of baby Geraldine was found behind the door, with a tie tightly knotted around her neck.

The Home Office pathologist, Dr Donald Teare, reported that both victims had died of strangulation. Beryl's right eye and upper lip were badly swollen and there were signs of bruising in her vagina, though Dr Teare omitted to take a vaginal swab. Had he done so, things might have turned out differently, in view of John Christie's sexual habits.

As it was, the police now viewed the case as a simple 'domestic' which had turned into murder. Evans was brought back to Notting Hill and made two lengthy statements in the course of the afternoon of Friday, 2 December.

In his first, he claimed to have strangled Beryl and Geraldine while the Christies were in bed. In the second, he added that Beryl had been getting deeper and deeper into debt. The Crown decided to proceed only on the killing of Geraldine, a crime for which Evans could expect little sympathy.

Timothy Evans's trial for murder began at Number One Court at the Old Bailey on 11 January 1950, before Mr Justice Lewis.

In the witness box, Christie won the judge's sympathy when he told him that First World War gas had left him with difficulty in speaking. He also impressed him with an account of his wartime service as a special constable.

In the end the jury took just forty minutes to find Evans guilty of murder, and he was sentenced to death.

Thereafter – to his solicitors, counsel, family, priests and prison officers – Evans maintained the story that Christie had killed both Beryl and Geraldine. Already there was some public disquiet, and a petition with about 1800 signatures was presented to the Home Secretary.

But no reprieve was forthcoming. On 9 March, 1950, a bewildered Timothy Evans walked to the gallows. To the end he repeated his protest: 'I didn't do it. Christie done it.'

Above: ***Timothy Evans, Christie's tragic dupe, gave himself up to police in Merthyr Vale and was shipped back to London to face murder charges.***

CHRISTIE ON THE LOOSE AGAIN

Almost two years after Timothy Evans's execution, the urge to kill came upon John Christie once again. This time, the victim was his wife Ethel.

On 14 December 1952, Christie was to claim that he was awakened by his prematurely elderly and arthritic wife having convulsions. To put her out of her misery 'in the kindest way', he strangled her. 'For two days I left my wife's body in bed. Then I pulled up the floorboards of the front room and buried her.' Afterwards, said Christie, he was sorry. 'From the first day I missed her. The quiet love she and I bore each other happens only once in a lifetime.'

During the few weeks after Ethel's killing, he sold most of his furniture and lived with a few bare essentials, accompanied only by his cat and mongrel bitch Judy, to which he was devoted. At Christmas he sent Ethel's sister and her husband in Sheffield a Christmas card signed 'From Ethel and Reg'.

That winter he prowled the streets and cafés of Notting Hill as he had done in wartime. By March 1953, he had lured three more women to their deaths in 10 Rillington Place.

The first was a twenty-six-year-old Southampton-born prostitute named Kathleen Maloney. After giving her the 'gas' treatment, as she lolled semi-conscious in a deckchair, Christie strangled her during sex. Then, after wrapping her in a blanket, he thrust her into the kitchen alcove and papered over the door.

A few days later, Christie struck again. This time his victim was a twenty-five-year-old Belfast street-walker named Rita Nelson whom he met in a café. She was gassed, strangled and ravished, then pushed in behind Kathleen Maloney.

Towards the end of February Christie came across Hectorina MacLennan, fated to be his last victim. Hectorina, a twenty-six-year-old originally from Scotland, was living with her lorry driver boyfriend Alexander Baker, but the couple had been locked out of their flat. Christie invited Hectorina back to Rillington Place, but was disconcerted when she turned up with Baker in tow.

The three of them spent an extremely uncomfortable three days together in the first week in March. Although the couple were lovers, Christie would not allow them to use his mattress. While one slept, the other sat up with him in the kitchen – for despite his necrophiliac preferences, a streak of puritanism from his long-gone Sunday school days in Halifax remained.

On 6 March Christie apparently accompanied the couple to the labour exchange. When Baker went in to sign for his dole money, Christie whisked Hectorina back to Rillington Place with him. When it was over, Christie shoved the still-warm MacLennan into the cupboard alcove, clipping her bra strap round Maloney's knees to hold her body upright. Then he sealed up the door again.

CONFESSION TIME

And then, it seemed, Christie had had enough of the dilapidated house and its mouldering ghosts. He fled, he was arrested and he began to confess – in letters to friends, to newspapers and to the police.

But even now the wily streak in his character was not subdued, for his very confessions were preparations towards the defence which he was convinced would see him clear of the gallows. He intended to prove that he was insane.

Christie's trial began on 22 June 1953 in the same Old Bailey court in which Evans had stood trial three years before.

Derek Curtis-Bennett QC, his distinguished defence counsel, was out to prove insanity on Christie's behalf. To this end Christie had admitted to all the women's murders, even that of Beryl Evans – 'The more the merrier,' he remarked. But, like Evans, he could expect scant sympathy for killing a child, so Curtis-Bennett tried to keep Geraldine's death out of the way.

The legal establishment were not, in any case, eager to awaken the spectre of a man who had perhaps been wrongly convicted and executed.

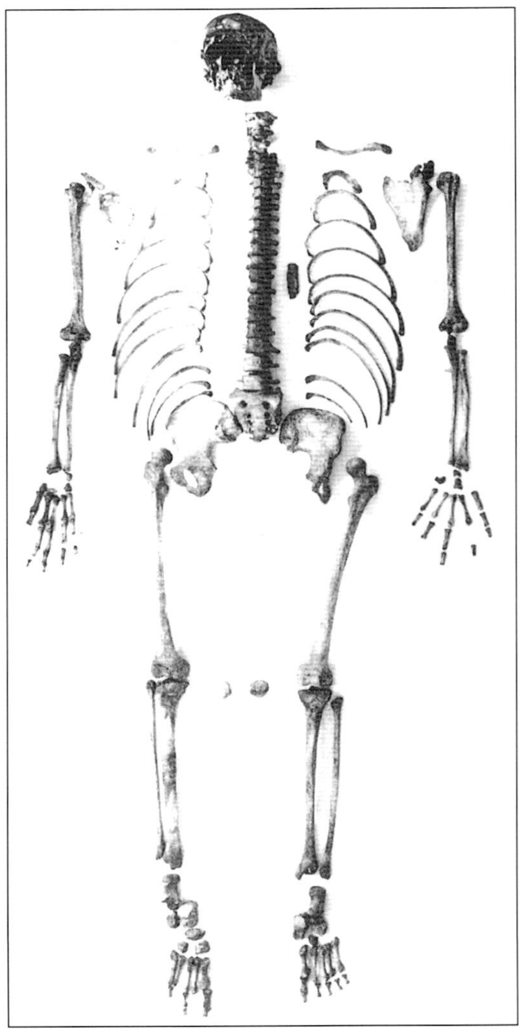

Right: ***The skeleton of Ruth Fuerst found in the garden at 10 Rillington Place.***

On 18 May, Beryl Evans's body had been exhumed from Kensington Borough Cemetery in Gunnersbury for examination by a trio of the leading Home Office consultant pathologists. The body of Geraldine, which lay alongside that of her mother, had not been exhumed.

The bones in the garden had been reassembled, and the heat-shattered skull of Ruth Fuerst was pieced together like a jigsaw puzzle. In post-mortem examinations, the bodies of Maloney, Nelson and MacLennan had been found to contain samples of Christie's sperm. But whether intercourse had taken place before, after or during the murders was impossible to prove.

In court, when he was asked if he had killed the baby Geraldine, Christie replied 'No.' He was constantly evasive about the evidence he had given in the Evans trial. In any case, despite the best efforts of his defence team, his trial lasted only four days, and at the end of it, on 25 June 1953, Christie was sentenced to death.

Above: ***The wash house where baby Geraldine's body was found.***

THE REVIEW OF THE TIMOTHY EVANS CASE HAD TO BE COMPLETED IN A STAGGERING TWENTY DAYS, BEFORE CHRISTIE WAS DUE TO BE EXECUTED

CAMPAIGN FOR TIMOTHY EVANS

Almost immediately, a clamour went up for a review of the Evans case. Under pressure from the Labour opposition the Home Secretary, Sir David Maxwell Fyfe, appointed the Recorder of Portsmouth, John Scott-Henderson, to study 'whether there is any ground for thinking there may have been a miscarriage of justice'. It was a monumental task which had to be completed in under twenty days, before sentence on Christie was carried out.

Surprisingly, when the hastily assembled report appeared it claimed that Evans had indeed carried out the murder of his daughter, as charged. But it added that he had also killed his wife. In other words, according to Scott-Henderson, Christie had told the truth at Evans's trial but lied at his own.

Although some criminologists have continued to have misgivings as to Evans's total innocence, a sustained campaign throughout the 1950s and into the 1960s by such journalists as Harold Evans and Ludovic Kennedy eventually bore fruit.

In 1966, a year after he had successfully called for the temporary abolition of capital punishment, Labour Home Secretary Roy Jenkins granted Timothy Evans a posthumous free pardon. On 18 October of that year, his remains were reburied at St Patrick's Cemetery in Leytonstone in east London. Four years later, capital punishment was abolished entirely.

Rillington Place lingered on for another half dozen years under a new name, Ruston Close. Finally it was demolished, and a new street, Bartle Road, built on its site. There is no number 10 at Bartle Road. A garden marks the spot, between number 9 and number 11, where the most infamous house in British criminal history once stood.

PETER KURTEN
Düsseldorf Monster

Vampirism, cannibalism, rape and torture were all part of the depraved Peter Kurten's repertoire. After forty years of violence, bestiality and blood-lust he became the first serial killer to be examined in depth by a criminal psychiatrist

Right: ***Passers-by read the news of another murder in Düsseldorf.***

Opposite: ***Peter Kurten was to become the most infamous murderer in the city's history.***

Below left: ***The flat in Düsseldorf where Kurten and his wife lived.***

Below: ***Kurten was regarded by his neighbours as a pleasant and likeable man.***

'I have no remorse. As to whether recollection of my deeds makes me feel ashamed, I will tell you. Thinking back to all the details is not at all unpleasant. I rather enjoy it.'

Thus, in the summer of 1931, spoke a polite, quiet-voiced, neat little man of forty-eight named Peter Kurten, who in a career spanning over thirty years had turned his adopted city of Düsseldorf into the murder centre of Europe. Kurten's name entered the annals of criminology through the fact that, after his conviction, he became the first serial killer ever interviewed in depth by a psychiatrist.

Professor Karl Berg concluded, after listening to Kurten's lucid and rational confession, that, though sane under German law, Kurten was a 'narcissistic psychopath' whose sole reason for being was the gratification of his own desires. It was the horrific variety of those desires that appalled the pre-Hitler German people: vampirism, cannibalism, bestiality, rape, sadism and murder in many forms.

PRECOCIOUS SEXUALITY

Peter Kurten was born in Köln-Mulheim in 1883 into a family of thirteen children. His father was a violent drunk, who often forced his wife to have sexual intercourse in front of his children. When finally he attempted sex with one of his daughters, his wife had him arrested and he was imprisoned.

But there is little doubt that a strange seed had been sown in the mind of Peter by the activities of his father. And that seed was nurtured by the town dog-catcher, who moved in as lodger when his father went to jail.

Kurten was a precociously sexual child. When his father was taken away he tried to molest the sister who had been attacked, imitating what he had seen his father do. The dog-catcher taught him to masturbate dogs and torture them.

Kurten was also a murderer very early on. At the age of nine, on a school outing in Düsseldorf, to which city the family had moved, he managed to push a friend off a raft. The friend could not swim, and when another boy dived in Kurten held his head under. Both boys drowned, but the blame was not lodged with Kurten until he confessed all to Professor Berg nearly forty years later.

At thirteen, Kurten began to practise bestiality with sheep, pigs and goats. Three years later he ran away from home to Koblenz, where he moved in with a prostitute. After stealing money from her he was jailed, the first of several prison sentences which were to take up over twenty years of his life.

EVIL FANTASIES

While in jail – much of the time in solitary confinement for insubordination – he began to fantasize. Once out, he tried an experiment by strangling a girl in a wood while having sex with her. As no body was ever found, it is presumed that this first victim, at least, escaped with her life and recovered.

By 1900 Kurten, just seventeen, was back in jail serving four years for theft. When he was released in 1904 his dark fantasies bore fruit. He committed his first recorded sex murder, getting away with it almost by fluke.

A ten-year-old girl named Christine Klein lived with her father in the family tavern at Köln-Mulheim, on the Rhine. One summer morning the girl was found dead, throttled into unconsciousness, and then slashed across the throat with a sharp knife. She had not been raped, but had suffered some sexual molestation.

Twice after the Klein killing, Peter Kurten struck down strangers in the street with an axe. Both victims survived. Kurten said he derived sexual pleasure from watching their blood flow.

In 1921 he was released from prison for burglary, and at his sister's house in Altenburg met his future wife. Posing as a prisoner of war recently released by the Russians, he wooed her with a mixture of sexual flattery and threats of violence.

Frau Kurten remains a shadowy figure. It appeared that she had been a prostitute for a time, and had been imprisoned for four years for shooting dead a man who had jilted her after promising marriage.

Kurten treated her with a kind of rough affection, and although he was unfaithful always returned. For four years the couple lived in Altenburg, and Kurten made an effort to reform. He worked as a moulder, became a trade unionist, and was politically active in the troubled days of the ill-fated Weimar Republic.

From time to time, however, he still went on the prowl, seeking out women either to beat or to strangle into submission. Often, if he achieved orgasm before they passed out, he would apologize, saying; 'Ah well, that's the way love is.' Occasionally his wife intervened to save him from charges of assault.

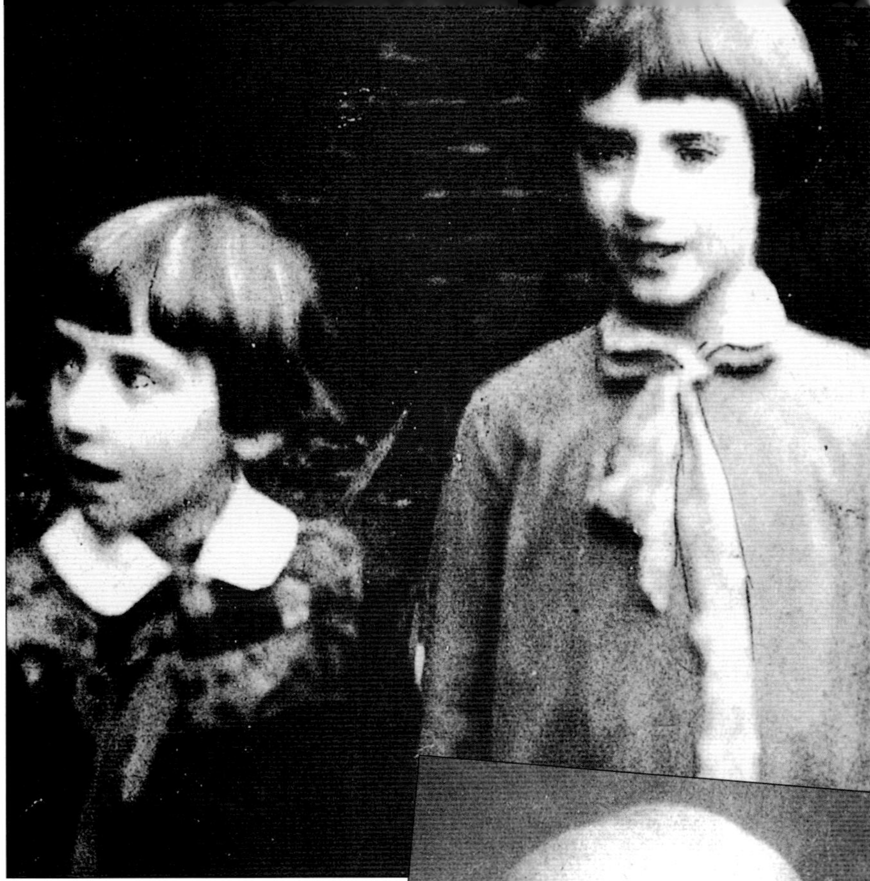

Above: ***Two of Kurten's intended victims who managed to refuse his enticements.***

Right: ***Frau Meurer was walking home one night when she was approached by a 'respectable' man.***

A MURDERER AT NINE, FOUR YEARS LATER KURTEN WAS INDULGING IN TORTURE AND BESTIALITY WITH FARMYARD ANIMALS

ARMED WITH AN AXE, KURTEN ATTACKED STRANGERS IN THE STREET - WATCHING THEIR BLOOD FLOW, HE SAID, GAVE HIM SEXUAL PLEASURE

NOCTURNAL ATROCITIES

Kurten realized, however, that his strange desires were growing again, and that Altenburg was too small a town for them to go undetected. In 1925 the Kurtens moved to Düsseldorf and settled in a top-floor flat at 71 Mettmannerstrasse. Almost at once, a series of sexual atrocities and murders made police aware that a maniac was roaming the streets.

They began on the night of 3 February 1929, when Kurten sprang from the shadows at a woman walking home and stabbed her twenty-four times with a pair of scissors. Miraculously, she survived. On 13 February, a forty-five-year-old mechanic named Rudolf Scheer was attacked on his way home from a beer cellar. He was stabbed repeatedly in the head and neck before being left to die in the road.

On the night of 9 March, Kurten had time to kill undisturbed. His victim was an eight-year-old girl named Rosa Ohliger, who was dragged behind a hedge and stabbed thirteen times.

Soon after this, Kurten had another lucky break. Two women were attacked by a man with a noose but escaped, badly bruised. They described their attacker as an 'idiot' with a hare-lip.

The police found a man named Stausberg who fitted the description. After confessing not only to the noose attacks but to the recent murders, he was confined to a mental home. For the next few months the attacks ceased and the police relaxed their vigilance.

But early in August 1929 they began again. Two women and a man were attacked as they walked home late at night. They survived.

Then, on the 24th, two children were found dead on an allotment in Düsseldorf. Like Christine Klein sixteen years before, they had been first throttled, then slashed across their throats.

That same afternoon, a serving maid named Gertrude Schulte was walking home when she was accosted by what she described as a 'pleasant-looking, ordinary man' of about forty. The man asked her outright to have sexual intercourse with her, walking by her side and almost pleading.

'I'd rather die!' said Gertrude. 'Well, die then!' said the man, and stabbed her several times before running off. She survived to give the police their first good description of the man they sought.

Kurten's next victim was not discovered until the late autumn. Another servant girl, twenty-year-old Maria Hahn, had been stabbed to death with twenty knife blows, and buried on the banks of the Rhine.

The following day Kurten returned to the site and dug up the body, intending, he said, to crucify it on a tree 'to shock passers-by'. But the body was too heavy, so, after stabbing it again, he dragged it to a new site for reburial.

Early in September a thirty-one-year-old servant girl named Ida Reuter was raped and battered to death with a hammer. A few days later yet another servant girl, a half-gypsy named Elisabeth Dorrier, suffered the same fate.

In October a housewife, Frau Meurer, was walking home when a 'respectable' man asked her if she was not afraid to be walking out alone so late at night. Before she could reply, he beat her to the ground with a hammer. The same day a prostitute was similarly attacked, but like Frau Meurer, she survived.

It was probably the sheer casual bravado of the attacks which kept Peter Kurten from arrest for so long, for by the end of 1929 he was the world's most

Above left: ***Gertrude Schulte survived an attack by Kurten despite being stabbed in the neck several times.***

Above: ***Frau Meurer was another who survived a vicious attack by Kurten.***

'I'D RATHER DIE!' SAID THE SHOCKED GIRL WHEN KURTEN BEGGED TO HAVE SEX WITH HER. 'WELL, DIE THEN!' HE REPLIED, STABBING HER

infamous murderer. Foreign journalists flocked to Düsseldorf, while police interviewed over nine thousand people and followed up a further two thousand clues. Still they got nowhere, and the attacks continued.

The last murder took place on 7 November, when five-year-old Gertrude Albermann disappeared. Two days later, Kurten wrote to the Communist newspaper *Freiheit* (Freedom). He enclosed a map showing the location of the body, along with a plan of the Pappendale Meadows with the position of another burial site marked.

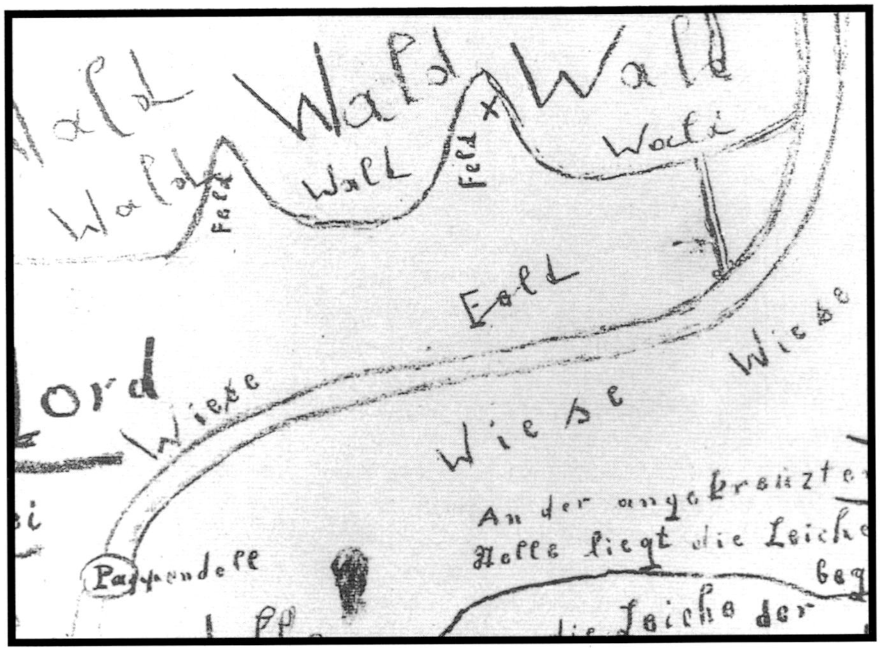

Left: ***Peter Kurten, the picture of respectability.***

Above: ***The map drawn by Kurten showing where two of his victims were buried.***

The police recovered Gertrude's body, strangled and stabbed thirty-five times. At Pappendale they exhumed the body of Maria Hahn. Among the hundreds of sightseers who watched as the police dug was, of course, Peter Kurten.

IDENTIFIED THROUGH A FLUKE

His capture came about by an unlikely chance. On 19 May 1930 a certain Frau Brugmann opened and read a letter which arrived wrongly at her address.

It was from a twenty-year-old servant girl named Maria Budlick who had gone back with a man to his apartment at Mettmannerstrasse.

During the course of the evening he had turned nasty, demanding sex. Frightened, Maria had complied, and the couple had copulated standing up in a doorway. He then led her back to a tram stop and left her to find her way to a convent, where the nuns had given her a bed.

In view of the intense police hunt then going on for a sex maniac, Fraù Brugmann felt she ought to hand this extraordinary letter to the authorities. A Chief Inspector Gennat, who was in charge of the case and was by now clutching at straws, sought out Maria Budlick. In turn, she led the policeman to the address 71 Mettmannerstrasse where the man had taken her, and showed

Gennat the empty room into which she had been led. On the way downstairs she met the man who had raped her. He went pale. Later, the landlady told her that his name was Peter Kurten.

Looking through his files, Gennat found that Kurten had been among the thousands of people interviewed after a woman had accused him of attacking her. So flimsy was the evidence against the respectable tradesman, however, that the police had fined the woman for wasting their time. When questioned, the neighbours assured Gennat that Kurten was a pleasant, likeable man whom children seemed to take to instantly.

Kurten heard of these enquiries and knew instinctively that the game was up. Indeed his behaviour suggests that, like many subsequent serial killers, he had reached a point where his principal urge was to be caught.

On 23 May he told his long-suffering wife that he was the 'monster of Düsseldorf' and had killed even more victims than the police thought – the final estimation was about twenty-two or twenty-three.

Frau Kurten's reaction was of horror and dismay and she suggested a suicide pact. But Kurten had a better idea. There was a large reward offered for the capture of the killer. If his wife could claim that, she could live in comfort. And so on the afternoon of 24 May, outside the St Rochus church and almost by appointment, Peter Kurten was finally arrested.

TEXTBOOK SERIAL KILLER

In prison, he gave a long and highly detailed confession to the police psychiatrist, Dr – later Professor – Karl Berg. He even admitted to setting a number of fatal fires in 1911 and 1912. Peter Kurten's confession was to provide the basis for later analysis into the minds of serial killers.

Most people, of course, were horrified when details of Kurten's career came to light, but many were not. For every letter abusing him which arrived at Düsseldorf jail, there was at least one other which was a love letter or a request for an autograph. Kurten revelled in them all.

His trial opened at Düsseldorf Criminal Court on 13 April 1931 and lasted ten days. His defence was insanity, but after listening to complex psychiatric evidence the jury retired for only ninety minutes before returning a Guilty verdict on nine counts of murder.

Kurten was sentenced to death. His lawyer formally appealed, but the appeal was turned down on 30 June, and the execution was set for 2 July at 6 a.m.

It was to be only two years before Adolf Hitler swept to power, but meanwhile liberalism ran deep in the dying Weimar republic and the death penalty was rarely used. The last condemned man actually to die was a double murderer named Bottcher, executed in Berlin in 1928. The German Humanitarian League protested against the Kurten sentence, and letters of support poured into the prison.

But for a killer of Kurten's notoriety there could be no reprieve – and in any case, the last person to wish for such an outcome was Peter Kurten himself. Execution in Germany was by guillotine, and he was fascinated by the instrument. Would he, he asked Dr Berg, be able – even for an instant – to hear the gushing of his own blood when the blade fell?

Berg said that he thought that this was physiologically possible, and Kurten was delighted. After eating an outsized last 'breakfast' of Wiener schnitzel, fried potatoes and white wine, the monster of Düsseldorf went to his fate smiling and replete.

UNABLE TO FACE BEING A MURDERER'S WIDOW, FRAU KURTEN SUGGESTED A SUICIDE PACT. NO, SAID KURTEN, SHE SHOULD TURN HIM IN AND COLLECT THE REWARD

KURTEN WAS FASCINATED BY THE PROSPECT OF HEARING HIS OWN BLOOD GUSH OUT AS THE GUILLOTINE FELL

Below: ***Kurten listening to proceedings during his trial.***

EDWARD GEIN
The Secret Hunter

Warped and perverted by an emotionally disturbed childhood, Edward Gein was to turn his small-town rural community into the centre of a ghoulish murder case – inspiration for *The Silence of the Lambs* and Hitchcock's thriller *Psycho*

Above: ***Mary Hogan, one of Gein's victims. She was running a local bar when she disappeared.***

Above right: ***Hogan's Tavern, a barn-like saloon, exalts its regulars to drink Blatz Beer.***

Opposite: ***Edward Gein, the handyman from Plainfield, Wisconsin, who was charged with mass murder.***

Below: ***The farmhouse where Edward Gein lived and killed. Bernice Worden's corpse was found here.***

The central plain of Wisconsin is one of the most melancholy and uninspiring tracts of land in the United States. It consists of flat, stony farmland about 120 miles square, fit only for raising scrubby cereal crops and equally lean livestock. In the 1950s it was scattered with dilapidated farmsteads clustered around a few small towns.

One of these was Plainfield, which, founded by German settlers in 1849, had grown in a hundred years to accommodate about 800 souls. In an area of clapboard houses and gloomy non-conformist chapels, about the only place of human warmth and interest was Hogan's Tavern, and even that was no stately pleasure-dome.

BLOODSTAINS AT HOGAN'S TAVERN

The tavern was presided over by its eponymous owner, Mary Hogan. She was a big, buxom woman in her early fifties with a broken nose and a colourful past.

She had come to Plainfield before the Second World War from Chicago, where, it was rumoured, she had run a speakeasy and brothel for one of the Prohibition

Above: ***Plainfield, Wisconsin was a small farming community. Founded in 1849, its population never reached a thousand.***

DURING THE DEER-HUNTING SEASON CARCASSES WERE DISEMBOWELLED IN THE OPEN AND THE BLOODSTAINED REMAINS ABANDONED IN THE SNOW

mobs. Most of the local menfolk would gather at Hogan's to drink beer and yarn away the long evenings.

On the afternoon of 8 December 1954, a local farmer named Seymour Lester entered the deserted bar room, stamping his boots on the floor and calling for service. There was no reply. Seymour's eye was drawn to a large dark patch on the floor leading into a back room. It was blood, soaking into the pine floorboards.

Seymour scuttled to the telephone and soon Wautoma County Sheriff Harold S. Thompson arrived, followed by a couple of deputies. A search of the premises revealed a .32 calibre rifle cartridge case near the blood patch. Further bloodstains led out through the back door and across the snow to where tyre tracks indicated that a vehicle about the size of a pick-up truck had been parked.

The cash register had not been interfered with, and it seemed to Sheriff Thompson that Mary Hogan had been shot down and spirited away.

UNEXPLAINED DISAPPEARANCES

It was not the first time that the area had experienced sudden disappearances. In May 1947 a schoolgirl from the nearby hamlet of Jefferson had vanished after being given a lift home by a neighbour. In November 1952 Victor 'Bunk' Travis, a Plainfield farmer, set off with his friend Ray Burgess to hunt deer during the Wisconsin open season. Both men subsequently vanished.

Of more interest to the men investigating the Hogan case was the affair of fifteen-year-old Evelyn Hartley, who had apparently been abducted while baby-sitting for a neighbour in November 1953. As in the Hogan disappearance, there were signs of a scuffle and bloodstains had been found leading from the house.

The Travis–Burgess case was perhaps the most explicable. During the nine-day deer-hunting season, tourists flocked in from Milwaukee and Chicago to track their prey through the snowy woodlands of central Wisconsin.

Many of them had little experience of either woodcraft or firearms, and accidents were frequent. In 1957, for instance, thirteen hunting visitors died in the Plainfield area from stray bullets.

At the best of times, the deer-hunting season was not for the squeamish. Hunters 'gralloched' their kill in the open, stringing up the carcasses from

trees, porches or any suitable structure, slitting up their abdomens. Edible portions such as liver, kidneys and hearts would be removed, and the rest of the offal abandoned. The empty husk of the carcase would then be lashed across the radiator of the hunter's truck and driven away for skinning and quartering elsewhere.

One of the few Plainfield farmers to express his disgust at this slaughter was a slightly built bachelor named Edward Theodore Gein.

LOVELESS CHILDHOOD

Gein was descended from the first wave of German settlers, though the two sides of his family were diametrically different in outlook. Edward's father, George Gein, was an orphan who had been brought up on a farm near the township of La Crosse by his god-fearing grandparents. In 1899 he had married. His wife, Augusta, ran the family grocery store in La Crosse.

A strict Lutheran, Augusta soon grew to dread and despise her husband's drinking and violence. Nevertheless the couple had two sons, Henry, born in 1902, and Edward Theodore, born on 27 August 1906.

In 1913 George Gein inherited his grandparents' farm near La Crosse, and the family moved out to work it. A year later they bought a larger spread just outside Plainfield. George Gein died of alcoholic excess in 1940, aged sixty-six, and was buried in the Plainfield cemetery.

George had given love to no one. Augusta seemed incapable of doing so. Instead of affection, she showered scriptural texts on her sons, reminding them constantly that they were sinners.

Above: ***Gein used Bernice Worden's own pick-up to move her body.***

Below: ***Sheriff Art Schley. The Gein investigation was his first murder case.***

Henry seemed able to detach himself from his mother's hide-bound views, but his brother Edward grew morose and solitary.

In the spring of 1944, Henry and Eddie Gein suffered a brush fire on their farm and were separated by the smoke. Eddie ran for help, and managed to lead a search party directly to where his brother lay dead. Henry had bruising to his forehead, but an autopsy gave the cause of death as smoke inhalation.

LONE SURVIVOR

Shortly after Henry's death, Augusta suffered a stroke. For twelve months Eddie nursed her tenderly back to what seemed like full health, but in December 1945 she suddenly collapsed and died. Eddie was left by himself in the big old 'L'-shaped timber farmhouse, with its annexe at the rear which he called his 'summer kitchen'.

He was known as a hard-working and honest man, but was not talkative. Unlike his father Eddie was never a heavy drinker, though he enjoyed the odd evening sitting over a beer or two down at Hogan's Tavern, and seemed to miss Mary Hogan when she was gone.

This point was made to Eddie one morning by Elmo Ueeck, who owned the Plainfield sawmill, when Eddie was over at the mill fixing fences some weeks after Mary's disappearance. If Eddie had taken a shine to Mary Hogan, Ueeck teased, why hadn't he said so when she was still around? Then maybe she would have been back at Gein's farm cooking supper for him, instead of being missing and maybe lying dead somewhere.

Gein, Ueeck was to recall later, rolled his eyes and shifted his weight from foot to foot, before giving one of his strange, tooth-baring, lopsided grins. 'She ain't missing,' he said after some deliberation. 'She's at the farm right now.'

Elmo Ueeck thought no more about Eddie's odd fancy. It was just the sort of strange remark he would make.

DEATH AT THE HARDWARE STORE

Three years went by, and the time of the annual deer cull approached again. One woman who always looked forward to the increased trade was Bernice Worden. A plump and homely widow in her late fifties, she ran Worden's Hardware and Implement Store, selling everything from agricultural tools to ammunition.

Bernice was now preparing to hand over the store to her son, Frank, who served as deputy sheriff of Plainfield, and settle down to enjoy her retirement in the company of her grandchildren.

Recently, Bernice had been vaguely troubled by the presence of Eddie Gein. For the last few weeks he had taken to sitting in his pick-up outside the store, or standing opposite, gazing across at her.

On Friday, 15 November 1957, just before she closed for the night, Gein had wandered in, looked around vaguely and asked her the price of anti-freeze. When she told him he wandered off again without a word.

Saturday, 16 November, was the first day of the deer-hunting season. When dawn broke, the town emptied of its menfolk as they made for the woods in their pick-up trucks, rifles racked behind them. Only one customer appeared at Worden's store as Bernice opened up at 8.30a.m.: Eddie Gein.

This time Eddie had an empty half-gallon jug, which he asked Bernice to fill with anti-freeze. He paid for it and left by the back door, while Bernice returned to the front of the store to fill out a sales slip with Eddie's name and purchase.

Above: ***Edward Gein adored his dominant mother. He professed to hating violence in any form.***

'SHE AIN'T MISSING,' SAID EDDIE OF THE MURDERED MARY. 'SHE'S AT THE FARM RIGHT NOW'

Below: ***Police found Mary Hogan's face and scalp behind rubbish stacked in Gein's summer house.***

At this point, according to Eddie's later testimony, he walked back in, picked up a hunting rifle and, while pretending to admire it, loaded it and shot Bernice. He then dragged her out to her own pick-up truck and drove off with her body.

Bernard Muschinski, who managed the filling station just down and across the street from Worden's store, looked out of his office at 8.45a.m. and saw Bernice's pick-up truck pull out from the store's back yard and roar away. At lunchtime he walked past the store and was surprised to see that the lights were still on, though the door was locked. Bernice he guessed was growing forgetful.

In mid-morning, Elmo Ueeck had caught sight of Eddie Gein in slightly embarrassing circumstances. The sawmill owner had chased a deer off his own property and on to Eddie's, where he had managed to shoot it.

He had brought his truck round on to Eddie's land to whisk the carcass away, when he saw Eddie's old Ford sedan bouncing down the rutted track towards him. Eddie clearly saw the dead deer tied across Ueeck's front fender, but merely gave a friendly wave and roared past in a flurry of frozen slush. At lunchtime he drove back to apologize, but Eddie

cheerfully waved away Elmo Ueeck's explanation.

That afternoon Bob Hill and his sister Darlene, Eddie's cousins, walked across to see him. They wanted him to run them into town to pick up a new car battery, as theirs had gone flat.

Gein stepped out briskly on to the porch to greet them. He was in his shirtsleeves and, to their surprise, his hands and arms were dappled with blood.

Bob knew of Gein's often expressed horror of blood and butchery, but his cousin seemed calm as he told them he had been dressing a deer. After going indoors to wash his hands, he came out and drove them into Plainfield. When he drove them back home, their mother, Irene, invited him to stay for supper.

Meanwhile, Frank Worden had called at Bernard Muschinski's gas station to fill up his car. There he heard that his mother's store was still locked, though the lights were on.

Frank opened the door with a spare key and viewed the scene with a sinking heart. There was a large patch of blood on the floor, and the cash register had been torn from its screws on the counter.

He rang the new sheriff of Wautoma County, thirty-two-year-old Art Schley, and then set about searching the store. By the time Schley arrived, Frank had found his mother's last sales slip. It had Gein's name on it.

'He's done something to her,' Worden told the sheriff and his deputy.

'Who?' the sheriff asked.

Worden held out the docket. 'Ed Gein,' he said. Sheriff Schley put out a radio call for Gein to be brought in, as news of the dramatic and not unprecedented events spread around the town.

Up at the Hills' farm, Eddie Gein was just finishing his supper when a neighbour called by with the news of the disappearance.

'It must have been somebody pretty cold-blooded,' commented Eddie.

Irene Hill turned to her cousin. 'How come,' she asked jocularly, 'that every time someone gets banged on the head and hauled away, you're always around?

In reply, she was to remember, Gein shrugged his shoulders and grinned his toothy grin.

Bob Hill suggested that he and Eddie should drive into town to see what was going on. Gein cheerfully agreed, but as the two men stepped across the freezing, starlit yard a police squad car skidded to a stop. Traffic Officer Dan Chase and

Above: ***A police officer sorts through trash in Gein's kitchen. It was described by one writer as 'mental disorder as decor'.***

A WOMAN'S BODY WAS HANGING BY ITS HEELS FROM THE RAFTERS – SHE HAD BEEN BEHEADED AND DISEMBOWELLED JUST LIKE A DEER

Deputy 'Poke' Spees got out, and Gein was taken in for questioning.

On the way into town, Chase asked him what he had been doing that day. Gein told him. Questioned on details, however, Gein became muddled, and then said: 'Somebody framed me.'

'Framed you for what?' Chase asked.

'Well, about Mrs Worden,' Gein replied. 'She's dead, ain't she? I heard it. They told me in there.'

SECRETS OF THE 'SUMMER KITCHEN'

With Gein in custody, Sheriff Schley called in a more experienced colleague, Captain Lloyd Schoephoerster of the nearby Green Lake County Sheriff's office. Together they drove to Gein's farmhouse. The yard was dark and deserted as the headlights of their car illuminated the dark wooden walls of Gein's 'summer kitchen'.

Flashlights in hand, the two men walked up the steps and pushed open the creaking door. As he entered the room, Art Schley felt something brush his shoulder. He whirled around. The beam of his torch fell on the bloody stump of a human neck. It belonged to the naked torso of a stout woman, hanging by the tendons of her heels from the rafters. She had been beheaded and cleanly disembowelled – 'gralloched' like a deer.

When the two officers had radioed for reinforcements, they ventured back into the house. They could find no lights, and until a mobile generator was rigged they and their helpers searched by torchlight.

THE HORRIFIED POLICE REALIZED THAT GEIN'S CLOTHING, FURNITURE AND HOUSEHOLD EFFECTS HAD ALL BEEN FASHIONED FROM HUMAN SKIN

It was a cesspit, a rotting rubbish dump of old metal and organic remains. Apart from the grisly corpse hanging from the ceiling there were piles of old clothes, dirty pans and dishes, broken chairs, dusty packages of half-eaten, mouldering food, and heaps of gaudy-covered magazines.

These proved to be a mixture of garish horror comics which dealt with stories of torture and flagellation, war crimes and 'true' detective magazines, and more or less 'straight' pornography. The kitchen sink was filled with sand, and there was a sinister, grinning row of dentures on the mantlepiece.

The full horror of the scene was only revealed when the generator was rigged. As the powerful light chased shadows away, it shone in the eye sockets of a number of skulls. Some lay tumbled under the table, others had been sawn in half and were apparently used as bowls. Two of them were impaled on the posts of a rag- and fur-strewn bed in which Gein presumably slept.

Then came the skin. As forensic scientists arrived and poked around in the growing dawn, they realized that a kitchen chair had a seat of human hide. Soon they had turned up lampshades, the sheath of a hunting knife, a drum, a bracelet and a wastepaper basket – all made from crudely tanned human skin.

There was a skin shirt, the pendulous dried breasts still attached, clearly made from the top half of a woman's body, and several pairs of human skin 'leggings'. And in cardboard boxes were bones and pieces of dried flesh, the debris of this ghoulish tannery.

But the biggest shocks were still to come, for Eddie Gein had a collection of 'shrunken heads'. They hung on the walls of his bedroom, some by their hair, some from hooks thrust through their ears. Gein had obviously peeled the flesh away from the skulls and stuffed the resulting faces and scalps with old rags and newspapers. All seemed, by the length of the hair, to be women's faces. One bore the still recognizable features of Mary Hogan.

By now the heat of the arc lamps had made the stench almost unbearable, despite the freezing weather outside. But the searchers had a few more vital items to discover. They finally found them in and around the cold and rusted kitchen stove.

Bernice Worden's heart was in a plastic bag and the rest of her entrails lay nearby, wrapped in an old coat. In a meal bag lay her head, bloodied around the nostrils but with a strangely peaceful expression on her face. Her ears, however, had already been pierced with hanging hooks...

Less dramatic, but still surprising, was the main part of the house. This, locked and boarded off from the chamber of horrors at the rear, proved to be a perfectly ordinary, though dust-covered,

Left: ***November 1957 – Edward Gein stands handcuffed on the farmland where human remains were discovered.***

family home. It was a shrine to Augusta Gein, untouched and unseen by outside eyes since her death over a decade previously.

During the morning of Sunday, 17 November, the human relics from Gein's hellish kitchen were bagged and tagged and despatched to Gault's Funeral Home for post-mortem examination. Gein, meanwhile, sat silently in the town's jailhouse, his stubbled jaw hanging and his eyes rolling damply.

For twelve hours he uttered not a word, even when Sheriff Schley, fresh from the mayhem of the ranch, lost control and struck him. During the afternoon, however, an initial autopsy showed that Bernice Worden had been shot in the head with a .22 bullet.

NEED FOR HUMAN REMAINS

On 18 November, Monday morning, Gein slowly began to reply to the questioning of the local District Attorney, Earl Kileen. He confessed to having shot Mrs Worden and loaded her body into her own pick-up truck, along with the cash register which, he said, he wanted to 'strip down to see how it worked'.

After dumping the pick-up in the woods near his home, he had transferred the body to his Ford sedan and strung it up with a sharpened branch through the ankle tendons. He had bled the corpse into a bucket, afterwards burying the fresh blood in the ground. Asked by Kileen if he thought he had been dressing a deer, he replied, 'That is the only explanation I can think of.'

Mrs Worden, he claimed, was the only person he ever remembered killing, but during the past few years he had felt the need for human remains. Sometimes he watched the newspapers for the funerals of people he knew had died, and then went to the graveyard and stole the corpses. He always, he claimed, 'then left the graves in apple-pie order'.

Which neatly introduced a topic that had preyed on Kileen's mind. Had Gein ever eaten any parts of the corpses?

The farmer looked genuinely horrified, and vigorously shook his head.

Had he then ever had sexual relations with any of them?

'No! No!' replied Gein. 'In any case, they smelt too bad.'

That afternoon Gein was held on a charge of armed robbery – stealing the cash register – and then spent the rest of the day helping the police with their enquiries.

He pointed out the spot where he had poured away Bernice Worden's blood. Later he was interviewed about the four-year mystery of the disappearance of Evelyn Hartley, the fifteen-year-old baby sitter. Gein seemed never to have heard of her.

When questioned about Mary Hogan, however, whose head had been found on his premises, Gein lapsed into silence again. Then, in a faltering voice, he admitted that he had 'called into her bar for a drink, once or twice'.

The following day, Tuesday, the hoard of pressmen which had converged on Plainfield and had been filing wildly speculative stories ever since, was finally allowed up to Gein's property. Sheriff Schley promptly got into a fist fight with a number of reporters.

Gein was taken to the State Central Crime Laboratory in the state capital, Madison, for lie detector tests. Strapped to the equipment for almost nine hours, Eddie Gein readily admitted to making and wearing the 'garments' of human skin, and said that he thought that he 'may have murdered Mary Hogan, but was very hazy' about it.

On the subject of Bernice Worden, however, he claimed that this was an accident. He was to keep up the protest for the remainder of his life.

On Thursday, 21 November, Gein was formally charged with the first degree murders of Worden and Hogan. His attorney entered a plea of insanity, and the judge committed the accused to the Central State Hospital for the Criminally Insane in Waupun, pending psychological tests.

By now, DA Kileen had obtained from Gein a list of the persons whose graves he remembered robbing, and the focus of interest moved to Plainfield Town Cemetery. Pat Danna, the sexton, claimed that none of the graves had been disturbed, but the exhumation party chose to examine the tomb of Mrs Eleanor Adams – who was, coincidentally, buried a few feet from Gein's parents. (Later it was explained that, had he tried to disturb his own mother, he would have to break into a concrete vault to get at her.)

As the frozen soil was scraped away from Mrs Adams's casket, the lid was seen to be split in two. The coffin itself proved to be empty except for rotting bits of burial shroud and a 12-inch steel crowbar.

Digging continued at Gein's farm. In a rubbish dump, the near complete skeleton of a woman with a gold tooth was discovered. In another burial trench a jumbled mass of bones had been interred.

After further lie detector and psychological tests, forensic scientist Joe Wilimovski became convinced that Gein had killed only Hogan and Worden, and had otherwise confined his hobby of

Above: ***Gein was incarcerated in Mendota Mental Health Institute, a gothic pile near Madison, Wisconsin.***

Right: ***Sheriff Art Schley steers Edward Gein into the Central State Hospital at Waupun, Wisconsin.***

GEIN WAS APPALLED WHEN THE DISTRICT ATTORNEY ASKED IF HE HAD EVER EATEN CORPSES OR MADE LOVE TO THEM

mutilation to the bodies of already dead women. Nine corpses had by now been assembled from the unidentified portions, all of them middle-aged women.

During his questioning, Gein spoke calmly and apparently rationally about the dismemberments and flayings. He seemed to find little wrong with what he had done, and was apparently rather proud of his unsuspected anatomical knowledge.

The standard Wechsler adult intelligence test showed that Eddie Gein was 'quite bright' and in some ways above average, except for his almost total inability to communicate with other people in any but the most basic terms.

Psychologists at the hospital put this down to a 'severe emotional disturbance' in his early development. This had retarded his normal sexual-emotional development causing him to retreat into a bizarre fantasy world in which his sexual urges became confused by grief over the death of his mother, combined with fear of transgressing the strait-laced moral code she had imbued in him while she was alive.

As one expert, Dr Milton Miller, put it: 'In many ways, the patient has lived a psychotic life for years. He has substituted human parts for the companionship of human beings.'

On 6 January 1958, as Eddie Gein sat blankly chewing gum, Circuit Judge Herbert Bunde briefly heard the comments of three psychologists and committed him indefinitely to the state hospital. Almost three months later Gein's farm, which was due to be put up for auction, was mysteriously consumed by fire while many of Plainfield's leading citizens – including Deputy Sheriff Frank Worden – looked on. Gein's comment was: 'Just as well.'

As the Gein case unfolded, Robert Bloch, a writer living in Weyauwega, 30 miles east of Plainfield, followed it with interest. He was intrigued by the psychologists' report that the influence of a long-dead mother could drive a man to commit such strange and inhuman crimes.

But, like other Mid-West dwellers, he was even more astonished that 'a ghoulish killer with perverted sexual appetites could flourish almost openly in a small rural community where everybody prides himself on knowing everyone else's business'.

Bloch's resulting novel *Psycho* was filmed by Alfred Hitchcock in 1960. And nearly thirty years later another novel-based film, *The Silence of the Lambs*, which featured a man who made suits out of female skin, also echoed the bizarre doings at Plainfield.

In January 1968, District Judge Robert Gollmar heard from the hospital authorities that their patient was now deemed sufficiently sane to stand trial, and Eddie Gein was marched into the dock. It was a short-lived appearance. Eddie was found guilty but insane, and returned to hospital.

There, despite being a model inmate, he was to remain for the rest of his life. He died in the geriatrics wing of Mendota Mental Health Institute on 26 July 1984, and was buried in an unmarked grave at Plainfield, beside his mother.

ONE NIGHT THE FARM BURNT DOWN, WATCHED BY PROMINENT PLAINFIELD CITIZENS. 'JUST AS WELL,' WAS GEIN'S COMMENT FROM THE MENTAL HOSPITAL

Below: ***Edward Gein awaits the start of his unsuccessful petition for release from Central State Hospital in 1974.***

ED KEMPER
The Headhunter

He started with family pets. Then he moved on to assorted hitch-hikers, his grandmother and mother, carving up the bodies to prevent detection.
Ed Kemper was a paranoid schizophrenic with a John Wayne macho fixation, and he was loose in California

Someone, in a state so conscious of psychiatry, psychotherapy and general mental maintainance as California, should have spotted Ed Kemper sooner. He started young enough, after all.

When he was nine years old, Ed buried the family cat alive in the back yard. Later he dug up its body, cut off its head, stuck it on a pole and, taking the strange totem to his bedroom, prayed to it.

In 1961, when he was thirteen and in summer camp, Ed was taught to shoot. He celebrated by shooting dead a

Left: ***Kemper arriving at court.***

Opposite: ***Edmund Emil Kemper III, the six-foot-nine giant who loved killing things.***

ALL HIS LIFE ED KEMPER BELIEVED HE BEHAVED REASONABLY SO LONG AS NO ONE CROSSED HIM – AND THE SIAMESE CAT HAD CROSSED HIM

Below: ***609A Ord Drive in Aptos, California was the Kempers' comfortable lower-middle-class home.***

classmate's pet dog. But instead of it giving him a macho image – his hero John Wayne was fast with a gun, but always popular – Kemper was reviled for the deed.

Shortly afterwards he wreaked revenge on the new family pet, a Siamese cat. This time he sliced off the top of the animal's skull with a machete, and then stabbed the body. Parts of the cat were hidden in his bedroom cupboard.

BIZARRE BACKGROUND

But if Ed was odd, his family were at least partly to blame.

Ed – Edmund Emil Kemper III, known at home as 'Guy' – was the only son of an ex-Marine who had served with the Special Forces Unit in Europe during the Second World War. Ed III was born on 18 December 1948, and worshipped his 6 ft 8 ins tall father.

In 1957 the father, who despite his size tended to be dominated by Ed's mother Clarnell, left his wife and three young children for another woman. Clarnell sold the family home in California, and moved to Helena, Montana.

Clarnell Kemper herself stood over 6 ft tall, and was a hard drinker. When Ed mourned the departure of his father, his mother feared that he was 'going soft' and might develop into a homosexual. To pre-empt this, she made him sleep in the cellar, locking him in and placing the kitchen table over the trapdoor.

In the summer of 1964, Ed's father felt that the boy needed a complete change. The answer seemed to be his own parents, Edmund and Maude Kemper.

Edmund Kemper I was a quiet, rather colourless man who had worked most of his life for the California State Division of Highways. Now, at seventy-one, he lived in retirement on his smallholding in the foothills of the Sierra Nevada. His wife Maude, sixty-five, was an entirely different creature. Everything and everyone within her sphere of influence was controlled with an iron hand.

On 8 August 1964, Maude's grandson Ed III arrived at the ranch. Maude took against her grandson from the outset. She had to suffer him, in the event, for just sixteen days.

Above: ***Anita Luchessa was eighteen and in her first year at Fresno State University when she made the fatal error of accepting a lift from Ed Kemper.***

TO PRE-EMPT ANY 'SOFTNESS' OR HOMOSEXUAL TENDENCIES ED'S MOTHER MADE HIM SLEEP LOCKED UP IN THE CELLAR

SHOOTING GRANDMA

On the hot, airless morning of 27 August 1964, old Ed Kemper set out to fetch the shopping while Maude settled to her typewriter at the kitchen table. Young Ed shuffled around listlessly in the yard for a while, then came in and took his grandfather's .22 rifle from the kitchen door. Loading it, he told his grandmother he was going out to shoot rabbits.

'Just don't shoot any birds,' she snapped. Young Kemper stopped on the threshold. Something about her tone induced an instant surge of white-hot rage. Whipping around he flung the rifle up to his shoulder and fired a shot into the back of her head. As she fell forward he loosed off two more into her back. Then he put down the gun, selected a sharp kitchen knife, and stabbed her repeatedly until his fury drained away.

Then he wrapped a towel around the dead woman's head to soak up the blood, and carried her body into the bedroom.

He realized that he was in trouble. As his grandfather drove up outside, Kemper killed him with a single shot to the head in order, he said later, to spare him the sight of his murdered wife.

After a desultory attempt to clean up the kitchen, Ed rang his mother Clarnell for help. 'There's been an accident,' he said. 'Grandma's dead. So is Grandpa.'

Clarnell, who immediately suspected that her son was responsible, told him to ring the local sheriff. When the lawman arrived, Ed admitted what he had done.

After a session with a court psychiatrist, Ed Kemper was pronounced a paranoid schizophrenic. Without much further examination, it was decided to send him to the State Hospital at Atascadero.

Above: ***Mary Ann Pesce was Anita Luchessa's roommate at university. The two girls were hitch-hiking when they met with Kemper.***

LISTENING TO THE SEX OFFENDERS, KEMPER UNDERSTOOD THAT TO GET AWAY WITH RAPE IT WAS NECESSARY TO KILL THE VICTIM

BAD INFLUENCE

The boy murderer was to stay at Atascadero for the next five years, and all in all he enjoyed the experience. The Research Director, Dr Frank Vanasek, took him under his wing and Ed soon became a trusted inmate.

Gradually he acquired a basic working knowledge of psychological conditions, including his own. He knew what the doctors wanted him to say, and he said it.

But he also learned a lot about sex. Eagerly he listened to sex offenders of every kind, fantasizing at night about their experiences. He was particularly interested in the testimony of the rapists, noting that almost all of them had been caught because a victim had identified them. The moral seemed to be that to get away with rape, the victim should not be allowed to live.

These, of course, were very private thoughts. To the doctors, he tried to present the portrait of a rapidly improving, integrated human being.

Although the possibility of explosiveness was 'certainly evident', the doctors decided that he would be safe in the community. He was first released into the care of the California Youth Authority in 1969, and stayed there for three months while he attended college.

Most of his reports at Atascadero had noted that his mother was probably a causative influence of his problems, and recommended that Ed should in future be kept apart from her. But on his final release from the halfway house he was placed back in the custody of the formidable Clarnell Kemper just in time for his twenty-first birthday.

His mother had by now moved to the coastal town of Santa Cruz. She had an administrative job at the University of California and an apartment in the suburb of Aptos.

Across from the courtroom at Aptos was a bar named the Jury Room, where off-duty local policemen congregated. Kemper began drinking there, and his size, clipped hair, short, police-style moustache and conservative attitudes helped him fit in very well. The police liked him, and he became known to them as 'Big Eddie'.

Kemper, with his John Wayne fixation, fancied the idea of a career as a lawman himself, but was told that he would be too big for the California law agencies. He became depressed and took a job as

Above: ***Fifteen-year-old Aiko Koo was standing at a bus stop in Berkeley, California when she was picked up by Ed Kemper.***

flagman with the Division of Highways.

His mother had other ideas. His marks had been good in college, during his treatment period, and she wanted him to enter university and 'better himself'. Inevitably they had rows.

The monotonous but steady job of flagman meant that Ed had independent money for the first time in his life. He bought a black and yellow 1969 Ford Galaxie sedan, and rented a room in a friend's flat in Alameda, a suburb of San Francisco.

PROWLING THE HIGHWAYS

For the next eighteen months or so, Ed Kemper spent his leisure time cruising the highways and byways of California, pondering in his unquiet mind lubriciously upon sex.

At the tail end of the 'flower power' era, San Francisco and its environs were full of free-spirited young women who habitually hitch-hiked. Ed made a practice of picking them up and chatting to them, using all the psychological wiles he had learned in Atascadero.

His 'straight' looks led girls to trust him, and he made things easier for himself by getting his mother to fix him up with a University of California permit for his windscreen, giving him access to the university's campuses. He had given about 150 girls 'safe' lifts before he was ready for what he had in mind.

On Sunday, 7 May 1972, Kemper took to the access roads around the freeways outside San Francisco in his Ford Galaxie. Under his seat were a hunting knife, a plastic bag, a pair of handcuffs and a Browning 9mm automatic pistol, borrowed from a workmate. At 4 p.m. he spotted two pretty young girls thumbing by the side of the road, and Kemper drew alongside them.

Mary Ann Pesce and Anita Luchessa were eighteen years old, first-year students at Fresno State College. They were, as they told Kemper, going to see a friend at Stanford University, about an hour's drive away. The girls were unfamiliar with those parts, they admitted, and did not know the area.

As they talked, Kemper had been taking advantage of the girls' lack of local knowledge to drive out of town. Now he pulled down a side road. Mary Ann suddenly realized something was wrong and asked, from the back seat, 'What do you want?'

Kemper held up the Browning pistol in reply and said: 'You know what I want.'

Mary Ann talked calmly to Kemper in the approved fashion that she had learnt during university safety lectures, trying to get her potential attacker to see her as a person rather than a victim. Unfortunately Kemper, with his experience at Atascadero, knew the ruse.

Above: ***Ed Kemper helps police locate the body of his victim, Aiko Koo.***

Below: ***Police dig up the remains of fifteen-year-old Aiko Koo.***

In fact he used a piece of psychology of his own. He told the girls that he was going to lock one of them in the boot and hide the other in the back seat, before taking them both back to his apartment. He had, of course, no such intention, but the girls went along with his wishes.

After locking the terrified Anita in the boot, he handcuffed Mary Ann's hands behind her back. Then he pulled a plastic bag over her head and began to strangle her with a dressing gown cord. Mary Ann put up a tremendous fight. She bit through the plastic bag and managed to get her mouth to the rope, keeping it from its choke-hold.

Kemper took up the hunting knife and stabbed her twice in the back. She turned over and he stabbed her once more, but she managed to shake the bag off and tried to sit upright. Finally Kemper grabbed her by the chin and slashed her throat.

With Mary Ann dead, Kemper went to deal with Anita, who must have heard the struggle and thus, he considered, would have to be slaughtered with despatch. He was right. When she saw the blood on his hands she began to scream and struggle and he stabbed frantically.

With both girls dead he drove the bodies back to his room in Alameda, knowing his flatmate was out. It was about 6 p.m. He carried them in, wrapped in blankets, and first undressed them, taking copious photographs with a Polaroid, and then dissected and decapitated them. He copied down the information from their ID cards and then destroyed their clothes and possessions, retaining only their ready cash – $8.28.

That same evening he took the segmented bodies out to the wilds of Santa Cruz, where he buried them. The heads he kept for a while. They were trophies, but they were also small guards against dental identification. Some time later he drove up into the hills and tumbled them into a ravine.

To the Californian police forces, the two girls were free spirits who had gone their own ways, regardless of parental admonitions. Mary Ann and Anita were, for a while, just a couple of runaways.

For four months Kemper gloated over his Polaroid photographs, slaking his sadistic urges by recalling in detail the things he had done to the two girls. Any intention to kill was further curbed by a motorcycle accident, which left him with a broken left arm.

Below: ***Eighteen-year-old Cindy Schall was picked up by Kemper on the outskirts of Santa Cruz.***

And Kemper had another priority on his mind. Any prospect of a better job was hampered by his record, for even in California few people fancied employing a double murderer who had served five years in a mental institution. Until he had his juvenile record declared sealed, he was unable to buy a gun easily. Meanwhile he had managed to borrow a .357 Magnum.

THE KILLER STRIKES AGAIN ... AND AGAIN

As dusk fell on 14 September, fifteen-year-old Aiko Koo was standing at a bus-stop in University Avenue, Berkeley, trying to thumb a lift.

Ed Kemper picked her up, but instead of taking her towards San Francisco, her destination, he set off fast down the coast highway. Aiko instantly realized she was in trouble and began to scream. Kemper pulled out his pistol and thrust it into her ribs, telling her that he meant her no harm. He was, he said, contemplating suicide, and wanted someone to talk to.

He drove her up into the mountains and stopped the car. Like her predecessors, Aiko struggled against his colossal weight, but in the end was overcome. He suffocated her into unconsciousness, raped her and then strangled her.

After wrapping the small body in a blanket and stowing it in the boot of his car Kemper drove off, glowing with satisfaction and the knowledge of his secret. A few miles down the road he stopped off at a bar for a beer, in order to savour his 'conquest' at leisure.

At about eleven that night he arrived back at Alameda and carried the body indoors.Then he dissected it and scattered the pieces in the Santa Cruz mountains. He retained only the head, which he carried around in the boot of his car.

On 15 September, a panel of juvenile psychiatrists examined Kemper and declared him mentally fit. Two months later a court, acting on the panel's instructions, 'sealed' his juvenile record. He was now entitled to go out to a gun shop, sign a form, wait five days and purchase a gun.

For the moment, however, Kemper had

Above: ***Student IDs of Rosalind Thorpe and Alice Liu, the last two students to fall prey to Ed Kemper.***

other problems. His broken arm had kept him off work, and he was unable to pay the rent in Alameda. Reluctantly, he moved back to his mother's flat at 609A Ord Drive in Apatos. They began to quarrel again almost instantly, and the old frustrations began to build up.

On 8 January 1973, Kemper bought a .22 Rutgers automatic with a 6 inch barrel. Itching to try it out, he took to cruising the roads that same evening. Weather conditions seemed ideal, with heavy rain forcing girls who would otherwise avoid the risk to get any ride they could. He picked up two or three, but the streets were busy and he decided to make no untoward moves.

KEMPER USED HIS MOTHER'S WHITE SHOE POLISH TO COVER UP THE BLOODSTAINS ON HIS PLASTER CAST

He had almost given up when, in Mission Avenue in Santa Cruz, he saw a short, shapely blonde named Cindy Schall.

Cindy was eighteen, a native of Marin County, near San Francisco. She was in her second year at Cabrillo College, on the outskirts of Santa Cruz, where she was studying to become a teacher. When Kemper picked her up she was on her way to an evening class.

As soon as she got into the car, he showed her the gun. Then he told her a similar 'suicide' story to the one he had told Aiko Koo. For three hours he drove, heading east to Watsonville and then turning into the hills at the township of Freedom. He persuaded her to get into the boot, and then killed her with a single shot to the head.

Kemper's mother was out for the evening, but even without the danger of prying eyes, Kemper had a difficult job manoeuvring the 11 stone corpse indoors with his injured arm. As it was, his plaster cast was splashed with blood, which he covered up with his mother's white shoe polish. Overnight, Cindy Schall lay in Kemper's bedroom cupboard.

The following morning, when his mother left for work, Kemper lugged the body into the bathroom and began cutting it into disposable pieces.

Later in the day, Kemper placed the pieces of flesh in plastic bags and threw them into a ravine near Monterey. As souvenirs he kept Cindy's outsize man's work shirt, and a small handmade ring. He also kept her head in his cupboard.

A day later, newspapers carried details of a Highway Patrolman's find on the road out of Monterey – two arms, a hand, and portions of two legs. Some time after that a ribcage was washed ashore. Enough of the body was recovered for Cindy Schall to be positively identified. Caution dictated that Ed get rid of the head, so he buried it outside his mother's window.

Just a month after the slaying of Cindy Schall, the Kempers – mother and son – had another mammoth row. The effect on Ed was familiar: rage and frustration. He stormed out of the house and threw himself into the Ford, tucking the pistol under his right thigh as he drove. It was another wet night.

Rosalind Thorpe was just emerging

from a lecture theatre as Kemper drove by. Normally the twenty-three-year-old linguistics and psychology student rode her bicycle everywhere, but tonight the rain had put paid to that, she told Kemper. Seeing his campus sticker, she assumed him to be a fellow student.

As they chatted, Kemper spotted a small Chinese girl thumbing by the side of the road. He stopped and she got into the back seat. She was, she said, Alice Liu. She was twenty-one.

As they reached the hill overlooking the town of Santa Cruz, Kemper slowed the car as if to admire the lights reflected in the ocean. Then he picked up his gun in his good right hand and shot Rosalind smartly in the temple.

As she fell he turned to Alice, who was writhing in the back, screaming. Kemper fired twice at her and missed, then managed to hit her in the head. Alice lay unconscious, though making soft moaning sounds, as he drove at speed out of town.

For the first time in his 'adventures' Kemper felt sick and frightened at what he had done. Alice's moaning did not help, and as soon as he was far from any street lights he stopped the car and shot her once more in the head. For a time she was quiet, and then the terrible moaning began again. He pulled off the road and carried both bodies to the boot of his car.

His plaster cast was again sprayed with blood by the 'blow-back' as the bullet entered Rosalind's skull, and he stopped in a filling station toilet to scrub it off as best he could. Then he went home.

His mother was up, watching TV. He told her that he was going out for cigarettes, but before going to the shop he stopped by the car, opened the boot and hastily decapitated both bodies with his hunting knife. It was between 10 and 11p.m., but no one was around.

The following morning he carried Alice's headless body into his bedroom and had sexual intercourse with it, before cutting off her hands 'as an afterthought'. Later that day he dumped the bodies near San Francisco, in the hope that police would think the perpetrator a local man. Then he drove back to the town of Pacifica and threw the heads and hands over a bluff called Devil's Slide.

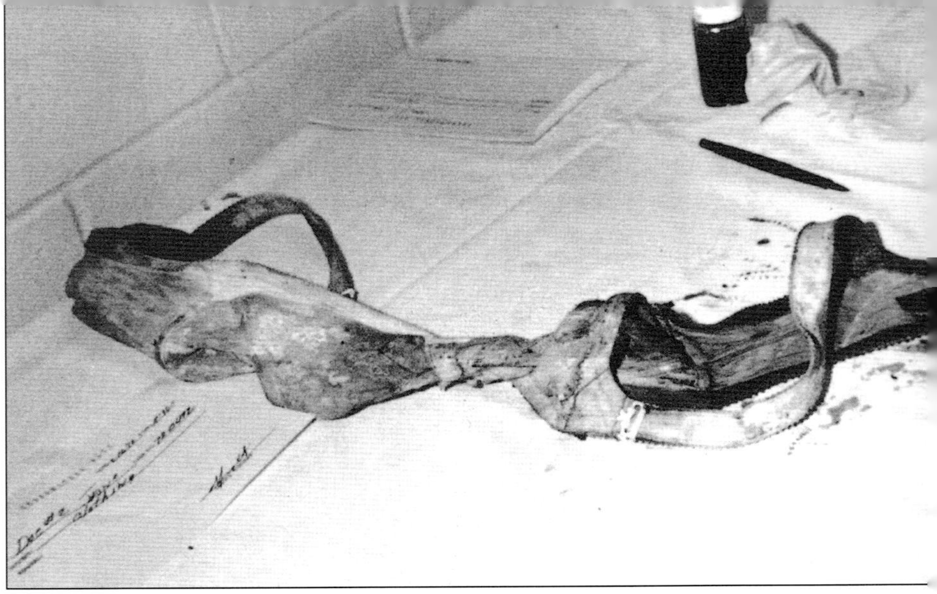

Above: ***Rosalind Thorpe's bloodstained bra was introduced as evidence at Kemper's trial.***

TROUBLE NOW CAME FROM AN UNEXPECTED QUARTER - ANOTHER MASS MURDERER WAS WORKING OUT OF SANTA CRUZ

He also felt that things were getting more difficult for him.At the end of January a woman's skeleton was found in the mountains. She was identified as Mary Guilfoyle, a twenty-three-year-old English student who, like Cindy Schall, had attended Cabrillo College.

She was a victim not of Kemper but of another mass murderer, Herbert Mullin, who had started killing at the same time as Kemper and also lived in Santa Cruz. Mullin was to kill thirteen victims and eventually ended up in the same prison as Ed Kemper. Meanwhile he was causing Kemper trouble.

FINAL BLOODBATH

In the middle of April, Kemper packed up all the documents and personal belongings he had taken from his victims, together with his prized .22 pistol, and threw them in the ocean. He had stomach trouble, which turned out to be ulcers, and his nerves were in shreds. It was time, he felt, to bring his career to a massive climax, perhaps killing everyone in his neighbourhood in one night of slaughter.

HIS MOTHER ASKED HER SON IF HE WANTED TO TALK. 'NO,' HE REPLIED, AND WENT TO FETCH A KNIFE AND HAMMER

On 20 April, Good Friday, Kemper went home and drank beer in front of the television while pondering what to do next; his mother was working late.At about four in the morning of Easter Saturday he went into his mother's bedroom. She was awake, and asked him if he wanted to talk. He told her no, and went back to his own room to fetch a pocket knife and a hammer.

When he was sure his mother was sleeping he crept back in and brought the hammer down with all his force on the right side of her head. She did not move, but as the blood welled up Ed saw that she was still breathing. Turning her over on to her back, he sawed into her trachea with his pocket knife, continuing to cut until the head rolled free.

For the rest of that day he felt sick, giddy and restless. The killing this time had done nothing to calm his confused feelings. He cleaned up the bloody mess as best he could, and then went out drinking with a friend.

Towards the evening, in a muddled attempt to disguise his mother's absence over the Easter holiday, he decided to kill her best friend, Mrs Sally Hallett. He hoped that the joint disappearance would confuse the police. Kemper rang Mrs Hallett, and told her he was preparing a surprise dinner for his mother. Mrs Hallett agreed to come over that evening.

She arrived exhausted after the journey. 'Let's sit down,' she said. 'I'm dead!' They were her last words.

After strangling and decapitating her, Kemper went for a drink at the Jury Room. He had, he knew, reached the very end of the trail. There was no way he could cover up the slaughter just across the road from the policemen's bar.

On Easter Sunday morning he packed Mrs Hallett's body into his bedroom cupboard, and then loaded his weapons into her car.

He headed east to Reno and then hired a car, leaving Mrs Hallett's vehicle at a garage. He drove for the rest of the day and night. Just before midnight on Monday, 23 April, he stopped at a pay-phone in the town of Pueblo, Colorado, 1200 miles away from Santa Cruz.

Then he rang the Santa Cruz police and asked for Lieutenant Charles Scherer, who was in charge of the student murder investigations. It was not until three telephone calls and five more hours had passed, however, that Ed Kemper convinced his old police drinking buddies that he was the man they were looking for. They sent a Colorado patrol car out to pick him up, and he was arrested in Denver by Santa Cruz police.

Ed Kemper's confession was long, articulate and complete in every detail, for he had savoured each killing over and over in his head. When the details of his release from Atascadero were made public there was sudden public loss of confidence in psychiatric criminal evaluation. It was already shaky after revelations that Herbert Mullin, the other Santa Cruz murderer, who had also been arrested, was likewise a former mental hospital inmate. Typically Ed Kemper detested Mullin because 'he had killed people for no good reason'.

On 25 October 1973 Ed Kemper was charged with eight counts of first degree murder at Santa Cruz Court House. On 8 November he was found guilty and sentenced to life imprisonment in California Medical Facility at Vacaville. He escaped the death penalty because it was suspended in California at that time.

All parole recommendations for Kemper have been turned down since then, and it is unlikely that he will ever be released. Since entering the Facility, Kemper has worked at recording books for the blind, supervising fifteen fellow inmates. He received a public service award for this work in 1981.

'LET'S SIT DOWN,' SAID HIS MOTHER'S FRIEND AFTER HER EXHAUSTING JOURNEY. 'I'M DEAD!' A FEW MINUTES LATER, SHE WAS

Below: ***Ed Kemper towers above his police escort in court.***

SARAH PAYNE
Forensic Fibres

The murder of an eight-year-old girl in July 2000, triggered one of the most high-profile police enquiries that lasted for well over a year. Following forensic evidence from fibres and a single hair, the case was finally closed.

Sarah Payne went missing on July 1, 2000 while she was staying with her grandparents in Kingston Gorse, near Littlehampton, in Sussex. The police started a massive search in which they asked for the help of the Forensic Science Service (FSS), the market leader in the supply of forensic science services to police forces in England and Wales.

A farm worker found Sarah's partly-covered body in a field in West Sussex, just a few yards away from the A29, 17 days after she disappeared. Her body was naked and had been lying there for some time. At first there appeared to be no sign of injury but a full forensic examination would be able to give the police more information. The body was badly decomposed but a full DNA profile was taken from her muscle tissue which matched exactly with a milk tooth that had been saved by Sarah's mother.

EXTENSIVE EVIDENCE

The investigation, which cost over £2 million, involved more than 1,000 people. Among these 1,000 were 20 experts employed in the field of forensics and between them they managed to obtain more than 500 items which were submitted for further examination.

While the forensic team carried out their tests the police concentrated on something that Sarah's brother, Lee, had said to them. When questioned, Lee told

Opposite page: *The* News of the World *printed names and pictures of convicted sex offenders over a period of two weeks in their 'Name and Shame' campaign, following the murder of schoolgirl Sarah Payne.*

Left: *The anguished faces of Sara and Michael Payne, parents of Sarah, following the court hearing on February 6, 2001.*

Above: *The memorial plaque for Sarah Payne, which was unveiled July 1, 2003 fixed to a tree in Pulborough, England.*

them that just after Sarah disappeared he noticed a white Transit van going down the lane past their grandparents' house. It wasn't long before a local man who was on the sex offenders' register became a prime suspect. A week before Sarah disappeared, Roy Whiting had bought a white Fiat Ducato van. When the police impounded his vehicle the police found it contained a red sweatshirt, a pair of socks, a chequered shirt, a clown-patterned curtain and a petrol receipt, which proved that Whiting had been in the area where Sarah's body had been found.

PROOF OF GUILT

The only piece of Sarah's clothing that the police managed to recover was a single black shoe. However, this one item contained 350 pieces of fibre which the forensic team examined one by one under a microscope.

There were fibres which proved the shoe belonged to Sarah because they matched those on her blue school sweatshirt. The turning point in the investigation, though, was when they examined just four dark red fibres which matched the red sweatshirt found in the back of Roy Whiting's van. This was the first piece of tangible evidence that actually linked Sarah to the van. Two single fibres from one of Whiting's socks were found on the driver's seat and also inside the body bag which had contained Sarah's body.

The forensic team then went painstakingly through all the fair hairs that they removed from the sweatshirt and the piece of clown curtain. From the 40 hairs removed, only one single hair was a full profile match to Sarah. Again, it was one single multi-coloured cotton fibre which was found on Sarah's shoe that was found to match the clown curtain found on the seat of the van.

In December 2001 Roy Whiting was found guilty and sentenced to life imprisonment. The trial judge, Mr Justice Richard Curtis said:

> *It was a rare case when he would recommend that a life sentence should mean life.*